The
Pier

The Pier

MATT BROLLY

 THOMAS & MERCER

Text copyright © 2022 by Matt Brolly
All rights reserved.

Published by Thomas & Mercer, Seattle

www.apub.com

Amazon, the Amazon logo, and Thomas & Mercer are trademarks of Amazon. com, Inc., or its affiliates.

ISBN-13: 9781542031431
ISBN-10: 1542031435

Cover design by Tom Sanderson

Printed in the United States of America

For Frank

Prologue

The assailant laughed, the shotgun swaying precariously in his hands. 'What, you want a confession before I kill you?'

'I'd settle for a confession,' said DI Louise Blackwell. It wasn't the first time she'd faced the barrel of a gun. Working on a missing girl case in Cheddar, she'd had a similar weapon pointed directly at her, but that didn't make the sight any more palatable. The real danger came from the person holding it – and if, as now seemed certain, the assailant was behind all the recent events in Weston, then it was conceivable that he was willing to use it. 'You need to tell me what's happening,' she said.

'What's happening is that I have a gun pointed at you which I am going to use,' said the assailant.

Louise looked over to DCI Robertson. 'Backup is just around the corner,' he said, sneaking a look at the shovel on the ground of the allotment which would be within his grasp if he bent down.

'Fuck the backup. I'm not getting out of here either way,' said the assailant, his laugh turning into a cough.

This had to be the moment. The assailant's cough was causing him to shake, and Louise wasted no time. She looked at Robertson, nodding towards the shovel, and taking her phone from her pocket she threw it towards the assailant, telling him to catch it, as she dropped to the floor.

The assailant's indecision was exacerbated by his coughing fit. He lifted the shotgun in the air, tracking the long trajectory of the phone as he watched it fall from the sky, before pointing it at Louise who was now lying on the ground.

Louise locked eyes with the man and for a split second wondered if this was the last thing she would ever see, before Robertson brought the blade of the shovel down hard on the assailant's wrists, the shotgun falling from his hands without making a sound.

The assailant appeared to be wounded, a gash in his forearm weeping open, but as Robertson bent down to secure him, he surprised both Robertson and Louise by jutting his elbow into Robertson's mouth.

The blow wasn't significant but was enough to take Robertson off guard. Before either of them knew it, the assailant had produced a thick steel wire from his pocket and was on top of Robertson. They were both on the ground, the man's knee in Robertson's back, as he wrapped the wire around his neck.

Backup was only seconds behind and Louise wasted no time in picking up the gun.

'You going to shoot me too?' said the assailant, the wire pulled into Robertson's flesh.

The gun was heavy in Louise's hands, the tension from the last few days making her back and neck ache, but she stood firm, her arms solid as she pointed the gun directly at the assailant's head. 'You don't think I will?'

'I'm unarmed,' he said.

'You let my colleague go and you'll be unharmed.'

'I could slit his throat before you had the chance to pull that trigger,' said the assailant, pulling harder on the wire.

The gun was already cocked, Louise taking a step forward. 'You want everyone to know your name, that's fine. But what's the point if you're dead?'

The words hit the assailant as hard as the shovel had hit his arms. He flinched, and stepped back, his eyes wide. 'OK, OK, I'll let him go,' he said, dropping the wire.

Robertson scrambled to his feet, and restrained the assailant. 'Louise,' he said.

The sound of her name drifted towards her but she was stuck in a moment of indecision. The man had caused so much harm.

'Louise,' said Robertson again.

Louise heard, but she kept the gun pointed at the assailant's head. He'd ruined so many lives. Would anyone blame her for pulling the trigger?

TWO WEEKS
EARLIER

Chapter One

Louise Blackwell woke with a jolt, a heavy feeling in her chest making her gasp for breath. Her subconscious had been tormenting her with dreams of Tim Finch, her ex-colleague who was now in prison awaiting trial for attempted murder. The dream was still fresh in her mind and she replayed it scene by scene. At first, she'd been back at the Walton farm chasing the serial killer and abuser, Max Walton, with Finch as her only ally. Finch telling her the man was armed. Louise shooting him dead. Then: late last summer at Finch's house. Finch tying up the police officer, Amira Hood, ready to kill her, when Louise had arrived and confronted him.

Louise couldn't help but smile at that particular memory: the fight that ensued, and the injury she had caused to Finch's leg.

'Tea for you. I need to get off soon.'

Louise looked over at Thomas who was already ready for work. 'How come you never dressed so well when you worked with me?' she said, taking the tea from him.

The last time she'd felt this way had been during a turbulent few months at university, when she'd fallen in love for the first time. She'd thought she'd grown hardened to such emotions since then, but here she was kissing Thomas goodbye with a fluttering feeling in her stomach. It saddened her to think that the moment was tarnished by thoughts of Finch.

She showered and changed in a rush. The nights over at Thomas's house were becoming more frequent. So much so that she had more than one change of clothes stored at his house. It still felt a little illicit, especially as she lived in the same house as her parents, albeit on her own separate floor.

It was also strange heading to work without Thomas. He'd started his new job as a security consultant in Thornbury but she hadn't got used to his absence. It was just one of many changes in the last few months. Louise worked out of Avon and Somerset's headquarters in Portishead, the CID team in Weston-super-Mare now defunct. She still had overall responsibility for the town where she now lived but had to make the daily trek to her new offices, which could take anything from thirty minutes to an hour depending on traffic.

As her car crawled on to the slow-moving rush-hour M5, it appeared that today's commute would be longer than normal. Somewhere else, she knew, Thomas was stuck in the same traffic jam. It was strange how easily her thoughts would return to him. They'd worked together for three years prior to hooking up, and although she'd often thought about him during that period, it had been nothing like the last few months. At first the situation had been a little awkward as they'd still been on the same team, and they had decided to keep it secret. But now that Thomas had left the police, after growing disillusioned with all the internal politics, she'd grown to realise how much she missed his presence during the day. He'd often been the person she'd turned to at work for comfort and balance, and it was taking some time to adjust to him not being around, especially with the move to headquarters.

However, now that their relationship was public, it seemed like it hadn't been much of a surprise to her colleagues. Her main friend at work, DI Tracey Pugh, had even claimed to have known about the ongoing fling since its inception. Tracey was the one person left at work she could confide in and had pointed out the plain fact that Thomas leaving was probably the best possible thing for their relationship. 'You don't want to be seeing your boyfriend twenty-four-seven now, do you?' she'd said.

Louise had agreed, although she'd been perturbed by Tracey's use of *boyfriend*, a term that still felt a little incongruous, as if Louise was too old for such things.

A call came in as the traffic began to thin out towards the junction for Clevedon. It was the news she'd been waiting to hear for some time, and the reason she'd been thinking about Finch so much over the last few days: a date finally being set for Tim Finch's court case. The call was from Kent Mooney, an officer from the Ghost Squad, the nickname given to the constabulary's internal investigation team. As Louise was due to be a witness, she had no role in the ongoing investigation into Finch, though she would have liked nothing more than to lead the prosecution against him.

But while she should have been buoyed by the news, a sense of melancholy overcame her as she left the motorway at the Portway and took the A369 to Portishead. Finch had been a torment ever since the night at the Walton farm. The fallout from Finch's lie about Walton holding a firearm had led to Louise's effective demotion to Weston-super-Mare. Not content with her leaving the major investigation team, Finch had harassed her both at work and in her social life, with the aim of getting her to leave the force. But she'd never let him win, and when it became apparent that he'd been doing the same and worse to other officers and civilian staff for a number of years, she'd finally managed to get him to account for his crimes.

She had no qualms about seeing him go down for what he'd done. If she had her way he'd rot in jail, and she didn't think of him as a former colleague. He was a bad apple who had conned everyone around him. That he'd blagged his way to becoming a police officer, and had corrupted some of those he'd worked with, was a shame she shared with her remaining colleagues. She had no doubts about any of that. However, none of it alleviated the dread she felt that, now it was close to ending, Finch would find a way to evade justice.

However unlikely that seemed, it wasn't beyond possibility.

By the time she reached her office in the CID, the thought had soured her mood. In the past, she would probably have grabbed a coffee and spent a couple of minutes venting to Thomas, but those days were gone. She looked out from her corner office through large glass panels on to the open area where her team worked, and reminded herself how far she'd come. She'd worked here before, alongside Finch, but following her move to Weston she'd never imagined she'd be back here and leading her own section of Major Crimes.

Despite arriving late, she still had thirty minutes left before the morning's briefing. With the restructuring, she was now lead detective of Major Crimes in north Somerset, which was much larger in scope than her work in Weston had been. The caseload was heavier and she was currently overseeing five major investigations, including a spate of racially motivated attacks in south Bristol. She was only the SIO on one case at present, an armed robbery in Brislington, where she'd already made a number of significant arrests. Although she'd understood her role would change significantly with her move back to HQ, she hadn't quite appreciated the amount of time she would spend behind her desk.

She noticed the increased activity as she was putting her things together, ready for the meeting. Everyone in the outer office seemed to be on their phones, suggesting something was going down. She didn't have the chance to check her phone before her office door was opened, and DCI Robertson barged in. If it was possible, his usual dour face appeared more sullen than normal. 'You haven't heard?' he said, squeezing his right hand open and shut.

Louise's first thought was that somehow Finch had escaped custody. It was the only thing that could explain her boss's agitation, but the truth was much worse.

'It's probably nothing to worry about, but we just received a call claiming that an explosive device has been placed in a primary school in Weston-super-Mare and will be detonated in twenty minutes.'

Such calls were far from daily occurrences but they weren't uncommon. That didn't stop Louise's heart hammering in her chest. 'What school, Iain?'

'We have already spoken to the headmistress and evacuation procedures have begun.'

'What school, Iain?'

The last time Louise had seen Robertson look so ashen had been the morning after the Christmas party. His lips were slightly parted, as if he'd been struck dumb. She wanted to grab him and shake the information from him, but she already knew what he had to say. 'It's Emily's school, isn't it?'

Louise's niece was in year 3 at Larkmead School in Weston.

Robertson closed his mouth and nodded.

Chapter Two

Being locked in his prison cell didn't bother Tim Finch. It wasn't that he took comfort from his isolation, or relished the false security of being away from the other inmates. It was more that he could see beyond his confines. His cell was a room he slept in, and admittedly spent too long in, nothing more than that. It was a room like any other, and as long as he kept seeing it in those terms then his incarceration wouldn't bother him.

He didn't stir as the bean slot opened, and one of the screws looked in on him. For now, he had the upper hand. He was still on remand, his full trial delayed, and most important of all he knew many of the screws from before. He had years of secrets buried away in his mind, and for now it made sense for most of them to keep him on side.

'Visitor for you.'

'Thanks, boss.'

Boss. The word stung in Finch's throat. It was laughable that the guard, a pale twenty-something called Derek Wilson, could be referred to as Finch's boss, but he had to play the game. As Wilson creaked opened the metallic door, he made eye contact with Finch, and at that moment Finch was certain they were both thinking about the same thing. A Christmas party two years ago where Finch had taken a group of police officers and prison guards to a little club he knew over in Keynsham, and introduced Wilson to a young woman.

A young woman who at the time had been underage.

Finch grabbed his walking stick, the annoying accessory a necessity after the attack that had shattered his leg. He sensed Wilson's uncertainty but it didn't come as a surprise. It radiated off nearly everyone he knew. They all thought they had him sussed out but the opposite was true. Like the rest of them, Wilson had his horrible little secrets and Finch knew every one, and was more than prepared to use them to his advantage.

The guard led him through the corridor of the beast wing where Finch was being kept for his own safety. He'd probably put away half of the monsters behind those doors and it was an insult to be associated with them. The paedophiles and rapists who acted from nothing but an uncontrolled instinct. They were so removed from him that they may as well have been a different species, but for now he was content to be among their number. If he was ever going to enter the prison populace proper, he needed to be ready. As an ex-copper – and worse, an ex-Serious Crimes DCI – it was never going to be straightforward, but he had the right connections. For now, it was important not to overplay his hand. It wasn't only the screws and his former officers he had the lowdown on. If he played things well, he could serve out his term with full protection and would be running things in the next few years.

Finch's solicitor put his back up by not standing to greet him. With the money Finch was paying the man's firm – a top defence firm from London – a little courtesy was the least he could expect. 'Rector,' he said, sitting down.

The solicitor lifted his eyebrow at the mention of his surname. 'Mr Finch. How are you?' he asked, as Wilson shut the door behind him.

'How the hell do you think I am? What's happening with my appeal?' As his court appearance had been delayed once more,

Rector and his cronies had been trying to get Finch out on bail, or if that didn't succeed, moved to a lower-category prison.

'I'm afraid you're still considered too much of a flight risk to be released, and too much of a security risk to be moved.'

'That's bullshit, for a start. Who's making these decisions?'

'It's not quite as simple as that, Mr Finch, as I'm sure you're aware.'

Finch wasn't aware of any such thing. If he'd been on the outside he would have known where to go; what pressure to put on what person. 'Then why the hell are you here, no doubt charging me for the privilege?'

'Two things. Neither wonderful, I'm afraid. First, there has been another allegation against you,' said Rector, placing a folder in front of him.

Finch glanced through the file. 'Constable Sally Margate. That's a blast from the past.'

'Mrs Margate claims you sexually harassed her at work when you were both probationary officers, leading her to leave the police force.'

Rector was looking at him as if expecting Finch to put up a defence. Finch ground his teeth. 'I presume she has no proof?'

'The police are investigating, gathering witness reports. Either way, an extra name doesn't look good. If you had anything to help us . . .'

Finch smiled. The poor bastard couldn't even bring himself to say that he wanted something to discredit the woman. He closed his eyes, focusing his memory. 'Neil Clarkson case. She lied under oath. Claimed to have witnessed an assault but was in another room at the time. Admittedly, I told her to lie, but if you check with the other officers involved, they will corroborate my story.'

'Even if it incriminates them?'

'They'll do it. What next?'

'Next, we have a date for your trial.'

After thirty minutes alone in the exercise yard, Finch was led back to his cell. Wilson didn't say a word to him as he opened the door, a wave of fetid air hitting him as he sat on his bed. 'Thanks, boss,' said Finch, picking up a book and turning his back to the guard, not even pretending to hide his disdain.

The door creaked shut and Finch clenched the spine of the book before throwing it against the stone wall. The court case announcement was expected but still a kick in the teeth. He was already over the legal maximum for months on remand – the CPS using a tried-and-tested loophole to keep him locked up – and had hoped that continued delays would mean he was released on bail before the case reached the Crown Court.

As for the latest accusation from another old colleague, what the hell difference did it make? They were crawling out of the woodwork like the worms they were, and one fresh accusation would make little difference.

The sight of the paperback on the floor was too much for him and he jumped from the bunk and placed it neatly on the shelf. From the sink, he took a bottle of aftershave and sprayed it over his neck and face. The citrus tang brought back so many positive memories that he felt invigorated. The court case could be a positive thing. There were still a number of anomalies to the investigation into him, and he was holding on to a lot of pivotal information that could threaten a successful prosecution against him.

Try as they might, they wouldn't break him. As the cell door opened again, Finch felt more positive than before. This time he didn't treat Wilson with any mock deference. 'What is it now?' he said.

Wilson looked intimidated, his head bowed. 'Someone wants to see you,' he said.

Finch got to his feet, his leg aching, immediately on alert. 'Who wants to see me?' he said, stopping short of grabbing the guard to shake the information out of him.

Wilson failed to make eye contact. It was obvious now that Finch wasn't the only inmate who had something on him. 'Terry Clemons.'

Finch nodded. 'You have been a naughty boy, Wilson, haven't you? What has Clemons got over you then?'

'Nothing.'

Finch hadn't needed to do any research before his incarceration. He'd always kept abreast of what was going on in the local prisons and knew the key players. He'd been expected to be placed in Horfield, and Terry Clemons was someone he'd previously identified. Although Horfield was a Category B prison, it still contained a number of undesirables. Clemons was a well-known gangland member from Tottenham in north London. He'd managed to wangle his way into the lighter Cat B prison in Bristol some time ago, which had alerted Finch's attention when he'd still been a police officer. He regretted not having spoken to Clemons. One thing was for sure, there was no way he was going to do so now unless under a severe form of duress. He glanced at the emergency button on the cell wall before replying. 'Right. Well then, you won't mind telling him I won't be speaking to him today then, will you?'

'I'm not sure he's going to take no for an answer,' said the guard.

'Is that so? Well, you're going to have to drag me out of this cell and along the corridor if you want me to go anywhere.'

'Didn't think you were scared of anything, Finch,' said Wilson.

'You are kidding me, aren't you, Wilson.'

'That's *boss* or *sir* to you.'

'*Boss* or *sir* nothing. I know what you did, Wilson, and I have the proof. I'm happy to play along with this charade for now, but

I can get word out about you like that,' said Finch, clicking his fingers. 'Maybe we could share a room together when they bring you in?'

Wilson's features seemed to slip a half centimetre down his face as he reached for the baton on his utility belt. Finch smirked and sat back on his bed.

'He said it would be worth your while,' said Wilson.

'I bet he did.'

'Said he had some important information he'd like to share with you.'

'Not this time, Wilson.'

Wilson squirmed, his indecision disgusting to behold. 'He says he can help you with Louise Blackwell.'

Chapter Three

Louise wasn't taking no for an answer. Robertson had done everything he could to stop her going to Weston, but she needed to be there to see for herself that Emily was safe. In the end, Robertson assigned the case to Tracey and reluctantly agreed to Louise tagging along. Within minutes they were heading back towards Weston. Tracey was driving, every now and then pulling at a loose thread of her wild curly hair as she steered through the traffic that was reacting to the blue lights and piercing siren. She knew better than to offer Louise any assurances. Louise knew as well as she did that it was probably little more than routine, but that didn't stop her urging Tracey to drive faster, and drumming her fingers on the dashboard in an ever-increasing tempo.

Although not as common as they had once been, bomb threats were still something the police had to deal with from time to time. But it was rare that any action needed to be taken. They were often prank calls, or cries for attention.

However, this time the threat appeared real. A device had been discovered in the school, and it was enough to have warranted action. None of that mattered at the moment. For now, Louise would only be content the second she saw that Emily was out of harm's way.

As Tracey raced down the M5, Louise radioed the first responder, PC David MacFarlane, again. 'David, what's happening?'

'The school has been evacuated, ma'am. Everyone is in the park across the road, teachers included. Fire service are here, waiting for instructions.'

Louise sensed her elevated heartbeat come to rest. She stopped short of asking the constable if he'd seen her niece. 'Is everyone accounted for?'

'All the registers have been submitted, as well as staff and guest lists. We don't believe anyone is inside the building.'

'No one is to go in before I get there,' said Louise, glancing at Tracey – who was supposedly in charge – before hanging up.

They arrived twenty minutes later, the surrounding area a sea of flashing lights and emergency vehicles. Avon and Somerset didn't have their own bomb disposal unit and always worked with the army's specialised team. Their van was already here. Louise knew the officer in charge, Lance Corporal Adam King, and accompanied him to the perimeter of the building as Tracey spoke to the headmistress, all the time trying to catch a glance of Emily in the throng of excited children across the road.

'As you know, much of our work is on counter terrorism. Can't remember the last time I've been called to a school,' said King.

'What's that? Sorry, Adam,' said Louise, distracted as she looked around for Emily.

King was a hulk of a man, well over six feet tall with a body-builder's physique. 'It doesn't matter,' he said, as together they went through the transcript of the call they'd received from the head-teacher. Joanne Harrison had been informed of an unusual-looking device located in the PE lock-up area. Fortunately, she'd had some training in the HOT – Hidden, Obviously suspicious, Typical – protocols used to determine the potential dangers of unattended objects, and had decided to accelerate things.

'I need to speak to her directly,' said King.

Louise summoned PC MacFarlane and told him to find the headmistress and Tracey. Sweat dripped down her forehead. It was early June and the south-west was on its fifth day of a relentless heatwave. The sky was cloudless, the heat Mediterranean-like. Although she knew Emily had to be safe, Louise kept glancing over at the throng of pupils and teachers, desperate for a sight of her niece.

Louise recognised the short, squat woman following Tracey across the road. She'd met Joanne Harrison on a couple of occasions when Emily had first started at Larkmead. She was accompanied by a man who could have been her twin.

Mrs Harrison gave Louise a brief smile. 'Emily is fine,' she said, before introducing the man with her, the caretaker Karl Insgrove.

'You discovered the object?' said King, wiping his mouth with the back of his hand.

'Mr Insgrove uncovered the object this morning and alerted me to it.'

'Can you tell me again what it looked like?' said King.

Mr Insgrove was in his element. 'I've seen undetonated bombs from the war before,' he said, stepping forward. 'There was one found over in Burnham, what, twenty years back, but I could tell this was different. More modern.'

Louise struggled to hide her frustration, exchanging a knowing look with King, as she urged the caretaker to get to the point.

'And what did it look like, sir?' said King.

'I didn't think much of it at first. I thought it was some new gym equipment wrapped in grey plastic, but then I saw the wires.'

'Neither of you managed to take a photograph?' asked Louise.

'I'm sorry, that was my mistake. My first concern was for the children, obviously,' said Mrs Harrison.

Louise couldn't begrudge the woman for that. Even with the headmistress's assurance that her niece was safe, she still felt an overwhelming need to see Emily for herself despite there not being any obvious immediate danger.

'Did you touch the package in any way?' asked King.

The caretaker shook his head. 'I got a closer look. The wires seemed to be connected to a smaller secondary section but I couldn't be sure. I knew the most sensible thing was not to touch it, so I asked Mrs Harrison to take a look.'

'You did the right thing,' said King, to the caretaker's delight.

'Still nothing called in?' he asked Louise, once the two civilians had been led away.

'Nothing yet. Does it sound plausible that it's an explosive device?'

'God only knows until we take a look. What sort of idiot would place it in a school though? I'll need this whole road cordoned off until we know what we're dealing with.'

Louise nodded and walked off as King instructed his colleague Corporal Mitch Norton to prepare the bomb disposal robot. After speaking to Tracey and PC MacFarlane, she went in search of Emily. Everything seemed to be under control, but she needed to see her niece. With the relocation and her relationship with Thomas developing, she'd made a special effort to spend more time with the girl. It had been over a year since Louise's parents and her niece had relocated to Weston and they'd all moved into the same house together. Prior to that Emily had experienced things a girl her age should never have to experience, and Louise's priority was to give her the best life possible. For now, that meant blocking off every Sunday in her calendar for her.

Louise felt her knees buckle as she caught sight of Emily playing with a group of girls in her class. The relief was physical, and she had to take a second to compose herself. She recognised the pent-up energy in her niece, Emily jumping up and down on the spot waiting for her turn before noticing Louise was there. 'Aunty Louise,' said Emily, running towards her.

Louise bent down to hug her smiling niece, her heart still thundering.

'What are you doing here?' asked Emily.

'A bit of police work, but mainly to see you,' said Louise, as Emily's friends edged nearer.

'Is that why we aren't in class?' asked one of the girls.

'Oh, there's nothing to worry about. Sometimes we're called out to see if everything is OK. You girls just enjoy your free time, and I'll see you later,' said Louise, kissing Emily on the cheek.

Tracey was in discussion with the headmistress and King as Louise returned. 'You've met Arnie?' said King, pointing to the bomb disposal robot being prepared by Norton. Louise had seen the machines before. This particular model had caterpillar tracks over six wheels, and a crane-like hydraulic arm. Louise didn't know if the reference to the Terminator was a joke or not – the machine was quite small – but wasn't about to question the men.

Minutes later, King had set up the radio control and Arnie made its way to the rear of the building. If any of the children or staff were spooked about the sight of the machine moving along unaided, they were hiding it well. The children continued playing, as the teachers began dealing with the parents who'd obviously found out about what was happening. The scene was so idyllic, it seemed absurd to think there might be an explosive device nearby.

King guided the robot via a joystick. The machine's cameras provided video playback. The enthusiastic caretaker, Karl Insgrove, was by his side giving directions to the PE storeroom where the device had been discovered.

Louise stayed back, close enough to see the screen as Arnie moved through the ghost-town school, coming to an abrupt stop as it reached the storeroom.

'We'll take it from here, Mr Insgrove,' said King.

The caretaker looked mortally wounded as he retreated, though he perked up when King added, 'Thank you for your invaluable help.'

Louise took the caretaker's spot next to King, feeling dwarfed by the sheer size of the man. King pressed a button and Arnie's huge hydraulics went into action, a metallic arm moving towards the door handle. King controlled the actions of the robot with his gloved hand, reaching forward and opening an imaginary door as the robot turned the real door handle.

The IED – Improvised Explosive Device – was easy to spot. A large plastic container was connected by wires to a battery-driven power source. The camera zoomed in on the grey plastic packaging, which contained a block of solid white material.

King conferred with his colleague before turning towards Tracey and Louise. They had to look up to speak to him. Louise was blinded by the sun hovering about King's head like a halo. 'Can't tell for sure if that's real though,' he said. 'It looks possibly like RDX to me – a plastic explosive.'

'What damage can it do?' asked Tracey.

'You wouldn't want to be standing next to it, that's for sure. It would take out that storeroom and anyone near it. Imagine some kids getting some equipment out of there and it going off. Doesn't bear thinking about. No one owned up to it yet?'

'No. What's the next step?' asked Louise, studying the screen.

'We'll use the disruptor on it,' said King.

'What does that entail?' said Louise, dismayed to realise she was thinking like management, assessing what the fallout would be from a bomb being detonated in a school. She really did need to get out of the office more.

'Think of it like a shotgun on a stick. It's water-based, and will take out the device's power source, neutralising it immediately,' said King, his tone matter-of-fact.

'Let us know what you need us to be doing,' said Tracey, glancing at Louise for her to follow.

Such had been her concern for Emily, Louise had forgotten she wasn't in charge of the case. As she stepped away, she noted a glint of something white protruding from the underside of the package. 'What's that?' she said, pointing to it on the screen.

'Mitch, zoom in on the left side of the package. Appears there's something jammed under it.'

The camera scrolled towards the device. 'Looks like a piece of paper, sir,' came the reply.

'You think you can extract it?' asked Louise.

'Sure can,' said King.

The camera zoomed out as an extendable metal rod moved towards the package. 'Metal rod thing,' King said to Louise, not so much as breaking a smile as the end of the rod opened up and a set of pincers grabbed the paper. 'Might be a good thing we waited to blow this thing up,' he added, as the rod retracted, carrying a piece of paper that clearly had writing on it.

'Don't keep us in suspense,' said Louise, enjoying herself a little more than she thought she should be.

'Here we go,' said King, turning the note towards the screen so they could read it:

> *Next time you won't be so lucky, DI Blackwell. Next time it will be live.*

Chapter Four

Louise called DCI Robertson before taking the obvious decision to close the school for the day. After neutralising the device, Adam King had informed her that the material in the container was fake, and not the plastic explosive they'd feared. Nevertheless, he'd insisted on a sweep of the school building and it made little sense to try to keep the school running when the potential risk was so high. That didn't stop the complaints Mrs Harrison had to field as the parents collected their children.

Tracey stayed with the search team as Louise waited with Emily for Louise's parents to arrive. Louise was still coming to terms with the note having been addressed to her. Tracey had suggested that she didn't get involved any further with the investigation – at least for the time being – and Louise had reluctantly agreed, not wanting Emily out of her sight until her parents arrived.

One of the dads from Emily's class, Graham Pritchard, was in a full-blown argument with the headteacher, and it was taking all of Louise's resolve not to get involved. 'I can't believe you would put our children in such danger,' he said to the harried-looking Mrs Harrison.

'We're only following protocols, Mr Pritchard. Now, if you'll excuse me,' said Mrs Harrison.

'This is not the last you'll hear of this,' said the man, as if he was the only one concerned for his child's safety.

Louise was about to point out the seriousness of the situation when her mother arrived. Even she was looking agitated. 'Is this necessary?' she asked Louise, under her breath.

'What exactly have you heard?' said Louise.

'A fake bomb of some sort.'

'Do you want to take the risk?' said Louise, stopping short of telling her mother about the warning that had come with the bomb. She would only worry. And then there was a risk that the information, inadvertently or not, would find its way to the WhatsApp groups.

'It's not me, Louise, it's the other parents. They're complaining on WhatsApp that it was all a hoax. Probably one of the kids did it.'

It never ceased to amaze Louise how quickly information could slip out, and how absurdly it could be interpreted.

'I don't think an eleven-year-old would have the wherewithal to pull this off, Mum. And why? To get out of a day in primary school?'

'Maybe. So what are we going to do with you, little miss?' asked her mum, grabbing Emily by the hand.

'Beach?' said Emily, giggling.

Louise's mum sighed. She loved being Emily's guardian – both Louise's parents did – but Louise understood the toll it could take on them. They'd expected at this time of their lives to be enjoying their retirement, not raising their only grandchild. Louise did her best to help out, but work made it difficult.

Louise kissed them both goodbye, holding Emily close until the girl gently pulled away. 'I need you to be careful, Mum,' she said.

Her mother frowned. 'I will be. Is there something you're not telling me?'

'No, just be careful, OK?'

Louise waited until they were out of sight before returning to the school. She would try to get back early tonight to help her parents out. It would be good to have an evening meal with them for once, though she had stopped short of telling her mother that in case she was delayed.

'Oh, did I miss my little Emily?' said Tracey, as Louise walked over to the PE storeroom where the device and note were being processed, ready for Forensics.

Tracey was like a second aunt to Emily and would occasionally take her out for the day. 'Sorry. I'm taking her out on Sunday if you fancy joining us?'

'Sam is taking me away this weekend. It's supposed to be a surprise, but he keeps asking me if I still have the time free.' Tracey pushed the hair away from her eyes. Sam was another officer, who worked out of Nailsea. They'd been together for a couple of years now, which had initially surprised Louise. Sam was about ten years younger than Tracey, and it was possibly the first proper relationship she remembered her friend having. There was also the fact that Tracey had once spent the night with Thomas, which was something Louise didn't like to dwell on.

'Do you know where he's whisking you away to?'

'I may have snuck a look at his emails,' said Tracey, with a grin that lit up her face.

'Always the detective. So?'

'Bognor Regis,' said Tracey, taking a sharp intake of breath. 'I know, when you say it out loud it doesn't sound that romantic, but he's booked a lovely boutique hotel by the sea. He's trying his best, bless him.' Tracey let out a sigh. 'So what do you think about all of this?'

Now that Emily was safe, Louise felt more able to focus on the details of the case. Although she'd dismissed her mother's suggestion that one of the children had done it, she wanted to believe it had all been a hoax and this would be the most they heard of it. All the staff and anyone who had been a guest at the school in the last week would have to be questioned, which meant it wasn't a small task. 'The note is a bit vague. No suggestion as to why they did this or what they want. But the implication is obvious. They intend to strike again.'

'Why do you think they mentioned you?'

It was Louise's turn to let out a sigh. She didn't want to think it was personal, but it was hard not to with her name on the note and the dummy bomb being found at Emily's school.

Finch's name sprang immediately to her mind. He might have been safely away on remand, but that didn't mean he was without influence on the outside. She decided to keep those thoughts to herself, for now. 'Could be that they thought I would be the investigating officer.'

'Or that they knew Emily went to the school.'

'I guess we have to consider both possibilities. My concern is that everything points to this being a dummy run. They were testing our responses. Whether or not this is personal to me, we need to speak to Counter Terrorism, see what they have going on in this area.'

'I've got the team calling the local schools just in case.'

'Let's make that region-wide. Keep everyone vigilant.'

If it had been a hoax, perhaps a disgruntled school employee getting revenge for some perceived injustice, it was a dangerous and highly disruptive one. The fallout would be felt beyond Weston-super-Mare. Louise supposed that was the way with all types of terrorism. Now there would be lots of frightened schoolchildren and anxious parents in the seaside town and the local area. It would have taken a distinct lack of awareness not to realise this would happen – and that, coupled with the note mentioning her name, suggested to Louise that whoever was responsible knew exactly what they were doing; that she could be the cause, and target, of the offender, was something she would need to speak to Robertson and the other senior officers about.

'Shit, I've got to get going,' said Louise, glancing at her watch. 'The problem with this relocation business is that I'm going back and forth to the city all the time,' she said to Tracey, before setting off.

'How about your place in Clifton?'

Louise had kept a two-bedroom flat in Bristol after being forced to move to Weston. She rented it out but there was no possibility of moving back in. Her parents had moved to Weston to be closer to her, and she had obligations to help look after her niece, which she was more than happy to do. 'That's the past now. Keep me informed of how things go here,' she said, walking off to where her car was parked.

A familiar face stopped her as she was about to get in the car. As always seemed to be the case, Dominic Garrett sounded out of breath. 'DI Blackwell? A second of your time?' asked the rud-dy-faced man who, despite the heat, was wearing a snugly fitted three-piece suit.

'Hello, Mr Garrett, how are you?' said Louise, unlocking her car. Garrett was the editor of the local paper, *The Mercury*. To Louise, Garrett was a man out of time. He seemed to be stuck somewhere in the eighties, his days consisting of liquid lunches that went on for hours. Despite which, he was usually very good company.

'I was hoping we could talk about the shocking developments at the school. Unexploded bombs, I hear? Innocent children, bank holiday weekend not far off. I'm sure you'd love to comment?'

Garrett was being purposely obtuse. He would never publish anything so alarming. It was his way of trying to get a sound bite from her. She decided to play along, wanting to find out how much

Garrett already knew. 'You know as well as I do, Mr Garrett, that you will need to speak to our press office. I can tell you, though, that no explosive device was found on the school property.'

'A hoax?'

'You know who to speak to.'

'Still a frightening development. You'll keep me informed?' He was smiling, but the expression looked more like a grimace as he squinted his eyes against the glare of the sun.

'Sure.'

'I understand a trial date has been set for DCI Finch,' said Garrett, as Louise sat down in the driver's seat.

So that was why he was here. Louise took a long breath and started the engine. 'Ex-DCI.'

'Innocent until proven guilty, and all that?'

'If you like,' said Louise.

'Are you still confident of a successful prosecution?'

He was clearly trying to provoke a response, but the question still irked her. There was no reason not to be confident, but the fact was Garrett was right. Finch was legally innocent until proven guilty, and no doubt would be doing everything in his power to circumvent justice if he was able. 'Press office, Mr Garrett,' said Louise.

'Would you mind if one of our freelancers got in contact to discuss in greater detail? An old friend of yours. Tania Elliot.'

'You're kidding me?'

Garrett's innocent look had morphed into smugness. 'You and Tania make such lovely stories together.'

'Goodbye, Dominic,' said Louise, pulling away before she said something she would regret.

Tania Elliot was the last name Louise wanted to hear. Elliot had been a local reporter at *The Mercury* when Louise had first met her, and had found nationwide fame reporting on a number of Louise's significant cases. She was supposedly located in London now and there was no way she'd been in contact with Garrett simply because of the device at the school. No, there was only one reason the journalist was back on the scene, and that had to do with the reason Louise was headed into Bristol: Tim Finch.

◆ ◆ ◆

The new senior prosecutor for the area's Crown Prosecution Service was a public-schoolboy type, Antony Meades. Meades had succeeded Natalie Gurgenstein, who had made the unfortunate decision to start dating the then DCI Finch a few weeks before his arrest. Gurgenstein had since moved up north and Meades had been promoted from the ranks.

Louise had worked with Meades on a number of investigations and had always enjoyed working with him. He was good company, and well mannered. She'd soon deduced he'd gone into working for the Crown out of choice. He came from a wealthy family, and she was sure he could have had his choice of any of the city solicitor firms.

The CPS building was in the heart of Redcliffe. Meades' office was large but cramped. It had the air of organised chaos: box folders, case files and books covering every inch of space, all precariously placed in towering piles. Louise apologised for being late, and removed a bunch of files from the seat opposite Meades.

'I heard about the incident at the school. Your niece goes there? I trust everything is OK?'

Louise decided not to share the information about the note, wanting to keep it as secret as possible. 'News travels fast. Yes, everyone is fine. Fake news and all that.'

'Still pretty damaging PR-wise, I imagine? Bombs in schools is never a good look.'

31

'Are you trying to improve my mood, Antony?'

Meades swept away the blond fringe from his forehead. 'Ah yes, sorry. Some more not-so-good news, I'm afraid.'

'I thought I was here to go through the Finch case?' said Louise.

'Yes and no. Mr Finch's prosecution is pretty much in hand. We can work through some of the details nearer the time. It was more that I wanted to talk to you about the potential fallout from Finch being convicted.'

'The only fallout I can see is that he won't be put away for long enough.'

'Hopefully that won't be the case. No, it's more about the reaction to his conviction. And I'm afraid that has already started. We've had notice from a number of legal representatives of convicts Finch had put away.'

'That's not so unusual, is it?' said Louise. A natural consequence of a corrupt officer being imprisoned was that everyone they had previously arrested would take the opportunity to claim that their prosecution had been unlawful. Sadly, this sometimes led to prosecutions being quashed. Louise didn't like it, and although she hoped that the majority of Finch's prosecutions would still stand, there was a risk that some would not.

'No, and although it looks like we will be facing a number of retrials, everything is well enough in hand. However, I have been alerted of an inquiry that has the potential to affect you personally. It is a bit out of my jurisdiction but we should try and get a handle on it together.'

Louise didn't like the way Meades' eyes were downcast. 'Spit it out, Antony.'

'We've had a relative of Max Walton get in touch with us. His nephew, Justin Walton. He's obviously heard about Finch's impending trial, and sees it as an opportunity to reopen the inquiry about what happened to his uncle.'

'I hope you told him where to go.'

'Thing is, Louise, it appears that he wants to open a case against you for unlawful killing. He says you were in a relationship with Finch and that you hunted and murdered his uncle.'

'Little shit. Did he mention that his beloved uncle was responsible for the murders of countless innocent people? No, I didn't think so. And anyway, I've already been cleared of that.'

'This is true. Unfortunately, the young Justin Walton has been getting some dubious advice and is considering bringing a private prosecution against you personally.'

Chapter Five

Clemons was the sort of con who could easily be underestimated. In his late fifties, he had the well-cushioned body of a man who enjoyed life to its full despite having spent the last ten years at Her Majesty's pleasure. He was all smiles, and although his bonhomie was clearly a fabrication, Finch was still impressed by the man. Like Finch, Clemons was meticulous in everything he did. The cleanliness of his cell was testimony to that, his bed made with military precision, his belongings kept in perfect symmetrical lines on his shelves.

Both of them were ruthless, only in it for themselves, and each would give the other up in a heartbeat. For now, they both had something the other wanted, so Finch was content to play along with the other man's game.

The lure of information on Louise Blackwell had been too much for Finch to turn down. Blackwell was the reason he was inside. She was an itch he should have scrubbed out at the beginning. He'd thought he'd done as much that night in Bridgwater when he'd made her shoot the unarmed Max Walton, but she kept coming back like the proverbial bad penny.

In retrospect, he'd been too lenient on Louise. She wasn't like the others, whom he'd manipulated and discarded as he'd wanted.

She'd survived things that would have broken most people, and he'd been foolish not to have finished her off when he'd had the chance.

He'd agreed to meet Clemons during a break period, when their interaction could be monitored by more than just the prison guards.

'Good to see you, Tim. Enjoying the books?'

The set of books Clemons had sent to Finch's cell was a nice touch, but Finch wasn't going to be bought so easily. Finch sat on the offered chair and nodded in thanks.

'You let me know if you need anything else to help you settle in,' said Clemons, glancing at his two henchmen, who then left the cell.

Finch no longer felt any imminent threat of violence. It had become apparent that Clemons ran the prison with an intelligence that meant little went down inside unless it was necessary. There were still beatings, some savage, but Clemons tried his best to avoid internal confrontation. He'd already demonstrated to Finch an encyclopaedic knowledge of his fellow inmates, which extended beyond the walls of the prison. He knew the prisoners' families, the circles they moved in, their value to him and most importantly their weaknesses. And it didn't stop with the prisoners. At least four of the guards were in his pocket, and he knew more about Wilson's predilections than Finch did. It was impressive, and again Finch regretted not making contact earlier with the man. They could have done some good business together.

'What do you know about Greg Farrell?' said Clemons, once they'd finished with the preliminaries.

'Farrell? I had my eye on him but he's straight as they come.'

'You had him moved from Weston CID.'

'That was more to piss off Blackwell but I thought I saw something in him. He's good. Smarmy bastard. But a good detective.'

'And Thomas Ireland?'

Ireland was worse than Farrell. Straight as the day was long. Finch had been surprised when he'd heard Farrell had left the force. The detective had the kind of attitude and brown-nosed intensity that led to promotions. 'Let's get to it, shall we? Ireland is just another ex-copper, Farrell is a rule-lover you want to avoid. I'm sure you know all this already.'

'Do you know Ireland is fucking Louise Blackwell?'

Finch took in a deep breath and tried to hide his surprise. He felt a familiar rage rise within him, and tried to keep it down. 'Dirty dog. No, I didn't know, and frankly I don't care. What has this to do with me?'

Clemons wrinkled his brow, as if momentarily thrown off course. What was he expecting from Finch? Some outpouring of grief that a woman he'd slept with on a couple of occasions was now giving it to someone else? Finch had learned early on in his career that there was no place for emotion if one was to get ahead. He'd only slept with Louise in the first place to try and gain some kind of control over her. They'd both been going for promotion to DCI at the time and he'd hoped he would be able to derail her ambitions. It hadn't worked, and he'd been fortunate that the Walton situation had arisen. He'd made a snap decision in telling her that Walton was carrying. He'd denied it afterwards, and Louise had escaped prosecution with her career in tatters, but somehow it had worked out for her in the long run. In retrospect, he wished that Walton had been carrying. If Walton had returned fire on Louise, Finch wouldn't be inside now and his fucking leg wouldn't ache every minute of the day.

Clemons settled himself. 'I'm taking a risk talking to you, you understand that. Coppers, bent or not, are not welcome around here.'

'I'm pretty sure you can deal with that, Clemons. I don't think anyone is going to start thinking you've changed sides. What is this all about? If this is some kind of trust thing, then I think you know what you're going to get from me. Neither of us are stupid. You know as well as I do that I'm in this for myself, but if we can help each other let's do it. Otherwise, I'll be off.'

'You put one of my team away once, you know that?'

'That can't be what this is about,' said Finch, searching his memory for anything that would have once linked him to Clemons.

'Charlie Litten. Assault charge.'

Finch nodded. 'Big bastard.'

'Said you stole a stash of drugs off him during the arrest.'

'Probably saved him a few years off his sentence.'

Clemons chuckled. 'You've got balls, Finch, I'll give you that. Normally if you steal from me, it doesn't work out very well for you.'

Finch still couldn't link Litten to Clemons. He'd been some lowlife flogging pills in a nightclub. He'd only taken him down because he'd put a fellow lowlife in hospital with irreversible head trauma. Nothing in the ensuing interrogation had suggested he'd had any links to organised crime, or even London for that matter. 'Is this where your heavies come in and give me a beating?' asked Finch. His nonchalance wasn't an act. He could take a beating if necessary but it wouldn't come to that. He'd already left a file with his solicitor with the details of Wilson's misdemeanours in it. If anything happened to him then the solicitor was to open that letter, and he'd let Wilson know exactly what would happen. As such, he trusted the prison guard was looking out for him.

'It would be more than a beating, but that's child's play. I think we can work together, Finch. But you need to know I'm serious. Any sign I get that you're crossing me, it will be over for you. I know you think you have friends in here, but I have more friends than you. Understand?'

Finch smirked. 'Okay, Clemons, whatever you say. Let's start,' he said.

Chapter Six

Both Louise's dreams and thoughts were once more haunted by the memory of Max Walton. The news of Walton's nephew, Justin, wanting to take out a private prosecution had forced her to remember that disturbing time in her past.

The investigation into Max Walton had started early in her career with the MIT. Walton been arrested once, five years prior to that night at the farm, on suspicion of an attempted abduction of a hitchhiker on the A38. The victim had failed to identify Walton from a line-up and they'd had to let him go, and it wasn't until a year later when a body was found close to Walton's farm that he had appeared on their radar again. Unfortunately, by then he'd disappeared, and five other bodies were found before his eventual death.

Afterwards, she'd relived those final moments on a daily basis. She'd known what Walton was, what he was capable of doing, but if Finch hadn't lied to her about him being armed, she would never have shot him. At least, that's what she'd thought to begin with. As the weeks had unravelled, Finch, and other senior officers who supported him, had made her doubt herself. They'd told her it was understandable, and that they would have done the same thing themselves in her situation. Thankfully she'd stayed firm, and over the coming months and years she'd managed to put the memory to the side. But it still occasionally returned to her, forcing her to relive those last seconds: the gun in her shaking hand, and the damage the ensuing bullet had caused.

Louise blinked herself back into the present. After her long day going back and forth from Bristol she'd thought she'd wanted to be alone, but Thomas had called and she'd ended up staying the night. Sometimes, she forgot that Thomas was no longer in the police, and she would blurt out the day's events as if they were still colleagues. She'd already told him about the note found at the school, and she was lying next to him now, telling him about her meeting with Antony Meades when she should have been sleeping.

'Does he think Justin Walton would have a chance?' said Thomas.

'It's more about the damage he could cause in the meantime. Antony thinks it's possible someone put him up to the task of messing with me.'

'Funny that he starts to speak up the same time Finch's trial date is announced.'

Thomas had worked with Finch and had as low an opinion of him as Louise did. 'Not sure if it's in Finch's interests either,' said Louise, wondering if she was trying to convince herself.

'He would use anything that could impact his case. What if he tries to use it as a means to undermine your credibility?'

Meades hadn't come directly out with it, but Louise had sensed his concern. 'I'm not sure even Finch would be that desperate.'

'Still, it's a bit of an uncomfortable coincidence.'

It wasn't the only supposed coincidence she was dealing with at present. Louise was reminded of her meeting with *The Mercury*'s editor, Dominic Garrett, and the news he'd given her that Tania Elliot was back in town. Tania had published a bestselling non-fiction book following Louise's first major investigation in Weston, and had been a constant presence in the area until last year. Now Louise understood why she was back. Garrett hadn't come out and said it, but Louise was sure Tania was working on a book featuring Finch, and that meant she would also have been dredging up the past. In particular, the Max Walton case.

'Listen, Tom, there is something you should know,' said Louise.

Thomas smiled. 'I can't quite get used to you calling me Tom,' he said, even though she'd been calling him it for the last six months.

Louise smiled back. 'I'm not your boss anymore.'

'Aren't you?' said Tom, his eyes wide in mock surprise.

'Listen, I don't know how much you know about what went on back then, but with Tania back on the scene, and if Justin Walton does go ahead with this private prosecution thing, then a lot of stuff is going to be dredged up from that time and I . . .'

Thomas shuffled closer to her. 'We did know each other then, remember? Different areas but we knew each other. I understood what Finch was back then, and I know he was lying about what happened.'

Louise pulled away from his embrace. 'It's not that. It's . . .Christ, this is so hard to say. I—'

Thomas interrupted her, giving her the out she realised she was hoping for. 'I know about you and him, Louise.'

Louise and Finch had slept together on an ad hoc basis during the time they worked together. It had never been serious, and in retrospect she suspected it was something Finch had engineered as a means of having control over her. She had no doubt that if she'd been as subservient as some of Finch's other conquests, then he would never have sacrificed her in the way he did at the Walton farm. 'You don't mind?'

'Well, I'm shocked that your taste in men was so bad but it's not any of my business. That's in the past. We've all done things we regret. I mean . . . Finch, come on,' said Thomas, placing his hand over his mouth.

Louise moved back towards him. 'What was I thinking?' she said, shuddering as she remembered the smell of Finch's overpowering aftershave.

'I was thinking . . . I have Noah this weekend. Maybe we could go out for the day, bring Emily along?'

'Sure, that would be nice,' said Louise, tensing as Thomas moved in closer. 'Right, shall we try and get to sleep?' she added.

Thomas looked surprised before moving back to his side of the bed. Louise wasn't sure why she was so thrown by the suggestion of Noah and Emily meeting. She'd been seeing Thomas for six months now, and it was a natural next step. She told herself that she'd simply been caught off guard by the suggestion, but wondered if she was kidding herself. Why something so innocent felt like such a massive step was unclear to her. All she knew was that she didn't feel ready, and that only sufficed to make her more confused.

'Night, Mr Security Man,' she said, flicking off the bedside light.

'Night,' said Thomas, sounding unsure, as if he was trying to work out what he'd done wrong.

◆ ◆ ◆

Louise was up in time to make the short drive to her house near Sand Bay. Emily was sitting at the dining table when she arrived, her mouth full of cereal as she called over, 'Aunty Louise!' The family's young Labrador, Molly, danced around Louise as if she hadn't seen her in months.

Louise's father playfully glanced at his watch and said, 'Weren't you wearing that yesterday?'

'You don't know what I was wearing yesterday, thank you very much.'

'I do,' said her mother.

41

'Fine, you've caught me out. I was about to pop upstairs to change. Just wanted to let you know that I can take Emily into school this morning.'

'You try to raise them properly,' said her father, winking at her.

'You two.' Louise shook her head.

She showered and changed and was back downstairs in fifteen minutes, Thomas's suggestion about taking Noah and Emily out together still bothering her.

'Any more information on what happened yesterday?' said her mother, under her breath, as they walked outside to Louise's car.

Following her meeting with Meades, it had been difficult to focus on the developments in Weston. Everyone was alert to the potential threat, and Louise had suffered a round of questioning by the hierarchy at headquarters before being allowed to work on the case. 'What's the latest on the WhatsApp groups?' said Louise, as Emily climbed into the car.

'I'm not prying, I'd just like to be kept abreast of any potential bomb threats at my granddaughter's school.'

'You know I can't give you any details, Mum. It was a hoax. As soon as I know more and I'm cleared to do so, I'll share details with you,' said Louise, getting into the driver's seat. She could imagine what her mum would think if she knew a note had been found at the school with Louise's name on it.

'And how is Thomas?' said her mother, a knowing look on her face.

Louise lowered her eyes, the awkwardness of last night's conversation still fresh in her mind. 'Have a good day, Mum.'

Louise drove Emily along the seafront before turning inland to her school. It was high tide, the water brushing against the stone wall of the promenade. Louise had once taken the sight of the murky sea for granted, but now couldn't get enough of it. It was part of the town's identity, at times like this, when it filled the shoreline, and when it retreated and left a stretch of mud in its absence. She felt connected to the town in its vicinity, and would have happily spent hours watching it if she ever had the time.

She rarely had the chance to drop Emily off at school, but the muted atmosphere in the playground was unmistakable. Parents were naturally concerned about yesterday's events, and the children could sense the hesitation in the air. Even Emily stuck close to her as they waited for the bell.

'I think a few parents are steering clear for a few days,' said the dad she'd seen at the school yesterday who'd been berating Mrs Harrison.

Graham Pritchard was a single dad, and every time Louise saw him, she felt he was on the verge of trying to ask her out. He was pleasant enough, but had little sense of personal space, always standing a few centimetres too close.

Instinctively, Louise took a sidestep away from him. 'I can understand that. These things can be very traumatic.'

'Are you here on official business?' asked Graham, with an awkward smile.

'I'm here to drop this young lady off,' said Louise, not about to divulge any work details with him.

'Some of those teachers will do anything to get some time off,' said Graham, wincing when Louise didn't smile. 'Sorry, not appropriate?'

Louise wanted to tell him to stop trying so hard, and was pleased when the headteacher rang the bell for the children to get into their respective lines.

'Will you pick me up today, Aunty Louise?' asked Emily, as Louise bent down to kiss her goodbye.

'Not today, but I'll try and get back for dinner if I can.'

Emily frowned, suggesting that they both knew that was unlikely. 'Go on now, I'll see you later,' said Louise, walking away before Graham could engage her in more conversation. She waited in her car until the crowd had thinned, and returned to the school where she was due to begin interviewing the staff.

◆ ◆ ◆

Joanne Harrison ran her hand through her unkempt hair as Louise was escorted into her office by the school receptionist. Dark circles hung under the headmistress's eyes like shadows. Louise imagined she'd spent the night replaying the previous day's events over in her mind, wondering if there was anything she could have done differently. 'Any luck from the fingerprints?' she asked, as Louise sat opposite her.

The SOCOs, now officially known in the region as CSIs – Crime Scene Investigators – but still referred to by their original acronym by those in the force, had arrived yesterday. They had stripped down the storeroom where the fake explosive unit had been discovered, testing for prints and other substances. At the same time, Louise's colleagues had taken prints from all staff and guests at the school during the day. It would be some time before everything was fully processed and any potential discrepancies investigated.

Mrs Harrison sighed as Louise explained, a day's worth of frustration coming out in the sound. 'I see.'

'I know I asked you yesterday, but I was wondering if you'd any more thought on who might be responsible for yesterday? Someone with a grudge against the school, perhaps. An ex-teacher, a disgruntled parent, anything that comes to mind?'

'I have been thinking about little else, Inspector.'

'Please, call me Louise.'

'Louise . . . Disgruntled parents are part and parcel of being a headteacher, I'm afraid. Naturally, everyone wants the best for their child, but that sometimes means that there are complaints over the most minor things.'

'Can you give me an example?'

Mrs Harrison sighed again, shuffling papers on her desk. 'Well, my latest complaint isn't minor. A parent of a boy in year six has lodged a bullying complaint. Apparently, the boy was picked on by a classmate for having long hair. The bully called him a girl and several other names I won't repeat.'

'Not very enlightened.'

'Not at all, and it is a thing we take seriously.'

'What are the steps you take in such a matter?'

'If the boy had come to us first, we would have spoken to the other child concerned and tried to reach a resolution. Whatever school you're in, these things are going to happen. Children will be children, and can be cruel. It's our job to help them explain the things they do wrong and help them understand and develop. As the complaint came from a parent, we had to get the other set of parents involved, which rarely goes to plan.'

Louise understood only too well. After Emily's father had died, her behaviour at her old school had become unruly, and Louise had had to speak to the headteacher on numerous occasions. Emily had bitten one of her classmates during an argument, and things with the parents had never been the same. It was Louise's parents who'd borne the brunt of things, her mother telling her how the other parents had looked at her in the playground as if she was raising a monster. 'I can imagine.'

'We have a zero-tolerance policy on bullying, but there are always little things going on. I speak to parents every day over one thing or another, and not everyone is satisfied with the responses I give.'

'Staff issues?'

'We've had a stable staff force for the last few years. I get the occasional request for grade raises, that sort of thing, but they are a lovely bunch. Both the teachers and support staff. I can't believe any of them would do something like this and scare the children so.'

It was Louise's turn to sigh. 'I'd still like to talk to them one by one,' she said.

'I have an office set up for you, and a list,' said Mrs Harrison, handing her a sheet of paper.

Louise followed her to a small box room with no window.

'Sorry, it's all I could find. I would have offered you the sports hall but I didn't want the children to see. I hope you understand?'

'That's fine, thank you. Mr Insgrove first?' asked Louise, glancing at the sheet.

'I'll just get him for you. There was one thing before I go. I received a call this morning from a journalist asking about yesterday. She wasn't the first, but she seemed to know you.'

Louise lowered her eyes. 'Tania Elliot?'

'That's her, yes. I didn't give her any details but thought you should know.'

'Thank you,' said Louise, clenching her hands. 'I'll make sure she doesn't bother you again.'

Chapter Seven

Louise called Tania Elliot later that morning, and arranged to meet her at the Kalimera restaurant across from the seafront at lunchtime. Louise smiled when she saw the restaurant owner, Georgina, who had been a sometime confidante in the years since she'd moved to Weston.

'Why are you meeting this woman again?' said Georgina, pointing over to Tania, who had arrived early and was sitting at a table and looking at her phone. Georgina placed a black coffee on the counter without asking. 'She brings trouble with her.'

'I'm trying to temper that as much as possible. Trust me, it would be worse if I didn't meet with her.'

Georgina frowned, flicking her black hair behind her shoulders. 'Sit, I'll bring it over.'

Louise was used to the woman's brusque manner and didn't take offence as she walked over and shook hands with Tania. The morning had been an exhausting onslaught of interview after interview. It was work she would normally have delegated, but as it was Emily's school she wanted to be involved first-hand. But it had taken some persuasion on her part. With the note being addressed to her, and the crime scene being Emily's school, Robertson had argued that Tracey should stay as lead investigator. Louise had argued that due to her own work in the area, she was a relatively well-known detective. Eventually, Robertson had reluctantly allowed her to investigate, with the proviso that he was the SIO.

Apart from some juicy gossip about two teachers allegedly in a secret relationship, she had to concede she was no further along in her investigation than she had been at the start. As Mrs Harrison had claimed, the staff were a relatively content bunch, and if there was a motive to have planted the device it wasn't an obvious one.

'You look well,' said Louise, taking a seat opposite the reporter. When she'd first met Tania she'd been a rookie hack, trying to make a name for herself. With Louise's inadvertent help, she'd done just that, and now had a regular column for a broadsheet newspaper to go alongside her non-fiction work. Her dress sense matched her elevated status. Where once she'd worn jeans and a hoodie, she was now wearing a sleek designer dress, her face subtly painted with make-up.

'It's good to see you, Louise, and thanks for taking the time to see me.'

'What are you working on now?' said Louise, smiling as Georgina placed her coffee in front of her.

'Your latest triumph.'

The scar on Louise's arm itched as she heard the words. Her last major case had been the prosecution of a killer who had been branding their targets in the Weston area, but Tania wasn't talking about that. 'You mean Tim Finch?'

'What bigger triumph than putting that arsehole away?'

That was something they could agree on. 'I only had a bit part to play in that,' said Louise, remembering a crazy twelve-hour period where she'd not only fought Finch – preventing him from killing Amira and resulting in his arrest – but she had also received the scar now pulsating on her arm after being attacked by a psychopath nicknamed the Branding Killer by the press.

'Modest as ever. I am working on something involving him. Obviously, lots will depend on what happens at his trial, but I think there is quite a story to tell there.'

Louise couldn't quite pinpoint what it was about Tania that antagonised her so. She'd had good relationships with journalists in the past and she accepted that being pushy was sometimes part of the job. With Tania, that pushiness transformed into something else. Louise always got the sense from her that she was only in it for herself, and at times she presented a ruthlessness and lack of empathy that would have shamed many of the criminals Louise had dealt with in the past.

'I hear there was a bomb threat at Larkmead School,' said Tania, sipping at a glass of iced water.

The incident had made local news but had so far stayed under the radar of the nationals. With no group coming forward to claim responsibility, Louise hoped it would soon become yesterday's news, and that the fact her name was on the note would never come to light. 'But you don't want to discuss that, Tania, do you?'

Tania's eyes narrowed. 'No small talk then. I was hoping we could chat some more about Finch.'

'I'd rather not.'

'You, probably more than most, knew him very well. You both worked together at MIT and continued working together following your move to Weston.'

Louise had no doubt that Tania knew everything there was to know about her and Finch, including their brief sexual relationship. It had never been a secret but wasn't something Louise wanted to read about in Tania's latest book. 'Finch is on remand, and I will soon be testifying against him. You can hardly expect me to talk about an active case.'

'Of course not. I was looking for something a little more . . . personal.'

49

Louise felt her pulse quicken, the scar on her arm throbbing even more intensely. 'Personal?'

'Tell me a little about what he was like, before all this came to light. He's been a very successful police officer prosecution-wise. Did you know he had this dark side from the beginning?'

'Did I know he would manipulate and abuse female officers, you mean? Before trying to kill one of them?'

'When did you first become suspicious that he was corrupt?'

It was a pertinent question, and one Louise didn't want to face. The truth was she had been duped as much as the others. Up until that evening at the Walton farm, she'd more or less trusted Finch. She knew he was a bit of a player. It was why their relationship had never become more serious. But he could be charming and funny, and as Tania suggested had also been a very good policeman, at least in terms of successful prosecutions. As she'd walked through the derelict farm building, the air fetid with the smell of pig shit, she'd trusted Finch with her life. 'My complaints about Finch are on record,' she said.

'I understand there was a conflict of opinion about what went down that evening at the Walton farm. You claim that Finch told you that Max Walton was armed, and he denies it.'

'It's no secret, Tania.'

'And you're sticking by that?'

'It's what happened. Why are you dredging this up again? What is it you actually want?'

'You were effectively demoted to Weston because of Finch. Didn't that make you angry?'

'Of course it made me fucking angry,' said Louise, through gritted teeth. She turned away, furious with herself for losing her temper. Her complaints at the time had fallen on deaf ears. Finch had stolen her promotion and wanted her gone. He'd hassled her even after she'd left HQ, sending her anonymous texts that had come close to threatening her sanity.

'I hate to ask you this, but do you think you could have done more to stop him?'

Louise met Tania's eyes. She had to hand it to her – Tania knew how to push her buttons. Louise rarely lost her temper, and now she was on the verge of reaching across the table to grab the journalist. 'I'm not talking about this any more.'

Tania nodded, as if she was doing Louise a favour by not continuing. 'Something you should be aware of, Louise. I was recently contacted by Justin Walton, Max Walton's nephew.'

Louise cursed inwardly. 'Why do I need to be aware of that?'

'He is claiming that, with Finch facing a prison sentence, the case of his uncle's unlawful death should be reopened.'

Louise snorted. 'His uncle, the depraved mass murderer?'

'Are you saying all suspected killers should be shot dead without investigation or context?'

'Don't put words into my mouth, Tania. There was a legitimate threat that night, and you know it.'

'You shot an unarmed man.'

Louise had only been armed because of a now-defunct national pilot scheme allowing senior detectives to carry firearms in potentially fatal situations. 'I've been cleared of all wrongdoing, and am not prepared to talk about it any more.'

'I believe Justin Walton is considering a private prosecution against you and Finch.'

'What do you want, Tania?'

'I want you to help yourself, Louise.'

Louise snorted again. 'Save that for those more easily manipulated.'

'I need to tell this story. And so far, I only have Mr Walton's side of things.'

'I'm sure your readers will welcome his input.'

'And I'll be getting Finch's perspective on things too.'

Louise sucked in a breath. In her peripheral vision, she caught Georgina staring over as if poised for attack.

'He's agreed to talk with me,' said Tania.

'Well, enjoy that,' said Louise.

Tania handed Louise her card. 'You can call me any time,' she said, as both their phones went off in unison.

Louise walked away, out of earshot. 'Tracey?'

'Hi, Lou. Are you in Weston?'

'Yes, why?'

'Probably best you get over to Kewstoke. A fire has broken out in one of the static caravans over there, and it looks like there might be a link to the incident at the school.'

Chapter Eight

Clemons' plan was mulled over in Finch's mind as he tidied his cell. The new television had arrived within an hour of his meeting, Wilson guiding one of Clemons' lackeys who proceeded to set the television up for him with an idiotic grin etched on to his face. Finch didn't care much for TV but wasn't about to divulge that to Clemons. It was a gesture and for now he was appreciative. What was important now was how he could best exploit the situation for his own ends.

The proposal had potential, but Finch understood Clemons wasn't talking to him out of the goodness of his own heart. From the sounds of it, he needed Finch, and if he did deliver what he promised then it indeed had the possibility of harming Louise Blackwell via her new squeeze, Thomas Ireland; and with Blackwell sidelined, his court case could be thrown into disarray. At the very least they would be forced to let him out of this remand hellhole, and that might be all he needed.

Finch didn't like to rush into things, but time wasn't on his side. He rearranged the line of legal texts on his shelf so they were symmetrical, before banging on the cell door, his knuckles making a satisfying noise against the cold metal.

Five minutes later, the bean hole opened and a voice said, 'What is it, Finch?'

'I'd like to speak with Officer Wilson, boss,' said Finch, his nails digging into his skin as he used the title for a man he didn't even recognise.

'Do you now. He's not around, you can make do with me.'

'Officer Wilson is my key worker,' said Finch.

'If you have an issue, you can either raise it with me or wait until Mr Wilson is available. What will it be?'

'When will he be available?'

'I'll let him know you'd like to speak to him,' said the guard, slamming the divider shut.

Finch sat at his desk and concentrated on his breathing. He refused to be riled by the likes of the nameless guard. It was a travesty that he was in this position, having to bow and beg to scum like him, but he had to be sensible. This was his life for the time being and he had to play the game like he always had. He would wait, and whenever he got out of this godforsaken place, he would savour taking revenge on all those who had ever wronged him.

Clemons wasn't the only one with a plan in motion.

Wilson arrived at Finch's cell an hour later like the obedient sheep he was. 'I need to see someone,' said Finch, stopping short of chastising the guard for his absence.

'You can put it on your weekly request,' said Wilson. 'You can't just summon me like this.'

'I need it to be arranged for tomorrow.'

'Don't be ridiculous. Even if I wanted to, it couldn't be done.'

'It's an ex-colleague of mine. I need you to phone him and tell him to make a request to see me. He'll know what to do to make it sound above board.'

'Is this to do with your meeting with Clemons?'

Finch stared Wilson down. 'Don't worry about letting Clemons down. It's me you need to be concerned with. Here's the number. I expect to see him tomorrow.'

'I always knew you were bad news,' said Wilson, snatching the note from him.

◆ ◆ ◆

Finch eased himself back on his bed and waited. He scanned his room five times and, content that nothing was out of place, closed his eyes.

Being inside was a battle of wills. They wanted you to break so that you were easier to manage. Finch understood that more than most. It would never happen to him because he was stronger than they were. He could accept his imprisonment. All it took was viewing it from a different perspective. If it had to be, this would be his head office for the next few years. There was still much to be gained from being inside and he would maximise his time here if necessary.

If necessary. Though he could accept his lot, it didn't mean he wouldn't be happy to get out, and the coming weeks would give him the best chance of that.

He kept his eyes closed but didn't sleep. He hated to use the term, but what he was doing was a type of meditation. In his head, he played through all possible scenarios from the obvious to the ludicrous. He tried to imagine how all the other parties would react to different types of pressure. Where were the weaknesses, where were the potential openings for exploitation? It was an approach he'd taken with his career from the start. He usually won because he was the only person aware he was in a competition. That wasn't the case this time, and his recent experiences with Louise and the others meant he had to be more thorough in his plans. He'd been sloppy on the outside with that Amira bitch, and that sloppiness had cost him.

His chest tightened, his anger causing his muscles to contract. He should have been more ruthless with Louise Blackwell when he'd had the chance. She had grown to become the folly of his existence. He wondered if he'd kept her around because of the challenge she brought with her. He'd beaten her once, had made her shoot an unarmed man, but the victory had been essentially worthless. He'd enjoyed her mini breakdown as she'd fought her case before being demoted to Weston, but hadn't expected her comeback.

And now she'd turned the tables on him, working with Amira and those other bitches to put him away.

One-all. The game was still afoot. And he promised himself this time he would be even more ruthless in his desire to win.

The rattle of the cell door tore him from his reverie. He'd forgotten where he was and he allowed a couple of seconds of silence to sink in before leaving the bed.

'Dinner, Finch.'

He took the offered tray with its childlike sections of barely edible food and spotted a note taped underneath:

Check the back of the TV.

Finch ripped the note into shreds before starting his meal. If there was something waiting for him inside the television then he wasn't going to be rushed into looking.

He waited until his tray had been collected before acting. He'd tried the TV earlier that day, watching the local news, and wasn't expecting much.

It took a bit of work but he managed to find a loose screw that held together a hidden panel. Removing the panel, Finch retrieved an old-style mobile phone with a charging wire connected directly to the TV.

Finch replaced the panel and switched on the handset. The volume was switched off and a message had been saved on the screen:

Another perk.

Finch smirked, recalling how he used to send Louise anonymous text messages when she'd first moved to Weston. He'd never known for sure the mental impact it had, but on occasions he'd even driven to the bungalow she'd lived in and waited for her to switch off her lights so he could catch her just as she was falling asleep.

One thing was for sure, he wasn't going to be manipulated in such a way. One number was stored on the phone, but he wasn't going to be rushed into using it. If Clemons wanted thanks for the gift, then he would have to wait.

He waited until the following morning after breakfast to retrieve the phone from the panel. Although the phone could come in handy, it was also a huge risk for him. Having a phone in his possession would mean him losing what privileges he had, and would also be detrimental to his case.

Clemons would know this, but still Finch called the number on the phone, and was surprised when a female voice answered.

Chapter Nine

Ten minutes into her journey, a flume of black smoke guided Louise to her destination, a static caravan park in Kewstoke less than a mile from her house.

Tracey was already at the scene, having been in the area on an unrelated investigation. 'Fortunately, the fire was contained to the one static caravan,' she said, wiping sweat from her forehead.

The fire was out now. The SOCOs were working with the fire brigade to ensure it was safe before entering.

'Someone call it in?' asked Louise, as she watched the remnants of the smoke snake into the clear sky.

'Here,' said Tracey, handing over her phone.

The voice sounded like it belonged to a middle-aged man. It would be analysed but Louise didn't think any voice modification software was being used. 'I told you, DI Blackwell, next time it would be real,' the voice said, before giving the caravan's address.

Louise felt a shiver at the mention of her name. 'When was this called in?'

'We received this notification eight minutes before the emergency call came in from one of the caravan owners. The woman in question, Merrill Letts, claims she heard a noise and looked out to see the fire. Said it was maybe two to three minutes from hearing the noise until the time she called it in.'

Louise knew the assistant chief fire officer, a rotund man called John McKee, who greeted her with his warm Welsh accent. 'Lucky we kept it to the one caravan. Could have spread like the proverbial if we hadn't got here sooner. I understand you had a hoax call yesterday at Larkmead School?'

Louise was about to answer when Tracey tapped her on her shoulder. She turned to see Tania Elliot pulling up in her sleek black coupé. 'Tell her to piss off, will you, Tracey. I'll arrest her if I have to speak to her.' It hadn't evaded Louise's attention that Tania's phone had gone off at the same time as hers. She didn't wish to overreact but she wondered if Tania had a source in the police or other emergency service who had tipped her off.

'What did you hear?' Louise asked McKee, as Tracey marched off to intercept Tania.

'I was at some stupid regional meeting but I heard about it. A pretend explosive device?'

'And a note.'

'No note this time, but he called it in?'

'Apparently so.'

'Look, we went inside when we arrived, to check no one was in danger. I'm happy to go back now and look for the source. The guys say there was a big smell of gasoline, and you only need to look at the smoke and the damage done to know some sort of accelerant was used. Wanted to check you're OK for us to go rummaging around now?'

Louise checked with Janice Sutton from the SOCO team before agreeing. Tracey had returned, Tania having been banished to her car. The journalist was still in eyeline and Louise felt a disproportionate amount of anger that she was still on site.

'Says she's doing no harm sitting in her car,' said Tracey, by way of explanation.

Louise could have pushed it but was already distracted. Up close the smell of gasoline was strong and sweet, and smoke clung to her clothes. Louise had been caught in a fire before, and had to fight her triggered feelings of being trapped and surrounded by engulfing flames as three of the fire team went back into the caravan.

It wasn't long before they were outside again, one of the team chatting to McKee before he walked over and showed her a grainy image that had been taken inside. It appeared to be the charcoal remains of an IED. 'Is that a phone?' said Louise.

'I'd get your bomb guys back here if I were you,' said McKee.

'How does it work?' said Louise, zooming in on the image.

'I can't be sure until we've had a closer look. Appears that the vibration function on the phone would have sparked the ignition, but the place had already been doused with petrol in advance. This was timed to go off when it did.'

'Remotely?'

'All they had to do was call,' said McKee.

'Isn't that quite sophisticated?' asked Louise, thinking about the potential damage such a system could do, and whether Emily was really safe having gone back to school.

'Unfortunately, not anymore. Frightening really. Of course, they would have to set up the thing in the first place, so someone must have planted the device and soaked the place with petrol.'

Louise thanked McKee, her teeth grinding. Through the glare of the sun, she could see Tania sitting behind the driver's wheel of her car chatting away on her mobile. The fallout from this could be enormous. Thankfully, no one was injured, but the thought of a rogue arsonist with such capabilities was more than unsettling.

'I have spoken with the owners of the caravan, Mr and Mrs Bastien. Retired couple, currently in Malta,' said Tracey.

'What did they say?' said Louise, distracted by thoughts of what her next steps should be.

'Naturally, they're a bit put out,' said Tracey.

'Sorry, stupid question,' said Louise, shaking her head as if to drag herself back into the present. 'When were they last here?'

'Not for six months. They pay the park a fee to keep their caravan maintained in their absence, but they don't like to let it out. The wife was very emotional on the phone. I asked all the obvious questions but she can't think of a reason why anyone would target them specifically.'

'Maybe it was because the arsonist knew they were away,' said Louise, almost to herself. 'We need to close this site down,' she added, snapping back into work mode. 'No one is to leave. Guess I better call it in.'

'I'll sort it, no problem,' said Tracey. 'The park owner's on her way as well.'

'Thanks, Tracey.'

'What shall we do with her?' asked Tracey, pointing to the figure of Tania Elliot, who was still on her phone.

'Let's cordon this whole area off, and make sure Tania can't see what's going on. I think we're going to be here a long time.'

◆ ◆ ◆

The news wasn't greeted with much enthusiasm by DCI Robertson. Louise could sense him pacing the office as she told him about the potential threat and her need for extra staff.

'You know I'm going to have to escalate this?' he said, his voice a low growl.

In the past that would have meant Finch was going to be called in, and Louise had to stop for a second as it dawned on her that he was safely behind bars and could no longer interfere. 'Do what you have to, boss.'

'As long as you realise we may lose the case. If this is seen as anything close to a terrorist threat it will be taken over.'

It wasn't the first time she'd risked losing an investigation. She understood the risk. 'This isn't terrorists. This is targeted, Iain.'

'Maybe so, but I'm not the one you'll need to convince. The caller mentioned your name again. I'm going to be asked if you should be in charge of this investigation.'

'I know you'll do your best for me,' said Louise, hanging up before he had the chance to argue. For now, she had control of the investigation, and that was all she could focus on. She had completed a counter-terrorism training course a few years back, and although she wasn't an expert, nothing about what was happening fell into the known patterns. That didn't rule it out, but Louise's first priority was to discover anything that linked the school and the caravan park.

As it was still term time, the caravan park wasn't at full capacity, but a couple of hours in and there was already a queue of caravan owners and renters wanting to get back on site. Backup staff from Portishead were arriving piecemeal and it was becoming a difficult situation to manage.

When the park's owner Mary Sutcliffe – a formidable-looking woman in her late sixties – arrived, she wasted no time in expressing her concerns at the way her tenants were being treated.

'I appreciate your concern, but we have no other option at present,' said Louise, following the woman to her office, a small prefab hut that overlooked the site.

'Tea?'

'I'm fine,' said Louise.

'I could do with something a little stronger. I guess you can't partake? Could never abide drinking on my own.'

Louise shook her head. 'You live in Bristol?'

'Westbury.'

'When were you last on the site?'

'Yesterday. I suppose I'm a suspect? Think this is an insurance job? Believe me, this will cost me much more than I'll ever make back.' The woman was well spoken, her neutral accent suggesting she wasn't from the south-west.

'No one is suggesting that,' said Louise. 'I need some more details on your security set-up. At some point someone has entered the Bastiens' caravan and planted the device, as well as soaking the place with accelerant. Realistically, with the smell of the gasoline, that must have happened in the last twenty-four hours.'

'Was the lock busted?'

'We're not sure. It appears that it wasn't forced open, but the lock could have been picked. Who would have access to the keys?'

Mary looked behind her to a wall safe. 'We have all the keys in there. It is the Bastiens' property, so they would have keys and could make and give out as many copies as they wished.'

'Could we see?' said Louise, looking at the wall safe.

'Of course.'

'Do you mind using these,' she said, handing the woman a pair of latex gloves. 'If you could open it but not touch anything inside, please.'

Mary frowned but did as she was asked. 'Two sets of keys for the Bastien property, all present and correct.'

'I will need to get this room checked for prints and DNA. Who has access to the safe?'

'I have a key, as does my partner, who is in the Seychelles at present on business,' said Mary, emphasising the last word as if it was made up.

'Anyone else?'

'I'm afraid so. We have a cleaning firm who come in who need access to the caravans, and a local handyman who comes in and helps us out.'

'I'll need a list of names,' said Louise. 'As well as a list of all owners, and people on site.'

'I can print that up for you now. With those on site, we're notified by the caravan owners about rentals and what have you. It's their responsibility to give us all the names, but they can be a bit slack – especially with family members.'

'I understand,' said Louise, remaining in her seat as Mary booted up her computer and began printing for her.

'Rentals list,' said Mary, handing her four sheets of A4 paper.

A musty smell seemed to permeate the room as Louise read through the list. Some of the names had already been interviewed, but there were over a hundred people and those were just the rentals.

Mary handed her some more paper. 'Owners who may or may not be on site. They're supposed to tell us but they rarely do if they're just turning up because of the weather. And staff list.'

Louise ignored the owners and went straight to the staff list. 'You have a lot of cleaners.'

'Transient job sometimes. We hire a firm. Those are the main contacts. To be fair, they've been pretty good. No complaints, and nothing seems to go missing.'

Louise stopped, a jet of adrenaline hitting her system. 'This man, Karl Insgrove?'

'Our handyman. What about him?'

'Do you know if he works at Larkmead School?'

'Yes, he's the caretaker there. As I said, he only helps out here now and then,' said Mary, but Louise had already stopped listening.

'You have an address for him?'

'Yes, here,' said Mary, printing up the sheet. 'You don't think he's . . .'

Louise was already on her feet. 'Thank you, and please don't touch anything else in here,' she said, as she headed for her car.

Chapter Ten

As Louise pulled up outside Larkmead, she saw her mother getting into her car with Emily.

'Louise, what are you doing here?' her mother asked, as Emily waved from the back seat.

Louise had called Joanne Harrison to confirm the caretaker was still at the school. 'Back for work, nothing to worry about.'

'Are you meeting Mrs Harrison again?' said Emily.

Louise's mother was staring at Louise with concentration, a familiar look that meant she was trying to analyse what her daughter was up to. 'Yes, darling. Not to talk about you though,' said Louise, sticking her head through the window to kiss her niece. 'Best you go home with Grandma now.'

Her mother frowned and mouthed, 'What's happening?'

'It's fine, Mum, I'll speak to you later. Please take Emily home now.'

Louise waited until the pair had driven away before crossing the road to the school at the same time as two backup patrol cars arrived. This grabbed everyone's attention, and Louise had to dodge past concerned parents as she made her way through to the school reception where Mrs Harrison was waiting.

'Is this absolutely necessary?' said the headteacher.

'I just need to speak to him. Where is he?'

'In my office.'

'Does he know I'm coming?'

'No, which is something else I don't like.' The headmistress glanced behind Louise. 'Now this,' she added through gritted teeth as two uniformed officers arrived.

Louise instructed the officers to guard the area, before walking with Mrs Harrison to her office where Karl Insgrove was waiting.

'Hello again,' said the caretaker.

'Hello, Mr Insgrove.' Louise stood, guarding the door, with the headmistress behind her.

'Karl,' said the caretaker, his smile fading as he glanced from Louise to Mrs Harrison. 'Everything OK?'

Louise studied Insgrove, trying to work out if there was anything in her past that linked her to him. The offender had used her name both in the warning note at the school and during the call. For him to single her out specifically suggested he held some sort of grudge against her, but the only interaction she could recall with Insgrove was seeing him occasionally when dropping Emily at school. 'There's been a fire at the Kewstoke Caravan Park,' said Louise.

Insgrove's look of concern was convincing. 'Oh dear, is everyone OK? Mrs Sutcliffe?'

'She's fine, and thankfully no one was hurt. We believe it was an act of arson. One of the caravans has burnt down.'

'My goodness.'

'Anything you'd like to tell me before I continue?' said Louise, her body tensed in anticipation of Karl trying to make a run for it. She'd been in this position too many times not to prepare for the worst.

'Would anyone like to tell me what the hell is going on here?' asked Mrs Harrison, still in the corridor.

'It's OK, Joanne. That's the place where I do my part-time work. I guess that's why you're here? You think I'm some sort of link?'

'An explosive device was found inside the caravan. It was similar to the one we found in the school PE storeroom.'

Insgrove nodded. 'I don't know what to say. I haven't been there since the weekend.'

'But you have access to the keys?'

Insgrove moved his hand to his belt and produced a set of keys. 'This opens the safe at the park where the keys are kept. Which caravan burnt down?'

'Does Mr Insgrove need a solicitor?' asked the headteacher.

'Not unless he wants one. The caravan belonged to the Bastien family.'

'Oh dear. As I said, I don't know what to tell you other than I have nothing to do with either of these incidents. The Bastiens are lovely people,' he added, glancing at Mrs Harrison, who had now stepped into the room. Again, Louise was struck by how similar the two people looked. It was in their eyes, and thin eyebrows, even in their squat body shapes. If she'd met them under different circumstances, she would have sworn they were related.

'This is quite preposterous. I have known Karl for nigh on forty years now,' said Mrs Harrison.

'You need to accompany me to the station, Mr Insgrove.'

'Am I under arrest?'

'No, but I would have no option but to arrest you if you didn't wish to accompany me.'

Karl looked at the headteacher again, pleading. 'I haven't done anything. And I don't want to go out in front of the children.'

If the caretaker was innocent of the charges, then Louise understood his concern. 'School's over now. Nearly everyone has gone home,' she said.

'You won't cuff him?' said Mrs Harrison.

Louise paused. The caretaker was in his sixties and looked out of shape, and she had two sets of officers positioned in the reception area and car park. 'You'll have to stay next to me at all times. If you deviate from that then I will arrest you on the spot. Do you understand?'

The caretaker was on the verge of tears as he got to his feet. It was a convincing act but Louise couldn't afford for sentimentality to get in the way of duty. She kept close to Insgrove and signalled for the uniformed officers to stand by.

As they left the building, Louise noted that Mrs Harrison looked dismayed to see some of the parents were still in the courtyard area at the front of the school. There was a collective hush as Louise walked past with Insgrove next to her. The caretaker offered the parents – and a few schoolchildren who were frozen to the spot, staring at the scene – a quick smile before Mrs Harrison interjected.

'Mr Insgrove is helping the police with some details regarding yesterday's incident,' said Mrs Harrison. If anything, this made things worse, as parents began talking over each other, questioning why the caretaker had been taken into custody.

Louise placed her hand on Insgrove's back and eased him forward, wanting everyone out of the awkward situation as soon as possible. At the patrol car, she helped him inside next to one of the officers. By this point, Insgrove was crying. Louise wasn't sure if it was from guilt, or at a perceived unfairness. That she would have to try and unravel back at the station. For now, she had more pressing problems.

Twenty metres away, Tania Elliot was leaning on the bonnet of her car. She'd been taking photos of the incident and was videoing Insgrove's arrest.

'Where are you taking him?' asked Mrs Harrison, breaking Louise out of her trance-like focus on the journalist.

'Weston station for now. In Worle.'

'I would like to be present for any interviews with Mr Insgrove. In lieu of a solicitor.'

'Due to your professional and personal relationship with Mr Insgrove, I'm afraid that won't be possible,' said Louise, hoping the headteacher wouldn't question how close Louise was to the investigation, with Emily being one of the pupils at the school. 'I will make sure Mr Insgrove has legal representation if he needs it, and of course you are welcome to wait for him at the station,' she added when Mrs Harrison didn't reply. 'If there was any other way, I would have taken it. Hopefully, Mr Insgrove will be able to answer our questions and we can get to the bottom of this. Would you like a lift to the station?'

'I can make my own way there, thank you,' said the head-teacher, heading back to the school where she was swarmed by parents and schoolchildren.

'Is Mr Insgrove under arrest?' asked Tania, sneaking up to Louise as Mrs Harrison retreated.

'No.'

'Helping with inquiries, I understand,' said Tania, taking notes with a small pencil held in her beautifully manicured hand. 'He's the handyman at the Kewstoke caravan site, I believe?'

'No comment.'

'No comment,' said Tania, mimicking Louise as she continued writing.

Louise refused to rise to the bait. Tania was purposely trying to antagonise her in the hope that she would lose her cool and blurt out something she shouldn't. 'What do you want, Tania?'

'After today's developments, this will be big news. Maybe even national. It's my duty to report what has happened.'

'Mr Insgrove isn't under arrest.'

'I know, he's helping police with inquiries. I'll be sure to mention it.'

'Maybe you could hold off for a day. We need to speak to him because of his links to both sites, nothing more, nothing less. It wouldn't be fair to drag his name through the media.'

'Fair? That's a good one. You didn't seem to mind dragging him out in front of his colleagues and the parents. In front of the children.'

'What do you want?' asked Louise, realising she sounded like a broken record.

'Exclusive access to this case, and for you to sit down and answer some questions about Finch.'

Louise looked away, her body tensing. 'I will give you daily updates about this investigation, that I can promise, but I won't be talking about Finch. He has a court appearance pending, as you well know.'

'Everything will be off the record until the verdict.'

'I can't do it. Take it or leave it but I won't be speaking about Finch.'

'I'll take it, Louise. You'll speak to me after your interview with Mr Insgrove?'

Louise's shoulder muscles were pulling. She hated making any deals with the journalist but didn't want Insgrove's name in the papers. 'If you don't publish anything from here just yet then I will speak to you.'

'Thank you, DI Blackwell, always a pleasure. Now excuse me, I have some people I need to speak to.'

Louise shook her head as Tania walked towards the group of parents, her notebook held out in front of her like a weapon.

Chapter Eleven

The exercise yard was overlooked on all sides. If it ever caught the sun, it must have been at a different time to when Finch had used the place. He only walked in shadows, and as he paced it now alone, reluctantly using his walking stick, counting each and every step with military precision, he felt eyes boring into him. Men on both sides of the prison divide wished harm upon him, but for now he was relatively safe. He was on remand, and the guards were happy waiting for his court appearance after which they hoped he would be assimilated into full prison life, more than likely somewhere worse than this. As for his fellow prisoners, even if they could get past the security that meant he ate, slept and exercised alone, no one would touch him because of his links to Terry Clemons.

Finch wasn't sure yet if Clemons was an opportunity or a hindrance. What he wanted of Finch was doable, as long as the deviant guard Wilson did what he was told.

If Finch succeeded in helping him out, Clemons had offered Finch a potential security blanket for his time inside. Finch could continue exploiting his old contacts to aid Clemons' business. It was a way of staying safe in an environment that only promised to get more hostile.

Finch counted to seventy-two and made a sharp left turn before starting his count again from zero.

Finch would be mad not to consider Clemons a risk. That was why he'd asked Wilson to summon his old colleague Edward Perkins. Perkins was perfect for the job and could be trusted to keep his mouth shut. More importantly, Finch had dirt on the man going back to the last decade. If he wanted, he could have Perkins accompanying him inside with a click of his fingers. That would keep Perkins loyal, and would mean he would be an ally if Clemons decided to turn.

He paced some more. A smell always seemed to accompany his little walks around the exercise yard, something akin to rotting vegetables even though no bins were in sight. It was ripe in the thick air today, repressive in the heat. Finch breathed through his mouth, trying to avoid the dead smell as he considered the other anomaly: the phone, and its pre-programmed number belonging to the journalist Tania Elliot.

Finch recalled the woman from his time spent in Weston. She was a pretty little thing, and he'd tried it on with her a couple of times to a general lack of interest. She was savvy, and had probably made a small fortune from recent events in the shitty little seaside town. On the phone she'd promised to make him famous.

'Infamous?' he'd asked.

'I think we can do better than that,' she'd said, her voice seductive as she asked to meet him.

Only when he'd reminded her why he was facing trial had she properly explained herself. Her real interest was with the dead psychopath Max Walton. She was writing a book on him and the fallout from that time. Central to her plans was Finch's recollection of that night at the farm when Louise had shot the unarmed man dead.

Christ, that was some fuck-up. They should never have been carrying anything in the first place. Some bigwig trying to make a name for himself had used Avon and Somerset as their guinea pigs, giving senior detectives firearm training and allowing them to carry weapons into potentially life-threatening scenarios.

Finch chuckled as he began his thirty-second lap of the prison yard. That experiment had soon ended after he'd given Louise the order to shoot. He'd had no qualms about giving the order, nor denying he had ever done so. He wanted Walton dead, wanted Louise to fuck up so he could secure his promotion to DCI, and both things had worked out in his favour. The world was a better place without Walton, and his had been a better world being a DCI.

Not that he'd told the journalist any of that. He'd never trusted their kind ever, had only tried to use them for his own ends. But he'd still agreed to meet her. He hoped he could slip a few stories about Louise into the public domain before the trial started.

'Time.'

Finch stopped walking at the command from the prison guard. It was the same guard who'd refused him permission to speak to Wilson the other day. Finch now knew him as Boss Kirkland, or *sir* as he preferred to be known.

'I'm going to cuff you, Finch. Hands behind your back,' said the guard, walking towards him.

'Cuff me, why?' It was a Cat B prison and Finch had never been cuffed going to or from the exercise yard before.

'You have a visitor,' said Kirkland, pulling Finch's right arm behind his back and placing the metal cuffs over his wrists.

'Easy, man.'

'Easy who?'

'Mr Kirkland,' said Finch, with a mock smile.

'You'd do well not to cross me, Finch. I'm not weak like Wilson. I despise people like you who abuse their power, and won't be putting up with any of that shit in my prison, do you understand?'

73

'Whatever happened to innocent until proven guilty?' asked Finch, as the guard pushed him through the doors and back inside the prison.

'Fuck you. That's what happened.'

Finch knew better than to respond. In a way, he admired the guard. He was taking the no-nonsense route Finch had favoured as a police officer, and it would be foolish to take it personally.

Kirkland guided him through three sets of gates before reaching an interview cell. He nodded to a second guard, who opened the metallic door to reveal the welcome face of Edward Perkins, who was sitting at a metal desk fixed to the floor.

'Eddie,' said Finch, as Kirkland shoved him through the opening and sat him down.

'That's DS Perkins now,' said his former colleague, stony-faced.

'You need me here?' said Kirkland.

'I'll be fine,' said Perkins.

'You can keep the cuffs on, Finch, for your insolence.'

Finch sighed but didn't argue. Kirkland locked them inside and they both waited a minute before breaking their silence.

'How's it going, guv?' said Perkins, his blank expression easing into a smile.

'Better for seeing a friendly face. *That's DS Perkins now*?' he asked, raising his eyebrows.

'Got to play the game, guv.'

'How did you get to see me?' asked Finch.

'Told them I needed your input on an old case. Didn't even bother to question me. Brought some files just in case,' said Perkins, placing a box file on to the desk.

'You speak to Wilson, then?'

'You need to watch him, boss. He's a talker.'

'Don't worry, he knows what will happen if he talks too much. I'd worry more about that Kirkland character. He's likely to check your story on the way out.'

Perkins pointed to his head. 'All up here.'

Finch nodded. 'So what's new in the world?'

'Headquarters is a piss-take now. That Weston lot are heading up one section, and Tracey is running Bristol.'

Tracey Pugh was one of the few female officers Finch hadn't tried to get rid of. Partly because she didn't fit into the little games he liked to play with female officers. He found her repulsive, and would no sooner have slept with her than pissed on her if she was on fire. But she was best friends with Louise, and that meant he could leverage her for information, usually without her direct knowledge. Sadly, the only dirt he had on her was a penchant for younger men in the department, and she'd sidestepped that possible indiscretion by dating a young plod who now worked out of Nailsea and had no direct work relationship with her. 'And Blackwell?'

'Still pushing her agenda. How can they justify putting proper detectives away when *she* is on the force,' he said, saying the things he knew Finch wanted to hear.

'You need to push for promotion, Perkins. Can't have that lot taking over.'

Perkins raised his head in acknowledgement. Finch was humouring the man and Perkins probably knew it. He was already a level too high on the pay scale, and no one with any sense was going to give him extra power, especially with his history with Finch. 'How can I help, boss?'

Despite their relative privacy, Finch was forced to speak in code. Perkins had been around the block enough to get the gist of what he was saying. With Perkins' help, the flow of drugs into the Cat B prison could be tied up. It was a big ask for the man but they both knew he had little choice but to accept.

'Nasty outfit. You sure you want to get involved?' said Perkins.

'You'll hardly know you're part of it, Eddie. Turn a blind eye and manage the guards. Wilson is on board so you can work with him.'

Perkins placed his hand to his mouth, the mood shifting in the cell. Finch knew better than to talk. Perkins wanted to negotiate and he wasn't going to break first. 'What's in this for you?' said his former colleague, after a prolonged silence.

'Don't need to worry about that, Eddie.'

'You heard about the fire over in Kewstoke?' asked Perkins, surprising Finch by changing topic.

'We have a deal, Eddie?' said Finch, ignoring him.

Perkins pursed his lips. He looked on edge, as if building himself up to say something. 'This will be it, boss. I'm out then. Paid my debt, you know.'

'Goes without saying, Eddie,' said Finch, sucking in his fury. The gall of the man, trying to bargain with him. Finch might be inside prison but to him that was little more than an illusion. Perkins had only an inkling of the trouble Finch could throw his way if he wanted. That Perkins was trying to play him – now that the officer thought he was in a stronger position than he had been when they were colleagues – was something Finch wouldn't forget in a hurry. But for now, he decided to promise the man what he was asking for. 'There is one more thing, and this will directly benefit you.'

'What's that, boss?' said Perkins, the tension in the room easing.

'It might not be that late for your promotion, after all,' said Finch, proceeding to tell his former colleague about Clemons' secondary plan to discredit Louise Blackwell.

Chapter Twelve

The tower block in Mead Vale was only a short walk from Thomas's house. Louise had been here before on a couple of drug raids, but since that time the place had been tidied up considerably. The stairwell was much better lit, and the damp problem had either been fixed or covered over with a fresh coat of paint.

Karl Insgrove had been relatively talkative during his interview. He'd denied involvement in either incident, but had agreed to his home being searched. Louise was undecided on his guilt or innocence for now. He certainly had the means to have been responsible, but she was struggling to find a motive.

And it wasn't only the school's headteacher who had vouched for the caretaker's character. After leaving her old station in Worle, Louise had received a call from her own mother telling her how helpful Mr Insgrove had been with her in the past when they'd first moved to the school. It was another distraction she didn't need. It was hard enough holding on to the investigation as it was, and this wasn't something she'd be sharing with Robertson any time soon. Louise imagined the parents' WhatsApp group was rife with speculation and had thanked her mother for her input, saying goodbye before an argument could start.

Tracey opened the door of the flat on the fifth floor, shining her torch until she located a light switch. After having witnessed first-hand the squalor that some of Insgrove's fellow residents lived in, Louise had feared the worst, but Insgrove's small flat was immaculate. The place had a very modern feel, the walls a neutral off-white, the floors laminated wood with patterned rugs. There was little clutter. In the living-room area, a small settee and arm-chair faced an old-style box television set. The floors were spotless throughout, the bathroom gleaming.

'Either he's very practical . . . or he was expecting visitors,' said Tracey, opening a door off the main room.

'He is a caretaker. His job is to look after things,' said Louise, following her colleague into Insgrove's bedroom.

'Military man,' said Tracey, touching the tight corners of the well-made bed.

Louise took a frame off the wall above the headboard of Insgrove's bed. Behind the glass were a number of military medals. 'He told us he was in the navy. Served in the Falklands.' She glanced at a number of pictures of Insgrove in full military garb with his old colleagues. The only recent photo she could see of Insgrove was him outside the Holy Trinity church, with five other men of a similar age. Louise recorded the image on her phone.

'He wasn't an explosives expert by any chance?' asked Tracey, raising her eyebrows in pretend hope.

'Sadly not. Technician on the boats. Ships,' said Louise, remembering Insgrove correcting her during the interview.

'Better get started then,' said Tracey.

After the interview, Louise had decided to detain Insgrove. His connection to the school and caravan park seemed too coinci-dental, and she couldn't risk letting him out until they'd exhausted all possibilities. That meant they had until tomorrow afternoon to find something more concrete to charge him with, or they would have to let him go.

Radioing to the search team waiting outside to begin with the front room, Louise began going through Insgrove's bedside tables. It was the type of search where they didn't know what they were looking for, but would know when they found it. The easy way Insgrove had submitted to the search suggested there wouldn't be anything incriminating. She doubted they were going to find an explosive device, or a can of petrol, but all they needed was something suggesting Insgrove had explosives knowledge, or had been present at the caravan site in the last twenty-four hours.

For now, the questioning over in Kewstoke had finished. No one in the park could recall seeing Insgrove since Friday. There were only limited CCTV cameras in the reception area, and those were easily avoided. Insgrove could have slipped in during the night, and have copied the key any time before that.

'Found a laptop,' said one of the constables who'd been searching the rest of the flat. He'd already placed the machine in a clear evidence bag.

'Where was it?' asked Louise.

'In the cupboard, there,' said the constable, shining his torch into a small cabinet in the bathroom.

'Strange place to keep your laptop.'

'Heavy too,' said the constable.

'OK, let's get that out for testing as soon as we can,' said Louise, as two people she'd never met before stepped into Insgrove's flat.

Louise was about to ask them who they were when her phone rang. It was DCI Robertson. Louise answered as Tracey questioned the pair as to what they were doing. 'Sir,' said Louise.

'You're about to get a visit,' said Robertson.

Louise turned her back on the pair, who were showing their ID to Tracey. 'I think we just have.'

'Counter Terrorism. Do you know them? Faulkner and Hartson?'

'Jesus,' said Louise, under her breath.

'Just want to talk, apparently. Procedure. Play along for now. If you can?' said Robertson.

'Sir,' said Louise, hanging up.

Tracey was handing the ID back and made eye contact with Louise as she walked over. 'DI Louise Blackwell,' she said.

'DCI Evelyn Hartson and DI David Faulkner, Counter Terrorism,' said the female agent, the pair offering their ID again.

Counter Terrorism were based out of headquarters, but didn't tend to mix with the other officers. She nodded her head. 'That's fine. How can I help you?'

'May we?' said Evelyn, nodding to outside the apartment.

Louise glanced at Tracey. Louise was technically in charge, but Tracey had as much right to be there as her.

'I'll supervise the others,' said Tracey, offering Louise a little nod of assurance as she walked away.

Louise felt a breeze as she stepped out into the corridor. 'Sorry to take you away from your work,' said Evelyn. 'We thought it best to introduce ourselves now, to avoid any complications later on.'

'You're going to tell me it's just procedure next?' said Louise.

DI Faulkner smiled. 'It is just procedure. Anything involving explosive devices, especially with notes and phone calls attached . . . well, you know how it is. We've read the case notes so far, but I don't believe we can eliminate possible terrorist involvement yet.'

'Perhaps not,' said Louise, 'but it's a long way to come to tell us.'

'Not at all,' said David, flashing her a smile he probably thought was charming.

'As David says, it is just procedure. We need to monitor the investigation and would like to help out as best we can. We're only here to support you at this stage,' said Evelyn.

They were being careful to stress they were not taking over the investigation, while leaving room for that distinct possibility. At any other time, Louise might have bristled at their involvement. In her last few major investigations, the threat of headquarters' major investigation team, and in particular DCI Finch, had loomed over everything. Here she was now heading the MIT herself, facing the threat of losing the case to another organisation. And she was already in a precarious situation. With it being Emily's school, and the note being addressed to her, there was enough concern over her being the lead detective. It was probably in part why the CTU officers were here, but there was no point second-guessing anyone at this stage. At least it was still hers for the time being. 'I'm happy to share all information, and you'll have access on the database.'

'Naturally, but we were hoping we could liaise in a more practical way,' said David.

Adrenaline spiked in Louise's bloodstream. It was a struggle not to respond dismissively. '*A more practical way?*'

'What my colleague means,' said Evelyn, giving the smiling male agent a dismissive sneer, 'is that we all know the limitation of formal reports. By *liaison*, we were hoping we could get your thoughts directly. Maybe catch up on a daily basis. Just a few minutes of your time.'

It was no secret that, since the Walton farm incident, Louise had found it harder than before to work as part of a team. When she'd first moved to Weston CID she'd been isolated, mostly through choice, and it had taken her time to trust her colleagues, and for them to trust her. The request wasn't unreasonable. Evelyn was right about the limitations of a system where you only recorded details of the crimes and the subsequent investigation. The CTU would have access to resources and information she didn't, and it made sense to utilise them as best she could.

Louise shared with them her thoughts about the attacks being personal in nature.

'What are your first impressions of Karl Insgrove?' asked Evelyn.

Louise considered her reply before answering. 'I haven't got a clear idea of him yet as he keeps defying expectations. He was quite passive when we spoke to him at the school, tearful as we led him away. A little bit more forceful when we questioned him, but there was still the occasional tear. Searching his flat, he seems very ordered, which I guess coincides with his military background.'

'You think he did it?' said David, as if it was that clear-cut.

Louise never liked to work on hunches or gut instinct. If she thought someone was guilty of a crime it was because of evidence, or a strong suggestion that the person involved was guilty. Like all police officers, she'd been wrong before, and it was simply too early to make such a call. 'Do you?'

There it was again, that smile. Louise wondered how many people the agent had charmed with it and if he relied on it a little too much. It reminded her of how Greg Farrell had acted earlier in his career – a cheeky smile masking his true thoughts.

'We can look at his military background if you like,' said Evelyn, when David didn't respond.

'That would be helpful,' said Louise, thanking them before returning to the Insgrove flat and shutting the door behind her.

Chapter Thirteen

For the first time in a few nights, Louise didn't stay at Thomas's house. The search at the Insgrove flat had gone on long into the night, and aside from the laptop little else had been found that felt relevant. Louise made herself a Malay Chai. A recent addition to her night-time routine, as suggested by Tracey, the tea was caffeine-free but full of flavour. She laughed to herself as she sat in front of the television, thinking how not so long ago the tea would have been a large measure of vodka from the bottle she kept in the freezer.

After switching on BBC News, Louise stood and stretched her legs. She would have gone to bed, but she could never sleep straight away after a busy day. Her legs ached, as if she'd been out running all evening, and she groaned as she stretched them. She'd been meaning to take up some form of exercise again – running, cycling or swimming – but the demands on her time made it difficult. If she wasn't working, she was either with Thomas or here at home with Emily.

She was surprised how much she enjoyed these few minutes of being alone. She loved being with Thomas, but it had been so long since she'd shared her life with anyone that she wasn't used to it. She worried she would never feel completely comfortable living with someone on a full-time basis, but that wasn't something she would have to worry about for now. Things were OK with Thomas, but neither of them was in a rush to move things along. Or so she'd thought. She'd yet to fully process his suggestion that Emily and Noah meet. It wasn't that unreasonable an idea. They had been seeing each other for some time, and the children were an integral part of their lives. Louise should have been pleased Thomas was ready to take that next step, so why did she feel as if she was being rushed?

Her phone rang as she made herself a second cup of tea. Her legs were still restless and she touched her toes, feeling a stretch in her calves, before picking up. It was nearly 1 a.m., and she didn't recognise the London phone number on the phone's screen.

'Louise Blackwell.'

'Louise, this is Glyn Rhinehart from *The Times*.'

Louise clicked her neck, the tension from her legs spreading to the rest of her body. Glyn was the crime desk editor from the national newspaper. They'd last spoken a couple of years back, when one of Louise's cases had made the national news. 'Glyn, how are you? I presume the reason you're calling me at one a.m. is bad news?'

'I'm very well, Louise, thank you. Not sure if it's bad news. But I wanted to give you a heads-up. We're running a small story tomorrow about the caravan fire in your neck of the woods.'

Louise carried her tea back to the living room, where she clicked on the *Times* website. 'Seriously? Slow news day?'

'I believe it follows hot on the heels of a potential bomb threat at a local school?'

The story was already on the site. Little more than a clickbait piece, it reported the fire at the caravan park and the threat at the school. 'I think you already know that, Glyn.'

Glyn chuckled. 'We also know you've spoken to Karl Insgrove. In fact, we have a picture.'

There was no byline on the article, but it was obvious who was responsible. 'Tania being shy, is she?' asked Louise.

'What can you tell me about Mr Insgrove?'

'Why isn't Tania asking me these questions?'

Glyn chuckled again. 'Not much gets past you, Louise. I wanted to speak to you before we print Mr Insgrove's name. We have a picture of him being led away as well.'

Louise picked up her tea, taking a sip before answering. 'I don't think that would be wise, Glyn. He's only helping us with inquiries at present.'

'But he's staying the night in the cells . . .'

Louise lowered her eyes, biting her tongue as her leg cramped up. Standing, she said, 'No comment, but I would appreciate it if you didn't use his name for the time being. He's a caretaker at a local school and there's no need to drag his name through the mud for no reason.'

'I understand he works at your niece's school?'

Louise clenched her hands. 'Not sure how that's relevant, Glyn,' she said, lowering her voice so that he would understand her displeasure.

'There are rumours that it could be a terrorist organisation behind all this. You have the big air event coming up soon. Are you worried about the potential impact on the town?'

'Now, I know you won't be printing that. At the moment, all we have is a fire at a caravan park—'

'An arson attack,' said Glyn, interrupting.

'A fire and a dummy explosive device. It could be kids playing silly games that got out of hand. To print anything else at this stage would be irresponsible. Now, if you could excuse me, it's been a long day.'

'Just one more thing, DI Blackwell,' said Glyn, but Louise was already in the process of removing the phone from her ear and had hit End Call before he had the chance to say any more.

◆ ◆ ◆

She was up by six, her mind too wired to sleep properly. After showering, she unlocked the dividing door and walked downstairs. She managed two or three steps before she heard Molly bounding towards her. 'You're getting too big,' said Louise, defending herself as the dog launched itself at her.

After giving the dog the attention it craved, Louise headed towards the kitchen area, Molly circling around her legs, to find her family eating their breakfast.

'Just got in?' said her father, deadpan.

Louise picked up a piece of toast and bit down on it. 'I can take Emily into school again today,' she said, noting her parents exchanging looks.

'Yes,' said Emily, in between mouthfuls of cereal.

'Not sure that's such a good idea, Louise,' said her mother.

Emily dropped her spoon and sat up straight. 'Yes it is,' she said, giving her face a concentrated look of seriousness.

'You just finish up and get the rest of your clothes on, young lady,' said Louise's mother, not elaborating until Emily had left the room.

'What's this about?' said Louise.

Her father frowned, and lifted the newspaper up to signal he was out of the conversation. 'It's just that you're not the most popular person at the school at the moment,' said her mother.

'WhatsApp?' said Louise.

'That's irrelevant, Lou, and you know it.'

'Is this because of Karl Insgrove?'

'Frankly, yes. People are a bit put-out you arrested him in front of the children and . . .'

Louise sighed. 'Took him in for questioning. And?'

'The parents can't believe he did anything.'

'Oh, I see. A group of strangers who have no knowledge about what has happened have determined Mr Insgrove's innocence.' Louise shook her head. 'I shouldn't be speaking about this, and you mustn't mention this conversation, Mum.'

'I'm not stupid, Louise.'

'Good, then you won't mind me taking Emily to school then. I've faced worse than the wrath of primary-school parents.'

'You sure about that?' said her father, poking his head up from behind his paper with a sly grin.

◆ ◆ ◆

Louise skimmed through her father's newspaper before leaving, thankful she was unable to find anything about the investigation.

'Do you want me to come with you?' said her mother, as Emily and Louise got into the car.

'What exactly do you think is going to happen, Mum?'

'I'm worried about her,' said her mother, under her breath, pointing to Emily who was sitting in the back seat, her legs kicking out in front of her.

'Mum, please. Nothing will happen in front of Emily, I promise you.'

'Come on, Aunty Louise, we'll be late,' said Emily.

'See, my customer is ready to depart.'

Her mother let out a long sigh and blew a kiss to Emily as Louise pulled away. Her mother's concerns aside, it was great to see Emily so keen to get to school. Part of the reason Louise's parents had made the move to Weston in the first place was the trouble Emily was having at school in Bristol. It was more than understandable, and the family had hoped moving to Weston would help Emily, and to a certain extent it had. Emily still saw a counsellor once a week, and Louise's parents had both suffered, in their own private ways, after the death of their son. But lately Louise had the sense that they were finally moving on with their lives, and Emily's eagerness not to be late seemed to be proof that she was as well.

'How has school been the last few days, Emily?' she asked, catching sight of her niece in the rear-view mirror.

'Bit strange really.'

Louise stifled a laugh at Emily's choice of words. 'Bit strange. How?'

'With that thing, you know. The bomb.'

'There wasn't a bomb, Emily. It was pretend.'

'I know, they told us. But . . . it was still frightening.'

Louise shuddered, her skin prickling. 'I am so sorry to hear that, Emily. It can be scary when these things happen, but it was only pretend, I promise.'

Emily paused, as if in thought. 'OK.'

'And you know who is here to protect you?'

Emily pretended to concentrate this time. Louise caught the half-smile in the rear-view mirror. 'Aunty Louise?'

'Darn tooting,' said Louise, making Emily laugh.

Despite Emily's concerns, they were early for school. Louise parked up opposite the seafront, deciding to take a short walk into school.

'Can I go on the beach?' asked Emily.

'Best not now. Don't want to have sand in your shoes all day.'

Emily nodded, accepting Louise's sage advice. 'This is nice,' she said, as they held hands and walked along the promenade, the sea already retreating.

'That was exactly what I was thinking,' said Louise. They crossed the road, Emily's hand soft in her palm. It had been too long since they'd spent such time together. If Louise could have been granted a wish at that moment, she would have requested the day off so she could spend the day with the girl.

They didn't say much else as they made the walk inland. Louise was content to enjoy the simple pleasure of holding Emily's hand. When she finally let go when they reached the playground, Louise felt a little ache of separation mixed with joy as Emily ran to play with her friends.

The feeling didn't last long. Graham Pritchard sidled over from out of nowhere. 'I saw you were in the papers this morning,' he said, cramping her space once more.

Louise took one step to the left, catching sight of a group of parents standing round a copy of *The Times*. 'Oh, shit. What did it say?'

'A bit sensationalised for my tastes, especially from such a newspaper. Seem to be covering all the possible angles. Disgruntled employee, terrorist organisation. That local journalist wrote it, can you believe? Tania Elliot.'

'I can well believe it,' said Louise, taking another step away as Graham edged closer. 'Did it mention any names?'

'Only yours and Mr Insgrove's.'

'Shit,' said Louise, sneaking another glance at the group of parents, who were looking over without reservation.

The bell couldn't come too soon, Mrs Harrison bringing it out and silencing the crowd. Louise managed to get a quick kiss goodbye from Emily and was heading out of the playground when someone called her name.

She turned to the source of the voice and stopped in her tracks. Everyone else was leaving the playground area, the pupils snaking their way to their classrooms behind their teachers, all oblivious to the potential threat.

'You don't have a child here,' said Louise, walking up to the man she'd never met before but recognised from photos.

'Maybe, maybe not.' Justin Walton had the same dead-eyed stare as his uncle. Aside from that, his appearance was far removed.

Max Walton had been a beast of a man, from his beard and wayward hair down to his thick, rugby-player physique, whereas Justin was little more than a bundle of sticks.

'What is it you want, Mr Walton? If this is anything to do with a potential lawsuit against me, I suggest you make contact through your solicitors.'

Walton grinned, and it was hard for Louise not to see the same malevolence and lack of humanity she'd seen all those years before. The fetid smell of pig shit and the decay she'd experienced that night at the farm reached her nose and made her want to retch. 'That? That was just a piss-take. No, I've got something much more serious I need to talk to you about.'

Louise was immediately on the defensive. He may not have looked like his uncle, but he was a blood relative of Max Walton. She reached for her duty belt, making sure her pepper spray was to hand as she demanded Walton tell her what he wanted.

Chapter Fourteen

As Finch made his way past the cells towards the main prison section, he was bombarded with catcalls and obscenities. It was the first day of the pre-trial and he was wearing a suit that felt a size looser than it had before he'd been put inside. Clemons had summoned him, and Wilson was leading him past the baying mob, Finch relishing every moment.

He recognised half the screeching inmates. He'd either put them away, used them as informants, or had simply come across them during his daily role dealing with the lowest of the low. The potential danger meant nothing to him. He was relatively safe with Wilson there, so he took the opportunity to look his enemies in the eye, making a mental note of those who looked away and those who kept ranting.

The same grinning idiot who'd brought him the television was waiting outside Clemons' cell. 'You have five minutes,' shouted Wilson, to no response, as Finch was ushered inside.

'Quite a reception,' said Clemons, offering Finch a seat. 'And don't you look sharp.'

Finch reached inside his jacket pocket, judging Clemons' reaction as he slowly removed the mobile phone he'd been given. He was impressed when the man didn't flinch. 'You can have this back,' he said.

'You don't like my gift?' said Clemons, pretending to be hurt as he took the phone off him.

'I can't risk taking it to court, and I'll be damned if I'm going to leave it in my cell.'

'You called the number?'

Finch nodded.

'Very persistent woman. Sounds like she wants to make you famous,' said Clemons.

Finch ignored him. He'd come across Tania Elliot before. He hadn't trusted her then, and he definitely didn't trust her now, but that didn't mean she couldn't be useful. 'So . . . what was so urgent?'

'I like a man who gets down to business. You seen this?' Clemons handed him a newspaper with a story about an arson attack in Weston and a bomb threat at a local school.

'What about it?'

'I was wondering if you were involved somehow,' said Clemons, studying him with the kind of intent that would have unnerved most people.

'Why would I set a caravan on fire, Clemons?'

'The school is where Louise Blackwell's niece attends.'

Finch wasn't sure what the man was suggesting. He was aware of Emily Blackwell. He had once threatened the girl in order to get Louise to back off, but to no avail. He would have no qualms about putting her in danger again, but wasn't about to discuss anything with the lowlife next to him. 'And?'

'I just find it interesting that these two incidents occurred so close to your court hearing.'

If Clemons was thinking it, he was sure similar connections would be made elsewhere. It made him smile to think that Blackwell and her cronies were getting distracted; that even from prison he was still exerting his influence. 'We're getting sidetracked,' said Finch. He was interested in what Clemons did and didn't know, but wasn't about to let on. 'I've spoken to my man. He knows what to do. The shipment should arrive soon.'

Clemons relaxed his gaze, taking a sip of water as he broke eye contact. 'I saw. Eddie Perkins came to visit you. Can he be trusted? He's a bigger criminal than anyone in here. Present company excluded, of course.'

The little fucker had some balls, that was for sure. It was easy to act the tough guy when the power dynamic was switched, but Finch was determined it wouldn't always be this way. 'He'll get the job done. And our side of the bargain?'

'That's already in progress, Mr Finch. We're watching their movements. As soon as we know for sure, we'll go in. Probably Wednesday.'

Finch stood. He half expected the cell door to open and for a load of Clemons' lackeys to funnel in and dole out some traditional prison justice. But they never materialised. Clemons led him to the door where an agitated Wilson was waiting, glancing at the corridor.

'Until next Wednesday,' said Clemons.

'Wednesday,' said Finch, feeling almost regal in his suit as he followed Wilson past the jeering inmates as if he was leaving the place for good.

Chapter Fifteen

'Do we have to do this here? You could at least buy me a cup of tea or something,' said Justin Walton, wiping his nose.

Louise didn't say anything. She kept reminding herself that this wasn't Max Walton, that he didn't offer the same kind of threat, but still her hand was in reaching distance of the pepper spray.

She hadn't noticed it before, but she saw the hints of addiction in Walton's dilated eyes and his inability to stand still. 'That's not going to happen. If we speak, we speak here now, otherwise you call your solicitor and we can go through more official channels.'

Walton moved from foot to foot as if the path was made of lava. 'I was hoping for your help,' he said, eyes focused on his shuffling feet.

'You want my help?'

'Yeah. I see all the trouble you're going through. The fire over in Kewstoke, the bomb at the school.'

'There wasn't any explosion, Justin.'

'You know what I mean. Anyway, got me thinking. The last thing you need is someone bringing a case against you.' Walton stopped moving and lifted his head.

'You're not serious. What are you after – money?' said Louise.

'Make your life that much easier I imagine?'

Louise could see he was desperate for his next fix. 'I can help you, Justin. Get you into rehab if that's what you need?'

Walton recoiled as if insulted. 'Fuck off,' he said, backing away with tired ambling steps. 'I'm not some sort of junkie, you know?'

'What is it you want then?'

Walton leaned in closer. 'Some money,' he said, as if Louise was stupid. 'Make this all go away.'

It was laughable and lamentable. She could have arrested him for attempting to bribe an officer, and if he kept going would have no option but to do so. It also came as a bit of a relief. Private prosecutions were self-funded, and if Walton was desperate for cash, it suggested he would never have the type of money to mount a case against Louise unless someone else was funding him. 'Would you like to repeat that?' said Louise, opening the recording app on her phone.

'You must think I'm stupid,' said Walton.

'It had crossed my mind. Where were you on the night of the sixth, Mr Walton?' she asked.

Walton's skin paled, his mouth hanging open. 'What?' he said, his voice devoid of the bravado he'd displayed up until that moment.

'The night of the sixth?'

'I have nothing to do with any of this, I was just trying to score . . . I was just trying to help you out.'

'Where are you staying at present, Mr Walton?' said Louise, ignoring his complaints now she was firmly in charge.

She was surprised by how easily he capitulated, giving her his address without any argument and an alibi for the last three evenings. 'I didn't have nothing to do with this,' he repeated.

Louise believed his last statement. He didn't seem to have the organisational skills to have pulled off something like this. What did concern her was the fact that he'd somehow hired a solicitor to begin the private prosecution. Admittedly, she'd only dealt with him for the last few minutes, but it didn't ring true to her. It further confirmed that someone else may have put him up to it.

'What is this all about, Justin? Who told you to take the private prosecution out against me?'

'I don't know what you mean.'

'We don't need to play these games, Justin. You don't have the money for that. Someone put you up to it, didn't they?' said Louise, her thoughts turning to Tania Elliot and Tim Finch.

'I don't know what you're talking about.'

'Someone paid you to do this. Cause a bit of trouble with the upcoming court case.'

Walton backed away, rubbing his nose.

'I can help you.'

'No, no, I'm out,' said Walton.

Louise let him walk off. Arresting the nephew of Max Walton at present would only bring more unwelcome attention her way. She was content to have his address and alibis she could check on, but it was clear to her now that someone had put him up to the job of bringing the private prosecution, and she was determined to find out who exactly had done so.

◆　◆　◆

She was back at Weston nick within twenty minutes, where she met Tracey in the old CID. Time was running out to interview Karl Insgrove again before they would have to formally charge or release him.

'Bought you a pain au chocolat,' said Tracey, handing her a paper bag patched with grease. 'And a black coffee, which should hopefully still be warm.'

Seeing Tracey always buoyed Louise's mood. Whatever the situation, Tracey was usually there with a smile. And after the run-in with Justin Walton, Tracey's smile was just what Louise needed to see.

'He was trying to buy you off?' said Tracey, after Louise explained what had happened.

Louise took a bite of the pain au chocolat, sugar rushing her system and giving her a delicious high. 'I'm not sure he knew what he wanted, really. I get the feeling someone put him up to it.'

'Which solicitors did he hire?'

'Barker Price. No way he could have afforded them, especially going forward.'

'Let me have a nose around. See if I can find out who paid the initial sum. I know a few people over there.'

'Appreciate that, thanks. He's definitely hiding something,' said Louise, stopping short of telling Tracey about the fear she'd seen in Walton's eyes when she'd suggested he could be linked to the ongoing investigation. It was one thing having suspicions about Walton, but with nothing more than a look to go on she wasn't prepared to involve Tracey yet. 'Don't suppose you have a copy of *The Times*?' she asked, telling Tracey about her late-night call with Glyn Rhinehart.

'I was going to ask about that. Tania playing silly buggers again.'

'I'd rather have kept Insgrove's name out of it if I could have.'

'Those CTU officers have anything to say about it?'

'Not yet,' said Louise.

'Not much we can do about it now, I guess. If Insgrove did start that fire then he deserves to be in the paper anyway,' said Tracey.

'Let's find out, then.'

Karl Insgrove was led to the interview room a few minutes later, having eaten his breakfast in his cell. The night of imprisonment didn't appear to have done him much harm, though he was a bit emotional when speaking to Louise. She still couldn't tell if the tears were a result of guilt or unhappiness at what had happened to him.

'You used to be in the army?' asked Louise, trying to catch Insgrove off guard by diving right into the questions.

'Not quite. Royal Navy,' said Insgrove, sinking back in his chair.

'We saw your medals. Very impressive. You served in the Falklands?'

'You went to my house?' said Insgrove, wiping his forehead.

'You gave us permission,' said Louise, glancing at his duty solicitor.

'You were a technician?' asked Tracey.

'You haven't taken anything, have you?'

'No need to worry, Karl. Everything is as it was except for your laptop which we have taken for testing and will return to you.'

Insgrove took in a deep breath. 'I was a technician. What has this to do with me being held here?'

Louise shrugged. 'We wanted to find out more about you.'

'What, you think I suffered hardship in the war, so years later out of nowhere I decided to start setting fires?'

It seemed a night in the cells had made Mr Insgrove a little bit more forceful in his responses. 'What other reason would you have for setting them?' asked Louise.

Insgrove was momentarily confused. 'Good try. It wasn't fair taking me away in front of the parents. They'll never trust me now.'

'I wouldn't worry about that,' said Louise, recalling the way the parents had looked at her earlier. 'Listen, Karl, as I explained to you last night, it would be so much better for you if you came clean now. We know you had access to both the school PE storeroom and the caravan park. This doesn't look good for you, and if you don't cooperate now then I'm not going to be able to help you.'

'I told you, I have nothing to do with any of it. Why would I put those children at risk? They mean everything to me,' said Insgrove, his eyes reddening.

'The children were never at risk, at least not physically.'

'Why set fire to the caravan park where I help out? They've always treated me very well, and they give me an extra few bob when I need it. I'd be mad to mess with that. And to what end?'

'Where were you the night before last?' asked Tracey.

'I've told you. At home. I went straight home from school. I was knackered after all that commotion.'

'But no one can vouch for that.'

'I live alone,' said Insgrove, who looked exasperated.

With time running out, Louise tried one last tack. 'Have you heard this before?' she said, before playing the voice message left before the fire at the caravan park.

'No,' said Insgrove, waiting until the end of the message before answering.

'Do we know each other, Mr Insgrove?' asked Louise.

'What do you mean?' asked the solicitor.

'Both the message at the dummy IED at the school and the voice message mention my name. Do we know each other?' said Louise.

'I've seen you at school. You're Emily's aunt,' said Insgrove.

'It's a very small school, so there is no reason why my client wouldn't know you,' said the solicitor, on the defensive.

'Beyond the school, Mr Insgrove. Have we ever met elsewhere?'

Insgrove looked at his solicitor for advice. 'I don't know what you mean.'

'I think that is you on the voice message, and I think you left that note in the dummy IED,' said Louise.

Insgrove began shaking his head. 'No, no, no,' he said, muttering to himself.

Louise took in a deep breath. 'Did someone put you up to this, Mr Insgrove?'

Insgrove shook his head five or six times. 'Why would someone do that?'

'Do you know Justin Walton?' asked Louise.

Insgrove hesitated before answering. 'Justin who?'

Louise exchanged looks with Tracey. It was clear they were getting nowhere, and they didn't have enough to hold him any longer. She asked a few more questions before ending the interview. She told Insgrove about the article in *The Times* and warned him that he would attract some media attention. His body appeared to deflate at the news, and his solicitor had to help him from his seat.

Joanne Harrison was waiting for him in reception. Louise watched from the window of the office as the headteacher put her arm around Insgrove and led him to the car. Again, she found it difficult to believe they weren't siblings.

Mrs Harrison's car was followed by an unmarked police car, Louise having decided to put Insgrove under surveillance for the next twenty-four hours.

The day had barely begun and already she felt knackered. A conference call was set up with headquarters and she briefed the team on the next movements, which now included checking Justin Walton's alibi for the last few days.

Satisfied that everything was accounted for, she made the journey to the Crown Court in Bristol, where she was due to meet the head of CPS, Antony Meades. As she was parking up, Thomas called, but she decided she didn't have time to answer. There was too much happening for her to worry about her personal life, and she was sure he would understand.

Chapter Sixteen

Antony Meades' robust mood was broken when Louise informed him about her run-in with Justin Walton. 'He tried to bribe you?' said the solicitor, running his hand through his fringe.

'Not exactly.'

'That's what it sounds like to me. Could you not have arrested him?'

'It would be my word against his, and with everything that's going on I thought the last thing we needed was more attention.'

Meades' fringe bounced back perfectly in place. He scratched his head, sighing. 'I'll get on to his solicitors. Find out what the hell is going on for you.'

'Thanks, Antony. I appreciate it.'

Meades offered her a smile. Tracey had a little crush on him, and now that he had turned his attention fully to her, Louise could understand why. He placed the following week's itinerary in front of her, with estimations about when she would be needed to testify against Finch.

'I would have liked to have been there for the whole thing, but with the present case that is going to be difficult.'

'We won't need you until Wednesday at the earliest. I've spoken to the defence barrister, and I'm sure he's going to drain every last billable minute out of this. Although I didn't say that, obviously.

For now, we need to go through your story and try to anticipate everything that will be thrown at you.'

Louise understood it would almost be like she was on trial when she took the witness stand. Finch was being tried for the attempted murder of Amira Hood and Louise was pivotal to the success of that prosecution, having been the one to rescue Amira. Not only would she be cross-examined about the incidents leading to Finch's arrest, she would no doubt be asked about the disciplinary fallout from Max Walton's death, as well as her relationship, past and present, with Finch.

If she couldn't answer Meades' questions now, then she wouldn't be able to do so in the witness box. Meades didn't go easy. Taking on the role of the defence team counsel, over the next thirty minutes he accused her of being a cold-hearted killer, a vigilante who took the law into her own hands, a spurned lover, and a police officer jealous of her colleague's success.

By the end, she was exhausted. But she felt more prepared for what lay ahead. Back outside the building, she was heading towards a sandwich shop she liked on Corn Street when she saw Amira, who wasted no time rushing over and placing her arms around Louise. 'How are you, Louise, it's so great to see you.'

'It's great to see you too. Are you here to see Antony?'

'Yep, I'm late already. I'm sure we can catch up next week?'

Amira had been the catalyst in bringing a case against Finch. A former officer from HQ, Amira had entered into a relationship with Finch that had turned abusive; his recurring pattern of behaviour, it seemed. Finch had all but forced her to leave Portishead for a post in South Wales. Last year, the young woman had approached Louise and suggested that together they bring Finch down, and eventually Louise had realised it was the push she needed.

'Give me a call when you're finished with Antony,' said Louise. 'It would be great to catch up. Everything OK though?'

'Everything is good,' said Amira, smiling once more before giving Louise a peck on the cheek.

Sometimes things worked out. The change in Amira was wonderful to see. On the night Finch was arrested, he had held Amira hostage in his house. She'd come close to losing her life but she'd survived. Louise had kept in contact and was so pleased to see her thriving.

Amira had quit the police force a few weeks after that night. Ironically, it had been what Finch had wanted all along. His MO – at least when it came to the police department – was to sleep with fellow officers and civilian staff, before trying to hound them out of the area. Part power game, part self-preservation, Finch had succeeded for so long. Louise was a victim as much as any of the others, but had managed to come out on top. Now all she needed was to make sure the other women destroyed by Finch could get the same sort of justice.

She glanced at her phone as she headed back to Weston, noting another missed call from Thomas. It wasn't really significant, and he would more than understand, but she wondered if her reluctance to answer earlier had something to do with her feelings that they were rushing into things. The fairest thing to do would be to talk to him, and she realised she was avoiding this. She was about to call him back when a call came in from the two officers assigned to watch Karl Insgrove.

'Mrs Harrison took him for something to eat then dropped him off at his flat. He came down earlier to pop to the newsagent then went back up. You want us to stay here?'

Louise could sense the boredom seeping through from the other end of the line. She'd been there so many times before and was glad it wasn't her having to stare into the empty distance for hours on end, on the off chance that Insgrove would leave his flat. Budget constraints meant the surveillance wasn't something that could last long, but she needed eyes on Insgrove for as long as possible. 'Let me know as soon as there are any more updates,' she said, hanging up.

Tracey called as Louise was pulling back into the caravan park in Kewstoke. 'Hello,' she said, distracted by the sight of the burnt-out shell of the Bastiens' holiday home. It was like a monstrous art installation, the blackened remains giving the impression of it still being on fire.

'Hi, thought I'd check in,' said Tracey. 'Been going through Justin Walton's alibi. Seems to check out for the most part. Has he officially dropped the case against you?'

'Not yet.'

'I've put the feelers out at his solicitors' firm. The guy I know there said at the very least Walton would have paid some sort of deposit for it to have got to this stage. Not particularly cheap, and I've just seen where he lives. Something is definitely off.'

'Could be dealing again?' said Louise.

'He lives in some sort of house share. Things are on edge there. I'd say there's a definite possibility that they're hiding something. Want me to look into it a bit more?'

'Maybe not for now. Think we need to keep it relevant,' said Louise. Checking Walton's alibi was related to the investigation, but anything else felt as if it was too close to Louise's private prosecution case. The last thing she needed was the threat of misappropriation of police services being thrown at her. If Walton was dealing drugs again then she would get a team to look into it, but for now Tracey was best utilised elsewhere.

'OK. Any news on Karl Insgrove?'

'Safely at home.'

'You think this is the end of it?'

'We can't watch him forever. If he is responsible then I hope it was all a cry for help and this is the end of it. Thankfully, no one got injured.'

It was true that the investigation was being given more prominence than perhaps it warranted, but that was always going to happen when a school was involved. 'If our luck is in, the voice analysis will get a result and we can charge him and wrap this up,' said Louise, hanging up.

Mary Sutcliffe was outside the burnt shell, accompanied by two elderly people. Most likely the Bastiens.

The fire had occurred over twenty-four hours ago, but the smell of the fumes and the smoke still hung in the air, as if the singular static caravan had its own micro-climate. Louise produced her warrant card and was introduced to Mr and Mrs Bastien.

'Terrible business,' said Mr Bastien, who was bent over so he appeared to be the same height as his much shorter wife.

Louise took the pair to Mrs Sutcliffe's office and went through some preliminary questions. Neither had any idea why someone would target their specific caravan. 'Thankfully, we didn't keep any personal belongings there,' said Mrs Bastien, who shook every time she spoke.

'Do you know the site's handyman?'

'Karl? Lovely fellow,' said Mr Bastien, with a look that bordered on the hostile. 'I understand he's been arrested. Preposterous thought.'

'He hasn't been charged with anything,' said Louise. 'You ever come across someone by the name of Justin Walton?' she added, mainly on the off chance.

The pair stared at her blankly and she soon wrapped things up. It had seemed unlikely from the start that the Bastiens would have any knowledge about what had happened. They didn't appear overly distraught, more a little put out by the inconvenience, but for now Louise didn't believe they had played a role in the fire.

Furthermore, she'd failed to uncover any animosity between the Bastiens and Karl Insgrove. That in itself didn't mean anything

– he would have known the caravan was unoccupied – but it made things less than clear-cut. Despite the old Occam's razor adage, the most obvious explanation wasn't always the correct one. Everything did point to Insgrove at the moment, but that didn't rule out other potential suspects. And although he was, for now, safely behind bars, Louise felt herself thinking more and more about the potential influence of Tim Finch.

Chapter Seventeen

Thomas stared at his phone as if sheer force of will would make it ring. He was behaving like a child, waiting for her call like some lovesick teenager. He'd worked in the police long enough to know that Louise could have a hundred other things more important to do than talking to him. It wasn't the first time she hadn't answered his call, and it wouldn't be the last. With the explosion in Weston, and Finch's upcoming court case, it was no surprise her mind was more than preoccupied. He picked the phone up and considered calling again, before putting it away and returning to his work.

In front of him, three large screens played back CCTV images from various sections of the warehouse and loading bays of Oblong Distribution. Monitoring the screens wasn't really his job as head of security – in another office elsewhere in the building, two of his staff would be analysing the videos with more vigour – but he liked to be able to keep track of things, and he thought it important that people knew he was keeping track as well.

When he'd joined, Oblong had been besieged with security issues. The company delivered shipments nationwide, and too many were either not getting delivered or were going missing in transit. His first few months had been spent conducting in-depth security checks on a number of staff, leading to a number of dismissals within the firm. Figures had improved since, but he sensed things were still not quite as they should be.

He watched pallets being loaded into a number of transit vans, every now and then glancing at the desk drawer hoping for a call from Louise. He smiled to himself, trying to recall the last time he'd felt so nervous about a woman. It was probably during the weeks leading up to his proposal to Rebecca. Back then, he'd thought there was no way she was going to say yes. He'd been wrong about that, but his insecurity this time felt more justified.

It was hard to pinpoint exactly, but he'd felt Louise slipping away over these last few weeks. They still spent time together – she'd spent the night before last at his – but she seemed distracted, and he was worried that he'd started moving a little fast. As he'd confessed to her, he'd felt something between them since the first day she'd arrived in Weston, when he'd still been married, and in the subsequent years his attraction had grown. He'd been as surprised as anyone when they'd eventually got together, and maybe he'd let his overenthusiasm get in the way.

The latest example of that had been his suggestion that he and Noah meet up with Louise and Emily that weekend. It had been an innocent enough suggestion, but in retrospect he understood how it might seem. As if he was trying to play happy families when he and Louise were barely six months into their relationship. He'd wanted to tell her on the phone that the suggestion had no significance to it, and now here he was, wracked by indecision. Not wanting to come over as needy, but desperate to speak to her again.

Telling himself to focus, he turned his attention back to the job of vetting a new delivery driver. He'd upscaled the security process since joining which, although giving him extra work, meant he could be completely satisfied with every new employee who joined the company.

After a quick scan of the candidate's work history, he found the number for his last employer and was about to call for a reference when a flicker of motion on one of the screens caught his eye. Cars began streaming into the parking area. Immediately he called one of his colleagues at the depot.

The phone kept ringing as the cars filtered in – at last count, there were seven. As Thomas zoomed in with the camera, he noted that the car number plates were covered over. He called the police as a group of men filtered out of the cars carrying baseball bats and various weapons and began smashing up the parked vans. Most of his staff had headed back inside the relative safety of the warehouse, but a few were holding their ground, shouting at the intruders and trying to protect the vehicles when Thomas would have much preferred them to join their colleagues inside.

Nothing had happened like this before, and Thomas had no real idea what was going on now. He gave his name to the emergency services operator, stopping short of telling him he was a former police officer. The second he hung up, the attackers got back in their cars and began driving away.

As far as Thomas could make out, nothing had been taken and, despite the stubborn bravery of some of the drivers and loading staff, no physical confrontations had taken place.

After a few minutes calling, he finally managed to get through to the depot and instructed everyone to vacate the area until the police arrived, before heading to the scene himself.

◆ ◆ ◆

'What sort of security do you guys have going on here?' said the plain-clothed policeman who appeared to be heading up the operation in Thornbury.

Thomas stared hard at the man, stone-faced for as long as he could before breaking into a smile. 'I might've known they'd send you over, Greg,' he said.

'How are you, Tom? It's good to see you.'

DS Greg Farrell was a former colleague of Thomas's from Weston CID who had made the transfer to HQ in Portishead a year before Louise. Thomas had worked with Farrell on a number of cases, and had seen him grow from a slightly annoying, precocious young man when he'd first joined the team, into something approaching a seasoned professional. Louise trusted Farrell, and that was all the character reference Thomas would ever need.

'Well, I could do without all this, but aside from that I'm well. How are things without me?'

'We're coping. So what the hell went down here?'

Thomas told him what he'd seen from the office. 'Seven saloon cars. Number plates covered up. I counted sixteen men in all. Baseball bats, iron bars, that sort of thing.'

'I guess this is what happens when you don't deliver people's shit on time,' said Farrell.

'I guess the general public can only take so much,' said Thomas.

'Any threats? I don't suppose you've had any disputes with rival firms?' asked Farrell, walking through the battered vehicles, avoiding the shattered glass from the windscreens and lights.

'I'd be surprised if the Royal Mail or DHL have a team of heavies on their payroll.' The damage seemed to be superficial. The vehicles wouldn't be back out on the roads for a few weeks, and the bill to fix them would be in the thousands, but only the bodywork had been targeted. Even the tyres on most of the vehicles remained intact.

'And your staff? Pissed anyone off?'

Thomas told him about the dismissals he'd been forced to make. 'Some of them have criminal records that hadn't been declared. Quite a lot of tidying was needed when I joined, and there's still some way to go.'

'So it could be disgruntled ex-employees?'

'Seems a bit extreme to me. A lot of trouble to go to – smashing up some vehicles. It feels very targeted, especially in broad daylight.'

'I agree,' said Farrell. 'Leave it to us. We'll need to speak to everyone here. Could you get that sorted for me?'

'Sure thing, DS Farrell.'

'It is a shame you left, Tom. I really mean that. I think you'd enjoy working at headquarters now.'

'Until today, I'd have told you I'd made the right decision,' said Thomas, looking at the graveyard of cars.

'And you and Louise . . .'

'All good.' It was no secret, and Thomas didn't mind speaking to Farrell, but Louise was Farrell's boss and it didn't feel right going into any detail about their relationship.

'I always knew you two would get together.'

'Of course you did. Right, I'll get that staff list for you—'

'Sir,' said one of the SOCOs, interrupting them. 'Think you might want to see this.'

Thomas followed the SOCO and Farrell to the back of one of his firm's transit vans. The windows were smashed and the SOCO prised open the door with her gloved hand. 'We've photographed the scene,' she said, pulling out a holdall. 'Found this,' she added, unzipping it to reveal a small, tightly wrapped bag of white powder.

Chapter Eighteen

This time, Louise answered when Thomas called. She wanted to hear his voice, but also needed someone to vent about Finch to. She'd just got off the phone with Antony Meades, who'd been in court watching the jury selection for the case. It had suddenly hit her that next week was a reality, and although the case against Finch appeared watertight there was always a chance that things could go wrong.

Thomas listened patiently as she told him about Justin Walton and her concerns about Finch. When she was finished, he hesitantly told her about the incident at his work. 'I missed this,' she said. 'Farrell was there?'

'Is here,' said Thomas. 'They found what appears to be cocaine in three of our vans. Only small amounts, but it was packaged as if ready for selling.'

'Any arrests?'

'Not yet. All the drivers and packers have to remain on site, which is a pain, even if it is understandable. I'll be questioned as well.'

Louise chuckled. 'I'll tell Greg to go easy on you.'

'Much appreciated,' said Thomas, his voice deflated.

'You think it could have been planted by the attackers? What's the estimated street value?'

'Farrell doesn't think it's that much. Twenty to fifty K depending on purity.'

'It's not nothing.'

'No,' said Thomas, before falling silent.

'Is there anything else you're not telling me?' asked Louise, wondering if now was a suitable time for them to discuss their weekend plans and the fact that she'd yet to confirm getting together on Sunday.

Thomas sighed. 'I'm sorry, Louise. I didn't want to bother you with this, not with all the stuff you have going on.'

'Don't be silly, Tom. You can tell me anything.'

'Still can't get used to you calling me . . . Anyway, Tania Elliot was here.'

Louise swore under her breath. 'This is like the bad old days when she was like my shadow. What did she want?'

'She'd been tipped off about the incident, naturally. Started questioning me about a drug-smuggling operation being carried out from here.'

'I hope you told her where to go.'

'I did, but you know how she is, won't shut up. Started asking me if a rival gang did this.'

'I wouldn't worry. It's the way she works. Grasps at straws until she finds one she can hold on to.'

'Normally I wouldn't have minded, but then she mentioned you.'

'Did she?' said Louise, heat rising to her face.

'Asked if we were in a relationship. Obviously, it was *no comment* all the way. Then she started going on about Finch's court case. I think she's going to run with this. I know it couldn't have come at a worse time for you.'

He was right about that but there was nothing they could do. 'Don't worry, I'll speak to her,' said Louise, already fantasising about the range of curse words she would use on the journalist the next time they spoke.

◆ ◆ ◆

The commotion at Thomas's firm was an unwelcome distraction, and Tania being there made things more challenging. Whatever the truth of the situation, the journalist would find a way of manipulating the story for her own agenda; and with Finch's trial beginning next week, it was obvious and worrying where that would lead.

Resisting the urge to travel to Thornbury to check on the situation, Louise returned to Portishead. Most of her team were out on other cases and the place lacked energy. A message had been left on her desk from Simon Coulson, one of the IT specialists at HQ. The laptop recovered at Insgrove's flat hadn't been used in four years, which was disappointing but unsurprising. After pouring coffee, she stuck her head into Robertson's office. The DCI glanced up before returning his gaze to his computer screen. 'I see your boyfriend is running a drugs operation now,' he said, smiling to himself.

'I thought you would have come up with something a little better than that, sir, with all this time on your hands.'

'Aye, right. Nothing but time here. Is there something you want, DI Blackwell?'

'Well, I don't want to burden you.'

Robertson sighed, and looked up. 'Double the responsibility, but not double the pay,' he said. 'You ever miss those halcyon days of being by the seaside?'

'I'm still there most of the time. And to be fair, it's only been a few months.'

'Feels like a lifetime. What's up?'

Louise took a seat. Her boss had red eyes and a couple of days of fine grey stubble on his face. The move had been an adjustment for all of them and, like her, Robertson had yet to find his equilibrium. She told him what she'd heard from Thomas, and the latest developments in Weston.

It didn't take Robertson long to work out what she really wanted to talk about. 'Finch next week?'

'Yep.'

'You worried about your testimony?'

'More worried that he's going to worm his way out of it somehow.'

'I think something like this is beyond even his means. He wants his day in court because he loves the sound of his own voice, and it will give him the chance to air his grievances. He won't be going anywhere.'

'I'm probably his main grievance,' said Louise.

'That you are, and that's a good thing. He wouldn't be where he is if it wasn't for you.'

Louise couldn't take all the credit for that. It had taken Amira's determination to really spur her into action, and the real reason Finch was behind bars was because of the Ghost Squad, who'd been running a secret operation on Finch for a number of months. She must be feeling fragile today. First needing to hear Thomas's voice, and now this pep talk from Robertson. 'I guess you're right,' she said, standing.

'You were cleared of all wrongdoing, Louise,' said Robertson, softly, as if reading her mind. 'For what it's worth, I believed you at the time and I sure as hell believe you now. Finch is an arch manipulator. Why he told you Max Walton was holding a gun I don't know. I suspect it was because he's not right up here.' Robertson pointed to his head with an absurdly comical look on his face.

It felt such a relief to laugh. Louise couldn't remember Robertson ever doing such a thing before. He usually had a bone-dry sense of humour, and in a heartbeat his crazy expression had disappeared and he was back studying his screen.

'Thanks, Iain,' she said, receiving a grunt of acknowledgement in response.

As she headed back into the main office, she caught sight of Simon Coulson loitering outside her office. 'You here to see me, or just getting out of work?'

Coulson smiled, shyly. 'I have the results back on the voice analysis from the phone call to the school. I rushed it through myself,' he said, handing her a set of papers.

'I appreciate that, Simon. Care to give me the lowdown?'

'As we expected, the call was sent from a voice over IP so it's all but untraceable. It was a great idea to get Mr Insgrove to repeat the phrase used during his interview. I won't bore you with the details, but our analysis suggests there is a seventy-eight per cent chance that it was Mr Insgrove who made the call using voice-changing software.'

◆ ◆ ◆

Coulson had given her some more detail on voice frequencies and modulators which hadn't made much sense to her. If he said it was a 78 per cent chance then she took that at face value. It would never be enough to secure a prosecution, or even warrant making another arrest, but it did give Louise good reason to question Karl Insgrove again.

She checked in with the patrol car as she headed back to Weston, and was told there had been no movement all day. The surveillance was due to end shortly, and there were no plans to extend it. The simple fact was it was too expensive to have a pair of officers watch the building of a suspect who at present was under suspicion for a case of arson. It was only the fact that a school had been an initial target, and that explosive devices were being used, that she'd been able to sign off on the surveillance in the first place. Despite Coulson's 78 per cent match, it was unlikely Robertson or those above him would be willing to keep spending money on it.

She was there in thirty minutes, dropping off a couple of petrol station coffees to the two officers. 'So you've not seen him all day?'

'Hasn't left since we last spoke. We do an hourly patrol around the building, but there is only one way in and one way out,' said the driver.

Louise knew that wasn't strictly true – there were a number of alarmed fire exits, as well as numerous ground-floor windows someone could leave from – but she didn't push the point. 'OK, I'm going up. One of you around the back, please,' said Louise, heading towards the entrance.

She hadn't called ahead, not wanting to give Insgrove the chance to prepare his story. If she could speak to him alone, instil in him how serious it was that his speech patterns were a 78 per cent match for the emergency call, then perhaps she could finally get some answers. It would be good to head into the weekend with a victory of sorts, especially considering what lay in store next week.

The lift smelled of damp and cigarettes despite the large no-smoking signs plastered up on all sides. It was a relief when the door pinged open and she reached the relative fresh air of the hallway. She knocked three times, calling Mr Insgrove's name when he didn't answer.

Louise had been concerned this would happen. She called the number they had for Insgrove, which rang seven times before going to answerphone, and knocked on the door once more.

Insgrove's neighbour, a young pregnant woman, opened her door and looked out. 'What's all the noise?'

'Sorry, ma'am. DI Blackwell. I'm trying to speak to Mr Insgrove. Have you seen him today?' said Louise, displaying her warrant card.

'No. I heard him playing his music earlier. I've been out.'

'Do you happen to have a key for him?'

'No,' said the woman, frowning at Louise as if she'd asked something preposterous before slamming her door shut.

'Mr Insgrove, please,' said Louise, banging on the door once more.

With still no answer, she called down to the two officers to double-check there had been no movement. Insgrove wasn't a prisoner and hadn't been told to stay in his apartment. The reason she had put a team on him was more to see what his next movements would be rather than a means of ensuring he stayed at home. She considered calling Mrs Harrison, whom Insgrove had put down as his emergency contact, but didn't want to get her involved yet. Instead, she called Robertson and explained the situation.

'Do you think he's in danger?' asked Robertson, giving an effective green light for her to break down the man's door.

'He doesn't appear to have left the building and isn't answering his phone. Considering everything that has happened of late I am concerned for his well-being,' said Louise, making sure she covered every base before going ahead.

'I agree,' said Robertson.

Louise called the patrol team up, instructing that they bring the battering ram with them. She tried Insgrove's phone again before banging on the door, once more attracting the attention of Insgrove's pregnant next-door neighbour, who opened her door, her mouth opening to speak, then closing it when she saw the two other officers running over with the battering ram.

'Mr Insgrove, I am going to count down from ten, and then I will be forced to break down the door as I fear for your safety,' said Louise. She counted to ten, and nodded to her colleagues.

The door caved in on the first hit, the frame splintering into pieces from the impact. Louise was first through the door, a familiar smell greeting her as she stepped into Insgrove's living room, something coppery and acrid hanging in the air, and immediately Louise was on alert. She withdrew her baton, her two colleagues following her inside. 'Hold your positions,' said Louise, fearing the worst and not wanting to contaminate a potential crime scene.

It wasn't the smell of blood but rather the sound of dripping water that led her to the bathroom. She prised open the door with her baton. She didn't need to check the body in the bath to know Karl Insgrove was dead.

His corpse sat in a pool of maroon liquid, a long vertical incision on his left wrist. On the bathroom floor was a cut-throat razor without the safety shield. The bath was three-quarters full and although the tap was still dripping there wasn't enough of a flood risk to necessitate her switching it off. Instead, Louise tiptoed backwards, instructing her colleagues to call it in.

As she moved backwards, she caught sight of an addressed envelope on the dining table. Unable to read the inscription on the front from her angle, she considered reaching over and opening it before deciding against it. Although the death had all the hallmarks of a suicide, it could be something else and the letter could hold some important forensic information so would have to be dealt with by the SOCOs.

'Secure the entry to the whole building. I don't want anyone coming in or leaving,' she said to her colleagues. Until she was told that suicide was confirmed, she had to treat it as a suspicious death and didn't want a potential witness or even attacker leaving before someone had spoken to them.

The SOCOs arrived within the hour. Louise was on friendly terms with the head of the team, Janice Sutton, and asked her if someone could process the note as a priority.

'Let's get set up in the bathroom first and I'll handle it personally for you,' said Janice, who understood the pressure Louise was under.

It was thirty minutes before Louise received the note. The envelope was addressed to Mrs Harrison and Louise gave Janice permission to open it. She did as instructed, photographing the letter, and sent it to Louise's phone:

> *Dear Joanne,*
>
> *I never thought things would end this way. I only wanted to help.*
>
> *Thank you for everything you gave to me over the years. It was a pleasure working at the school and I am sorry for the distress I must have caused to the staff, the children, and most importantly you.*
>
> *Whatever you do, please do not open the school Monday.*
>
> *Yours for ever,*
>
> *Karl*

Chapter Nineteen

Outside, night had descended. The still air was filled with the smell of marijuana and cigarette smoke. The residents were growing restless as more emergency vehicles arrived. Louise joined Tracey, who was sharing a cigarette with Greg Farrell. Seeing Farrell reminded her that she hadn't called Thomas since speaking to him earlier. 'Thought you'd still be in Thornbury,' she said to Farrell.

'This sounds much more exciting,' said Farrell. 'And we're all but wrapped up there.'

'Thomas OK?' asked Louise, watching the pair for an exchange of looks.

'Decided not to arrest him this time,' said Farrell, receiving a chuckle from Tracey.

'Glad you can see the funny side of it,' said Louise. 'What do you think? Was it planted?'

'If it was, it wasn't during the raid. The depot was covered with CCTV cameras – your boyfriend's doing, apparently – and I've watched the attack numerous times from various angles and they just smash the place up.'

'Good timing on their part,' said Tracey.

'Exactly. We did get a bit of luck. The covering came off one of the number plates and we got a partial match. Looking at that at the moment.'

'Any idea who the attackers were?' asked Louise.

'Everyone is playing dumb about the drugs but I'd be amazed if there wasn't a link. Either suppliers or rivals.'

'Rivals?'

'Tom has got his work cut out there. We've had to block all the vans and lorries leaving his depot until we've searched the whole place. He wasn't best pleased, and neither were his bosses.'

Louise rubbed her brow. The job had been going so well for him, and now this. It made her feel guilty for the lacklustre way she'd reacted to his suggestion of getting the kids to meet. He was astute enough to have noticed her reluctance, and this would be an extra problem he wouldn't want to deal with. 'I'll call him.'

'What's the latest?' said Tracey, finishing her cigarette and extinguishing it on the ground with the sole of her shoe.

For a second, Louise thought she was asking about her relationship with Thomas before remembering the corpse in the bathtub. 'Everything points to suicide. We'll know for sure after the post-mortem.'

'And the note?'

'That is a massive headache we could do without. Robbo's talking to the brass about it. I'm waiting for the CTU and I need to tell Mrs Harrison about all this. You take over here, Trace?'

Tracey nodded.

'You need some company?' asked Farrell.

'I'm OK, best I see her alone for this one,' said Louise. She called Thomas as she headed for her car, sidestepping an ongoing argument between a uniformed officer and two women who were trying to get back inside. She offered her colleague a nod of encouragement as she placed her phone back in her pocket, Thomas not answering.

122

Louise thought about the note as she drove to the home address for Mrs Harrison in Congresbury, which was a short journey along the A370 from Worle. It created more questions than answers. Notwithstanding the implied threat that there would be another explosion on Monday, the note hadn't mentioned Louise specifically. The note found at the school had included her name, and the caller – who was more than likely Insgrove – had also used her name directly. So why had he not used it now? The absence of her name on the suicide note would make it easier to justify her position on the investigation, but it also made her wonder if she'd been approaching things the wrong way.

Louise pulled up outside a small cottage in the heart of the village. The front garden was adorned with plants and bushes that Louise imagined would look spectacular in the daytime. Although it was June the air had an autumnal feel, the smell of burning wood drifting towards her as she knocked on the door. This was the job all police officers dreaded. Even though Mrs Harrison wasn't related to Insgrove, there was no telling what her reaction would be to the news of his death, especially considering recent events.

The sound of dogs barking accompanied footsteps, then Mrs Harrison opened the door and took a couple of seconds to realise who was there. 'DI Blackwell?' she said, hesitantly.

'Mrs Harrison, can I come in?'

'Of course, what's this about?' asked Mrs Harrison, her confusion growing to concern.

Louise waited until they were in the living room and Mrs Harrison was sitting down to tell her the news. She studied the headteacher as she told her of Karl Insgrove's death. The evident shock was soon replaced by disbelief. 'When? How? I only saw him this morning.'

'I needed to speak to Mr Insgrove. When he didn't answer my phone call, I decided to visit him in his flat. That was when I discovered his body.'

'What . . . what happened?'

'It's still too early to know for sure, but it appears that Mr Insgrove took his own life sometime earlier today.'

A high-pitched sound escaped Mrs Harrison's lips as she processed this information. 'Suicide? No, I can't believe . . . Wait, how did you find him? Was the door open?'

'I had grounds to be concerned about Mr Insgrove's safety and decided to force down his door.'

'You,' shouted Mrs Harrison, getting to her feet. 'This is all your doing. He killed himself because you arrested him. In front of our parents, for crying out loud.'

Louise remained sitting. 'Please, Mrs Harrison, take a seat.'

'Why did you think he was in danger?' Mrs Harrison was still shouting, her body rigid as she thrust her chin towards Louise.

The gesture was reminiscent of the caretaker, and the image of him in the bathtub flashed into Louise's mind. She blinked away the sight of the maroon bathwater, the savage incision in the man's wrist, and the blood-splattered walls. 'Please, this isn't doing either of us any good. Sit, and I'll explain.'

Mrs Harrison stood rigid for a few more seconds before deflating like a balloon and collapsing on to the armchair opposite Louise as if all the strength had vanished from her body.

Louise told her about the voice-recognition match and the patrol team she'd had stationed outside Insgrove's building.

'I can't quite believe it. He was a troubled man in some ways but he would never hurt anyone.'

'In what way was he troubled?' said Louise, stopping short of asking the woman why she hadn't offered this information previously.

'I've known Karl for a number of years. We were at school together, actually. He's a very bright man.' Mrs Harrison closed her eyes for a few seconds. 'He *was* a very bright man. But he lacked some of the opportunities I was fortunate to be given. That was why he joined the navy. To get a trade, see the world. You know . . . all that nonsense.'

'Were you still friends with him when he joined the navy?'

'I knew him before he joined. I didn't know him when he returned. At least not to begin with.'

'What do you mean?'

'They sent him off to the Falklands in eighty-two. To this day, he has never talked about it, but he must have seen some things that have haunted him since. When he returned, he couldn't hold down a job, and took to alcohol then latterly drugs. We lost contact.' She sighed, scratching her forehead. 'We were once . . . you know . . . intimate with one another. That was before he went away. I'd had these notions about us being together when he returned, but that was a different Karl. It was only when I saw him ten or so years ago, begging on the high street, that I knew I needed to help him. It's to my eternal shame that I didn't do so before.'

Louise showed the headteacher the note Karl had left for her, and for the first time since Louise had arrived, Mrs Harrison began to cry. At first she just sobbed, but soon she was inconsolable as if she'd been holding all her pain in for years.

Louise wanted to comfort the woman, but she had to remain detached and professional.

It sounded as if both Mrs Harrison's and Karl Insgrove's lives had been irrevocably changed by Insgrove going away to war. In their own different ways, neither of them had come to terms with that, and had lived in the shadow of that decision.

Louise waited until the other woman had regained her composure before asking her if there was anyone else in Insgrove's life they should talk to.

Mrs Harrison shook her head vigorously, as if she thought Louise hadn't been listening. 'He was a very solitary person. Like me, he regularly attended Holy Trinity. He used to help out there as well. Always busy, always of service. Our pastor, Reverend Lancaster, loved him. He was a very quiet man but everyone loved him.'

'Anyone else you can think of? It would really help.'

'There is a war veterans group he met with once a week in the church hall. Ex-servicemen like him. I know he took a lot of comfort from that.'

Louise was reminded of one of the photos she'd seen at Insgrove's flat. 'Is this the group?' she asked, showing Mrs Harrison the picture of Insgrove and the other five elderly men.

'Yes, that's it. That man there, Bryce Milner, is the organiser. The other man there, Ben Coles, is also a regular parishioner at Holy Trinity. I have Bryce's number if that would help?' Louise took the details from Mrs Harrison before asking if she knew the significance of Insgrove's mention of Monday in his suicide note.

Mrs Harrison broke down again, crying as Louise waited for her to answer. Insgrove's death had affected the headteacher much more than Louise had expected, and it was a shame she had to push her so much. 'I apologise,' said Mrs Harrison, after a couple of minutes, wiping her nose. 'No, I have no idea what that note means. I don't understand any of it.'

'Are there any places in Weston that you think could be of significance to Karl?'

Mrs Harrison shook her head before a smile appeared on her face. 'I imagine you're too young to remember the Tropicana on the seafront?'

'No, I remember it. Even went there as a child.' The Tropicana was the old outdoor swimming complex that had once captured the imagination of the young Louise, with its fibreglass giant pineapple housing waterslides that in retrospect were anything but spectacular. The building still existed and occasionally staged events, including a Banksy installation a few years back.

'Karl used to work as a lifeguard there before he joined the navy, though that was before it became the Tropicana. He was an excellent swimmer. I can picture him now, sitting on that high chair looking down on everyone. It's hard to imagine they're the same people. Funny that, isn't it? How we grow old, how we change?'

Louise thanked the woman, telling her she would be in touch about a possible school closure on Monday. As she left the building, she called Robertson and suggested the Tropicana building be searched for explosives.

Chapter Twenty

Louise had suspected there was something beyond an employer/ employee relationship with the headteacher and Karl Insgrove, but she hadn't expected the story that Mrs Harrison had just told. Due to their similarity in appearance, Louise had half expected to find out that Insgrove was Mrs Harrison's cousin twice removed, not that they had once been lovers.

The sadness had been evident in Mrs Harrison's eyes when she'd told the story. Louise hadn't wanted to pry but it was clear the woman lived alone, and she wondered if in some way she'd spent her life pining over what could have been between her and Insgrove. She'd come to his rescue after finding him sleeping on the streets and had obviously struggled to come to terms with what had happened to him. That she so easily remembered him as a lifeguard, young and with his life ahead of him, was telling, and Louise hoped she would still be able to remember him fondly in the years to come.

Thomas's phone went straight to answerphone again as she drove to the Tropicana. She regretted not being able to be there for him on such a trying day, the guilt over her hesitant approach to their relationship still playing on her mind, but with Insgrove's note it was unlikely she was going anywhere in the foreseeable future.

Pulling up at the seafront, she called Bryce Milner, the organiser of the war veterans group Insgrove had attended. He had a gruff North Wales accent. 'I can't quite believe all this,' he said.

'You knew Mr Insgrove well?'

'He's been attending our war veterans group for some time. I didn't really see him outside of the group except at church.'

They agreed to meet the following day, and Milner supplied her with the names and numbers of the other men she'd seen in the photograph at Insgrove's flat.

As she left the car, she caught sight of Robertson waiting outside the Tropicana building, his arms folded as he all but scowled at anyone who looked his way.

'Going for a swim, sir?' said Louise.

'Now's not the best time to test me.'

'How did you get here so quick?'

'It's my superpower. What does it matter?'

'You've been to Insgrove's flat?'

'Yes, I've enjoyed that particular shitshow. Now tell me again why we're here.'

Louise relayed the information she'd received from Mrs Harrison.

'You can't be serious,' said Robertson. 'We're here because this guy was a lifeguard in the bloody seventies?'

'He worked at the school and the caravan park. It would make sense that he targeted somewhere else that meant something to him.'

'Why target anywhere at all if he was going to end his life?'

'Could be that this was all planned in advance. You know how it is. Building up his confidence, one step at a time. If we hadn't caught on to him then who knows when he would have stopped?'

'But why now?'

'That's something I'll find out.'

'So we clear this place, then what if there's nothing here? Vacate the whole of Weston for Monday?'

'I'm afraid that is a decision for upper management,' said Louise, with a slight tilt of the head.

'Don't push it. Nothing will be happening tonight though, that's for sure. And we can't ask the army back in. Not on this evidence. We'll get a team here tomorrow morning, search the place ourselves.'

Louise walked along the seafront as Robertson headed back to his car. The Tropicana building extended on to the beach that was now fully submerged. The promenade lights reflected the rippling water, and in the distance the silhouette of Steep Holm emerged from the sea, reminding Louise of her first major case in the town, when she'd tracked a vicious serial killer to the small, uninhabited island. She headed back inland, waiting for a group of runners to pass her by before crossing the road to her car where Tania Elliot was waiting.

'Me and my shadow,' said Louise.

'What brings you here tonight, DI Blackwell?' asked Tania, who was wrapped in a beautifully tailored three-quarter-length coat.

'I could ask you the same question. Did you follow me from Congresbury?'

'Care to comment on the death of Karl Insgrove?' said the journalist, ignoring the question.

Louise had promised Tania full access if she kept Insgrove's name out of the press, which she'd failed to do. 'Press office.'

'We know it was suicide. Any note?'

'Nothing that I can share at present.'

'Do you think Mr Insgrove was responsible for the hoax at the school, and the fire at the caravan park?'

'You're nothing but direct, aren't you, Tania?' When she wasn't being annoyed by the journalist's interference, Louise held a grudging respect for her. She'd often thought that Tania would make a good copper, and she was definitely better at finding out information than some detectives Louise knew.

'Just doing my job.'

'The investigation is still ongoing.'

'And the reason you're here tonight?'

'I had to speak to someone.'

Tania smiled as if she was in the know. Chances were high she'd seen Louise meet with Robertson earlier and was fishing for information. 'It's Tim Finch's trial date on Monday.'

Louise resisted the desire to walk away. She didn't want to discuss the court case with Tania, but was interested in what she might have to say. 'I'm aware of that.'

'You'll be there?'

'Other cases permitting.'

'You'll be giving evidence though?'

Tania knew full well she would be giving evidence. She was a pivotal witness in the charge of attempted murder. 'When called upon.'

'Are you ready to relive what happened at the Walton farm?'

Louise hadn't expected the question, and answered quickly. 'Did you speak to Finch?' she asked.

'I can't divulge my sources, Louise, you know that.'

'He's not a source, Tania. He's a psychotic woman-hater,' said Louise, regretting the words as they left her mouth. 'That was off the record and I'm leaving.'

Tania waited until Louise had reached her car before calling over: 'Is it true your former colleague Thomas Ireland was the subject of an arrest today for suspected drug running?'

Louise stopped in her tracks. Her body was rigid, a pain spreading from her left shoulder to her neck. 'Why do you do this, Tania? From the beginning I have helped your career. We could be allies rather than enemies,' she said, walking back towards the journalist until she was close enough to smell the perfume on the woman.

Tania instinctively took a step back. 'I don't think we're enemies.'

'Thomas hasn't been arrested, and you know that. Why waste my time?'

'But you are in a relationship with him?'

Louise lowered her eyes. 'Whether we are together or not is immaterial and that's all you're getting from me. Anything else, you go through the press office.'

'Aren't you worried that Finch will use this to discredit you?' said Tania.

Louise ignored the comment, getting in her car and driving off before she had the chance to say or do something else she regretted.

◆ ◆ ◆

By the time she returned to Karl Insgrove's block of flats, his body was being placed into the back of an ambulance for transport to the mortuary. Residents were being allowed in and out now, and in a few hours there would be no evidence that anything had happened in the building that day.

'SOCOs are still going through all his possessions,' said Tracey as she walked over.

Louise updated her on her meeting with Mrs Harrison, and the possibility that the Tropicana building could be a potential target.

'There are a couple of people who would be interested in hearing about that, I'm afraid.'

'CTU?'

'Got here ten minutes ago. I've stopped them going into the flat, and I don't know where they've got to. They were keen to speak to you directly.'

'I'm sure they'll find me when they're ready,' said Louise, noticing Farrell by the entrance to the flats. 'Excuse me,' she added, walking over to the DS.

'Greg, can I have a word?'

Farrell nodded. 'Of course.'

'You didn't have any contact with Tania Elliot today, did you?'

'No, not really. She was in Thornbury earlier, but I didn't talk to her.'

'Check if any of your team spoke to her, would you,' said Louise, telling him about Tania's accusation regarding Thomas.

'Jesus. I'll find out who spoke to her. Obviously we're not treating Tom as a suspect,' said Farrell, as the two CTU officers rounded the corner. 'I'll go help Tracey,' he added, walking off.

'Tough day,' said DI David Faulkner with his practised smile.

'You could say that. I presume you've heard about everything?'

'We've read the note,' said Evelyn. 'Any idea of what he means about Monday?'

Louise told them about her conversation with Mrs Harrison, and what she'd said about the Tropicana building. 'It's vague, I know, but it was important to him.'

The CTU officers exchanged a look. 'Are you going to examine the site?' asked Faulkner.

'Above my pay grade, but I am hoping we'll start tomorrow. Unless you have any suggestions?'

'Do you think Mr Insgrove could have been working with someone?' asked Evelyn.

'It has crossed my mind, though nothing suggests it. He was quite an isolated figure. Aside from Mrs Harrison, we don't know of any close friendships. That said, he was a popular figure at the school and the caravan site.'

'Any correspondence aside from the suicide note?'

'The SOCOs will keep us informed. His laptop has been sent along for analysis.'

'Headquarters?' asked Evelyn.

'Yes. Simon Coulson. We already know it hasn't been used in the last four years.'

Evelyn glanced over at her colleague. 'We'd still like to assist with that if we may?'

'Anything you're not telling me?' asked Louise.

'It could be nothing, could be something. The fact is that there is a risk of an explosion somewhere on Monday. As you can appreciate, we have our eyes on a number of people in the region. We'll be speaking to them.'

'Did you have your eyes on Karl Insgrove?' asked Louise.

'We're here to help,' said David, as if she hadn't asked the question. 'I'll make sure we liaise with the Tropicana development. Sounds like a good place to start, though I would suggest another sweep of the school first. Would you be able to keep us in the loop with anything you uncover in the flat?'

Faulkner's charm fell flat on her, but Louise agreed to cooperate. Just because she couldn't see the link to a terrorist threat didn't mean there wasn't one, though she was convinced they were hedging their bets. To Louise, it looked like a last desperate attempt for a lonely old man to make his mark. From what Mrs Harrison had told her, and certainly by his subsequent actions, it was apparent Insgrove had suffered with mental health issues that had gone unchecked. It was a familiar tale of neglect which, as was so often the case, could have been prevented.

It was after midnight when she left the site. She wanted as many residents questioned as was feasible and needed to stay to make sure the job was done properly. She'd sent Tracey and Farrell home long before, and as she got into her car it dawned on her that Thomas lived less than half a mile away. Such had been Louise's focus on the block of flats that she'd forgotten they were in the middle of Worle, and that her old bungalow was only a short walk away.

She drove to his house, parked outside and sent a text message. He'd given her a key and told her she could visit any time she wanted, but it didn't feel right to go inside now. He was either asleep or still at work. Deciding he would contact her when he was ready, she drove home, every now and then checking for a message that never arrived.

Chapter Twenty-One

The next time Louise looked at her phone was the following morning, to answer the persistent ringing from Tracey. 'Morning,' she said, surprised by her own croaking voice.

'Sorry to bother you so early, Lou. Just got wind that the business in Thornbury has somehow hit the tabloids.'

The news startled Louise and now Tracey had her full attention. 'I take it there's more to the story?'

'Both you and Thomas are named, and not in a good way. They've been clever but the insinuation is that Thomas is either involved or negligent.'

'And me?' said Louise, putting Tracey on speakerphone and searching for the story online.

'Not good I'm afraid.'

'No, it's not,' said Louise, finding the headline:

Killer Cop's Boyfriend in Drug Ambush Scandal

'There's misleading headlines, then there's that,' she added. She could hear Tracey smoking on the other end of the phone as she read the hatchet piece that mentioned that Thomas had been questioned by police. The article went on to state that Louise had been cleared of any wrongdoing in connection with Max Walton's death, but she doubted many people would read that far into the article. 'They've certainly covered all bases. Don't need to guess who wrote it.'

'That woman is a menace. This could easily prejudice the jurors.'

Louise was already thinking along those lines. 'Maybe that's exactly what she wants to happen,' she said, before hanging up.

◆ ◆ ◆

She called Thomas as she changed, pleased to hear his phone ringing even though he didn't answer until the tenth ring.

'Hello?' he said, as if it was a question.

'Hello, stranger. Still in bed?'

'Hey. I may be,' said Thomas, sounding even more croaky than she had earlier.

'Everything OK?'

'Nursing a hangover of titanic proportions.'

'I popped over to yours last night, but the lights were out, and I didn't want to disturb you.'

'That's probably a good thing. Didn't get in till about three. Had to leave my car and got a taxi from Bristol. Went with some of the guys to drown our sorrows after that shitstorm yesterday. Not a great look for the new head of security.'

'They can't put this on you.'

'Last in, first out. I don't know. I feel too sick to think about it at the moment.'

Louise paused. She didn't want to compound his misery, but it was best he heard it from her directly. 'I'm afraid it made the papers,' she said, telling him about the hatchet article.

'I'm so sorry, Louise.'

'What do you mean?'

'This is the last thing you need before next week, and with what's going on in Weston at the moment.'

'Don't be ridiculous, this isn't your fault.'

'Well, if we weren't . . .'

'Stop it. They would still have connected us. Did you see Tania yesterday?'

'She tried to ask me some questions, but I told her where to go. Probably foolish in retrospect.'

The journalist was becoming a problem. It wouldn't be long before Robertson or someone higher up the food chain was on at her about the article. It was bad enough having an ex-DCI in the dock next week, and this sort of publicity made everything ten times worse.

'We'll sort it. I tried calling yesterday,' said Louise.

'Sorry, I was getting so many calls I switched it off. I knew what you were dealing with in Weston so didn't think you'd want to hear from me.'

'Now that is silly. Look, I'd better go. I'll probably be working all weekend now but we can catch up tonight at some point.'

'That would be good. Think I need some sleep now.'

'Wasn't Noah staying this weekend?'

'Had to take a rain check on that after yesterday. Rebecca wasn't best pleased. We'll have to do the meet-up with Emily some other time?'

'Yes, that sounds good. See you later,' said Louise.

◆ ◆ ◆

Should she have been more supportive? Thomas had been apologetic about their names being in the paper, but she should have been the one apologising to him. She was the 'killer cop' as the paper so crudely described her. If it wasn't for her, and the Finch court case, she doubted the incident would have made the news.

And then there was the guilt at feeling relieved that Noah wasn't staying over that weekend. What was she so scared of? Spending a few hours with Noah and Emily in tow didn't constitute a marriage. It was a perfectly sensible idea that shouldn't have troubled her in any way. Yet she did feel relieved, despite knowing she had to break the news to her parents that she wouldn't be able to look after Emily that Sunday.

◆ ◆ ◆

'Is it true?' asked her mother when she joined them for breakfast. 'About Mr Insgrove?' She mouthed the last part silently while glancing at Emily, who was too busy eating toast to care what anyone was saying.

'I'm afraid so. Yesterday,' said Louise.

Her mother stood up, her face breaking as if she was hearing that a relative had died. 'What is it?' asked her dad, who had eased himself off his dining-room chair.

'They're going to blame you for this, you know,' said her mother, stumbling to the living room to get out of earshot of Emily.

'Oh, come on, love, that's not true,' said her dad.

'It is,' said her mother, with venom. 'You pulled that poor man out of the school in handcuffs in front of all the parents and pupils.'

'I appreciate you're upset, Mum, but that wasn't what happened. He wasn't cuffed, and nearly everyone had gone home by that point.'

'Oh whatever. They'll blame you, and then that blame will turn towards us and Emily.'

'*Us and Emily?*' said Louise.

'Oh, you know what I mean. Every time we come close to settling in, something happens. How do you think she's going to deal with this?'

In the midst of all the drama, Louise hadn't given much thought to the fallout beyond what had been revealed in the newspaper articles. The fact was, Insgrove had been the caretaker at Emily's school. Whether he was responsible or not for the dummy device and the fire, he would be mourned by the school. Her mother was right, some blame would come her way, but she couldn't feel guilty about that now. She'd only been doing her job, and had followed her guidelines properly. She had never wished any ill will towards Insgrove, but chances were high he was responsible for both the dummy bomb and the fire at the caravan park.

What she couldn't tell her mother was that the threat was far from over. Insgrove's cryptic warning about Monday was still a major concern. Even though the man was dead, the fire at the caravan park indicated someone with the ability to trigger an explosion remotely, and it was more than feasible he'd set a timer up for Monday. And the fact that Insgrove's suicide note hadn't mentioned her was still an issue. She had to wonder if Insgrove had been working with someone else. 'I'm sorry you feel that way, but we did the right thing in taking him in for questioning. No one wanted this to happen.'

'Try explaining that in the playground on Monday morning,' said her mother, standing. 'Excuse me,' she added, before walking off.

'Let her go,' said Louise's father. 'She's just upset.'

Louise kissed him goodbye, stopping short of telling him that if they didn't find something over the weekend, there might not be any Monday morning at the school.

'That's the last thing you want to see on a Saturday morning,' said Robertson, as they watched a van park up on the promenade in front of the Tropicana.

'It does take away the mystery a bit,' said Louise, as Lance Corporal Adam King left the van – which was emblazoned with the words *Bomb Disposal Unit* – accompanied by his colleague Mitch Norton.

'Louise. Iain,' said King.

'Thanks for coming, Adam,' Louise said. 'As I mentioned on the phone, hopefully we won't need you but thought it best to have you here in case we do find something.' After consulting with the council and the owners of the Tropicana, it had been agreed that the café on site would be closed for the day while they did a sweep of the place.

'Better safe than sorry,' said King. 'Where do you want us to start?'

Insgrove's suicide note had begged the headteacher not to open the school on Monday, but Louise wasn't going to wait until then. 'The school has to be the starting point. I know you checked it when the dummy bomb went off but it's been open since then.'

'No problem, I'll head over now. Get your team to do an initial sweep of the Tropicana first. You know the drill, stop if anything remotely suspicious is found.'

As King and Norton covered the short distance to the school, the area surrounding the Tropicana was cordoned off, and soon a small crowd had gathered nearby. There was a mixture of morbid curiosity and apprehension on their faces as the uniformed police moved in, coordinated by Inspector Dan Baker from Weston nick. Louise knew it was probably alarmist, but she would never have been able to rest if they hadn't secured the site.

'Come. You can buy me a coffee,' said Robertson, walking off down the promenade, ignoring the glances of anxious bystanders.

'Is it wrong to hope they find something?' said Louise, handing Robertson a coffee she'd bought from the café on the site of the old aquarium.

'I guess that would be a result. Unless he's got something else planned from the grave.'

'Let's hope it's just Monday,' said Louise, glancing back along the seafront to the Tropicana. An uneasiness hung in the air, as if any second something momentous was going to happen.

'A lot of people are pissed off by this. The air show starts this time next week. I don't need to tell you it's one of the biggest earning weekends of the year,' said Robertson, snarling as he sipped his coffee.

'So inconsiderate, these arsonists.'

Robertson shot her a withering look. 'Don't think I haven't read the morning papers,' he said, before taking another drink.

'What can I say? I love keeping local journalists in employment.'

Robertson sucked in a breath. 'Ever think you could just humour the woman? This is a hatchet job of the highest order.'

'I've tried my best, Iain. I offer exclusive access then she does something like this. It's the way she is. She's all about maximising readers, and it will only get worse with this book she's working on.'

'Is this book on you, or Finch?'

It was a question Louise had been considering ever since the journalist had reappeared in town the other day. 'I think that will depend on the outcome of the court case. She'll need an ending, I suppose.'

'I take it you've thought about the timing of all this?' said Robertson.

It was unfortunate that the Insgrove case coincided with Finch's imminent court date, but if it wasn't that there would be something else. As for what was happening with Thomas at Oblong, it was serious but would never have reached the papers if it wasn't for their relationship. 'I don't think Finch is masterminding all this from his prison cell, if that's what you're thinking,' said Louise, even though the idea was something she hadn't fully eliminated.

'No, but I don't like all this happening at the same time. You need to stay focused.'

'I've been here before, Iain. I know what I'm doing.'

'I know, I know, all I'm saying is don't let this distract you. I know it's important, and that you'll do a good job. But Monday is important too. We need that bastard sent away, and for a long time. For you, and everyone else he did over. For the police. And like it or not, Louise, you are pivotal to this happening.'

Louise pictured Finch in a tiny prison cell, plotting against her. But the image became much clearer when she pictured him back out in the world. Maybe she was being paranoid, but despite the overwhelming evidence against him, she still worried that somehow he was going to wangle his way out of things. Her character was going to come under question, and the newspaper article, with its exaggerated headline, wasn't going to make things any easier. But things went wrong sometimes, and although she appreciated Robertson's pep talk, nothing was going to distract her from keeping Finch where he belonged. 'Better get back,' she said.

'You'd never think we'd left this town, would you?' said Robertson, as they walked back to the Tropicana.

'I'm more of a local than I ever was,' said Louise, turning at the sound of a siren in the distance at the same second her phone began to ring.

Robertson had stopped in his tracks. 'You going to answer that?'

'Blackwell,' said Louise, eyes on Robertson as she listened to the information given to her from the station. 'An explosion,' she said, hanging up.

'Where? Not the Tropicana?' said Robertson, glancing down the promenade.

'No,' said Louise, shaking her head. 'The school.'

Chapter Twenty-Two

It was a Saturday, but Louise called her parents anyway as she began running back to her car. 'Where are you?' she said, trying to keep the panic out of her voice as her dad answered.

'Home. Everything OK?'

Louise threw the car keys to Robertson. 'Mum and Emily with you?'

'Mum has taken her and the dog for a walk. What's the matter, you're beginning to scare me.'

The scar on Louise's arm began to throb and itch. Her dad had been the first on the scene on the night she'd received the wound. He'd already gone through so much because of her, and she regretted causing him any further undue concern. 'Sorry, Dad. There's been a fire at Emily's school. I just wanted to check you hadn't gone in for any reason.'

'Jesus,' said her dad, his voice dropping. 'No, they only left five minutes ago. Is anyone hurt?'

'I'm making my way there now.'

'Thank God it wasn't a weekday.'

'Will you double-check they're OK and text me? I'd better not call Mum or she'll worry.'

'I'll do it now. Please stay safe, darling.'

'I will, Dad. Love you.'

Robertson was driving like a rally driver, and they made it to the school in under five minutes, guided in part by a plume of black smoke funnelling up from the main building. He skidded to a halt on the road outside, next to King's BDU van, and they jumped out and headed towards the first of the two fire trucks, where King was standing next to the assistant chief fire officer John McKee. McKee was handing out instructions as his team tried to contain the spread.

'Went off as we arrived,' said King.

'Anyone inside?' asked Louise.

'We're checking now. I've sent a team around the back,' said McKee.

Louise called the headteacher and was relieved when she answered, seemingly unconcerned. 'I'm sorry to tell you this, Mrs Harrison, but there has been a fire at the school. I need to know if anyone is due to be inside today.'

'What?' said Mrs Harrison.

'Please, it's important that you think. Does anyone have access to the school?'

Mrs Harrison began mumbling, as if trying to order her thoughts. 'We use a contract cleaning service. They were due to arrive this morning. They're from the council so they have keys, though Karl is usually there to supervise . . .' she said, her words trailing off.

'There could be people inside. Cleaning staff,' said Louise.

'How many?' said McKee, summoning two of his colleagues.

Louise asked the question to a clearly shell-shocked Mrs Harrison. 'They normally have a team of six or seven,' she said, relaying the information. Louise hung up, Mrs Harrison telling her she was on her way.

Robertson took Louise aside. 'We had this place thoroughly searched?' he asked.

'Adam and Mitch searched every inch after the dummy bomb but the school has been open since then,' said Louise, repeating what she'd said to King earlier.

'That's why we're here,' said King.

'Better get on to the caravan park. Send a team over just in case,' said Robertson, as the fire team began leading people out of the front door to the waiting paramedics.

Louise rushed towards the entrance of the school, ignoring McKee's objections. She'd counted four people so far, all women. They all looked unhurt, bar some smoke inhalation which was making them cough and splutter. 'How many of you came to work today?' she asked one of them, as a paramedic wrapped the woman in a foil coat and offered her oxygen.

'Six,' said the woman. 'I think Hana was there when . . .' The woman hesitated. Louise couldn't tell if the tears streaming from her eyes were from anguish or were a result of the black smoke. 'I think she was near the explosion.'

Another woman was led out, and Louise shouted over to McKee, 'One more. She was possibly near the origin of the explosion.'

'We have this in hand, DI Blackwell,' said McKee, who was in communication with his team by radio.

Minutes went by without anything happening. The fire was under control now, the area near the entrance to the school clouded by the thick smoke. Louise began coughing, hot tears streaming down her face as McKee and Robertson ushered her back to a safe distance.

'We're bringing her out now,' said the chief. 'Doesn't sound good.'

Seconds later, two firemen emerged from the shadowy smoke carrying a gurney. They walked steadily to one of the waiting ambulances, where the body was placed in the back and driven away.

Fifteen minutes later the call came in from the hospital. The woman, identified as Hana Sanchez, was dead on arrival.

Chapter Twenty-Three

Greg Farrell adjusted his tie and took a seat in the CID office. It was a Saturday, but he was wearing his suit as usual. Appearance was something he prided himself on. Just as crime didn't stop at the weekend, neither did his professionalism.

Following a house search on one of the drivers questioned in Thornbury the day before, an arrest had been made and Farrell was due to interview the suspect – Lloyd Bradshaw – now. Although he didn't have a record for any drug offences, Bradshaw had been arrested twice on suspicion to supply, but both times had escaped charge. Some of the cocaine recovered yesterday had been found in his van, and that, partnered with his record, had been enough to get a search warrant for the man's flat in Knowle West. Half a kilo of cocaine had been found, and Bradshaw had been subsequently charged and brought to the station for questioning.

Farrell nursed his coffee. After assisting Louise in Weston yesterday and the arrest that morning, he hadn't had much sleep. Now he felt a sudden lull, as the words on his screen merged into one another.

'Keeping you up, are we, Farrell?'

Farrell turned to the source of the comment, DS Eddie Perkins. 'You do know it's a Saturday, Ed?'

Perkins smiled, but the lack of humour in his eyes suggested he hadn't taken kindly to the joke. Not that it was a joke. Farrell couldn't remember the last time he'd seen Perkins in on the weekend, especially since his old boss DCI Finch had been arrested.

'Heard you got someone for that drug bust over in Thornbury?' asked Perkins.

Farrell stopped what he was doing, taking another sip of coffee before answering. Perkins worked in a separate department and wasn't much of a cross-department team player. That made it evident he wanted something. 'Questioning him now. Why?'

'Just curious.'

'Just curious?' said Farrell, incredulous.

'Excuse me for passing the time of day with you, Greg. Sounds like it was a good bust.'

Farrell squinted his eyes. Perkins had barely spoken to him for the first few months when he'd moved to headquarters. He'd been part of DCI Finch's team then, and it had become obvious that newbies were not to Perkins' liking. Aside from Tracey, Perkins was the only survivor of Finch's old team. The others had either transferred or left under suspicious circumstances. Farrell hadn't trusted Perkins then, and he trusted him less now and wasn't falling for any false compliments from the man. 'It was. Thanks for your interest,' he said, turning back to his screen.

'We had an arrest earlier in the year down by the docks. Similar MO, a number of cars turned up and there was a bit of a scuffle.'

Farrell recalled the incident but didn't see the relevance. A number of arrests had been made following CCTV evidence that had revealed the assailants' number plates. There had been a suspicion that those involved had links to a local drug gang, but aside from a few charges for possession nothing much had come from the incident. 'You know Lloyd Bradshaw?' said Farrell, keen to find out what angle Perkins was trying to take with him.

'Bit of a lowlife. Came across him a few times before. Wriggly little bastard, always seems to get out of it.'

Farrell could have accused Perkins' old boss of the same thing up until his arrest last year. 'OK, well, thanks Ed. If you have anything specific you think can help, then let me know.'

'Sure thing,' said Perkins, walking away.

'That was fucking weird,' said Farrell to himself, as he closed down his computer and went in search of more caffeine.

◆ ◆ ◆

Tracey was in the staff kitchen area filling a flask with coffee. 'Leave some of that for me, will you?' Farrell asked.

'Have you heard?' said Tracey, leaving a cupful of unappetising-looking brown liquid swirling in the bottom of the pot.

'What?' said Farrell, frowning as he poured the lukewarm coffee into his mug.

'There's been another explosion in Weston. This time, someone died.'

'Shit. So that's where you're off to with all my coffee?'

'It's a long journey. You not coming?'

'No, I'm still dealing with this Thornbury case. Made an arrest first thing this morning.'

'So I heard. Must have been weird speaking to Thomas yesterday?'

'He was cool about it. Knew what I was going to say before I'd even asked the questions.' Farrell had known Thomas ever since his probationary years on the streets of Weston. Thomas had been in CID back then, and held the sort of position Farrell had targeted. They'd clashed at times, and Farrell had to concede most of that had been due to his own youthful arrogance. They'd been getting on much better by the time Thomas resigned, and although by then they'd worked in different towns, Farrell had been sorry to see him go.

'I take it you've seen the newspaper this morning?'

'I wouldn't call it a newspaper, but I've seen it. Timing couldn't be worse I guess. I'll speak to public relations, see if we can put something out that takes the heat off Thomas and Louise. I'm going to interview Bradshaw now. Hopefully that will help.'

Tracey nodded. 'Thanks, Greg.'

It wasn't surprising Tracey had survived the cull of Finch's old colleagues. She was diligent and probably the hardest-working copper he'd met at HQ. Farrell knew she'd also had a thing with Thomas at one point, and wondered if that would make the news soon.

Bradshaw was in the interview room with his brief. Farrell went through the formalities before asking Bradshaw where he'd got the cocaine found in his flat from.

'Personal use.'

Farrell chuckled. 'You must have some constitution, Lloyd. And the heroin in your van?'

'That was a plant, and you know it.'

'I'll be straight with you, Lloyd, and you can ask your solicitor about this, but we have enough on you for a successful prosecution. No judge is going to believe you were holding that stuff for personal use.'

Bradshaw shrugged, his eyes blinking as he shuffled in his seat. He didn't look at his brief before answering. 'Personal use.'

Farrell rubbed his chin and opened Bradshaw's file. 'Been here before, haven't we, Lloyd? You know how this works. I see you're not averse to providing a little police cooperation.'

'I'm not a grass,' said Bradshaw, turning to his solicitor for support.

'I don't care what you are, Lloyd. All I want to know is where you got this from. Tell us who you're working for, and I'd be more inclined to believe the drugs we found at your flat, and in your van, were for personal use.'

The solicitor twitched his nose, but didn't say anything. Farrell had expected him to request some more formal confirmation that charges would be dropped against his client.

'No comment,' said Bradshaw.

'Think carefully, Lloyd. This isn't your first time round the block. All I need is a name. No one will know it came from you. Do yourself a favour or you'll be up in front of the magistrates Monday morning.'

Bradshaw sat back in his chair. 'I was holding it for someone,' he said.

'Good, Lloyd, we're getting somewhere. Who were you holding it for?'

'This can't get back to me.'

'It won't, Lloyd, just tell me.'

Bradshaw bared his teeth. 'It's that bloody security bloke.'

'Security bloke?' said Farrell, a shiver running through him.

'Yeah. He was there that day. Tommy. Tommy Ireland.'

Chapter Twenty-Four

Louise remained at the school, coordinating the arrival of Janice Sutton and the SOCOs, while Robertson left for Portishead in anticipation of further developments. The school was now potentially a murder scene. Adam King had rushed over from the Tropicana and was working with the SOCOs and fire department to determine what had happened.

King was the first to emerge from the school, dressed in a white protective SOCO suit. He pulled down his mask and sucked in air as if it was nectar. Louise glanced down to the evidence bag in his hand, trying hard not to make assumptions about the contents.

'It was deliberate,' said King. 'We found it in the school hall. I believe it was planted inside a wooden pommel horse. Military-issue with remote detonation.' He held the bag aloft as if the charred device within would mean something to her.

'Remote detonation?'

'Mobile phone. Call could have come in from, well, anywhere in the world. Similar in a way to the detonation in Kewstoke. Except this time the power source was connected to plastic explosives. I've taken some swabs, and a scene examiner will be here soon. We'll need the clothes from the victim as well.'

'Could it have been on a timer, or detonated by accident?' Louise asked. 'Insgrove said it was happening Monday.' She tried to shake the image of Karl Insgrove in the bloodied water of his bath from her mind.

King's eyes widened. 'Timer, possibly. Accident unlikely. You would need a charge to set it off. The call could be programmed in advance so the auto dial goes through at a specific time. Less chance of being traced that way, though the chances of that are next to nothing anyway. However, my guess is someone called this in.'

'But Insgrove could have planted this device and set a timer so it was called this morning.'

'Could have done so, yes.'

'And the explosives, where would you get them?'

'If you know where to look, it's possible. Military contacts, or the dark web. Not easy though. We'll have a better idea when we get the results back from the swabs as to what was used.'

'The explosion killed Hana Sanchez?'

'The autopsy will tell us more. This sort of blast . . . If she was standing too close,' said King, shaking his head, 'the force would have just sucked the oxygen out of her.'

'As for the fire, the explosion set light to the curtains in the school hall. That caused most of the damage. We got there in good time, and most of the damage is superficial,' said McKee.

Louise had managed to question some of the other cleaners. The deceased woman, Hana Sanchez, had been alone in the school hall at the time of the explosion, polishing the floor. 'I have to ask—' said Louise.

King nodded before she could finish the sentence. 'We checked everywhere when we came here last time, including the pommel horse. As good a place as any to hide something. Everything is on tape, so we're covered, though I appreciate that isn't much of a consolation at this point.'

It had been three days since the school had been reopened, which would have given Insgrove the chance to plant the device.

'Thanks, Adam. Can you get this processed for me with anything else you find?'

'Sure thing. I'll probably get the rest of the team down to help secure both sites. If we can keep staff to a minimum – and it might be worth putting up an exclusion area at the Tropicana in case there is something active there.'

Louise thanked him again and began making calls. The last thing anyone wanted to see was a part of the promenade cordoned off due to the threat of an explosion, but what option did she have? Better that than risk another fatality.

Behind her, she heard commotion at the barriers set up on the road. She turned to see Mrs Harrison arguing with one of the uniformed team.

'Let her through, please,' said Louise.

Mrs Harrison stumbled beneath the police tape towards Louise. 'What has happened to my school?' she said, her face ashen.

'My team has told me the damage is mainly superficial. The curtains caught fire, and the explosion has caused some impact to the walls and ceilings which you'll need to get examined. I'm sorry to have to tell you that one of the cleaning staff was caught in the blast and subsequently lost her life.'

Mrs Harrison looked at her dumbfounded, as if she couldn't make sense of her words, before her legs gave way and she fell to the ground.

Louise dropped to her haunches. She was trying to remain detached. She didn't know why the offender was involving her, but the note and the phone call were enough to make her feel, if not responsible, then somehow complicit in what was happening. 'Mrs Harrison, are you OK?' she said, signalling over one of the paramedics. The headteacher was breathless, her skin ghost-white as her forehead bristled with sweat. The paramedic sat with her and took her pulse as colour began to return to her face.

'I'm sorry about that.'

'Please, just stay there for a few minutes. Get your breath back,' said the paramedic.

Louise sat down on the ground next to the headmistress and thanked the paramedic. 'This must be a shock, just take your time.'

'I truly can't believe it. The other day was hard enough. We've spent the last three days dealing with the fears and concerns of the children. They internalise these things in ways we don't often appreciate.'

Louise understood all too well. She'd seen it in Emily when Paul had died – the anger and resentment bubbling under the surface, and occasionally revealing itself in random acts of violence. 'It's not going to be easy,' said Louise, unable to find the words to sugar-coat the situation.

'I just don't know what the parents are going to think,' said Mrs Harrison, looking at Louise as if only then remembering that her niece was at the school. 'What do you think? What do your parents think? Would you want to send Emily here on Monday?'

'It is a terrible tragedy, but the school will get through this. It's such a wonderful little community. We all felt that from the beginning, that's why we sent her here. The parents will know it's nobody's fault. They'll rally round.' Again, the image of Karl Insgrove in his bathtub popped into her mind.

She told Mrs Harrison where they believed the device had been planted. 'I presume Mr Insgrove would have had access to the school hall prior to his arrest?'

'Of course, but you're not suggesting . . .'

Louise let the headteacher dwell on the situation. Insgrove had taken his life and all but admitted to his involvement, then a day later a device exploded in the school. What else were they to think?

'He wouldn't harm anyone. He was so gentle, you don't understand.'

Louise didn't argue. She was content to accept Mrs Harrison's denial for the time being. The headmistress had been through so much that week already. Insgrove had meant more to her than she'd been prepared to accept, and the enormity of this happening the day after his death would have knocked the strongest of people.

The only anomaly bothering Louise was the lack of a warning. The suicide note had stated Monday. The first incident had been a hoax, and the second time it appeared that precautions were taken to stop anyone getting hurt, so why had this happened now?

Louise's thoughts were interrupted by the sight of Tania Elliot talking to one of the constables guarding the barrier tape. 'Excuse me, Mrs Harrison. Will you be OK if I pop over there for a second?'

'I'm fine, thank you.'

Louise tried to run as she watched the journalist interrogate the junior officer, her phone held out to record the interaction.

'You know better than that, Tania,' said Louise, nodding to the constable to leave them alone.

Tania pressed the screen of her phone and placed it inside her jacket's interior pocket. 'I could see that you were busy.'

'Is that thing on?'

'No. I'm not recording this conversation, though I would appreciate a comment on the death of Hana Sanchez.'

Louise lowered her eyes. It wasn't a surprise that Tania already knew, but that didn't make it any less irksome. 'It's part of an ongoing investigation.'

'Murder investigation?'

'There was a fire in the school, and sadly Mrs Hana Sanchez died as a result.'

Tania laughed, the hollow sound echoing on the stone walls of the school's forecourt. 'Fire? How long do you think you can keep that going? We know the fire at the caravan park was from a detonation, and look . . .' she said, pointing at Adam King's bomb disposal unit van.

'For now, we're trying not to alarm anyone.'

'But shouldn't we be alarmed? Next weekend is the air show and there'll be thousands of visitors here. Do you think the event should be cancelled?'

Louise had to hand it to Tania. She could dramatise any situation to its full extent. 'We believe the person responsible took his own life yesterday. We can't confirm that at present though, and I would hope that you might respect the situation and not print anything until post-mortems have been conducted on Karl Insgrove and Hana Sanchez.'

In normal circumstances Louise wouldn't have shared so much, but the alternative was risking a scare-campaign piece, which no one wanted at the moment. She couldn't confirm Insgrove's guilt at this point, but she didn't want it to get into people's heads that there was still a threat in town.

'I think that would be the sensible approach for now,' said Tania.

Louise knew better than to thank her. Too many times she'd say one thing and do another. If it was in Tania's best interests, then Tania would print it.

'There was one more thing,' said Tania, as Louise was returning to the scene.

Louise paused before looking back, utilising all her willpower not to snap. 'What is it?'

'That incident in Thornbury yesterday. The drugs raid. Any news on that?'

'Not my case, Tania.'

'But your boyfriend is involved.'

'As I said, it's not my case.'

'Do you think he's involved though? Thomas?'

'Don't be ridiculous, Tania. See you later.'

'You know how this will look, don't you?'

Louise stopped again. 'Is this some sort of tactic they tell you about in journalist school? Annoy someone enough, and you'll get a reaction?'

Tania laughed. Louise couldn't tell if she truly thought this was all a game. 'I want to get to the truth, Louise. It is DCI Finch's trial next week, after all.'

'He isn't a DCI anymore.'

'You'll be called as a witness. You were there on the night of the arrest?'

'You know all this, Tania. Spit it out.'

'It eats away at your credibility a bit, doesn't it?'

'What does?' said Louise, raising her voice.

'Sleeping with the accused, and then a man who may be guilty of drug running.'

Louise was used to this type of onslaught from the journalist. It was a technique Tania had begun to master after her first success in Weston, reporting the Pensioner Killer case. It was taking all of Louise's strength not to respond. She had enough to worry about without having to deal with Tania Elliot's provocation. 'Goodbye, Tania,' she said, before returning to the school.

Standing by the entrance, she wanted to retch at the sulphur-like smell coming from the burnt-out school hall. She could sense Tania's eyes still on her, and she stood straight as if demonstrating her resolve, when all she wanted to do was crouch to the ground and ease the tension in her shoulders and neck. An innocent woman had just died, but because of Tania Elliot, Louise's thoughts were drifting to other concerns. She knew she shouldn't let Tania's taunting get to her but what if she had a point? She had slept with Finch in the past, and to a certain extent she had trusted him. She couldn't believe she was thinking this way, but what if

Tania was right about Thomas? And if that was the case, what did it say about her? How could she be expected to run a successful investigation when she couldn't even make the right choices in her personal life?

Her focus changed as she recalled Hana Sanchez's body being wheeled out of the school building towards the waiting ambulance. Her role was simple. Find out who was responsible for this death and for the terror spreading through the town.

Everything else, for now, could wait.

Chapter Twenty-Five

After his earlier revelation about his drugs being supplied by Thomas Ireland – or, as he'd called him, Tommy Ireland – Lloyd Bradshaw wasn't saying anything more. Farrell spent another thirty minutes pushing him for information but he clammed up. Farrell wasn't giving his words much credence. Bradshaw would know Thomas was an ex-copper, and giving his name was almost definitely a diversionary tactic. He couldn't back up his claim that he was holding the drugs for Thomas, but unfortunately that didn't mean Farrell could ignore it. Thomas would need to be spoken to, and that would bring a headache of its own.

Farrell's old boss, DCI Robertson, headed Louise's section. Due to recent events in Weston, he was also at the station. He felt like the right person to speak to about this. Louise would find out at some point, but Farrell wanted the situation handled as discreetly as possible.

As he walked over to Robertson's office, one of the support staff called to him. 'If you're going to see DCI Robertson, I'd leave it. He's in a foul mood.'

'Why's that?'

'There's been another explosion in Weston. A cleaner from the school has died.'

'I knew that.' Farrell ran his hand over his face. 'I hate weekends,' he said, ignoring the advice and knocking on Robertson's door.

'The prodigal son returns,' said Robertson, as if they hadn't seen each other since Weston CID had moved to headquarters. Even more so than Thomas, Robertson had been a mentor to Farrell from the beginning and had helped him secure a place in the CID after his two years on the beat.

'Can I have a word, sir?'

'Take a seat, son. What is it?'

Farrell explained the situation with Bradshaw and Thomas, Robertson's face unreadable. 'I'm going to need to bring Tom in for questioning.'

'You need to look at what Bradshaw stands to gain from this first. Nothing else points to Ireland being involved?'

Tommy Ireland. Farrell had never once heard his former colleague referred to by the moniker Tommy. He was sure it was an affectation created by Bradshaw, but he couldn't shake the chilling thought that Thomas wasn't the person he believed he knew. Given what they knew about his ex-boss, DCI Finch, who was in the dock next week, it wasn't an inconceivable proposition. Finch had managed to hoodwink people over a number of years, but then there had always been doubts about his character. His womanising ways had gone unchecked, and the incident at the Walton farm with Louise had changed many people's perceptions of him, even if most had kept their negative opinions about him to themselves.

The same, however, couldn't be said of Thomas Ireland. He wasn't exactly a stick-in-the-mud, play-by-numbers guy, but he had always been reliable and trustworthy. Farrell had never known anyone raise a concern about the man's professionalism, and that was one of the reasons he was finding Bradshaw's testimony hard to believe. 'Nothing whatsoever.'

'This is the last thing we need with that wanker Finch being in court next week. My advice would be to go for Bradshaw. Find out who he knows, who he's working with. Leave Thomas for now until we have some more information.'

'Shall I speak to Louise?'

Robertson shook his head. 'She has enough to be worried about for now. Bradshaw is probably chancing his luck. No point stirring things up unless he can offer us some proof, which I presume he can't.'

'Won't speak any further on it.'

'Then follow normal procedures. Obviously, we can't rule Ireland out, but I'm not going to start messing his life up on the say-so of this chancer.'

◆ ◆ ◆

Farrell charged Bradshaw with possession with intent, and secured a place for him until Monday when he would be put in front of the magistrates. Although he agreed in principle with Robertson's advice, he didn't feel comfortable keeping anything from Louise. He knew Robertson wouldn't say anything, but things had a way of leaking in the station, and at some point he would have to talk to Thomas directly about it.

He spent the rest of the day speaking again to drivers from Oblong. He never mentioned Thomas directly, but angled his questions so that everyone had the opportunity to name the head of security as someone who could have been indirectly involved in Friday's incident. No one did.

The only further development came from an unlikely source. DS Eddie Perkins had been following up a lead on another drug-related incident in Fishponds when he'd arrested a well-known local thug by the name of Michael Sinclair. During the arrest, Perkins had searched Sinclair's van and noticed the back number plate had been blanked out. A quick check of the CCTV images from the attack in Thornbury had revealed that Sinclair's car shared the characteristic of a slight dent to the rear wheel arch.

'You want to sit in?' asked Perkins, after telling Farrell about the arrest.

This was the second time that day – a Saturday no less – that Perkins had taken an interest in him. It wasn't Perkins-like behaviour. They'd barely ever interacted, and Farrell wasn't falling for it. It could be that Perkins was trying to make allegiances, now that he didn't have Finch to rely on, but it was a little too late for that.

'Thanks, Ed, but I don't want to step on your toes. I'll watch it on video and speak to him if I need to. You'll push on the Thornbury incident though?'

'Yeah, of course. Are you're sure? Happy for you to take some of the glory,' said Perkins.

'Cheers, mate, but all yours.' It wasn't magnanimousness stopping him from joining the interview. Whether Perkins was trying to ingratiate himself or not, the last thing Farrell wanted to do was question Sinclair about Thomas in front of the other detective.

He watched the interview from the viewing room as Perkins interrogated Sinclair; firstly over an unrelated drug haul in Avonmouth docks, and then about Thornbury. When Sinclair went to deny his involvement, Perkins pointed out they had CCTV footage.

A less switched-on suspect would have mentioned that all the attackers had been wearing masks, but Sinclair wasn't going to be fooled by such a simple trap. 'A white car. How many thousands of those do you think there are in Bristol?' he said.

'With exactly the same dent, in the same spot? I would say a total of one exactly, and that belongs to you.'

Sinclair shrugged.

'Why were you there? Why cause all that damage?'

Shrug.

'For the tape, Mr Sinclair shrugged. Rival gang perhaps?'

'I don't know what you're talking about.'

'A quantity of drugs was found in three of the vans at the Thornbury depot. My question for you though is: why leave the drugs on the scene? You obviously knew they were there. Why smash the vans up? Why not take the goods?'

'No comment.'

'Good luck telling that to a judge, Sinclair. Your plate was blanked out when we came to yours and the video evidence is enough to link you to the attack. With your record, you're looking at a stretch.'

'Is that so?'

'Help me and I'll help you. Why were you targeting the Thornbury depot?'

Farrell had asked Perkins to question Sinclair over the Thornbury incident, but it now appeared to be his sole concern. Farrell couldn't shake the feeling that somehow he was being manipulated, as if Perkins knew something he didn't.

'You know as well as I do that there has been something going on from there for some time, Perkins.'

Perkins appeared to be shocked by the suggestion, and it certainly didn't tally with anything Farrell knew about. None of the van drivers had any previous aside from Lloyd Bradshaw, who only had a caution to his name. And there was something about Sinclair's claim that something had been going on at the Thornbury depot that didn't sound genuine. He was probably trying to cover his back, shift thoughts elsewhere, but it sounded contrived – as if the whole conversation was leading to this revelation. 'Don't presume anything about me, Michael. Now, I'll ask you one last time, what were you doing in Thornbury?'

Sinclair leaned forward, as if he'd spotted some hesitation in Perkins and wanted to exploit it to his own end. 'Not so hard without your boyfriend around, are you, DS Perkins?' he said, with a snarl.

'I'm warning you,' said Perkins, the heightened tone in his voice suggesting he was losing control of the interview.

'It's not Finch's manor anymore. No one cares about you, and this,' said Sinclair, throwing his arms into the air, 'ain't fooling nobody.'

It was only there for a second, but Farrell saw the flicker of indecision in Perkins' eyes. This was clearly not panning out the way he'd intended, and his body was tensing as a result. 'Don't you talk to me that way,' he said, through gritted teeth.

Sinclair looked up at the camera and smiled, before Perkins ended the interview.

'Little shit,' said Perkins to Farrell as they met in the viewing room.

'Don't let it get to you,' said Farrell, bemused by how Perkins was, all of a sudden, treating him as a confidant.

'Just winds me up. Finch gets put away, and just because I worked with him, I have to deal with the fallout.'

It was the first time Farrell had heard Perkins mention Finch since his old boss's arrest. It was no secret that the Ghost Squad had been looking into Perkins as well as Finch, but they didn't have enough evidence against him to mount a prosecution. It made no difference to Farrell, who would always associate him with his sociopath of a former boss, but it was interesting he was mentioning him now. 'You have enough to charge Sinclair?'

'Not really. He's right about the dent in his van. Everything I have on him is circumstantial at the moment. But I know he was at the scene. Sorry I couldn't help you more.'

'You tried, Ed. Appreciate it.'

But Farrell didn't appreciate it. Perkins had pushed his hand a little too far at the end, making it so obvious that he was trying to do Farrell a favour. It was out of character and Farrell needed to know why. It could be that Sinclair had been right, and that Perkins was out on a limb without Finch, but it felt more likely that Perkins was trying to force his way into the investigation. Did he know that Lloyd Bradshaw had mentioned Thomas as a potential ringleader? Farrell imagined that would be quite the success story for Perkins. Bringing down a former fellow officer would take away the bad feeling people had for him at present, and would banish the heat from his friendship with the disgraced Finch.

Farrell decided to follow him as he left the station in the early evening. It proved to be a relatively easy job, Perkins making the short journey to a car park off the seafront in Clevedon.

Farrell watched from across the road as Perkins paced the car park, smoking, waiting for someone to arrive. Five minutes later, a sleek Mercedes coupé pulled up and out stepped the journalist Tania Elliot.

Chapter Twenty-Six

Louise kept glancing at her phone as she left the hospital where Hana Sanchez's body had been taken. Try as she might, she still couldn't get Tania's words out of her mind. The suggestion that Thomas was somehow involved in the drug operation was laughable, but still she'd let Tania's words get to her. What she should have done was call Thomas and checked he was OK, so why was she hesitating? Her natural instincts were to suspect everyone, and what if she heard something in his voice? What if the last few months had all been a lie?

After viewing the body of Hana Sanchez, it was now her duty to inform the woman's family. A second death notice in less than a week would be hard for any officer to contend with, and Louise couldn't help but shoulder the responsibility. That first note at the school had contained her name and the caller had mentioned her specifically. That alone made her culpable. It could all be a distraction, but if the offender was doing this simply to hurt her then she would find it hard to forgive herself.

It made the journey to Hana's small, terraced house in Yatton feel like a penance. Records showed she was married to a Marco Sanchez, who was currently claiming jobseeker's allowance. They had two children in their thirties, Abby and Marco Jr, who lived in the local area.

A man in a thick navy dressing gown answered the door. The smell of alcohol drifted off him as though he'd doused himself in it. 'Mr Sanchez?' she asked.

The man took a few seconds to answer as he struggled to focus on her. 'Yes,' he said, eventually, the word sounding like a question.

'May I come in?' asked Louise, displaying her warrant card.

The house was a bizarre mix of perfect cleanliness and chaos. Louise peeked into the immaculate kitchen area as she followed Mr Sanchez to the living room, which was a graveyard of takeaway boxes and beer cans.

'Excuse the mess,' he said, slumping down on the sofa.

'Please, can we sit?' said Louise, proceeding to tell the man about the incident at the school.

When she was finished, Mr Sanchez twitched before standing and filling a china cup with supermarket-brand whisky. 'She's gone?' he said, wincing as he downed the drink.

Louise nodded. 'Is there anyone who can be with you?' she asked.

'My girl comes around every now and then.'

'Your daughter – Abby?'

'Abby,' repeated Mr Sanchez, filling his cup once more.

Louise eased the bottle from his grasp and helped him sit down. She found Abby's phone number and experienced the pain of telling the woman about her mother's death, before calling a family liaison officer to attend the house and offer some help to Mr Sanchez. Nothing suggested that Hana Sanchez had been specifically targeted. She'd simply been in the wrong place at the wrong time, and for that, Louise wanted to give her family all the help she could.

◆ ◆ ◆

Two hours later, Louise was standing outside Weston General. Abby Sanchez had identified the body of her mother, and Louise had made arrangements for it to be moved to the county morgue tomorrow morning. Louise was debating whether or not to drive home when Greg Farrell tapped her on the shoulder. 'I was told you were here,' he said, in response to her look of shock.

'What are you doing here, Greg?'

'I've had a hell of a day, can't deny it,' said Farrell. He told her about the interview with Lloyd Bradshaw and his claim that Thomas was responsible for the drug running within the delivery company. 'Called him Tommy Ireland.'

'Tommy Ireland?' said Louise, hearing a hint of panic in her laugh. 'You can't possibly believe him,' she added, her thoughts turning to Tania Elliot's words earlier that day.

'No. Something weird is going down. You know Ed Perkins? Of course you do. Anyway, he starts speaking to me this morning. All buddy-like, as if we're best friends. All of a sudden, he's found one of the drivers from the incident in Thornbury. Asks me to sit in on it. Then has the audacity to complain about his unfair treatment because Finch has been put away.'

Perkins was one of Finch's sycophants, possibly the last one left at the station. He'd been a detective constable during Louise's time at MIT, and promoted not long after her departure. She hadn't had many dealings with him since then, but he'd always made his allegiances well known. It wasn't a surprise he was trying to forge new alliances now Finch was facing trial, and it wasn't a surprise that he was poking his nose into an investigation that was having an impact on Thomas. 'Did you sit in on it?'

'I watched it. Something about it didn't ring true to me, as if he was going through the motions. The suspect, Michael Sinclair, turned on him at one point which he didn't like. But that's not really why I'm here. This evening, I decided to follow him afterwards and he ended up going to see that journalist, Tania Elliot.'

'Did he now? What time was this?'

'About eight p.m.'

'Not long after I spoke to her last. What's Perkins playing at? Does he know about Bradshaw's accusation?'

'Not that I'm aware of. So far, it's only you, me and Robertson. But you know how it is; it could easily be round the station by now.'

'Funny that Tania had already asked me about it.'

'She knew Thomas was head of security for Oblong, though?' asked Farrell.

'Yeah, but she out and out suggested that he was under suspicion of drug running. This was before you'd got Bradshaw's statement.'

'You think she knew Bradshaw was going to say it?'

'That, or she thought someone was going to,' said Louise.

'I'll keep an eye on him,' said Farrell, looking away.

It was obvious what he was concerned about, and she decided to rescue him. 'You're going to have to bring Thomas in at some point, I presume?' she said.

'We'll make it as low-key as we can. I'll arrange to see him at work first thing Monday.'

Louise sighed. It was the last thing they needed at present. 'Maybe you should do it sooner. Any hint of favouritism will reflect badly, and with Tom and I . . .'

'Understood,' said Farrell, shaking his head. 'I'll guess I'll get on to it tomorrow. You think all this stuff is over now Insgrove is out of the picture?'

'I hope so, though I still don't know why he did it, beyond it being a cry for help,' said Louise. 'And we still have the threat of Monday looming over us.'

She thanked Farrell for making the journey, and watched him drive away before deciding what to do next. It was too late to go back to headquarters, but she was restless and knew she wouldn't be able to sleep. She knew what she needed to do but was putting it off. She hadn't spoken to Thomas since earlier that day, but if she called him now, she would have to tell him about Lloyd Bradshaw's accusation.

She decided to drive to his house. She considered herself an excellent judge of character who could occasionally get things wrong, but she couldn't believe she'd been wrong about Thomas. Even if it wasn't against his character, she just couldn't see how he would have hidden that side from her over the years.

As she drove up the Locking Road, she reminded herself that all of this was to do with a lowlife who'd been found with cocaine in his possession. Bradshaw would know Thomas was ex-police and probably thought the accusation would benefit him in some way.

That only made her feel more guilty. The fact that she was even considering Thomas's involvement said much more about her than it did him.

Her phone rang as she was heading past Baytree Rec. Hers was the only car on the road at that point, and the piercing ringtone made her jolt in her seat. The phone was connected to the dashboard, the name *DCI Robertson* flashing on the screen.

'Sir?' she said, answering.

Robertson's voice came out as a low-pitched grumble from the car speakers. 'Where are you, Louise?'

'Driving through Weston towards Worle,' said Louise, stopping short of telling her boss she was on her way to Thomas's house.

'Keep driving to Portishead. There have been some developments,' said Robertson, hanging up.

Louise didn't bother ringing back. By the sound of it, Robertson had either just been dragged from bed or the bar, and if he didn't want to speak to her over the phone nothing was going to change that. She made good time to headquarters, arriving to see the DCI heading into the main building.

It was too late to call Tracey or Farrell to see if they knew what was happening, so she followed Robertson into the building not knowing what to expect. Robertson had stopped to get a coffee from the vending machine and handed her a cup. She'd been right about him getting dragged out of bed. He was wearing jeans and a dark pullover, his hair dishevelled, his eyes sunken. It was rare to see him in casual clothes but she knew better than to mention anything. 'Thanks,' she said, taking the coffee.

'Call came in not long before I called you. As head of department, I was alerted to it,' said Robertson, as they took the lift to the CID. He took out his phone and played the message, which sounded like it used the same voice-altering software as the call from Insgrove, despite the voice sounding slightly higher in pitch:

> *The explosion at the school will not be the last until DI Louise Blackwell has paid for all her crimes.*

Chapter Twenty-Seven

Assistant Chief Constable Alan Brightman and the two officers from CTU were waiting for Louise in the incident room. She was still coming to terms with the anonymous message as she followed Robertson through into the office. It potentially turned everything on its head. Not only did it suggest that Insgrove was either working with someone else or wasn't involved at all, it confirmed that the party or parties involved had a particular grievance with her which risked making her position on the investigation untenable.

The explosion at the school will not be the last until DI Louise Blackwell has paid for all her crimes.

Louise didn't know what her supposed crimes were, but people had died, and she had to shoulder that blame. No doubt that was why she was there, and the walk to the oval table where the three were sitting felt never-ending.

'DCI Robertson, DI Blackwell, thank you for coming in at this ungodly hour,' said Brightman – who, like Robertson, was dressed in his civilian garb.

This time last year, it would probably have been Assistant Chief Constable Morley who was holding court. Thankfully, that dinosaur had resigned after Finch's arrest. Brightman had a progressive reputation, and at the very least wasn't predisposed to a hatred of

Louise. 'Sir,' said Louise, taking a seat and nodding to the two CTU officers.

'You'll have heard the voice call. Seems almost impossible that it was pre-recorded as the operator had a conversation with them. This, of course, rules out Karl Insgrove unless he is calling from the dead. Anything in your dealings with Mr Insgrove to suggest he was working with someone else?' said Brightman.

'Nothing, sir. Insgrove denied any involvement from the beginning. The strongest piece of evidence we had against him, aside from his connection to the school and caravan park, was the voice-recognition analysis we did on the initial call.'

Brightman searched through his papers. 'Seventy-eight per cent probability?'

'Sir.'

'You still think he was responsible?'

The question was loaded. Insgrove had taken his own life, and if he was subsequently found not to have played a part in this then the blame for his death would fall on Louise. That didn't mean she wasn't going to say what she thought. Everything had pointed to Insgrove's involvement and she stood by what she'd done. 'Up until this message, I believed he was solely responsible. I still think he's involved, but it seems he wasn't working alone.'

'Did Mr Insgrove have a specific grudge against you?' asked DI David Faulkner.

Louise looked first at Robertson, before turning to the assistant chief. She'd expected the question, and it was a pertinent one. But she wasn't sure it was coming from the right person. 'With all due respect, sir, why am I being questioned by CTU?'

'We're all colleagues here, Louise. Please answer the question,' said Brightman.

'Cooperation goes both ways, sir. They haven't offered me anything, and in return they want me to start answering their questions?' It was a risky move, but she was fed up of being dictated to on her own case. Now that Finch and Morley were gone, she needed to make her position clear. She refused to be trampled on, and Brightman needed to understand that.

The assistant chief tilted his head towards the CTU officers. 'Well?'

'What would you like to know?' said Faulkner, focusing his magnanimous smile on Louise.

'First of all, you can tell me what your file says about Insgrove.'

'We don't have a file on Karl Insgrove,' said DCI Evelyn Hartson, speaking for the first time.

'Who do you have a file on?' asked Robertson.

'Some information we can't share. We liaise with MI5 and are prevented from disclosing it. All I can tell you is that none of our intelligence suggests any attacks were planned in the area, and our subsequent information backs this up,' said Faulkner.

'And if you don't mind me saying, DI Blackwell, this anonymous call suggests you are a specific target for the offenders. Especially if you take into account the previous call we believe most likely came from Insgrove, and the note found at Larkmead School,' said Evelyn.

'That's hard to deny. My niece goes to Larkmead School, though I have no direct link to the caravan park.'

'Do you think this could have anything to do with Finch's court case next week?' asked Brightman.

Louise's focus so far had been on Insgrove. And then, with the emergence of Justin Walton, she'd thought even less about the possibility of Finch's involvement. But she'd yet to rule it out. Finch certainly had connections in the criminal fraternity, and even from a prison cell it was feasible he could have some part to play. 'My feeling is no, he's not involved. I don't think even Finch would stoop this low. And I don't know how it would benefit him to kill innocent civilians. It would be a bit much just to piss me off.'

'He could be trying to discredit you,' said Evelyn. 'Read a newspaper recently?'

'That's uncalled for,' said Robertson.

Louise frowned. Robertson understood she didn't need protecting, but he hated the bullshit as much as anyone. DCI Hartson had been off with her since the first time Louise had met her, as if the events were beneath her pay grade. 'I'm not ruling out Finch's involvement completely, but I would like to state that Finch's prosecution isn't solely dependent upon my testimony. Many of the charges are cut and dry, and the attempted murder case is watertight,' she argued, despite her private worries about the case. 'We can place Amira Hood at his house, and there is enough visual and verbal evidence to suggest that Finch planned to kill her. There's also all the other women he systematically abused, who are just as important in providing a successful prosecution. Even if somehow all this discredits me, and again I'm not sure how or why it would, Finch won't really benefit. And believe me, I'm not sticking up for him. But at this moment, I just don't think this is his handiwork.'

She decided not to declare her knowledge about Perkins and the clandestine meeting with Tania Elliot. It might or might not mean anything at this stage, and she didn't want to cloud things further until she had more information.

'Then who would have a grudge against you, that they would target you this way? What so-called crimes do you need to answer for?' asked Brightman.

Louise's mind had been made up on that the second she'd heard the message. In a way, it was linked to the Finch case, but perhaps more indirectly than she might have expected. 'I believe the caller is alluding to the incident at Walton farm.'

'Where you shot an unarmed man?' said Evelyn.

Beside her, Louise felt Robertson tense up. For all the talk of cooperation, DCI Hartson was being purposely confrontational.

'I think what Evelyn means is, when you were forced to confront the serial killer Max Walton. Isn't that right, Evelyn?' said Faulkner, with an encouraging smile.

Evelyn's expression didn't break. 'I'm not accusing anyone of anything. You were cleared of all charges. I'm saying an unarmed man was shot, and it is natural that someone might be aggrieved by it. The question is, who?'

Louise wasn't inclined to share any information with the officers, but the way the assistant chief was looking at her it was inevitable they would find out one way or another. 'Walton's nephew, Justin Walton, has threatened a civil case against me for Max Walton's death.'

'Did we know about this?' asked Brightman, seemingly addressing the room in general.

'It is not confirmed at this stage, and I have come to understand that Mr Walton will no longer be pursuing the claim,' said Louise.

'You've spoken to him recently?' asked Faulkner.

Louise wasn't about to announce to the room that Walton had all but tried to blackmail her. 'I have already questioned him over the explosions and his connection to Karl Insgrove. We checked his whereabouts during, after and prior to the events in Weston. I didn't believe he is a credible suspect.'

'And you do now?' asked Faulkner.

Louise frowned. 'Not really. I'm pretty sure he's a drug addict and is all but destitute. I don't think he has the means, intellectually or even financially, to pull something like this off.'

'But maybe if he was working with Insgrove?' said Brightman.

'Or someone else?' said Hartson.

'What do we know about the rest of his family?' asked Robertson.

'At the time of his death, Max Walton had an estranged wife, Claudia Walton, and a sixteen-year-old son, Martyn. The wife had suffered years of emotional and physical abuse from him. She was originally from South Africa and they both moved back two years ago. Walton's brother, Justin's father, died seven years ago. Hit and run.'

'In light of this new information, namely the anonymous phone message, I think we should up our surveillance on Justin Walton. Are we agreed?' said Brightman.

'I'll check on the wife and son. Make sure they're both safely in South Africa,' said Louise. 'I don't want to rule out the possibility that this is all diversionary. We don't know for sure that any of this is related to Max Walton. Thanks to Tania Elliot, Finch's court case next week is making the headlines. Maybe the bomber is using this as a means to distract us. Dredging up the Walton case to send us in the wrong direction.'

Louise hoped she didn't have to spell it out for the CTU officers. Despite their talk of cooperation, they hadn't given her anything. She simply didn't believe they didn't have their eyes on at least one person in the area.

Faulkner smiled again, and this time it felt natural. 'Very astute, DI Blackwell. Rest assured we are taking this very seriously,' he said, exchanging looks with Hartson and Brightman.

'As a reminder, we have officers risking their lives out there,' said Robertson. 'We had a civilian casualty today, and that could easily have been one of my team. So if you know anything now, best share.'

'David?' said Brightman.

'There is a group from Withywood in Bristol we have a very close eye on. Nothing points to them staging anything in Weston, but there isn't a lot of talk between them internally. As soon as we hear anything that would jeopardise the lives of your officers, you have my word you'll be informed immediately. That has always been the case. Always will be,' said Evelyn.

Louise wanted the meeting to end, but it wasn't over just yet. There was an unmistakable tension in the air, with too much being left unsaid.

It was DCI Hartson who eventually broke the silence. 'I have to come out and say it, sir, I don't think DI Blackwell should remain in charge of this case.'

The tension in Louise's body returned. She turned her neck, hearing a click and a pop that she hoped wasn't audible to everyone else in the room. Despite Evelyn's obvious dislike of her, she couldn't blame the CTU officer. If Louise viewed the situation dispassionately, she had to concede that she was potentially too close to the case. The offender was now pinning the blame on her for the latest atrocity. If Morley had still been in charge, she would have been taken off the case, but the new ACC looked at her with his eyebrows raised, giving her a chance to explain herself.

Louise took a deep breath. 'I appreciate it seems that I am too close to the case, but taking me off now would be a backwards step. What if this is what the offender wants? Me off the case because I'm the most knowledgeable person on it.'

'Oh, come on,' said Evelyn, sitting back in her chair in an overly dramatic show of exasperation.

Louise leaned forward. 'The only thing that links me personally is my name on the note at the school and the messages. No demands have been made of me. And you think they're going to stop if I'm taken off the case? They want me to pay for whatever it is they think I've done. You think we should just do what the offender says because they think I'm guilty of a crime? That doesn't make any sense.' She turned her attention to Brightman. 'I know that town and these people better than anyone, sir. It would be the wrong move to bring someone in now. It would cost too much time. I'm one hundred per cent focused.'

Brightman rubbed his chin. 'Iain?'

'Louise's record speaks for itself, sir,' said Robertson, as if the question wasn't even worth asking.

Brightman nodded. 'We'll keep things the way they are, but I want a daily update, DI Blackwell, understand?' he said, clapping his hands once to wrap things up. 'Right. I think we could all do with some sleep. Tomorrow is almost here.'

◆ ◆ ◆

'Could have been worse,' said Robertson, once the others had left the room.

'How so?'

'No one was talking about giving the case to CTU. That feels like progress.' Robertson hesitated, and Louise knew what was coming. 'Have you seen Thomas today?'

'No. I saw Farrell, though. Told me about the accusation against Thomas.'

'Nonsense, obviously. But we'll have to speak to him.'

'Farrell is going to speak to him,' said Louise.

'And you?'

Louise sighed. It felt like an eternity since she'd seen Thomas. She understood Robertson's unsaid request not to speak to Thomas before his meeting with Farrell, and was sad to admit to herself that she felt a bit relieved. She didn't think Thomas had any involvement in what had happened, but she was still worried about seeing him face to face in case she saw something in his eyes that suggested he was involved in any way.

'I'm going home, sir,' she said.

Chapter Twenty-Eight

It was only procedure, but Louise couldn't shake her sense of guilt for not contacting Thomas last night. It felt like a betrayal and later Thomas would have to endure questioning from one of his old work colleagues about his role in a drug-distribution scheme.

'Are you OK, Aunty Louise?'

Louise was with Emily on the beach in Sand Bay, Molly sprinting to and from the sea, barking at the small breaking waves. 'What do you mean, darling?'

'You look pale,' said Emily.

'Just tired,' said Louise, who felt as if she was nursing a hangover, despite not having drunk anything alcoholic in months. It was the toil of recent days, and a combination of a lack of sleep and rushed meals. If the Insgrove case wasn't enough, Finch's Crown Court case began tomorrow. She'd yet to tell Emily that she couldn't spend the whole day with her, and it felt as if everything was threatening to overwhelm her.

'We can go back if you like,' said Emily, her face breaking into a look of heartbreaking compassion.

'No way. I'm not going to cut short a walk with my two best girls like that,' said Louise, fighting her lethargy as she jogged towards the shoreline where Molly was still barking at the tide as if she could reverse it.

After breakfast, Louise called Farrell before driving to head-quarters. Thomas had agreed to speak to him that morning and had attended the station earlier. 'How was he?' she asked, glancing at her phone to see if Thomas had rung.

'You know what he's like. Pretty relaxed about it. He understood we had to ask him the questions. It's clear there's no love lost between him and Bradshaw, so he wasn't surprised he'd made the accusation. He's offered us access to everything, phone and computer records, even offered for us to search his house. Obviously we'll check it all to cover our backs, but it is as we thought: a non-starter.'

Louise gave Emily a kiss goodbye. It was always a wrench saying goodbye to her on a weekend, and she held on to her a little longer than usual.

'Everything OK?' asked her mother.

'It's just the business with the school.'

Her mother shook her head. 'No, with you. Emily said you were poorly at the beach.'

'I'm fine.'

'They work you too hard. Even more so now you have to trek to Portishead every day. And you didn't even touch your breakfast.'

Louise was glad her mother had stopped drinking, but it did mean she had more energy to focus on other things, which now seemed to centre around Louise's well-being. 'I'll get something at the station. Thanks again, sorry to leave at such short notice.'

Her mother followed her to the car. 'When will you know about the school?' she asked. 'The parents are sure they're going to close it for the week.'

'I think that's a matter for the school. I'm sure they'll notify you. It's just the hall that's damaged, so I don't think they'll necessarily have to shut it.'

'Someone died there, Louise. It's hardly great for the kids.'

'I know, Mum, believe me. It sounds horrible, but life has to go on. You can't expect the whole school to stay off for the week. And I imagine most of the parents would kick off if it did.'

The last comment warranted a frown from her mother.

'Sorry, I know that sounds callous. We're doing everything we can. I need to go. Love you, Mum.'

Her mother nodded. 'Get something to eat,' she said, as Louise pulled away.

◆ ◆ ◆

Louise took her usual diversion through the town centre before heading towards Portishead. Although she'd already been to the beach in Sand Bay that morning with Emily, she wanted a glimpse of Weston before going to work. She felt as if she was checking in on the town as she made a lap of the seafront – taking in the Tropicana, its café now open – before heading back towards Emily's school, where a building team had already begun work on the damaged school hall.

She should have headed to the bypass, but decided to drive through Milton towards the M5. Taking this route meant she would pass the turning to Thomas's house.

Her pulse quickened as she passed Worle rec. It was ludicrous to feel this way but she was nervous about seeing him again. It felt awkward having not seen him for the last couple of days, the uneasiness intensified by Farrell having questioned him that morning. Thomas wouldn't know for sure, but would have wondered if Louise had known about it in advance.

She slowed down as the turning approached. Now she was in the peculiar situation of wanting to talk to him while also worrying that any conversation would end in an argument.

She carried on past the turning, deciding she was overthinking the situation. She'd been told not to speak to him, after all, and Thomas knew how things worked with the job. He wasn't the type of person to sulk. He would know she had been busy with work, and he would call her when he was ready. Besides, she had more pressing matters to contend with. But still, she checked her phone another ten times before she reached the station.

◆ ◆ ◆

Crime didn't stop for the weekend, and the car park at headquarters was full. Louise still felt like a bit of an outsider every time she stepped through the main doors. It wasn't the same place she'd left a few years ago when she'd moved to Weston, but there were still personnel within who would remember that time and the fallout from Max Walton's death. And as unpalatable as it seemed, some of them were on Finch's side. They had been during the Walton case, and had even remained loyal after Finch's arrest. The majority of the officers at the station had been glad to see Finch go. Corrupt officers only sufficed to make everyone's jobs harder. But there was still the odd old-school copper who saw Finch's arrest as a betrayal, and Louise wasn't sure what camp everyone fell into. She was forced to endure the occasional stare and muttered word behind her back. She'd been used to it for so long, but it never made it any easier.

She was glad to reach the CID, where Farrell and Tracey were together in the incident room, staring down at the table.

'What are we looking at?' asked Louise.

'National news again,' said Tracey, moving aside so Louise could see a small headline inside one of the Sunday broadsheets:

Suspected Murder in School

A photograph of the fire at Emily's school took up a quarter of the page, Louise seeing her name as she scanned the article. 'Where the hell are they getting "suspected murder" from?' she asked, noting Tania's name on the byline.

'Probably an anonymous source,' said Farrell. 'Did you manage to speak to Thomas yet?' he added.

Louise shook her head. 'Not yet,' she said, a little sharper than intended, before updating them on her late-night meeting with Brightman and the CTU officers, and the anonymous message that had been sent to the station stating that Louise had to pay for her crimes.

'Imagine if Morley had still been here. He'd have suggested you resign,' said Tracey.

'Even he wouldn't be stupid enough to give in to demands like that. Brightman was doing his best to be on my side, but I can imagine the pressure he's under. I'm worried CTU will get their hands on the investigation.'

'You think?' said Farrell. 'This isn't a terrorism thing.'

Louise was pleased that neither of her colleagues had even raised the question of what her supposed crimes were. 'Perhaps not, but that doesn't mean they don't want to get involved. With the air show next weekend, they want to cover everything. If we don't get something in the next few days, they'll either take the case from us or be forced to cancel the event.'

'Can you imagine the fallout from that?' said Tracey.

Tracey was right. Local businesses would lose thousands of pounds if the event was cancelled, and for an area that relied on cyclical trade that would be all but impossible to contend with. Whoever had sent that message was putting all the responsibility on Louise's shoulders, and however unjust that was, it was something she would have to accept. Not that she was going to resign, even if that was an option.

'I take it news of this threat is being kept amongst ourselves?' said Farrell.

'Yes, but I think it's out there in the station, and if the last few news days have taught us anything it's that someone likes to talk. Tracey, would you be able to get Justin Walton in? I think we should get his voice tested against the message. Also, be good to see if there are any other relatives out there,' said Louise, reminding herself that she'd yet to speak to South Africa.

Louise waited for Tracey to leave before speaking to Farrell. 'So how was he really?' she said.

'You haven't come in all this way just to read my face, have you?' said Farrell. 'He was fine, happy to cooperate. He knows how this all works so it wasn't an issue.'

'Must have been awkward for him.'

Farrell straightened his tie. It was a Sunday morning, and he must have been the smartest-dressed person in the station. 'He's not involved, I'm certain, and I'm not saying that because he's an ex-copper, or he's . . . you know . . .'

'My boyfriend?' said Louise, the word still sounding awkward to her ears.

'Yes. Bradshaw is deflecting and saw an obvious chance to take a bit of limelight off himself, and it's backfired. I've charged him and he'll be in front of the magistrates tomorrow.'

'Thanks, Greg.'

Farrell nodded, handing her the newspaper before walking off.

It took a number of calls before Louise managed to locate the address for Max Walton's ex-wife. Claudia Walton had changed her name to Kim Renwick before leaving the country of her birth. Louise appreciated the significance of changing both her first and last names, understanding the desire to completely obliterate the person she'd been while married to Max Walton. She located the woman in Menlo Park, a suburb of Pretoria, where she lived with her son, Martyn, whose surname had also changed from Walton to Renwick.

Louise called the local police office and explained the situation to a Detective Sergeant Connah Graves, who agreed to locate and speak to the pair. Louise tapped the table as she spoke to the detective. It was hard to decipher from his clipped accent whether or not he was taking this as seriously as it deserved. She stressed the importance and urgency, and he agreed to treat it as a priority while never once changing the tone of his voice.

She hung up and rubbed her forehead where a headache was forming. She hated having to wait on other people. If she had her own way, and an unlimited amount of time at her disposal, she would handle every miniscule aspect of each investigation. As it was, she was already restless for Tracey to get back to her with news from Justin Walton, and Graves to tell her that he'd spoken to Kim and Martyn Renwick.

Nothing could be achieved by waiting so she headed back into Weston, calling Mrs Harrison on her way. As she'd expected, the headteacher was at the school organising the renovations.

'The worst thing is the smell. You take one step into the school hall and you come out stinking of a bonfire,' said Mrs Harrison, taking a sniff of her cardigan as they met in her office.

'So you're planning to remain open tomorrow?'

'Of course, it would take something extraordinary to keep us closed. We owe it to the pupils, and to Karl, to keep going.'

'Mr Insgrove?' said Louise, unable to hide her incredulousness.

'Karl Insgrove was a long-standing member of this community, and we'll honour his death in the appropriate way.'

'Even though he could be responsible for what happened here?'

'May I remind you that Mr Insgrove had passed away by the time the fire started,' said Mrs Harrison.

'It was a staged explosion, Mrs Harrison. Not a fire that got out of hand. We think it's possible that Mr Insgrove called us prior to the dummy bomb being found. As you know, he left you a note to warn you about a potential future threat.'

Mrs Harrison pursed her lips. 'That could have been for anything. As far as I am concerned, Karl never did anything wrong. He was clearly suffering from some mental health problems and that, coupled with the pressure of the last few days, led to his untimely death.'

At least this time she'd stopped short of blaming Louise. 'Did Mr Insgrove have any close friends he may have mentioned to you?'

'Not really, he was a very solitary man, as I mentioned before. Why do you ask?'

Louise knew she had to handle the situation carefully. Mrs Harrison was blinded by her relationship with Insgrove, and was struggling with the concept of his involvement. 'We need to rule everything out. It could be that Mr Insgrove was working with someone else. Was perhaps being coerced into behaving against his will,' she added, hoping to pacify the headteacher.

Mrs Harrison considered this for a few seconds. 'Well, I guess I could possibly understand that. However, I don't think he had much of a social life beyond working at the school and the caravan site. And the vets group, of course.'

Louise had been supposed to meet the organiser of the group – Bryce Milner, with his deep Welsh accent – yesterday but had been forced to cancel after the explosion. 'There was no one else? No one he was closer to?'

Mrs Harrison seemed to squirm at the very thought and Louise didn't push her any more. She thanked her, and was on her way to visit Bryce Milner when her phone rang, the number withheld.

For a moment, Louise was transported back in time to the period when she'd first moved to Weston. One of Finch's little games at the time had been sending her anonymous text messages, and seeing *Unknown Number* on her phone always sent a jolt of adrenaline through her. 'DI Blackwell.'

'DI Blackwell, this is Connah Graves from Menlo Park police.'

'Hi Connah, thanks for getting back to me so quickly.'

'That's fine. I managed to track down Kim Renwick. She has moved from the area and lives a good ninety minutes away, so thought I'd call her first.'

Louise sighed inwardly. It wasn't the way she would have done it. 'What did she say?'

'That's the thing. She hasn't been back to the UK since leaving, but her son, Martyn, he's nineteen now and he's taking one of those gap years.'

'He's travelling?'

'Yes, that's right. That's the thing in fact. Kim spoke to him last night. He's been travelling around Europe, and for the last three weeks he's been staying in the UK.'

Chapter Twenty-Nine

Graves didn't have an address for Martyn Walton in the UK. 'They talk via WhatsApp,' he said, as if that was an explanation.

Louise's mind was a whirl of possibilities. Could it really be that Martyn Walton, now Renwick, had returned to the UK simply to torment her? And if so, why had he gone about it this way? She reiterated the importance of the situation to the South African detective. 'We need a UK address for him, and ideally a photograph.'

'I have a photo of him. He's on our database,' said Graves, maintaining the same monotone speech pattern.

'He has a record?'

'Yes.'

'Care to share the details?' said Louise, exasperated by the detective's seeming indifference.

'Let's see. A bit of shoplifting. A couple of fights including a charge of ABH.'

Louise was waiting for him to say something about arson but he stopped talking. 'Is that it?'

'Last in trouble two years ago. He was under threat of a custodial sentence, so looks like he's sorted himself out.'

'Could you send me the file?'

'Yes.'

Louise took in a deep breath. 'Connah, I do appreciate your help on this. Would it be possible for you to travel to Kim Renwick's house and speak to her face to face? We need to find out where Martyn is staying. One person has already lost their life here. If Martyn is anything like his father and he is involved, this could get much worse.'

'I can do that,' said Graves.

Louise thanked the detective before calling Tracey and telling her about Max Walton's son being in the UK.

'Just left Justin Walton's place. He's coming down off something. Something horrendous by the state of him.'

'OK, wait for me there. I think we need to speak to him about his cousin.'

◆ ◆ ◆

Louise rearranged her appointment with Bryce Milner from Insgrove's veterans group, and made the short journey to Bournville where Tracey was waiting. The emergence of Martyn Walton-Renwick as a potential suspect changed everything, and it tied in perfectly with the last message. If anyone thought Louise was guilty of a crime, it would be Max Walton's son.

'The last thing we need is another Walton hanging around,' said Tracey, as if reading her mind, as they made their way to the terraced house where Justin lived. 'I have to warn you, it's not a pretty sight in there. And as for the smell,' said Tracey, shaking her head.

Louise laughed, but as she entered the property, she realised Tracey had been underselling the place. The floor was a carpet of growing garbage. Crisp packets, pizza boxes, energy drink cans and empty bottles of alcohol covered every visible inch except where that space was taken up by a comatose human. The smell in the house was a torrid mix of body odour, weed, excrement and urine. 'Jesus, I should be wearing a mask,' said Louise, trying to breathe only through her mouth.

'Watch out for needles,' said Tracey, stepping over a young woman lying at the foot of the staircase. 'Walton is upstairs.'

'We should get Environmental Health out here,' said Louise, as she made her way up the stairs, though they both knew that wouldn't achieve anything. The building was council-owned. The state of the place and its inhabitants was part of a much larger problem not only in Weston but nationwide, and Louise had to reluctantly accept it wasn't something she could deal with now.

'I'm back, Justin,' said Tracey, barging open a door to a dingy room with yellowing wallpaper. Justin Walton was lying on a single bed. He glanced over at them before making a gun sign with his fingers and pointing them at Louise. 'You've brought the killer with you.'

Louise jammed open a window. 'What have you taken, Justin?'

'What haven't I taken?' he answered with a laugh.

Walton appeared to be naked underneath the sheet, his torso stick-thin and devoid of muscle. 'I need to talk to you about your cousin, Martyn Walton. Or Martyn Renwick as he is now known.'

Walton couldn't have hidden the flicker of recognition if he'd tried. 'I don't know any cousin,' he said, pulling the sheet over his bony shoulders.

'You know your dad had a brother?' said Louise.

'Of course I do. You killed him,' said Walton with a sneer, as the sheet rose up further until all she could see was his gaunt face, his skin pitted with blemishes.

Louise turned to Tracey, who shrugged. 'Shall we take him in?' she said.

'No, no,' said Walton, squirming beneath the sheet.

'Your uncle, Max Walton, had a son. Martyn.'

'Yes, yes,' said Walton, resigned.

'When did you last see him?'

'Ages ago. When we were kids. Before they left for wherever it was they went.'

'South Africa?'

'If you say so.'

It was Louise's turn to shake her head. 'Where's your phone?' she said.

Walton looked down to the garbage on the floor before reaching his arm out, but Tracey was too quick for him. 'I need a shower,' she said, grimacing as she pulled a phone with a smashed screen out from a heap of soiled clothes. 'Out of battery.'

'Are we going to find any message from Martyn Walton on this phone?' asked Louise.

'No,' said Walton, as if the suggestion was ludicrous.

'So you're giving us permission to take the phone away to be analysed?'

'No.'

'Right, let's get him to the station.'

Walton appeared to either be on the verge of tears or about to be sick. His pale skin appeared to lose another degree of colour. 'OK, OK, you can take it.'

'You do know what's going on here, Justin?' said Louise, softening her tone. 'Someone died yesterday. Someone was murdered. If we find out Martyn had anything to do with this, we'll be coming for you. Aiding and abetting a murderer is almost as bad as committing the crime itself, and the courts will definitely see it that way.'

'He messaged me, OK? On Facebook,' said Walton, mustering all his strength to shout at her.

'Now we're getting somewhere,' said Louise. She would have sat on his bed if it hadn't looked so filthy. Despite the window being open, the smell of decay hung in the air. 'When did you speak?'

'A couple of months back. He said he was coming to England and wanted to meet up.'

'And when did you meet up?'

'Walton lifted his head. 'Good one. We haven't met up.'

'When did he arrive?'

'I think he got to the UK four weeks ago, but honestly, I haven't seen him.'

'His number on the phone?' asked Tracey.

'Yeah.'

'Great, where's the charger?'

Louise did a sweep of the house as Tracey waited for the phone to charge. The partygoers were slowly coming back to life, and she counted eight of them as she went from room to room. She questioned them as best she could, their answers mainly monosyllabic, each denying any knowledge of Martyn Walton-Renwick, three of them even denying they knew Justin.

The phone had some charge by the time she reached upstairs. Tracey was scrolling through Justin's messages and phone records. 'Call history's been deleted. Apart from yesterday,' she said.

'We have Martyn's number?'

Tracey showed her the screen with a number on it. The contact was listed as 'M'.

'Like James Bond,' said Walton.

'You know, when we take this in, we'll be able to find your missing messages.'

'Good luck with that.'

'And when you last spoke to Martyn.'

'And with that.'

Louise sighed. If they had used an encrypted Wi-Fi app to make the calls then it would be impossible to trace anything. That Justin had deleted his records suggested he was maybe a bit more aware than he was making out. She took the phone off the charger and signalled Tracey into the hallway.

'You going to call now?' asked Tracey.

'No, he'll probably hang up the second he hears my voice. I was thinking we take it to Coulson and see if he can put a trace on it.'

'What about hunky through there?'

'We'll have to bring him with us. See if we can sweet-talk him into making the call.'

A crashing sound came from the other room and they both turned and ran back inside. The sight was the most nausea-inducing thing she'd experienced that day. Stark naked, Justin Walton had tried to escape from the bedroom window, but had slipped and was now face down on the bedroom floor.

Chapter Thirty

Louise brewed a fresh pot of coffee as she and Tracey waited for Simon Coulson to arrive. After his laughable escape attempt, they had arrested Justin Walton and taken him to the cells at Weston nick, where he was still recovering. He'd refused to cooperate any further, but once Coulson arrived, they planned to give him one more try.

The station was a little sleepier on a Sunday than Portishead had been; the whole building manned by a skeleton crew. After CID's departure, it was more of a community policing hub, and without the energy of her old team the place felt tired and rundown.

Tracey held Justin Walton's phone in her hand and was trying to retrieve his browsing history, to no avail. 'It's as if he was expecting us,' she said, as Louise handed her a new cup of coffee.

'Or it's a procedure he does on a daily basis.'

Before leaving, they had called in a team to search Walton's place from top to bottom, and had already been notified of drugs being found on site, though nothing substantial enough to suggest he was dealing.

'Have you spoken to Thomas yet?' said Tracey, surprising Louise with her bluntness as she innocently sipped her drink.

'Been a bit busy.'

Tracey smiled and nodded. 'I see.'

'You see nothing,' said Louise, smiling.

'Honestly, you are foolish sometimes.'

'Me?' said Louise.

'Yes, you. You've had the hots for this man for years, and you finally get together . . . and now you're going to throw it away over a misunderstanding?'

'I think you're reading more into this than there is,' said Louise, crossing her arms.

'Have you spoken to him since the attack in Thornbury?'

'Yes.'

'And today? After Greg spoke to him.'

'Not yet, but I've been busy,' said Louise, annoyed by the knowing look on Tracey's face.

'You know he's not involved in this. He would have to be a master of disguises to have got this past you. Us, for that matter. I've known him almost as long as you and I know he has nothing to do with it. You know it too.'

'I haven't said I did think he's responsible,' said Louise, a little too quickly.

'Lou, I know you. You're always looking for an excuse. That pathologist guy.'

'Dempsey? Come on.'

'He's a nice guy. You didn't even give him a try. Blamed it on the wine and on what was going on with your life.'

Louise had slept with Dempsey on one of her first nights in Weston after being transferred. Tracey was correct that she had blamed it on a night of drinking, but it had been a mistake and she'd felt right to dissuade his further advances. 'I was having a hard time of it.'

'I know, I know. But don't you ever think you might be this way because of Finch? You trusted him, or at least I think you did, and we know how that worked out. Maybe that's why you find it hard to trust someone now. Even Thomas. Maybe you're trying to self-sabotage your relationship. And this bullshit with the drug bust in Thornbury gave you the perfect opportunity to get out of giving it a try.'

'OK, Dr Phil. You been reading some relationship how-to guides or something?'

Tracey smirked. 'Maybe, but that's not the point.'

Louise laughed. Tracey was right, but her actions had nothing to do with Finch. She hadn't truly ever trusted him, though she'd also never appreciated the monster he was until it was too late. But if she was being honest, she knew she was using the Thornbury situation to put the brakes on things with Thomas. It all stemmed from his suggestion that the kids meet, though she wasn't going to give Tracey any more ammunition by telling her that. 'OK, I'll call him,' she said, about to pick up her phone as Simon Coulson arrived.

'To be continued,' mouthed Tracey.

Louise went to take a drink of her coffee before leaving it on the side.

'Thanks for coming in, Simon,' she said.

'No problem. I hate Sundays as a rule.'

From anyone else she would have taken that as a joke, but Coulson lived for his work and appeared never to be happier than when he was in front of a screen. Louise reiterated the situation to him. 'If needs be, I am going to ask Justin Walton one more time if he will try and speak to his cousin on the phone. If he refuses, then I'll have to call him directly.'

'If his phone is on, I should be able to get a location for him. Might be worth trying that before calling. As for the deleted calls and messages, that will depend on whether or not they were encrypted – and it sounds like they probably were?'

'According to Justin Walton, yes.'

'I'll try. You have the number?'

Louise gave him the phone. 'Under "M".'

'OK, let me get set up.'

'I'll have a final word with Walton,' said Louise.

'Your coffee,' said Tracey, holding out the cup.

Louise shook her head, the thought of coffee at that moment making her stomach hurt.

◆ ◆ ◆

'This is your last chance,' said Louise, speaking to Justin Walton in interview room three.

They'd given him some food and drink, but Walton looked worse than he had at the house a couple of hours earlier. He was on one hell of a comedown, his nicotine-yellowed fingers shaking as he did everything he could not to look directly at her.

'Tell us where Martyn is now, and you won't be obstructing our inquiry.'

'I don't know where he is.'

'We have someone going through your phone as we speak. Not only will we find Martyn's location, we will recover all correspondence between you. This will be your last chance to come clean about what you've been up to, your involvement with the fires.'

Walton's body tensed but he didn't respond. Louise wondered what Max Walton would have made of his nephew. Max had been a large, burly type who preyed on other people's weaknesses for fun. Had he taunted Justin as a child and made him turn on to the path he was on now? Or had it been much more of an abusive relationship, like Max's relationship with his wife?

'I told you I don't know nothing about any of it. Martyn called me to see if we could meet up. That's it.'

It was pointless going any further. She signalled to the uniformed guard to take him away before returning to the office where

Coulson looked as animated as she'd ever seen him, almost hopping on the spot when he turned his screen so Tracey could see. 'I've got a location for Walton-Renwick,' he said, as Louise approached. 'Up to the second as well. His phone just sent a ping to one of the nearby towers. He's at the Hampstead Park campsite in Locking.'

Louise tried to contain her mounting excitement. If Walton-Renwick had used his phone so close to Weston then there was a real chance they could get to him and end everything before it worsened. 'What are we waiting for?' she said, rushing to the door with Tracey and Coulson close behind.

Chapter Thirty-One

Tracey drove Louise and Coulson to the campsite. In the car, Louise arranged backup patrol teams to remain on standby on the edge of the village, while Coulson tried to locate an owner or manager of the site.

'I've a number here. Mr Joseph Dalby. Down as manager of the site,' said Coulson, showing Louise the number, which she punched into her phone.

'Hello,' came the reply, four rings later.

Louise introduced herself to Mr Dalby, who confirmed he was the site manager. 'I'm at home now,' he said.

'Is anyone on site at present?' asked Louise, her body straining against her seat belt as Tracey took a corner at an alarming speed.

'Not today. I'm down as an emergency contact, and for bookings. I make a stop in the morning and am due over there at six tonight. We only serve campers and those with motorhomes. Nothing fixed on site.'

'Do you have a list of who is staying on site?'

'Yes. At least, I have the names of those who booked. They're supposed to tell us everyone who is staying, but especially with those in tents it isn't always the case,' said Dalby, echoing the words of the site owner in Kewstoke.

'Do you have the name Martyn Renwick, or Martyn Walton, registered?'

'Bear with me,' said Dalby, the line going quiet.

'Less than half a mile away now, Lou.'

'Sir, are you there?' said Louise.

'Yes, sorry. No. No one by the name of Walton, or Renwick. Though, as I said, that doesn't mean they're not there.'

Louise asked Mr Dalby to join them as Tracey drove down the dirt track towards the site. The place was a stark contrast to the caravan park in Kewstoke. The campsite was literally a bordered-off field, with a small tarmac area for cars and motorhomes. As she left the car, Louise counted thirty tents spread out in random patterns on the field. She imagined it must be cheap to stay there, as she couldn't see any other attraction. The air was full of the smell of muck-spreading from a nearby farm, and to the east you could both see and hear the traffic on the motorway. 'Any luck?' she said to Coulson, who was checking the latest tracking information on his iPad.

'It's offline at the moment, possibly on airplane mode, but its last location was definitely here, and that was twenty minutes ago.'

'Best get knocking on some doors,' said Louise, stepping out on to the field, thankful that it hadn't been raining recently as she tromped over the dry mud. She tried a few empty tents before reaching a group of young men who had made a mini village of six tents next to the dilapidated toilet block. Sitting on deckchairs, sipping energy drinks and cans of lager, they had the same wide-eyed look she'd seen on Justin Walton that morning.

'I was wondering if you could help me,' she said, approaching.

'I'll help you, love,' said one of the boys, who sported perox-ide-blond hair.

His friends chuckled at his response until Louise took out her warrant card. 'That's good to know,' she said, holding up the photo from Martyn Renwick's driving licence she'd been sent by Graves in South Africa. 'I'm looking for this man. Might go by the name of Martyn.'

Peroxide Blond was now hyper-compliant. 'No, I don't think so,' he said, shaking his head. 'There were a couple of lads in those two tents over there,' he said, pointing a hundred yards down the field.

'What's he done?' said one of the others. Short and stocky with a shaved head, he'd been the only one not to laugh at Peroxide's joke.

'It's very important that we speak to him.'

The young man considered that for a moment. 'Can I see that photo again, please,' he said. His politeness and clear way of speaking made Louise think he might be military. She showed him the photo on her mobile again, which he zoomed in on.

'I can't be sure if it was him, but there was a guy staying in a small tent on his own over there. I only noticed him as he was packing in a rush a few hours ago, and looking at that driving licence he's from South Africa?'

'Yes,' said Louise.

The man shrugged. 'Could be nothing, but he was wearing a South Africa rugby shirt.'

Louise called over Coulson and Tracey, and asked the young man to lead them to the spot on the edge of the site.

'Probably there,' said the man, pointing to the discarded tent pegs.

Coulson sent another ping to see if the phone was still in the area, only for Tracey to step into the trees and then return a few moments later, having recovered the remains of an old Nokia brick phone.

Chapter Thirty-Two

Alone in the courtyard, wearing his suit, Finch could have easily believed that he was free. Only the sight of the prison guard Wilson in his periphery, and the locked gates, dispelled that notion. He counted as he paced, waiting for his transportation to the court for the first day of his trial.

The early-morning air still had a cold snap to it, but he kept the same steady pace he did every time he was ushered to this place, refusing to bend even to the weather. Hearing the rattle of the gates, and some muted voices, he continued his circuit, not looking over until his name was called.

'Clemons,' he said, as the man moved past Wilson and towards Finch.

Clemons was in his prison garb. The contrast between this and Finch's suit made it appear as if things were back to normal, that Finch was here to interrogate Clemons. He held his ground but tensed his body, anticipating an attack.

'Leaving us?' said Clemons, stopping a few metres short so they were not in touching distance.

'Day out for good behaviour.'

'Fancy your chances?'

Finch knew he was going to be guilty of something. The charges against him were numerous and his counsel had all but admitted that the proof was unarguable. His main concern was the charge of the attempted murder of Amira Hood. If a guilty verdict was reached for that then he would be expecting a good decade-plus inside – more if the sentencing judge had a thing against corrupt police, which most of them did. 'We'll see,' he said, not willing to give anything away. His best chance of escaping the charge was by discrediting Louise Blackwell's testimony. She had been present on the evening when he had tried to kill Amira Hood. Because of their history, in particular their fallout at the Walton farm, his plan had been to allege that everything had been set up by Louise and he was a victim of entrapment. It was a long shot, but he needed to put doubt into the jurors' minds.

'Things went smoothly last week. I believe your ex-colleague Thomas Ireland was arrested,' said Clemons.

The drug raid in Thornbury had been Clemons' idea. In return for seeing to it that DS Eddie Perkins turned a blind eye to a drug delivery in the Avonmouth docks, Clemons had arranged for a small stash of drugs to be placed in the vans that belonged to Ireland's delivery crew, as well as the attack that had alerted the police. Finch knew that Thomas hadn't been arrested, but he had been called in for questioning and Finch had been able to exploit that fact with the help of the journalist Tania Elliot.

Finch nodded.

'You think I'm wearing a wire,' said Clemons, pulling up his jumper.

'What do you want?'

Clemons pretended to recoil as if hurt by Finch's comment. 'Don't be like that, DCI Finch,' he said.

'Wilson,' said Finch, calling over to the prison guard.

'OK, OK. Listen, that was a good bit of work we did together. It's fine, you don't have to admit it out loud,' said Clemons, holding up his hand. 'Our shipment arrived perfectly, and your man Perkins cleared the way for us.'

'I have no idea what you're talking about,' said Finch.

'Blackwell's boyfriend has had his reputation ruined, and I'm sure you could use that during your trial.'

Finch unbuttoned the top button of his shirt. 'Do you have a point, Clemons?'

'Whether you stay in or you go, I think we could work together. Don't you?'

Under any other circumstances, Finch would have laughed in the man's face or done something much worse. But like it or not, things had changed. Even if he could get off the attempted murder charge, he was bound to face some time inside, and that meant humouring people like the man before him. 'What do you want?'

'Your friend, Eddie Perkins. I'd like to add him to the payroll.'

'What has that to do with me?'

'You would get a cut, naturally. On the outside or in. Inside, you would be guaranteed our protection which, if you are released into the wild, could be worth its weight in gold.'

Finch recalled Perkins' last words: *This will be it, boss.* He'd known then that those words meant very little. Perkins would bend to his will with a little pressure, and if applying that pressure meant Finch had to cosy up to Clemons, then so be it.

'I'll be seeing Perkins this week,' he said.

'Good, good. We'll get the details to you,' said Clemons.

Finch dropped his head a half-inch. 'Now, if you could excuse me, I have a date with my biographer,' he said, leaving Clemons in the middle of the prison yard as he walked back towards the gates.

Chapter Thirty-Three

A police presence was already in force when Louise drove Emily to school. Patrol cars and vans were spread along the promenade, and officers were visible on the street. Despite the explosion at the school on Saturday, the implied threat in Karl Insgrove's suicide note was being taken seriously. More so now they had another credible suspect in Martyn Walton-Renwick.

After the discarded phone had been discovered, a search team had recovered the remains of a SIM card, broken into numerous pieces. Coulson had been unable to recover any data from the card and had spent the evening working on Justin Walton's phone, but no messages between Justin Walton and Martyn Walton-Renwick had been recovered.

Holds had been placed on Martyn's debit and credit cards, but since his entry into the UK he hadn't used either – which suggested he had other, untraceable means of funding himself.

Louise pulled up outside the school, parking next to a patrol car she'd insisted stay outside the building all day. She'd initially wanted to keep Emily off, but Adam King had agreed to do another sweep of the building earlier that morning, and his findings had reassured her that there was no imminent threat to the school.

It was still difficult letting Emily go after hugging her good-bye in the playground, which was as full as Louise had ever seen it. Once again, she sensed the parents converging, shooting odd glances her way as if she was to blame for the situation.

'Strange times,' said Graham Pritchard, stepping towards her as she was about to get in her car. He was dressed in a smart-looking suit that she'd never seen him wear before.

'Sure is,' she said, pulling her car door open.

'Do you know what happened to the school hall?' he asked, as if they were co-conspirators.

'As much as you, Graham.'

'I doubt that's true,' he said, moving a step closer so she could smell his aftershave.

'I can't talk about it.'

'You must think they're safe though. If you're bringing Emily here. I guess it was a final passing shot from the caretaker?'

'I told you, I can't talk about it,' said Louise, trying not to lose her cool. Everyone was naturally a little on edge and she understood his concern. The truth was, she didn't yet fully understand Karl Insgrove's involvement in any of this. In many ways, she hoped Graham was right. That Insgrove had been responsible from the beginning, that the explosion on Saturday was his last act and that they could all be free of worry. Unfortunately, Max Walton's son being in the country meant this was far from a definite reality.

'I understand. It's such a shame about that cleaner.'

'Hana Sanchez,' said Louise.

'Yes. I hope the school do something special for her and her family. Have you told Emily about what actually happened?'

Emily was too familiar with death and tragedy for any age, let alone her seven years. She'd lost both her parents and had seen things in her time that would have tested any adult, Louise included. She'd wanted to talk to Emily about Hana, but had been forced to pass that duty on to Emily's grandparents as she'd been at work until the early hours. 'We explained that there was a terrible accident. And you, with Toby?'

'Same. It's so difficult. He was with his mum this weekend, so she spoke to him,' said Graham. 'It's horrible that they have to deal with this.'

'It is. Have a nice day, Graham. Off anywhere special?' asked Louise, stepping into the car.

Graham's face lit up as if she'd offered him the greatest compliment of his life. 'Oh this,' he said, pulling at his suit. 'Job interview.'

'Best of luck,' said Louise, shutting the door and glancing at her phone as she waited for the dad to leave.

Instinctively, she went to her text thread with Thomas. Both of them had been keen to take their relationship slowly, but this felt like the longest time they hadn't properly spoken since they'd got together. It was understandable with recent events and her excessive workload, but she felt as if it was coming to some sort of breaking point. 'This is ridiculous,' she said to herself, typing out a text message:

Hi, feels like I haven't seen you in ages. Shall we try and meet up tonight x

She waited a couple of minutes but the message remained unread, so she set off for her next port of call: the Crown Court, where Finch's trial was due to begin.

◆ ◆ ◆

Louise had been present at court for hundreds of cases over the years, but this wasn't like anything she'd faced before. It was the first time she'd be called as a witness rather than as an arresting officer. There were so many charges, and so many credible witnesses, that it was almost inevitable Finch would face a custodial sentence, yet she felt a sense of trepidation as she entered the building. Her chest tightened at the thought that Finch could somehow wrangle his way out of the charge of attempted murder. Yes, she would be pleased if he was found guilty of his other crimes, but she needed the attempted murder charge to stick more than any of the others.

After that night at his house when she'd rescued Amira and broken Finch's leg, she'd thought it had been the end of things. Finch had all but ruined her life ever since Max Walton's death, and at last she'd felt as if she'd got some closure. But now she realised that closure would only come if he went down for the longest time possible; and if the world finally knew who Finch truly was.

Amira was waiting for her in one of the small interview rooms. She was with Antony Meades, and the prosecution barrister for the trial, Amanda Knight. Knight was a first-rate barrister who'd worked on cases with Louise before, as well as occasionally being an opposing defence barrister. 'Mr Finch has hired some bigwig QC from London, who I can assure you will not be working on legal aid,' she said, as they talked through the procedure for the coming week.

'I wonder where he got the money from for that,' said Louise, exchanging a knowing look with Amira, who was biting her nails.

'It makes no difference to our case. Facts are facts. As long as you're both singing from the same hymn sheet, we'll be fine,' said Knight, who'd grilled them both on numerous occasions over the last few months in preparation for this week.

'When do you think I'll be needed?' asked Louise.

'Depends how long Charles Boothroyd QC intends to pro-long events, although I don't imagine it will be until Wednesday or Thursday at the earliest. We have a lot to get through before then, so my guess would be Thursday. Of course, they may decide to target only one or two of our witnesses, so could keep the cross-examination to a minimum. We'll know better later in the day.'

'I'm going to struggle to be here most of the time.'

Knight bit her lower lip and looked over at Meades, as if for support. 'I understand, but the more you can be here the better. I want the jury to see you as much as possible, to understand what you've gone through. Both of you,' she added, looking at Amira.

The clerk knocked on the door and told them to get ready. Louise walked with Amira to the court. 'You OK?' she asked.

'Yes. It's just I haven't seen him since that night. Not sure I want to see him again.'

Louise leaned in close to Amira. 'Fuck him, Amira. This isn't about him. This is about all the women whose lives he's destroyed. He tried to kill you, but he's behind bars now. There's a reason for that, remember? You. If you hadn't had the bravery to come to me in the first place, we would never be here. A few more days, and he'll be out of our lives for good. Yes?'

'OK,' said Amira, forcing a smile.

Louise reached out for the other woman's hand as Finch was led in. It was strange seeing him again, especially under custody. She'd hoped that his time on remand and the injury she had inflicted on him that night would have had a greater effect. But aside from the affectation of a walking stick, he looked no different to when she'd last seen him. He was dressed in one of the suits he'd always worn for work, and it was hard for her to truly believe he was on trial and wasn't there working.

As they stood for the judge, Finch sneaked a look at Louise. She might have been imagining it but she was sure she could smell his citrus aftershave drifting towards her as he looked away, not acknowledging her presence.

Louise tried not to stare back at Finch as Amanda Knight set out the prosecution's case and the various charges against him. As she'd expected, Finch was impossible to read. He remained passive as Knight accused him of betraying the trust not only of those he'd worked with, but the general public.

Louise glanced around the viewing gallery as name after name was read out of the women Finch had abused over the years.

'And finally, we will provide evidence that Mr Finch forcibly took hostage a former colleague of his, Ms Amira Hood, and planned on taking Ms Hood's life and that of one of his other former colleagues, DI Louise Blackwell,' said Knight.

Louise did her best not to react, taking hold of Amira's arm once more and tightening her grip, as she kept her gaze forwards towards the judge.

She let out a breath as Knight took a seat, memories from that night – Amira tied up, Finch waving the kitchen knife around like a baton, and the cracking sound as Finch planted his leg and she kicked out at his knee – flashing through her mind. She glanced over at Finch, who'd stirred enough to slowly shake his head in denial of the charges. It was this more than anything else at that moment that provoked her anger. How dare he, after everything he'd done, sit there with that look of victimhood, as if he'd done nothing wrong?

Charles Boothroyd QC made a relaxed introduction that Louise had heard a hundred times before. As most defence barristers did, he amplified the fact that the jurors had to be certain beyond all reasonable doubt that his client was guilty of the charges. Louise wanted to stand and argue when he went on to paint Finch as a victim. A hard-working police officer of nearly two decades, Finch had had to deal with the type of hardened criminals that most people, even most police officers, would not deal with, he argued. According to Boothroyd, Finch had endured peak psychological damage during his time in the force that had led to a breakdown, during which he'd had the altercation with Amira and Louise. He'd never meant to hurt anyone, and since his time on remand he'd been having daily meetings with a psychologist. The QC stopped short of blaming Louise for Finch's situation, but hinted that he'd been unfairly treated and even went so far as to mention the injury he'd sustained to his leg.

It was laughable, and Louise had heard it all before. But it was still galling to hear such a defence. What Boothroyd failed to mention was that Finch had received his broken leg during his knife attack on Louise, as Amira was tied up in the kitchen. She looked forward to explaining that to the jury later in the proceedings, but for now had to reluctantly keep quiet.

It became apparent from the opening witness statement that Boothroyd was going to interrogate each and every prosecution witness for all his worth. He was trying to put doubt into the minds of the jurors, and was prepared to do whatever he could to make that happen – including character assassination to make their testimony appear unsound. The first woman on the stand, Lindsey Saunders, had worked as a civilian office manager in Portishead during the period when Finch had first started in CID. She told the court how Finch had seduced her before trying to hound her out of the department.

The QC tried to turn it round on the woman, and by the time he'd finished with her, and the judge had called recess, she was in a flood of tears.

Louise met with Antony Meades in the coffee shop area. 'He's not going to go easy, is he?' she said to the solicitor.

'We never expected it any other way. It doesn't make a difference. He can try that with all the witnesses, but the fact is we have overwhelming evidence. He can try and paint Finch as this victim but it isn't going to work . . . as long as . . .'

'Amira and I don't fuck up?'

'That wasn't going to be my choice of words exactly,' said Meades, with a grin. 'We have the recording from that night, and I would suggest that Finch all but incriminates himself. However, there will be pressure on you. But I think you know that?'

Louise nodded. 'I need to get back to Weston. You'll keep me updated?'

'Blow by blow,' said Meades.

Louise took a coffee up to Amira before leaving. She was about to enter the briefing room, when along the corridor she caught sight of Tania Elliot leaving another office. The journalist hadn't seen her and Louise ducked behind a pillar as she moved off. It didn't take long to find out who Tania had been talking to. A couple of minutes later, Finch's solicitor left the same office.

Chapter Thirty-Four

Louise watched Tania Elliot head back into court before Louise returned outside. What the hell was the journalist playing at? Louise knew for certain that Tania had posted articles on the Finch case already. Louise could accept that the woman was talking to Finch's brief, but if she'd been talking to Finch himself . . .

She took a deep breath. Finch's legal team would never have been so stupid as to have allowed that to happen. If Tania had spoken to Finch and was using her articles as a means of influencing the case, it could throw the whole trial in the air.

Louise had more pressing problems to deal with, however. A haggle of journalists, TV cameras included, were outside the courthouse as if waiting in ambush. Louise started with the only words she was going to use, 'No comment,' as the questions kept coming. Some were regarding the case: *What was it like seeing your former colleague in the box? Do you think DCI Finch will face a prison sentence?* And Louise's personal favourite: *Do you think he's guilty?*

But as she walked briskly towards the car park, the questions became more personal: *Is it true you're in a relationship with Thomas Ireland?* And as she was getting into her car, she heard: *Do you think the previous accusation of unlawful killing will count against you?*

So there it was. If it was already a question on the lips of the journalists, then it was sure to be an angle used for the defence team. Louise slammed the car door shut, when what she wanted to do was to hold an impromptu press conference and explain again that she'd already been cleared of any wrongdoing.

She checked her phone before setting off, not surprised but frustrated to see Thomas hadn't responded.

Visions of the night at the Walton farm played on her mind as she made her way back to Weston. The remoteness of the place with its abandoned farming equipment, its sties and stables reeking of the rotting corpses of dead animals, was never far from her thoughts. She'd visited many times, but that night it had felt more sinister than before. More than likely it was hindsight talking, but as she'd moved through the pig sheds and up to the main farmhouse, she'd been sure something momentous was about to happen.

'You will not let this get to you,' she said, shaking her head to get rid of the unwanted memories. Somehow, she'd already arrived in Weston. She could barely recall the journey, her body and mind working on autopilot as she pulled up outside the Holy Trinity church hall.

She took another look at her phone – still no message from Thomas – before walking over to the church hall. A thin, wiry man in his seventies greeted her as she opened the door. 'DI Blackwell,' he said.

Louise nodded. 'And you must be Bryce Milner?' she said, recalling the man's Welsh accent from their brief phone call.

'I am indeed. Please come in. Can I get you anything? We have the finest breakfast tea and instant coffee you can get.'

'I'm fine, Mr Milner, thank you.'

Mr Milner headed the war veterans group that Karl Insgrove had attended. 'When was the last time you saw Mr Insgrove?' asked Louise, as she sat down on one of the chairs in the middle of the hall.

'Bryce, please. He called me, after that hoax bomb was found at the school,' said Bryce, leaving a one-chair gap between them as he sat down. 'Told me he was unlikely to attend the meeting that week.'

'It's Thursday nights you usually meet?'

'That's correct. I asked him if everything was OK. He sounded a bit shook up but I never expected he would . . .' Bryce looked away, as if caught in a distant memory. 'Then again, I didn't expect he would be subjected to such an ordeal in the first place. I presume there will be an inquiry?'

Louise wasn't sure if Bryce was accusing her of something. His tone was blunt and there was an underlying suggestion that the police's involvement had resulted in Insgrove's death. 'It's an ongoing investigation,' she said, not willing to get into a discussion about it.

'There was an explosion at the school after he died, though, wasn't there?'

'That is true. I can't discuss that any further, but I can assure you everything will be getting our fullest attention.'

Bryce murmured something under his breath, as if half satisfied by what he'd been told. 'A terrible loss.'

'Had you known Karl for long?'

'I set up this group about ten years ago. I'd recently moved to the area and used to attend a similar group in Taunton where I'd been living. The thing is, for those not from a military background, that type of life is unimaginable. It's not like the movies or television shows, you see. You probably understand a bit, being in the police, I don't know.' He paused again, lost in thought. 'I guess it's a cliché, but war changes you, whatever your direct involvement. It's not just the death, the terrible injuries, though that would do it, wouldn't it?' said Bryce, laughing.

'I'm sure this group was a great comfort to Karl.'

'Oh, it was. That's why he called me, you see. Hated to miss a meeting. Hated it. We have some young lads who attend nowadays.

Respectful boys. They listen to what Karl and us old-timers have to say. Karl used to like that. Gave him the opportunity to pass on his experience, and at the same time to discuss things he wouldn't usually share.'

'Could you tell me some more about Karl? I know he used to be in the navy and was involved in the Falklands conflict.'

Bryce's eyes narrowed, and as he studied her, she saw his age in the deep grooves on his face. He seemed to oscillate between friendliness and distrust, as if he didn't quite know how to take her. 'You know I can't share details about what goes on here,' he said.

'I understand there are matters of confidentiality you have to uphold, but there are parts of Karl's life we don't know enough about. We haven't ruled out the possibility of something happening again in town,' she said, not yet willing to divulge details about the latest phone message.

Bryce appeared to mull that over. Concentrating, his face was a canvas of lines, but despite his age she sensed an underlying strength to the man. 'He served on HMS *Coventry*, did you know that? He was on it when those bombs were dropped. He was lucky to escape.'

'I didn't know that. I thought he was serving on a different ship?'

'He was on HMS *Bristol*, but he'd been transferred a few days before to the *Coventry*. He was trapped on board for twenty minutes as it was going down. He saw some terrible things,' said Bryce, scowling. 'His friends burning,' he added, displaying his teeth as he shook his head.

The connection was obvious, and she could see in Bryce's eyes that he understood it too. Mrs Harrison had told her about Insgrove's drug problems after leaving the navy, but had never been clear on the actual details. 'Did he ever get help for what happened to him? Beyond this group, obviously?'

'There was less help available back then, and it's not much better nowadays. I'm sure you're aware the path Karl took with the drink and the drugs, but he'd put that all behind him. And I know what you're thinking about his experiences defining his subsequent actions but I simply can't imagine it.'

'He was involved, Bryce. There's no way to get away from that. Our concern now is that he may have been working with someone, and that person remains a potential threat.'

'What? No,' said Bryce, shaking his head.

'Is there anyone in the group Karl was particularly close to?'

'As I said, Karl got along with everyone. The younger guys looked up to him.'

'And the older guys?'

'Us older guys liked him too,' said Bryce, with a smile.

'Did any of you serve with him? Or were in the Falklands at the same time?'

Bryce placed his hand over his mouth in consideration. 'You think we're running some sort of terrorism cell here? Is that it? Old men getting back on a society that failed them. Blowing up school buildings in a desperate bid to get attention. Don't talk stupid.'

'No one is saying that, Bryce, but it is highly likely that Mr Insgrove wasn't working alone, so I think it is a legitimate question to ask.'

'The only other guy who was in the Falklands was Ben. Ben Coles. But he was a paratrooper. They'd never met before this group was formed.'

'You have an address for Mr Coles?'

'This is ludicrous,' said Bryce, getting up and retrieving an old address book which he opened for her.

Louise took a photo of Coles' address before handing her card to Bryce. 'I realise this is a horrible reality to consider, but if you can think of anything else that could help us, please call me.'

'You're only doing your job, I know that. If you'd only heard him talk here, you would be as surprised as I am. Still trying to get my head around it.'

'I do understand. If it's any comfort, I believe Karl was highly conflicted over what happened. He knew he was acting out of character. That's why it's important we find whoever was helping him.'

'I'll speak to the others, see what I can do,' said Bryce, his eyes reddening as he saw her to the door.

Chapter Thirty-Five

It was fun being on the other side for once. Finch was well aware that being the defendant played to his ego, but he didn't care about that. He was happy to be centre-stage. Relished the challenge that fat bitch of a barrister had set out with her opening statement. He had to be careful, though, his team had advised him, as if he'd been born yesterday. He tried to look contrite but not guilty, as if he knew he'd done something wrong but it wasn't as bad as they were making out. Now and again, he would sneak shy glances at the jurors to impress upon them his fragility. It was an act, but he'd been acting most of his life.

Blackwell had fucked off after recess. He was glad not to feel her eyes boring into him. During the break, he'd arranged for his solicitor to meet the journalist Tania Elliot. She'd always been an aggravating presence in his working life, but now the tables had turned. The quality he'd once so detested in her – her single-mindedness – could potentially do him a favour. She'd already begun the work she'd promised, and with the information he'd supplied her today the hope was that by the time Louise Blackwell came to the dock she would be a wreck in the eyes of the jurors and everyone involved in the case.

For now, Finch had to be content watching his QC ripping to shreds every witness they put before him. Finch had been careful over the years. He'd used untraceable phones for all his conquests and so much of the evidence being given was circumstantial, and Boothroyd was using that to his advantage.

Where he'd royally fucked up was keeping images of the women he'd manipulated on his laptop. He'd tried to delete them moments before he'd been ambushed by Blackwell, but everything had happened too fast. The plan in these circumstances was to get the jurors to believe he'd had permission to take those images – in most of the cases, that was true enough – and it was Boothroyd's job to create just enough doubt that they considered that a possibility.

The judge ended the day just as Knight was getting going with the evidence surrounding Ruby Williams, a once-pretty little redhead who'd worked in the PR team at headquarters. It must have only been six or seven years ago, but how the woman had let herself go. In some ways, it was embarrassing having her up there. She'd either had kids or had been eating her feelings over these last few years and the look was not a good one. The only consolation was that it must be difficult for the jurors to accept her tale of sex and deception, as it was hard enough to imagine anyone wanting to have sex with her in the first place.

Finch stood like a good boy as the judge did his thing before breaking for lunch. *Be contrite and respectful.* He was taken to a holding cell where he was given his daily gruel, before being led to the prison van where Wilson had arranged for him to meet Eddie Perkins.

'Give us five, Wilson, will you?' said Finch.

Wilson knew better than to argue, and the guard in the driver's seat was keen to be literally looking the other way.

'What the hell am I doing here?' said Perkins.

'Calm down, Eddie, I wanted to see you while we still have time. Who knows where they'll end up sending me if this goes tits up.'

Perkins pursed his lips, doing his best to pretend he had the power of thought. 'Everything went smooth,' he said, no doubt calculating what the chances actually were of Finch being moved out of the region.

'I know, Eddie. Mr Clemons was very impressed. That's why I wanted to speak to you.

'*Mr* Clemons?' said Perkins.

'That's what he'd like you to call him from now on, Eddie. Now that you're going into business with him.'

Chapter Thirty-Six

Whatever Farrell's thoughts were about Eddie Perkins, he was unsure about the ethics of tailing another officer. He'd done it the first time out of nagging doubt, and now he was struggling to justify it to himself. Yes, Perkins had met with Tania Elliot, but that was hardly a crime. Farrell had spoken to her on a number of occasions himself. Although Perkins' meeting with her had occurred around the same time articles were appearing in the paper about Thomas and Louise, that in itself didn't justify the off-the-books surveillance.

He'd convinced himself that there was something off about Perkins, but had to concede he was working on little more than a hunch. He had to admit, too, that he was naturally biased against the man as he was the last man standing of Finch's inner circle. None of which made the confines of the front seat of his car any easier to bear.

He'd expected Perkins to end up at the courthouse at some point that day, taking a chance, parking close to the building, with a sightline to the main entrance on Small Street. Perkins had arrived shortly before Louise left for the day. Farrell decided to await the man's return in the car, as there was little to be gained from watching Perkins inside where, no doubt, he was going to watch the freak show that was the Finch trial.

He'd had to endure watching Louise being harassed by reporters as she'd made her way to her car, when he'd wanted to jump out and smash some heads together. They had no idea what Louise had gone through with Finch, not that they'd care if they did. He only hoped that soon they would be seeing the back of the man for good, and that Perkins and his ilk would become a thing of the past.

Farrell received notification that Finch's trial was done for the day thirty minutes before Perkins left the building. Perkins appeared to be in a furious mood, his body tensed as he barged past the reporters who were paying him no attention. Farrell didn't have time to ponder why, but as he pulled away to follow Perkins, who was on foot, a prison van pulled out of the car park beneath the courthouse. Farrell couldn't tell for sure if Finch was in the back of the van, but he did wonder if Perkins had managed to speak to his old colleague before leaving. It wasn't allowed, but wasn't beyond the realm of possibility.

Farrell watched the van pull away, and arrived on Quay Street in time to see Perkins get in his car. Farrell had thought ahead and borrowed a friend's car for the day, but it was still a risky procedure. Perkins wouldn't be expecting it, but if he had his wits about him, he would notice at some point that he was being followed. It was a way of thinking ingrained into them in the police, so Farrell had to stay as far back as he was able without risking losing him. Fortunately, his job was made easier by the slow-moving traffic out of the centre. He was at least ten cars behind Perkins as they made their way past Anchor Road.

Farrell kept far back, and was relieved when – a few minutes later – Perkins took the turning to Brandon Hill, the public park that was the home of the Cabot Tower. Farrell parked on the road and waited until Perkins left his car before following on foot.

One thing Farrell knew for sure was that Perkins was not a lover of exercise or the outside. This wasn't a recreational visit, and he doubted Perkins would have chosen the park as a suitable meeting venue. Farrell had decided on a pair of hiking boots that morning, though as he followed along the pathway the decision felt like overkill.

Perkins was moving at a tragically slow pace, and twice Farrell had to drop to his knee to pretend to tie his shoe as the other detective stopped to catch his breath. As Perkins reached the adventure playground area, Farrell checked his watch. Children of all ages swarmed the playground, and on the surrounding fields they played ball games and threw Frisbees beneath the June sunshine. Some of the parents joined in with their offspring, while others took welcome breaks on the park benches, a few of them reading, but most stuck to their phones or in conversation with one another.

Farrell took the long way round, as Perkins made his way over to a group of three men huddled beneath a giant oak tree. All three of the men were smoking and paid no attention to any of the children as Perkins sauntered over to them.

Farrell had witnessed these types of exchanges before. He could see from the men's body language that Perkins wasn't welcome, two of the men looking him up and down as they dragged on their cigarettes. Farrell wanted to get nearer, both to see what was going on but also to be there in case Perkins was in danger, but it would be impossible to explain his presence if he got caught. He'd brought a camera with him and began taking snaps of the numerous squirrels, trying not to stand out as he turned the camera to Perkins and his friends, the zoom lens close to maximum.

Heart pumping, he put the camera on burst mode and took a set of pictures before looking away. Scrolling through the images, he could see he'd been fortunate enough to get some good shots.

He had to zoom in on the image to make sure he wasn't mistaken. He didn't recognise two of the men, but the third was definitely Michael Sinclair, the lowlife Perkins had arrested in Thornbury. The same lowlife who had tried to implicate Thomas Ireland as a drug dealer.

Chapter Thirty-Seven

As Louise stepped out of the church hall, she checked her phone, adrenaline rushing through her body as she saw the five missed calls from her mother. She was on the verge of calling back when she checked her text messages and saw that she'd only been calling to tell her that Emily had been picked up from school. Why her mother had to try and call five times was beyond Louise's understanding at that moment, though her annoyance was tempered by relief.

Now wasn't the time to be resting on their laurels, but the later it got the more she could hope that Karl Insgrove's farewell warning had already been honoured by the explosion on Saturday at the school.

It didn't mean they were at the end of the investigation, but the knot she'd felt in the pit of her stomach all day was easing. Now all they had to do was find out who had made the threat call following Insgrove's death. It would be wonderful if they could explain that away as a hoax, although everything pointed to it being the desperate bid of Martyn Walton-Renwick, in an effort to cause some disruption in the Finch trial.

If, and why, Walton-Renwick had been working with Insgrove was a question they would need to answer sooner or later. But it was still painful to know they'd been so close the day before. What made her feel worse was that she now had to relive that experience in front of Assistant Chief Constable Brightman and the officers from CTU.

◆ ◆ ◆

She called Thomas as she parked up in Portishead thirty minutes later, and was so surprised when he picked up that she took a couple of seconds spluttering her response to his 'Hey'.

'Hey, yourself,' she finally managed.

'Sorry, I was going to call you. It was the first day of the trial today, wasn't it? How did it go?'

He was speaking as if nothing was amiss between them, which made the exchange even more confusing. It had been so long since she'd had a serious relationship that she'd forgotten how the day-to-day interactions could be. Had she been reading too much into recent events? Thomas had so much on his plate that it was inevitable he'd be a little bit distracted. Could it be that all the negative thoughts swarming her head had just been her overactive imagination?

'It wasn't too bad. Bit weird seeing Finch. Though I have to say it helped a bit by seeing him with a walking stick.'

'Good. Let's hope he has that for the rest of his life.'

'How have you been? I know Greg had to speak to you.'

'That was a bit shitty but I can understand it. I have to be honest, I'm just about hanging on. With all the negative publicity, I think I'll be the one that takes the fall for this.'

'Oh no, Tom, that's terrible. They can't do that. It wasn't your fault.'

'I'm head of security. Anyway, when do I get to see you next?' The question sounded light, but Louise sensed an awkwardness, as if it was just a little forced.

'I'm full on with this explosion stuff in Weston. Probably won't be until after the air show now.'

'OK,' said Thomas, his disappointment obvious in his deflated voice.

She regretted the words as soon as she'd put the phone down. She was busy, but could have made time to see him before the end of the week. She wasn't sure why she wanted to avoid him. She tried to convince herself it had nothing to do with what had happened in Thornbury, and Farrell being forced to interview him. She'd made mistakes in her past, but in general she was a good judge of character, and she knew Thomas better than most. It wasn't in him to get involved in any kind of illegal activity. He'd spent so many years battling against those in the drug trade and had seen first-hand the effects on both the end users and those involved in the production and distribution at all levels. The fact was, he wasn't stupid enough to go down that route, and with his new job he was earning more than he'd ever had in the police so nothing about it added up.

Somewhere in the back of her mind, she was nagged by the idea that her fears were all down to her trust issues. She didn't want it to be true, but seeing Finch at the courthouse had reminded her of how foolish she'd been in the past. Now wasn't the time to dwell on that, and she forced thoughts of Finch and Thomas from her mind as she made her way to the incident room.

◆ ◆ ◆

Faulkner and Hartson were already there, sitting next to each other as if they were inseparable. 'Coffee, DI Blackwell?' said Faulkner, getting to his feet.

'No thanks,' said Louise. She couldn't tell if his charm was an act or not.

'How was the trial this morning?' he asked, as Louise sat down.

'It was fine, thank you,' said Louise. It was an innocuous enough question, but Louise didn't want to discuss what was happening with them. After the Walton farm fiasco, she'd had the feeling that she was being monitored much more closely than before. And not without good reason. For the first year or so, she had been sure Finch was tracking her somehow, waging a campaign of anonymous text messages to try and drive her from the police.

But it hadn't been just Finch. The assistant chief constable at the time, Terrence Morley, had been a continual thorn in her side. He'd made no secret of the fact that he'd wanted her out after Max Walton's death, and did his utmost to pass any of her significant cases over to MIT. In fact, if it hadn't been for DCI Robertson, she imagined every major case during her time in Weston CID would have been handed to Finch.

As if summoned by her thoughts, Robertson arrived, nodding at everyone in the room by way of greeting. 'Let's get going,' he said, sitting down before anyone had the chance to respond.

As she'd promised, Louise updated them with the developments, which mainly centred on Martyn Walton-Renwick and her recent conversation with Bryce Milner from the veterans group. 'We'll be interviewing everyone from that group, today and tomorrow,' she said. 'I've arranged to speak to Ben Coles who was in the Falklands at the same time as Karl Insgrove.'

'Where are we on locating Max Walton's son?' asked Evelyn Hartson, speaking for the first time since Louise had arrived.

'We have a notice on him. As he is not using any of his own bank cards, he is proving hard to find,' said Robertson.

'But you found his whereabouts yesterday?' said Hartson, eyebrows raised as she looked at Louise.

Louise bit her lower lip before replying. 'We have teams going to all the local campsites, hotels, bed and breakfast establishments, even Airbnbs.'

'But he could be anywhere?' said Hartson.

The DCI's reaction was needless and purposely provocative, but Louise refused to be drawn into an argument. It was clear to her that CTU wanted to take over the case and Hartson was trying to find excuses to snatch the investigation away. 'What do you have for us?' said Louise, reminding the pair that it was a two-way agreement.

Taking on the role of good cop, Faulkner replied, with his charming smile, 'Nothing suggests an imminent attack this weekend from the groups we're monitoring. I can't get into too many details, but the threat level is moderate.'

'With the groups you're monitoring?' said Louise.

'Moderate in general for the region. Of course, there may be other groups or individuals, but nothing is reaching our ears as of yet.' Faulkner interlinked his hands, sucking in his breath before glancing at his colleague, who nodded. 'There is one more thing that might be of interest to you. It's related to what you just told us about Karl Insgrove.'

Louise glanced at Robertson, who shrugged. 'Go on.'

'We requested some files on Max Walton, after Karl Insgrove's death. We knew he was ex-military, but part of his record was blanked out.'

'Spit it out, son,' said Robertson.

'We needed clearance, so it has only come to light just now. Max Walton was part of a covert team working in the Falklands War.'

Louise closed her eyes and shook her head. 'You're only finding this out now.'

'Much of this stuff stays classified unless someone requests it. I've read through the file – the parts that aren't redacted. I can send you the details but can tell you for certain that Max Walton, like Karl Insgrove, was aboard HMS *Coventry* the day it sank.'

Chapter Thirty-Eight

Although Monday had passed without incident, everyone was still on high alert. There was now a definite link between Max Walton and Karl Insgrove, and with Walton's son in the country it felt inevitable to Louise that things were far from over.

She'd arrived twenty minutes earlier at the house of Karl Insgrove's former groupmate, Ben Coles, in Blagdon, but had yet to leave her car. After the CTU's revelation yesterday that both Insgrove and Max Walton had been on HMS *Coventry*, everyone from Insgrove's vet group was under the closest scrutiny. Their records and relationships were being examined by CTU, and as Coles had served in the Falklands, she wanted to speak to him first.

Every now and then she went to take a sip of coffee from her thermal cup, only to forget about it. She would have left the car if she wasn't distracted by the newspaper on the passenger seat with Tania's latest article in it. Ever since the article had been published, she'd been inundated with calls from other journalists. It had got to the point that she'd been forced to put her phone on silent and was now reliant on her police radio. The sensationalism of the last article – *Suspected Murder in School* – felt tame in comparison:

Accused Is Lover of Serving Police Officer

It had only been a matter of time before the story about her previous relationship with Finch came out. She'd expected it to come to light during her testimony, but Tania had obviously been sitting on it and decided to release it now, for maximum exposure. Although she knew it word for word, Louise read the article again, wincing as Tania stated how Louise and Finch were lovers prior to the killing of Max Walton in Bridgwater. In an absurd turn of events, Tania claimed to have a source stating that Finch had been devastated after Walton's death when their relationship had gone sour.

Louise suspected Tania's 'source' was Finch himself. The cynic in Louise was sure Tania knew Finch was lying and was manipulating the story to his own ends, but what could Louise do? It now seemed conceivable that Finch might try and use this sob story during his own testimony.

She hadn't spoken to Thomas since the article had come out. He'd previously told her he was OK with what had happened with her and Finch, but she wondered how he'd feel about it being plastered over the papers.

Forgetting she was off coffee at the moment, she went to drink from the flask again before turning up her nose at the smell. She shouldn't let the news story distract her. It was exactly what Finch would have wanted, and she had bigger priorities at that moment.

Throwing the paper in the back seat, she left the car and walked over to the small bungalow where Ben Coles lived. The grey-brick building, one of many identical houses, reminded her of the place she'd rented in Tavistock Road when she'd first moved to Weston.

A flower basket hung outside the front door, the plant inside long dead. She pressed the doorbell, a novelty tune playing as she waited for the door to be opened.

The man who answered appeared much younger and was definitely in much better shape than both Bryce Milner and Karl

Insgrove had been. He was over six foot, slim and muscular, his head shaven. He was wearing jeans and a dark T-shirt, tattoos prominent on each forearm. 'Mr Coles?' asked Louise.

'That's me. You the copper asking all the stupid questions?' said Coles.

Louise sighed inwardly. 'DI Blackwell. May I come in?'

Coles nodded and led her through a small hallway to an immaculately tidy living area. Nothing was out of place, not that there was much furniture aside from two double sofas and a large-screen television. 'Tea?' said Coles.

'Thank you for taking the time to see me,' said Louise. She waited while the kettle boiled, accepting the mug of tea, the dark-brown liquid still swirling inside.

'You spoke to Bryce last night. He told me. Asking lots of questions about Karl.'

'I'm sure you appreciate the necessity of that, Mr Coles.'

Coles sat down, a groan of effort betraying his age. 'He's dead, ain't he? Not much of a threat anymore.'

Louise knew all too well the damage people could do from beyond the grave but wasn't about to get in a debate with the man over it. 'You were in the Falklands together?' she asked.

Coles tensed at the question, his back straightening as his forearms locked in place. 'We served at the same time. There is a significant difference.'

'So you never came across Karl Insgrove during that period?'

'The first time I met Karl was at one of the vets meetings Bryce set up. You know how many people died over there?'

Louise had read the stats but let Coles answer his own question.

'Two hundred and fifty-three British, six hundred and fifty Argies. Anyway, I was a para and he worked in electronics on the ships. Hardly likely to run into each other.'

Louise nodded, sipping the tea and appreciating the strong, bitter taste. 'I know Karl suffered from PTS after his time there. Do you mind if I ask about your experiences?'

Coles grinned, Louise noticing a faded tattoo on the side of his neck. 'Is that a nice way of asking if the war fucked me up as much as it did Karl?'

Louise didn't answer, smiling in response as she waited for the man to continue.

'It wasn't a picnic for me either. We all deal with it in different ways but if you truly think about it, it's such an unnatural experience. If you haven't been there, you can't explain it. I imagine you've seen some things in your time working?'

'Of course.'

'Well, think of the worst thing you've seen. A mutilated body perhaps, then multiply that imagery a hundredfold and imagine it's going on all around you for hours on end with your own life in the balance, and you'll have an idea. Like Karl, I turned to the booze when I got back. Thankfully I never got into drugs in the way he did, but I was still fucked up. Fifteen years sober now, but I still get those flashbacks. I saw my friends blown apart, literally blown apart metres from where I was standing. Never seen a war movie in my life that truly depicts that.'

'I can only imagine, Mr Coles,' said Louise, though she didn't have to imagine. She'd seen and endured enough horror in her time not to have her credentials questioned.

Coles smiled and moved his head, as if acknowledging her experience. 'I was surprised when I found out Karl had become involved in all this nonsense. I know he was still suffering, but it must have been worse than I imagined.'

'Did he ever talk about wanting to do this before? Did you know if he had access to that kind of equipment?'

'No, of course not. I mean, we all harbour grudges. There is a lot of pent-up anger, even at our age. I've seen some vets turn to violence, always aimed in the wrong way at the wrong people. That's why the group is so valuable to us, it gives us an opportunity to discuss those things that would otherwise eat away at us. Maybe Karl was that much better at hiding things.'

Louise drank some more of the tea. Coles was a difficult man to fathom. His earlier hostility had faded but it was still bubbling away beneath the surface. She had to push him more, but needed to do so in a way that didn't bring the hostile side of him back. 'I'm sure you heard about the explosion on Saturday?'

'That poor woman. You think Karl really left that bomb there? One thing I can say is that he loved working at that school. He lived for those kids . . .'

'We can't be sure, but we think Karl was probably working with someone else.'

'Someone else?' said Coles, as if the thought had never occurred to him.

'Yes, and we think that person is still at large. Aside from your group, do you know who else Karl may have had contact with?'

Coles stuck out his lower lip, shaking his head. 'No. I mean he had the school and the other job but he kept himself to himself. We have one of them WhatsApp things but he rarely posted anything. Very private guy. Find that hard to believe.'

Louise took a deep breath. 'When you were in the Falklands, would you ever have come across the SAS, that kind of thing?'

'The paras are the special forces,' said Coles, sitting back in the chair. 'But yes, we worked with other units, SAS included.'

Louise studied the man's face. 'Have you heard of Max Walton?'

Coles maintained eye contact. 'If I hadn't, I would have this week. It's in the papers. You were the one who shot him?'

He didn't say the words confrontationally. If anything, there was a hint of sadness in his question.

'Max Walton was a mass murderer. A serial killer. He was also a member of the SAS, who was active in the Falklands around the same time as yourself and Karl.'

Coles sat up straight. 'What? I don't understand. I never met Walton. I remember when you shot him. You were in the papers. I read about all the shit he'd done. I was relieved when he was dead, let me tell you that. I had no idea he was ex-service. He was a fucking disgrace,' said Coles, clearly agitated.

'Could it be that your paths crossed? I mean, can you recall everyone you worked with?'

Coles allowed his breathing to return to normal. 'It's possible, but the SAS are sneaky beaky, you know? You weren't supposed to know they were there. Those guys were close-knit, as you would expect. Our paths would occasionally cross, and I knew some of their names, at least their nicknames, but never a Walton. I remember faces and I've seen his, and I didn't see him over there.'

'You're sure you would have remembered? It was a long time ago.'

'Trust me, I would have remembered.'

'Did Karl ever mention him?'

'Max Walton? God, no. Maybe in passing.' Coles shrugged. 'Anyway, there is no way their paths would have crossed. Not in the Falklands anyway. I don't know what you've been told but Karl spent the war on board those ships. The SAS were flown in. He would never have met Walton. And if by chance they were on the same ship, they would never have spoken to one another.'

The last sentence stayed with Louise as she made her way back to Portishead. Until that point, everything Coles had said had sounded reasonable, but he had no way of knowing for sure if Walton and Insgrove would have spoken during Walton's stay on board the ship.

What she really wanted to do now was go to court and watch developments with Finch. Instead, she went back to the station and forced herself to relive the most momentous investigation in her history.

Reading through the file, Louise was reminded that they had spoken to a number of Walton's ex-colleagues from the armed forces but nothing in the notes suggested he'd had a period in the SAS. She ran a cross search of Insgrove, Coles, Milner and the other members of the vets counselling group, but no one appeared.

The irony that the one person who would be worth talking to was currently in court on an attempted murder charge wasn't lost on her. Looking back, there was nothing about Finch's contribution to the investigation that could be trusted anymore. For all she knew, he could have spoken to Ben Coles and Karl Insgrove during their investigation into Walton and not reported it; either because he hadn't thought it relevant or because he wanted to keep it from her.

Accused Is Lover of Serving Police Officer

It made her sick to the stomach that she'd ever had anything to do with the man. Everything bad that had happened in her life felt like it stemmed from that mistake, and still there was no escaping him. She was in the newspaper because of him, and one way or another he was tied to this current investigation. That Karl Insgrove and Max Walton had been serving in the Falklands was one coincidence too many, and that the fires had happened the week before Finch was in court made her wonder what role he had to play in everything.

The smell of coffee drifted towards her, her reaction making her wonder if she was coming down with something. 'Is your phone off?' said Tracey, knocking on the door and placing a cup in front of her.

'Shit, it's on silent,' said Louise, pulling her phone from her jacket and turning the volume on.

'I think Thomas has been trying to contact you.'

'He called you?'

'He's worried. He read that article.'

Louise glanced at her phone. Amongst the numerous missed calls from journalists and unknown numbers were four from Thomas. 'I'll call him,' said Louise.

Tracey lifted her head in acknowledgement. 'Everything OK between you two?'

'Of course,' said Louise.

'Hey,' she said, when Thomas answered the phone. 'Sorry I missed you. I had my phone on silent while interviewing. I'm the most popular copper in town at present.'

'You're always my most popular copper,' said Thomas. 'You OK? I can't believe Tania published that article today.'

'It was bound to come out at some point. The timing couldn't be better for Finch though,' said Louise, stopping short of telling Thomas she'd seen the journalist at the courthouse.

'I can't wait until this is over.'

'You and me both.'

'Anyway, I'm afraid I have some more bad news for you.'

Louise felt a flutter in her stomach as she tried to anticipate what he was going to say.

'I lost my job today,' he said, before she had the chance to ask him anything.

She went quiet. 'You're kidding?' she said, after she'd processed the information.

'No. They're calling it restructuring, but I know where the truth lies. I just wanted to let you know in case it causes you more grief.'

'You've lost your job and you're concerned about the effect it has on me?'

'I don't want them to use this against you.'

Louise was momentarily lost for words. It shouldn't have taken something like this for her to be reminded of Thomas's selflessness. That his major concern was the effect his dismissal would have on her said so much about him – and, she feared, said a little about her too. 'I'll get Greg to speak to them. He can explain it was nothing to do with you.'

'I'm not sure even DS Farrell can get me out of this one. Don't suppose there are any jobs going back in headquarters,' he said, with a laugh.

'We could certainly do with you at the moment,' said Louise. 'I really am sorry this has happened, Tom.'

'It's not your fault. Bad timing, I guess.'

Louise sensed his hesitancy, as if he wanted to say more but either didn't know what to say or was scared to do so. It had never felt awkward speaking to Thomas before, but now there was a divide growing between them that was of her own making. 'I wish I could be there for you. It's just . . .'

'You don't have to explain. I was thinking though. I'm sure to have some time off now, so maybe when this stuff with Finch is over we could go away somewhere together? Since I've known you, I can't remember you ever having a holiday.'

'That would be lovely,' said Louise, doubting her own words as she said them.

Chapter Thirty-Nine

Farrell had followed Perkins back to the station after watching his heated meeting with Michael Sinclair. Sinclair had been released without charge after Perkins' questioning had stalled, so why the hell was he meeting with the man now?

Something was clearly amiss, but Farrell had to be careful about his next move. Perkins was more sidelined in the station than before with Finch's incarceration, but that didn't mean he didn't have allies within the force.

Farrell wasn't able to look into Perkins' files, but unless he was working on something ultra-secret there didn't appear to be any logical reason for Perkins to be speaking to Sinclair.

Positive identification had just come in for the two other men Perkins had met. Etienne Hoffman and Grant Frame were two known villains from north London who'd been making a name for themselves in Bristol and the surrounding area. It didn't take Farrell long to link them to Terry Clemons, who was holed up at the same prison where Tim Finch was on remand.

Farrell wasn't sure if there was a worthwhile connection, but he knew for certain Perkins had been in court watching Finch's trial before meeting with Sinclair and two of Clemons' former colleagues, and that had to mean something.

Farrell's options were limited at this stage. He knew an officer in the Ghost Squad, but it was too early to even mention his suspicions to them. They may already be running something on Perkins, but if he raised this issue now it would change everything. No one wanted corrupt officers on their team – the widespread condemnation of Finch was proof enough of that – but being known as a potential grass would effectively ruin Farrell's career. However well intentioned, going against Perkins at this stage would mean that he would never be fully trusted again.

If she wasn't directly involved, as well as under enough pressure of her own at the moment, he would have gone to Louise. She was one of a handful of officers he trusted beyond question, and given her dealings with Finch had the perfect experience to know what to do next. DCI Robertson was another he could have gone to but he would be duty-bound to make something official out of it.

With Thomas no longer part of the team, there was only one other officer he could speak to: Tracey Pugh.

Farrell had worked with Tracey on her sabbatical to Weston during the Pensioner Killer murders a few years back, and he'd since got to know her very well. She was Louise's closest friend in the police, and that alone meant he was able to trust her.

She was working in the Major Crimes office searching through a database of photofits. 'Dating profiles?' he asked, sitting down next to her.

Tracey turned to him as if in a daze before breaking into a smile. 'Very funny,' she said. 'Though this one looks a bit tasty,' she added, pointing to a stick-thin man with the complexion of a teenager.

'Still trying to locate our South African fugitive?'

'There's something about this Walton family I just don't like. Can't quite put my finger on it. Anyway, what the hell are you doing in my department?'

'I was wondering if I could buy you a coffee?' said Farrell.

Tracey frowned, before realising he meant he wanted to speak to her in private. 'I know just the place,' she said.

Five minutes later they were sitting in Louise's office, Farrell having poured two cups from the staff machine. He told her about following Eddie Perkins and his run-in with Sinclair and two of Clemons' men.

'Eddie Perkins is no good, I can confirm that. It's an open secret he's on the take, though everyone turned a blind eye under Finch's reign.'

'There's no feasible reason he would be meeting with Sinclair is there?'

'He told you he didn't know him?' asked Tracey.

'Pretty much. And on the day of his release.'

'I know his team leader, Jake Chester. I'll have a discreet word, see if I can find out what he's working on. What did you want to do?'

'Ideally, I want to keep eyes on him. See what he does next, but sooner or later he's going to spot me.'

'You want me to help you?'

'Two eyes are better than one.'

Tracey seemed to consider the suggestion. 'Have you heard that Thomas lost his job? I just spoke to Louise.'

'No way,' said Farrell. 'Just because of what happened? We haven't charged him, and we're not going to. This isn't because of Lloyd Bradshaw's accusation, is it? Bradshaw was clearly bullshitting us.'

'Sounds like they don't want to take any chances. Maybe we can get some answers with Sinclair and Perkins. Count me in.'

◆ ◆ ◆

It was still light when Perkins left the office. Farrell had been loitering in the main foyer so he could keep an eye on the door, while Tracey had been waiting in her car. Perkins didn't notice him as he left, and Farrell called Tracey and told her to get ready.

They took separate cars, following Perkins from a distance. Despite what Farrell knew about Perkins, it still felt wrong following a fellow officer. Disloyalty was something not tolerated in the police, and that message had been drummed into him since his first training day at Hendon. He had to remind himself that Perkins was potentially doing something illegal, and that his actions were jeopardising the safety and future of his friends and colleagues.

'Perkins lives over by Bedminster, doesn't he?' said Tracey, on the phone.

'Believe so,' said Farrell, noticing in the distance that Perkins was taking a turning for Avonmouth.

'I'll hold back,' said Tracey, allowing Farrell to overtake her.

Farrell was still using his friend's car which he'd parked away from the station, but that in itself was a risk should Perkins have noticed it yesterday.

The traffic between his car and Perkins' began to thin, and Farrell was forced to pull over. 'He's making his way to the docklands,' he said to Tracey, who drove past him two minutes later.

'I've eyes on him,' said Tracey, ten minutes later. 'He's parked up in the transit area of South Docks Five.'

Farrell had Tracey's location on his phone and parked up next to her. 'You drive down, I'll go by foot?'

Tracey nodded, and set off as Farrell left the car. The docks may not have contained the thriving industry it once had, but there was still a hive of activity in the area which currently contained a seemingly endless tanker and a large ocean liner. Perkins had parked up in an area containing hundreds of shipping containers. 'He's leaving his car now,' Farrell told Tracey, who waited a couple of minutes before driving into the car park.

Farrell pulled his hoodie over his head, feeling more conspicuous walking down the hill than he had in the car. He still had a sightline of Perkins, who was constantly checking his surroundings.

He made his way to the entrance of the shipping containers where three men had just emerged.

'Company,' said Farrell, dropping to his haunches as he pulled out a long-lens camera from his holdall.

'You recognise them?' said Tracey.

'Same three. Sinclair, Hoffman and Frame.'

'What is he playing at? You want me to move in?'

Farrell adjusted his sight. The four men were standing firm. Sinclair appeared to be talking, Perkins stood rigid as he listened to what the man had to say. 'You'll be compromised if you move,' said Farrell, snapping photos of the four men. He zoomed in on Sinclair who was definitely the most agitated, gesturing with his arms as he spoke to Perkins.

Sinclair stopped speaking and the four men stood looking at one another before Perkins reached inside his jacket. Farrell's heartbeat spiked as he began clicking on the camera once more, only for Perkins to bring out a phone.

As Perkins went to tap on it, the phone was knocked from his hand by Hoffman. Sinclair shook his head as Farrell relayed the information to Tracey. 'Shall we go in?' she asked.

'Not yet,' said Farrell. The movement by Hoffman had been aggressive, but Perkins hadn't reacted. The phone lay on the ground between the four men as Perkins seemed to consider the situation. Eventually he said something to Sinclair, Farrell managing to capture Sinclair's grin as he went into his own coat pocket and retrieved something.

Farrell focused all his attention on the item. He couldn't help but chuckle at the sight of the clichéd brown envelope. He'd thought bungs were a thing of the past, reserved for eighties football managers in public toilets. But here was Sinclair, in daylight, seemingly handing Perkins an envelope stuffed with cash.

Chapter Forty

Preparations for the air show were in full swing in the centre of Weston. In readiness for the two-day festival, the lawns opposite the seafront to the west of the Grand Pier were full of stalls, and a number of activities had been planned for the beach. Alongside the annual beach motocross, it was the highest-attended weekend of the season, and the local hotels and bed and breakfasts were all at capacity.

Security procedures were in place throughout the town, but no one seemed to mind. It was Hana Sanchez's funeral tomorrow, and although the woman hadn't been forgotten – a memorial day had been planned – the town was moving on.

Louise sensed the excitement as she moved from site to site, checking the security protocols were being followed while searching for a hint, however small, of something untoward. She knew it could come down to one chance. She was sure that the offender, be it Martyn Walton-Renwick or not, would reveal themselves at some juncture, and she wanted to be there for that moment.

She walked past the various stalls on the lawns, stopping at a booth set up by the RAF. Her father had once been a sergeant in the air force, leaving a couple of years after her brother, Paul, had been born. As children, they would make the short journey from Bristol for the annual air show in Weston, the highlight of which was always the display by the air force's aerobatic airplane squad, the Red Arrows. Louise could vividly recall the childhood glee of watching the airplanes make their daredevil moves through the sky, the joy she'd experienced holding her father's hand as the planes rushed towards each other only to turn away with a split second to spare.

The memory made her think of Thomas and his suggestion about the holiday, which had come so close on the heels of her all but rebuffing his suggestion to take the kids out together. Until recently, they'd taken things slowly, neither feeling the need to make plans for any future together. It was now clear he wanted to move things along, and again she was forced to wonder where her reluctance came from.

◆ ◆ ◆

After checking the rest of the area, Louise made her way back to Bristol, arriving in time for the afternoon session. She put her phone on vibrate and stood for the judge. She'd made a special effort to be there that afternoon, as Terri Marsden was about to take the stand. Along with Amira, Terri had been one of the first to come forward to help the fight against Finch. She still worked at headquarters as a temp. Finch had struck up a relationship with her only to dump her like the others. He'd waited a few months before suggesting she leave her job – a common ploy he'd tried with all his conquests, either by force or suggestion – and when she'd refused, he'd threatened to distribute naked pictures he'd taken of her to the station and members of her family.

Amanda Knight talked to Terri with sensitivity and compassion. Terri broke down more than once as she told her story. Louise fumed as Terri recounted Finch's subtle threats, and the fact that she'd ultimately had to leave her job like so many others. Unfortunately, Louise knew there was worse to come for her today.

The defence barrister, Charles Boothroyd, was also sensitive during the questioning. At first glance it appeared he was on Terri's side, asking similar questions to Amanda Knight's. But Louise could tell he was softening his witness up. Yet when the first tough question arrived it came as a shock – both to her and to Terri, who was visibly trembling in the witness box.

'You agreed to have these photos taken by my client?' asked Boothroyd.

'Yes, but I didn't—'

'How long had you been seeing Mr Finch at this point?' said Boothroyd, interrupting.

Terri was already flustered. 'I don't know if that matters,' she said, turning to the judge for support.

'Please answer the question,' said the judge, not unkindly but with an assured authority that suggested she wasn't going to be messed with.

'About six weeks.'

Boothroyd frowned and glanced at the jury before continuing. 'Six weeks and you allowed him to take naked pictures of you. Do you make a habit of such behaviour?'

'Objection,' said Knight, getting to her feet.

'Withdrawn. So, six weeks into your relationship, and you allow Mr Finch to take pictures of you. That is correct?'

'Yes.'

'And you . . .' Boothroyd stopped to look down at his notes. 'Claim,' he added, with emphasis, 'that after your relationship ended, what must have been two weeks later, Mr Finch threatened to show these photos to your colleagues around the station?'

'That is correct.'

'But you have no proof of that.'

Terri glanced at the judge again. 'No, I—'

'And Mr Finch ended the relationship with you?'

'Yes, but—'

'I put it to you, Miss Marsden, that after Mr Finch ended your brief relationship you were somewhat taken aback. When approached by DC Amira Hood and DI Blackwell you saw a perfect opportunity to get your own back on Mr Finch. Is that correct?'

Terri's shaking intensified. 'No, of course not. I—'

'No more questions,' said Boothroyd, sitting down just as Louise's phone began to vibrate.

Enraged by Boothroyd's questioning, a clear indication of how the defence was going to proceed with the case, Louise glanced at the phone to see DCI Robertson was calling. She tiptoed out of the viewing gallery, not the most courteous behaviour with the trial in mid-flow, catching Tania Elliot's eye as she walked by, and managed to respond before the call went through to her answering service.

'I know you're at court, Louise, but thought you'd want to know. We have just had a sighting of Martyn Walton at a youth hostel around the corner from you.'

Louise didn't even hesitate. She left the courthouse with speed and began running towards the hostel.

Chapter Forty-One

The youth hostel at Narrow Quay was less than half a mile away. As Louise ran towards Corn Street, she saw a familiar face behind the wheel of a less familiar car. She shot Greg Farrell a quizzical look, Farrell responding with a firm shake of his head as if he didn't want to be disturbed. Louise looked behind her to decipher Farrell's sightline to see that he had a perfect view of the court entrance.

Why he was there was anyone's guess, but she couldn't dwell on that now. Martyn Walton-Renwick had checked into the youth hostel yesterday evening under his own name and was possibly in the building now. Robertson had sent two patrol cars to the place with instructions to secure the building, but Louise wanted to be present for this herself.

She ignored the stares as she jogged through Marsh Street, bemused that Walton-Renwick had seemingly used his own name to make the booking. That meant he either didn't know he was wanted – which felt unlikely after his last-minute escape from the campsite in Locking – or that perhaps he wasn't the smartest of people.

A third possibility struck Louise as she rounded the corner to Prince Street. That he wanted to get caught. He wouldn't be the first criminal she'd chased who, consciously or not, wanted to hand themselves in.

Blue lights heralded her arrival at the hostel. Outside, a number of young people were milling about waiting to be let back in as police officers interviewed them. A uniformed officer was inside talking to a young man she introduced as John Carpenter. 'It was Mr Carpenter who called us this morning, ma'am,' said the officer.

'I was just saying to your colleague that I was watching the news when a picture of Martyn Renwick came up. It sounded familiar and when they said he was South African it clicked. When I came into work today, I checked through the bookings, and sure enough there he was in room thirty-two.'

The young man seemed exorbitantly pleased with himself, and Louise hoped that he hadn't delayed his call too much. 'What identification do you require to stay here?' asked Louise.

'Usually a passport or photo ID of some sort.'

'You keep records on file?'

'Yes, I have a passport photo of him if you like,' said Carpenter, going behind the counter and punching a few buttons before Walton-Renwick's face appeared on the screen.

'Is room thirty-two a single room?'

'No, it's a shared dormitory. We currently have seven total in the room.'

'Are they in?'

'We don't track their movements I'm afraid.'

'I need a list of who is staying in that dormitory. No one is to leave this building,' said Louise, calling over to the two uniformed officers guarding the door.

The receptionist printed a list and showed it to them. 'Are these all single bookings?'

Carpenter scrutinised the list. 'The first four are booked in together. A group of German lads, very nice guys. The other three are single bookings.'

'Can you take us to the room please,' said Louise.

The hostel was more like a small boutique hotel than what Louise would expect of a hostel. They passed a canteen area where four young women sat on benches opposite one another, each staring intently at their phone. Carpenter led them up a flight of wood-panelled stairs and along the corridor to room 32.

'Is there any other exit from that room?'

'There is a window, but we have security locks on it so no one can get out.'

'I want you to knock on the door, whatever your usual routine is, and ask to go in. And tell me if he's in there. Can you do that for me?' said Louise.

The young man adjusted his glasses. 'Sure thing,' he said, knocking on the door.

A few seconds later, the door opened and a man who appeared to be in his twenties stood in the doorway, looking from Carpenter to Louise and back again. 'Hello,' he said, in what sounded like a German accent.

'Hi. Ludo, isn't it?'

'Yes, hi,' said Ludo, his eyes still darting from one person to the other.

'Just a quick registration check. Mind if I come in?'

'Of course not,' said Ludo, holding the door open.

'I'm going in,' said Louise into her radio, following Carpenter inside.

The room consisted of four sets of bunk beds. To the side was a small bathroom area, the door open. Aside from Ludo, there were three other men in the room, none of whom was Walton-Renwick. 'Just you four?' asked Louise.

'Yes,' said Ludo. 'Is there anything we can help you with?'

'This man,' said Louise, showing Ludo a picture of Walton-Renwick. 'He was staying here?'

'Yes. He was there,' said Ludo, pointing to the lower bunk of a bed by the window.

The bed was made up but looked slept in. 'When was the last time you saw the man staying here?' asked Louise.

Ludo shook his head. 'Last night?' he said, before speaking to his friends in German.

'I saw him this morning,' said one of the other men, perched on the top bunk opposite where Walton-Renwick would have been sleeping. 'Heard him packing his bag. He was trying to be quiet. I had my watch on,' said the man, turning his wrist as evidence. 'It was six a.m.'

They cleared the dormitory, Louise insisting on a full search of the building before she was willing to allow anyone in or out.

'Must have packed in a rush,' said one of the uniformed team she'd sent into Walton-Renwick's dormitory a few minutes later, handing Louise a folded A3 leaflet for the museum in Weston-super-Mare.

'Where was this?'

'Underneath his mattress.'

'Look,' said the officer, opening the leaflet up. On the back page was a layout of the museum. In three separate locations, Walton-Renwick had marked three red crosses.

For now, Louise had to assume they were perfect locations for potential IEDs.

Chapter Forty-Two

After watching Eddie Perkins take what they presumed to have been a bribe yesterday, Farrell and Tracey had some tough decisions to make. The photos Farrell had taken of the exchange were clear but didn't count for much. It was still feasible that Perkins was working on a case, and that information on it hadn't been shared with headquarters, though the involvement of Michael Sinclair made that seem highly unlikely.

For now, they agreed to keep up the surveillance. Which was how Farrell found himself back outside the courthouse while Tracey was watching the movements of Sinclair.

Farrell's heart had run cold when he saw Louise catch sight of him twenty minutes earlier. In that split second, he'd imagined Perkins leaving the courthouse and catching them looking at one another, and the situation blowing apart. Thankfully, Louise had readily acknowledged the heated shake of his head before leaving for the waterside, where Farrell had heard on the radio that Walton-Renwick had been located.

Earlier in the day, Farrell had seen Tania Elliot enter the courthouse five minutes after Perkins. Although both had legitimate reasons for being there, Farrell was sure Perkins was feeding information to Tania from Finch. He imagined the latest story about Finch and Louise being lovers had been leaked to the journalist that way, and for that alone Perkins deserved the surveillance and hopefully everything else that was coming his way.

Tania Elliot first. From what Farrell could see, she'd yet to miss a second of the trial. He'd always got on quite well with the woman, and most of the time he appreciated that she was just doing her job. It was only when she veered into the more personal side of things that he started to have a problem with her. And he couldn't believe that her clandestine meeting with Perkins was innocuous. Her focus was on the Finch case, as well as the sideshow of the explosions in Weston that had grown around it. It was arguable that she'd spoken to Perkins to get his view of things, but the secretive way they'd talked to one another suggested something else.

He watched her drive away in her sleek sports car, another thirty minutes passing with no sign of Perkins.

Finch left first. Farrell heard the security clearance call, and the prison van pull off. Two minutes later, Perkins left the courthouse. Farrell wasn't buying this coincidence. Was Perkins somehow managing to speak to Finch inside the building?

Farrell didn't have time to ponder the question long. Perkins was walking with purpose, his face a permanent scowl as he crossed Corn Street with barely a concern for the traffic as he got into his car. He sped out of the parking lot, forcing the driver of an SUV to slam on their brakes to avoid a collision.

Farrell eased into the traffic as smoothly as possible, calling Tracey to tell her he was on the move. 'He seems to be in a rush, or is taking out his anger on his car,' he said, following Perkins out of the city.

'Do you think he's heading back to Cabot Tower?'

'Could be, why?'

'Just followed Sinclair there.'

'Another collection?' said Farrell.

'We could get a team in?' said Tracey.

Perkins headed along Anchor Road, his speed and impatience only curtailed by the cars in front of him. It would be the perfect opportunity to catch Perkins and the others in the act, but again it would be a huge risk. They couldn't even confirm they were meeting yet, and had no way of knowing what that meeting would entail. Chances of it being nothing were too high at the moment, and if they got it wrong not only would it ruin any chance of them finding out what Perkins was up to, it would jeopardise their relationships with everyone else on the force.

Tracey understood that as well as he did, and didn't argue when he decided against it. 'Is it the same meeting place?' he asked.

'Looks that way.'

'OK, I'll hang back so there's no risk of him spotting me. Let me know when he arrives.'

◆ ◆ ◆

Farrell was still five minutes from the park when Tracey called again. 'He's on his way back to the car,' she said.

'What do you mean?'

'Just what I said. Perkins parked up, went to speak to Sinclair, took something off him and is now storming back to his car as if he's been told some bad news. Do you want me to follow or stay on Sinclair?'

'Follow. I'll wait on the main road and join.'

He managed to pull over a minute before Perkins left the car park and headed towards the Portway. 'I've got eyes on him,' he said to Tracey, pulling into the traffic.

'Right behind you,' said Tracey.

Perkins was more agitated than before, at one point trying to overtake a saloon car that must have been going thirty-five miles an hour. 'Did you see what they exchanged?' said Farrell, catching sight of Tracey's car in his rear-view mirror.

'Same as before. Perkins didn't even bother hiding it this time, all but snatching it from Sinclair's hand.'

'Cash?'

'Yep.'

'Shit,' said Farrell, as Perkins pulled off the road. 'You take it, I'll park up,' he added.

Tracey followed Perkins down the left turn. 'I'm going to park up too. You know what's over there, don't you?'

Farrell was already parked and running back towards her. He felt conspicuous in his suit, thankful that he was wearing his walking shoes. The turning Perkins had taken was to the head office of Oblong Distribution, the company where, until recently, Thomas had worked as head of security. 'Sure do.'

'He's pulled in there. What the hell is this about?'

Farrell didn't think it would happen, but a part of him was dreading hearing Tracey mention that Thomas was waiting to meet Perkins. 'Can you go in?'

'Not easily. He's already parked up and moving . . . Hang on.'

Farrell rounded a corner, seeing Tracey near the entrance to the car park. She was leaning behind a tree, her camera poised. 'Looks like Perkins is now a delivery boy,' she said.

Farrell caught up, ducking behind the tree as Tracey snapped away. 'Recognise him?' she said, showing him the screen of the camera.

'Yes, I interviewed him. That's Trent Wheatley. He's the MD of the business.'

'The guy who sacked Thomas?'

'I guess so,' said Farrell.

'Then why the hell is he taking a package from DS Perkins?'

Chapter Forty-Three

Returning to the prison each night was harder than Finch had anticipated. On remand, he had no option but to get on with it. He knew where he was and where he would be staying, and as such he had trained his brain accordingly. But with each day that he was transported to the courthouse, his mind began to trick itself that freedom was within reach.

If he ignored his position in the dock, it was easy enough to believe he was back at the courthouse on police business, watching the liars spread their nonsense about him. Despite relishing the hardship his barrister was putting the so-called witnesses through, part of him just wanted this to be over. Whether he was found guilty or not was almost an irrelevance; he just wanted the decision taken away from him so he could make plans for what came next.

No sooner was he processed than Wilson was banging on his cell and leading him over to see his puppet master, Terry Clemons. The Clemons situation was another conundrum he wanted to put to bed. If they ever let him out of this place, then Finch would call in every waiting favour, would leverage every single piece of information he had to bring Clemons and his crew down. Not through any sense of justice, but more for the fact that Clemons had the temerity to treat him the way he did: as if they were allies; or worse, as if Finch was some kind of errand boy.

The big lug of muscle stood aside as Finch was escorted to Clemons' cell. 'Must be nice to be back in a jogging suit,' said Clemons, by way of greeting, glancing down at the prison-issued outfit Finch was wearing.

'Always great to see you, Clemons.'

'Take a seat.'

Finch looked behind him, preparing himself as he always did in this situation for a potential beating, before sitting on the wooden chair next to Clemons' bunk bed.

'DS Perkins has delivered the package.'

'That was quick,' said Finch. He'd seen Perkins straight after the court had concluded for the day. Perkins had still been whining about his newfound role, though that hadn't stopped him accepting his payment the other day. Finch knew as well as Clemons that he hadn't needed to send Perkins to drop off the payment to Trent Wheatley. It was a test of power on Clemons' part, and more than likely a security measure. By having Perkins hand over the bribe to Wheatley, the detective would be made complicit.

Perkins had understood this, and had tried to refuse. This had continued for a few minutes until Finch had been forced to remind Perkins about what he held over him. He'd endured a minute's silence then, as he'd waited for Perkins to decide whether or not to call his bluff. In the end, the man had submitted as Finch knew he would.

'Everything is in place. Everyone paid off. We should have started working together years ago, Finch.'

Finch had worked with numerous cons in his time. It funded his interests, and up until the end had only helped his career. He'd known things other coppers didn't and that intel had served him well. But this was different. With Clemons, the roles were reversed. They weren't working together and never would be. Finch was working for Clemons, and when he was no longer needed, he would be dispensed with. 'Here's to the future,' said Finch, wondering if the wardens or Clemons' henchman would reach the cell first if he took Clemons' life where he sat.

◆ ◆ ◆

Back in his cell, Finch straightened his few meagre belongings and lay down on his bed, his arms folded across his chest. At first, he began plotting how he could take Clemons out of the equation. There were people inside, even in this Cat B prison, who owed him. And, more importantly, who he held dirt on. He was sure it could easily be arranged. It had happened before. A slip in the bathroom, an assisted suicide. It needn't ever be connected to Finch. But, no. The power-dynamic battle with Clemons would have to wait for now. To his credit, the man had done everything he'd promised. Thomas Ireland had lost his job, and Tania Elliot was now in direct contact with Finch and was helping spread the propaganda that would hopefully ruin the prosecution's case.

The plan from the beginning had been to undermine the witnesses. Although there were lots of them, the real focus was on Louise and Amira Hood. The attack on Thomas Ireland's character had only been a primer. By the time he was finished with Blackwell and Hood, they would be lucky to come out of the courtroom with their dignity intact.

The thought gave Finch comfort. He closed his eyes and fell immediately into a deep and dreamless sleep.

Chapter Forty-Four

Louise reached the museum in Burlington Street an hour before it was due to close. She'd called Robertson on her way and deployed additional staff to search for Martyn Walton-Renwick in the area surrounding the youth hostel. She was still at a loss as to why Walton-Renwick would take the risk of booking into the hostel under his own name. He'd gone to the lengths of using cash instead of a card to pay, so why hadn't he used fake identification? As for the leaflet they'd found under his mattress, she still wasn't sure if that was a huge oversight, a cry for help, or a misdirection. For now, her money was on the latter. Chances were that Walton-Renwick had got wind that he'd been spotted and left the leaflet as a diversionary tactic.

Not that they could take any chances. The manager of the museum had asked if they could wait until closing time, but there was no way they were taking that risk. She demanded an immediate evacuation of the building, regardless of the disruption and inevitable attention it would draw.

'Tourist board must love you.'

Louise had been so intent talking to the museum's manager that she hadn't seen Adam King arrive. 'Where's the van?'

'I'm incognito. Didn't want to scare the locals. Slight issue though.'

Louise sighed. The tension from the last few days felt as if it had taken root in her back and shoulders and was spreading to her stomach and chest. It was some time since she'd last had a hangover, but she felt as if she'd been living through one this last week. 'I think I need a coffee,' she said.

'Those,' said King, pointing to the row of houses to the side of the museum.

The museum was an old Victorian building wedged in between two sets of terraced houses. Opposite were garages with cars parked out front. 'What about them?'

'I'll do a preliminary search but we're going to need them evacuated immediately. This whole street needs to be closed down.'

'Great.'

'Not the end of it, I'm afraid.'

'You want me to shut the whole town, Adam?' asked Louise, with a little bit more bite than she'd intended.

If he took any offence, it wasn't apparent. 'Not quite, but the buildings to the rear have to be evacuated as well. If we have no way of telling where any devices have been planted, we can only guess as to the blast range – and there's a lot of glass inside if I recollect.'

'The courtyard has a glass ceiling,' said Louise, handing King the leaflet found under Walton-Renwick's mattress.

'Nice of him to point out the areas of danger for us,' said King, glancing at the crosses on the museum map. 'If only all arsonists were so helpful.'

The TV cameras began arriving as King and his team set up. Burlington Street had been blocked at both ends, and Louise had ordered the whole row to be evacuated. Whoever was responsible had already demonstrated their willingness to be more than just a threat. They'd already lost one life, and Louise wasn't willing to risk another.

DCI Robertson had arrived in the museum's reception, and together they watched the body-cam footage of King and Mitch Norton as they made a preliminary sweep of the building, moving through the reception area of the museum into the courtyard. 'This is where the first cross was marked,' said Louise, over the microphone.

'Shame they couldn't be more specific,' said King, his body cam scanning the open area that spanned nearly the whole length of the museum.

'I know you don't want to hear this, but I am getting grief from the council. They don't know what to do,' said Robertson, eyes glued to the screen as the bomb disposal team made painfully slow progress through the courtyard area.

'Don't know what to do about what?'

'About the air show,' said Robertson, a growl in his voice.

Louise wanted to say 'Fuck the air show', but found she was lacking the energy for complaint. A short stabbing pain was making its way up from her right ankle, as if she'd been sitting awkwardly on it, towards her stomach. She thought about Thomas's suggestion to take a short break away, and at that moment would have loved nothing more. 'Until we find Walton-Renwick, I think it is a risk but I don't imagine anyone wants to close the whole town down.'

'No, they don't,' said Robertson, as King cleared one section of the courtyard. 'Careless of him. Leading us here. You think he wants to get caught?'

'I'll be honest, Iain. I'm still not sure what is going on. Beyond the link of Insgrove and Max Walton being in the Falklands, I don't see how or why the two could be working together.'

Robertson nodded silently. He knew better than to question her approach. He'd been that way from the beginning, trusting her and letting her get on with work and offering help where it was needed. 'We sure he was at the youth hostel?'

'We've downloaded the CCTV files. Simon Coulson is heading up the search through that.'

'And that other thing?' added Robertson after a period of silence, King's team's methodical work having a hypnotising effect on them.

'Finch? He's trying to derail everything as we expected. He'll get what's coming to him.'

'I know you don't need to hear this, but remember you were in the right from the beginning. Something lots of people forget about. We'll all be here for you. OK?'

Louise turned to her boss, surprised at the waver in his voice. 'Not getting all emotional on me, are you, sir?' she said, placing her hand on his shoulder in thanks.

'Shit,' said King through their earpieces, sending them crashing back into the moment. 'I think I've found something.'

Chapter Forty-Five

Louise couldn't fully make out what King was looking at, as he worked on his discovery. 'Shit,' he repeated, his tone now heightened as if he was doing something she hadn't seen him do before: succumb to panic.

'What is it, Adam?' said Louise.

'IED. Homemade with a timer. Not sure we have time for Arnie to disrupt it.' The bomb disposal robot was in reception, waiting to be activated.

'How long?' said Robertson.

'Two minutes, forty-two seconds and counting. It's packed with a load of crap as well. Nuts and bolts. You need to push the cordon back . . . especially on the right side of the building. That includes you and everyone else.'

'What are you going to do?' asked Louise.

'I'm getting the hell out of here first, and then we'll get Arnie in. Mitch, let's go.'

Robertson began organising the officers with military precision as Louise watched King and Norton leave the building, running over to her to activate Arnie.

It was a miracle they had got to the device in time. When they'd arrived, they'd been forced to escort children and families from the area, and if the timer had been set for earlier, it was horrendous to think what could have happened.

From what King had told them, the IED was packed with material that would spread out from the blast and kill or severely injure anyone nearby.

That said, it was now after closing time at the museum. Louise didn't know how late the staff would usually stay on, but it seemed that the offender had deliberately set the timer for a period when the place would be shut. That supported the possibility that Walton-Renwick, if he was responsible, was not intent on causing maximum damage. If he'd wanted to do that, then he could have set the timer a couple of hours earlier. She tried to hope that this IED was another dummy bomb, like the one they'd initially found at the school, but it felt as if things had escalated beyond that point now. The offender had already killed someone, intentionally or not, and hope as she might it was highly unlikely that they were about to take a step back.

Captivated, they watched on the screen as Arnie made its way on its caterpillar tracks to the area where the bag had been found jammed behind one of the exhibits. Louise jumped as behind her a car alarm was activated, her heartbeat thumping as she prepared herself for the worst.

'Damn it,' screamed King, as he controlled the arm of the robot, trying to unfasten the bag.

'Fifty-two seconds,' said Louise, over her earpiece.

'Everyone needs to get down,' said King, still working on the bag. 'I need an eyeline on the power source.'

Robertson repeated the instructions to the officers manning the check lines, the area mercifully free of civilians. In the distance Louise heard the sound of traffic, people going about their business oblivious to the danger so close by.

Louise's arm itched, and it was only then she realised the area where they were taking refuge was a few doors down from the tattoo parlour where the woman who had given her the scar had worked.

'Eight seconds,' said Louise, staring at her watch as if she could hold back time.

The countdown ended – Louise, and by the looks of it the others, having mentally counted back from eight. The quiet was tangible, even the distant sound of the traffic fading in a snapshot of time, before the explosion ripped into the sky.

It was like nothing Louise had ever heard before. A few years back, she had been part of a rescue team at the Old Pier on Birnbeck Island and had seen the already derelict building go up in flames, but nothing had prepared her for this.

Even from the safety of this position, the noise was overwhelming. To begin with, it sounded like a train, before morphing into a raging thunder as the explosion tore through the front of the building. The damage was substantial, and Louise struggled to block out the mental images she had of the museum being full of families, and the deaths and injuries that would have caused.

◆ ◆ ◆

It was an hour before they even attempted to get near the site. King and Nolan went first, scanning the area for any more devices.

As they stepped into the building, the full extent of the damage became apparent on their body cams. The explosion had all but destroyed the front right-hand side of the courtyard and had pushed upwards, ripping out the glass ceiling. Shards of glass hung from metal stanchions like deadly stalactites, and those parts of the building still standing were peppered with shrapnel from the blast.

'Be careful,' said Louise through the earpiece, not caring how pointless the words were as the BDU stepped through the area, each a split second away from being killed by either the glass or a second explosion.

'Here,' said Robertson, appearing from nowhere and handing her a coffee.

Louise took one sniff and handed it back. 'No offence, sir, but that smells off.'

Robertson frowned and took the drink back, sniffing it as if Louise had lost her mind. 'Nothing wrong with this,' he said, pouring the contents into his cup. 'Janice Sutton and her team are here.'

'OK, I'll speak to them, but Adam says no one goes in until he's secured the area.'

With Robertson having being ever-present for the last couple of hours, Louise wondered at the absence of Tracey and Farrell. She'd hadn't spoken to Farrell since seeing him outside the courthouse where he'd obviously been working on something. They had their own cases but would usually have turned up for something like this by now. She realised she missed not only having them around, but Thomas as well. Even though both Farrell and Tracey had been at headquarters for some time now, the move out of Weston had changed the dynamic completely. Louise was used to change, especially in her working life, but part of her missed the old CID in Worle.

Even as she thought it, she realised that who she really missed was Thomas. Why was she so loath to accept that? She didn't have time to explore that question, her phone going off just as she reached Janice and the rest of the SOCOs.

'Blackwell,' she said, presuming the withheld number was work-related.

'DI Blackwell?' said the voice on the other end.

'Who is this?'

The caller was male, his voice modulated by some form of software. 'I think you know.'

Louise clicked her fingers, signalling Janice over. 'I think it's the offender,' she said, under her breath. 'Could you tell me your name?'

'You were warned. I've been lenient on you so far, but you haven't done what I asked of you.'

'You mean my resignation? What would that achieve?'

'This is your final chance. Resign now and there need be no more deaths.'

'Martyn, is that you? I can help,' said Louise, but the caller had already hung up.

Chapter Forty-Six

Farrell poured the last remnants of coffee from his flask and lamented his life decisions. He'd been tracking DS Perkins ever since his last meeting with Sinclair, and had spent the night on unofficial observation outside Perkins' house in Hartcliffe.

Perkins was nothing if not predictable. His life seemed to be an endless loop of routine: wake, work, pub, sleep, repeat. Twice already, Farrell was sure he could have pulled him over and arrested him for being drunk in charge of a motor vehicle. That Perkins could get up every morning after spending a good four or five hours in the local bar was a wonder, but here he was again shutting the front door behind him as he dragged himself to his car.

Farrell checked himself in the mirror before pulling away, noting he wasn't looking any better than his colleague. He'd managed to get a few minutes' sleep here and there during the night, waking every time a car engine started. It wasn't ideal, but the surveillance was unofficial and he was already at breaking point. His eyes were pitted with red lines and his reflection looked dazed, reminding him of photos he'd seen of himself when drunk.

'Morning,' he said, answering the call from Tracey. 'Perkins is on the move.'

'No movement here,' said Tracey, who'd been watching Sinclair. They'd decided they would watch the men until the end of the week and re-evaluate their options then. If it hadn't been for the involvement of Thomas, however tenuous that probably was, and his links with Louise, they would have done things differently. As it was, they were waiting to see what Perkins did next before deciding on their next move.

'And your handsome young man?' asked Farrell, smiling as Tracey groaned in response. Tracey had enlisted the help of her boyfriend, Sam, to watch over Thomas's ex-boss Trent Wheatley. Sam was a few years Tracey's junior, and Farrell was able to risk sending the occasional teasing comment her way, though he usually preferred doing it from the safe distance of a phone call.

'You're just jealous,' said Tracey. 'He's fine. Wheatley was up bright and early and is already at work. Nothing out of the ordinary yesterday. Are we going to keep this going for the rest of the day? I'm knackered.' This type of surveillance would usually involve a large number of officers. With just the three of them it was a thankless task that couldn't go on much longer.

'Looks like Perkins is headed back into court. We could switch targets?'

'I can last a few more hours if you can.'

'OK, let's reconvene at lunch or hopefully sooner,' said Farrell, hanging up.

He followed Perkins to a multi-storey car park near the centre. Parking outside, he was going to wait until Perkins made his way to the courthouse, when Tania Elliot pulled into the car park. Farrell rarely believed in coincidences and left his car to follow the journalist.

The more he dealt with her, the more he disliked Tania Elliot. He'd known her since she'd been a cub reporter on *The Mercury* and hardly recognised the person she'd become. Even Perkins wouldn't be stupid enough to trust her, but that didn't mean he wouldn't drip-feed her information. Farrell was amazed by some of the stuff she was getting away with. She'd done a hatchet job on Louise over the past week, and it was ratcheting everything up during Finch's trial. It was almost as if she wanted Finch to be found not guilty – and, blockbuster ending to her book or not, Farrell couldn't understand what was motivating her.

Farrell found the staircase as Tania headed up the first ramp. He decided to take a lift to the top floor and work his way down. If Perkins saw him then he could explain he was parking there before heading to the courthouse. It would be awkward but explicable.

He took a deep breath as the lift door opened, his lungs filling with the smell of stale nicotine and urine. Slipping out of the mobile prison, he stepped through the swing doors to the top of the building, thankful to get a bit of fresh air. He couldn't have timed it any better, Tania pulling into a space next to Perkins as Farrell walked in the opposite direction and pretended to tie his laces behind the cover of a black Land Rover.

He wasn't sure what he hoped to achieve. The top floor of the car park was a quarter full, and if he stepped out from behind the Land Rover he would be noticed. Ideally, he would have liked to get close enough to hear what they were talking about. Nowadays, clandestine meetings with journalists were actively discouraged. Everything was supposed to go directly through the press office. Such meetings still took place, but this was the second time he'd seen Perkins with Tania and, as far as Farrell could tell, there didn't seem to be a legitimate reason for them to be meeting.

He took photos as best he could, hoping that at some point they would come in useful. Tania and Perkins were close together. From Farrell's vantage point, it appeared that Perkins was encroaching on the journalist's personal space but Tania was holding her ground. Both were straight-faced, the only animation coming from Perkins' hand movements. Tania turned away, and Perkins pulled on her arm keeping his hand in place as she turned back to look at him. Tania shrugged his hand away as he reached for something inside the car to hand to her.

Tania shook her head just as Farrell was distracted by an incoming call on his phone. 'Shit,' he mumbled, keeping his eyes on the two as he answered.

'Greg, Wheatley is on the move. Looks like he's heading to Weston,' said Tracey.

Farrell had only turned away for a split second but had missed the chance to take a photo of Perkins handing something to Tania. 'Is Sam following?'

'As best he can.'

'OK, give me a few minutes and I'll get back to you,' said Farrell, hanging up as Tania got back in her car and drove off.

Ten minutes later, after watching Perkins enter the courthouse, he called Tracey back and explained what he'd seen.

'Did he definitely hand her something?' asked Tracey.

'I can't be sure. How is Sam doing?'

'Driving past Nailsea,' said Tracey. 'Look, I think we've got to the point where we need to go to Professional Standards about this. We've already done enough.'

Farrell agreed it was the sensible thing to do, though at this stage it had its own risks. The approach they'd taken was in itself highly unprofessional, and they would possibly face sanctions for their actions, however well meaning.

'Hang on,' said Tracey, interrupting his train of thought. 'Call coming in from Sam. I'll put you on conference.'

'He's just pulled up outside Tamar Road in Worle. He's leaving his car, and walking up the pathway.'

Farrell didn't need to check his notes to know the address. 'That's Thomas's house,' he said.

'Ringing the bell,' said Sam. 'This is the guy who sacked Thomas, right?'

'It's his company,' said Farrell.

'Hang on. He's taking something from his coat. Can't make it out, looks quite bulky. OK, he's posted it through the door and is heading back to his car. Shall I follow?'

'Fuck,' said Farrell, under his breath. What the hell was going on? 'Yes please, Sam,' he said, waiting until he'd hung up before speaking to Tracey. 'You know what this looks like?'

'Why would he sack Thomas, and then give him something?'

'Blackmail? A thank you?' said Farrell.

'We could pull Wheatley over and interrogate him?'

'That would blow everything open.'

'What else can we do?'

Farrell sighed. 'I need to locate Thomas, and give him the chance to explain himself,' he said. 'Give me an hour,' he added, hanging up before Tracey could convince him to take another course of action.

Chapter Forty-Seven

Louise did her best to ignore the flashing cameras, and the call of the journalists, as she headed into the courthouse. After the BDU had finally cleared the museum and surrounding area early in the morning, she'd driven home and spent a few uneasy hours half sleeping as her mind raced with thoughts of what could happen next.

It was a wonder that Hana Sanchez had been the only person to lose her life so far. Whether it was blind luck or not that had led them to the museum on time, she didn't know. They had been unable to track the call from the previous night but she was sure it had been Martyn Walton-Renwick. Maybe she was searching for things that weren't there, but hadn't there been a pleading quality to his request last night? Rather than tell her she must resign, it had been as if he was begging her. As if he was desperate not to cause any more damage than he'd already done.

She'd been dwelling on that question ever since. Her working theory was that Walton-Renwick was doing this for his father – that much felt obvious – but that his role was a reluctant one. She could understand the impact of not having a father growing up. In some twisted way, Walton-Renwick might see it as his duty to avenge his father's death. But if that was the case, why hadn't he targeted Louise more specifically? That he wanted her to resign, as some sort of punishment, suggested he didn't have the type of violent drive his father had possessed. That didn't mean he wouldn't strike again, but it gave her hope that if she could make contact with him he could be stopped.

Amira was waiting for her in the court canteen. She was going to be called to testify today, and with Louise being next on the call sheet there was a chance Louise would have to testify that day as well. Louise brought over two cups of tea and sat down opposite. From the bags under her eyes, it seemed Amira had had the same amount of sleep as her last night. Louise leaned across the table and placed her hand on Amira's. 'It's going to be OK,' she said.

Amira gave her a weak smile, and placed her free hand over Louise's before pulling back to drink her tea. 'I've been waiting for this for so long, it feels weird that we're almost at the end of it. In a way, I don't want it to be over. I'd rather he rotted on remand than have to suffer waiting for the jury to make its decision.'

'I understand. We both know what it's like waiting for a decision, but imagine how it's going to feel when he's put away for good.'

'If,' said Amira.

Louise understood her negativity. Everything had been leading to these last few days, and now that it was all a reality it was easy to focus on what could go wrong. 'All you have to do is tell the jury what happened. Antony has prepped you for the questions the defence team will ask. We both know they're grasping at straws. As long as you don't get rattled, you'll be fine, and Finch will go down for all this.'

Amira's smile was stronger this time, and she held Louise's gaze a little bit longer before Antony Meades approached and told them the court would shortly be in session.

Robertson was waiting in the corridor, looking like he'd made an effort with his suit. 'The museum is cleared,' he said, by way of greeting. 'It'll be some time before it's open for business again though.'

'You coming to watch the show, sir?'

'Thought I'd give you some moral support. And I'd like to look that fucker in the eye,' said Robertson, holding the court door open for her.

They sat in the front row of the viewing gallery, Robertson making a show of turning to Finch as he hobbled into view. 'How's that little niece of yours?' asked Robertson, turning back.

'She's fine. Hard to faze her nowadays. They had a memorial for Hana Sanchez yesterday at the school. I managed to drive her to school this morning, but haven't really spent any time with her for ages.'

'It can be hard at times. Give it a week and this will blow over. You must be owed some leave? When this bastard is put away you should go away for a couple of weeks.'

Louise briefly wondered if Robertson had been talking to Thomas, before dismissing the idea. It was a surprise that he was being so open with her, but she couldn't quite imagine him reaching out to talk to Thomas. 'Sounds great in practice.'

'Sounds great in reality. You'll be better for it,' said Robertson, as the clerk told them to stand.

As the jury filtered in, Louise speculated how many of them had been reading Tania's trash pieces about her over the last week. The journalist had managed to stay on the right side of what was permissible, shrewdly not going into too much detail about Finch's case. Everything she could get away with, she had, dragging Thomas through the mud about the incident in Thornbury – today's paper also leaking the story that he had been fired – questioning Louise's handling of the current attacks in Weston, and highlighting her role in Max Walton's death. Louise knew she was biased, but nothing Tania wrote appeared to be balanced. Certain rules prevented her from going into too much detail about Finch's case, but she had barely mentioned his role in Max Walton's death and the subsequent fallout. That would probably all change when Finch was found guilty, but at present it was as if Tania wanted to see Finch go free.

Amira held her shoulders up as she walked to the witness box. Louise had reminded her how strong she'd been on so many occasions. They had reached this position because of her determination, and Amira had only to access that resolve and she wouldn't have anything to worry about.

The young woman did her proud as Amanda Knight set out the case against Finch. It was difficult hearing Amira's testimony, from the initial period when she'd first started seeing Finch, to the final moments in his house where she had been tied up and thought she was going to die.

Louise stole looks at Finch as Amira detailed the last harrowing moments of that evening, when Louise had arrived and confronted Finch, their clash ending in Finch's broken leg. She could almost hear the sound of his bone breaking as Amira recounted the kick Louise had given to Finch. She stifled a smile at the memory.

Amanda Knight sat down as Charles Boothroyd took centre stage. This would be the real test for Amira. Louise nodded in encouragement as Amira primed herself for the onslaught. Meades and Knight had already prepped Amira and Louise for everything Boothroyd could ask, but no amount of training could fully prepare a witness for the pressure of being cross-examined in front of a jury.

Boothroyd continued in the same vein he had throughout the case, coming across as compassionate and understanding. He questioned Amira over her relationship with Finch, getting her to admit that she had been happy with him at one point and also that she had agreed for him to take salacious pictures of her – omitting the part where Finch had later used the same pictures to blackmail her. Boothroyd was never forceful, giving Amira time to answer his questions.

It was only when it came to the point when Amira had told the court that Finch had tried to force her to leave the police that the barrister's approach changed. It was a subtle shift in tone, his voice dropping ever so slightly as his questions became more urgent, his patience for Amira's responses wavering. 'I put it to you that the reason you were asked to leave had nothing to do with your relationship with Mr Finch,' he said.

'That's not true,' said Amira.

'The truth is you were out of your depth in the workplace, reflected in the fact that you have subsequently left the police.'

'No.'

'And that you were reeling from Mr Finch breaking up your relationship, a relationship that you have just admitted you were very happy in.'

'I was happy to begin with—'

'By your admittance you consented to the pictures Mr Finch took of you.'

'I didn't consent to—'

'And when he ended your relationship, you felt humiliated and useless and decided to hatch a plan against Mr Finch.'

'Don't be ridiculous.'

'Mr Finch, in your own words, was "a very popular man in the office", had a number of ex-relationships, and you decided to manipulate his former partner as a means of getting your own back at him.'

Amira stood with her mouth open, dumbfounded, and wasn't given the chance to answer.

'I put it to you, that you approached Detective Louise Blackwell and together you hatched a plan to force Mr Finch from his position as DCI. And when things didn't work out for you, you took things a bit further.'

'That's not the case—'

'I put it to you, Ms Hood,' said Boothroyd, his voice now at full volume, 'that on the night in question you and Louise Blackwell set out to attack Mr Finch, and had the police not arrived in time, his broken leg would have been the least of his injuries. You were once suspended on a charge of unlawful use of physical force during an arrest, is that not the case?'

Amira looked confused, muttering that she was cleared of the charge as Amanda Knight shouted, 'Objection.'

'Sustained,' said the judge.

'But it is the case that DI Blackwell was responsible for the death of an unarmed civilian, is it not?'

'Objection,' screamed Knight, but Louise could tell the doubt had already been placed in the jurors' minds.

'Mr Boothroyd, are we going to get to our point?' asked the judge.

'Yes, Your Honour,' said Boothroyd, milking every second for what it was worth, glancing at every gawping face on the jury before turning his attention back to Amira. 'Is it not the case, Ms Hood, that it isn't Mr Finch who should be standing here accused of attempted murder, but you and DI Louise Blackwell?'

Chapter Forty-Eight

Farrell was not so egocentric that he couldn't admit he was out of his depth. He should never have involved Tracey, and inadvertently Sam, with his off-the-books surveillance. Especially now, through sheer fluke, that it appeared as though Thomas might be a suspect once more.

Setting his friendship with Thomas aside, Farrell tried to make sense of the situation. It was feasible Thomas had been involved from the beginning, but why had Trent Wheatley sacked him only to deliver something to his house? Farrell didn't know for sure what had been posted through the door, but he doubted it was redundancy papers.

He parked up and walked to the courthouse. He had to run things by Louise. She would be annoyed that they had conducted an unauthorised surveillance operation, but he needed to let her know what had happened with Thomas.

Finch's case had resumed for the day by the time he arrived, and he sat at the back of the viewing gallery, Louise a few rows in front watching the former police officer Amira Hood give her testimony. The night Finch had cracked and nearly killed Amira had been a turning point for the whole department. Finch had recruited him directly from Weston, but Farrell's loyalty had always been with Louise. With Finch gone, and the Weston team relocating, headquarters had become a completely different place in which to work. There was an optimism he hadn't noticed before, and it wasn't until Finch had been sent on remand that Farrell had truly understood the man's negative impact on everything he came in contact with. And with Perkins also in attendance, Farrell wondered how much of a role Finch had to play in these recent developments.

Farrell realised he'd made a mistake when Finch's barrister began cross-examining Amira. It was clear he was trying to turn the tables on her and Louise, and the last thing he wanted to do was burden Louise with any more worries. He left the courthouse after the barrister accused Amira and Louise of plotting against Finch, not wanting to hear any more of the nonsense.

Outside, he decided to call Thomas and confront him directly about what he'd seen.

'I feel like I've spoken more to you since I stopped being a copper than I ever did when I was one.'

'Sorry to bother you, Thomas. Up to anything interesting?'

Farrell heard a split second of hesitation before Thomas answered. 'I'm a man of leisure at the moment, as you know. Just dropped Noah off at school. Might go crazy and grab a coffee later. Why?' said Thomas, clearly suspicious.

What Farrell really wanted to know was whether or not Thomas was home yet, but he couldn't come out directly and ask that. 'I know it's a pain but I need you to come in later. Talk over a few things.'

'Something you're not telling me, Greg?'

'No, just the normal shit.'

The hesitation was there again. Farrell didn't know if it was because he was hiding something, or if he was pissed off at the inconvenience. 'I'm picking Noah up later, now that I don't have a job. I could come over now or . . .'

'After will be fine. I'm not in the office anyway. Sometime after four thirty p.m.?'

'All right,' said Thomas, hanging up.

◆ ◆ ◆

Tracey was less than pleased when he told her about the conversation. 'What are you going to do, ask if he's had anything interesting posted through his door of late?' she asked, as they sat together in the staff canteen at headquarters.

'Any better suggestions?'

'Yes. We go straight to Standards, tell them what we know about Perkins and let them sort this out. If we don't, Greg, it will be them coming after us.'

◆ ◆ ◆

Ten minutes later it seemed the decision had been made for them. They were heading back to the CID when Robertson rushed past them, having returned from the courthouse. 'You haven't heard?' he said, taking them aside.

'What, sir?' said Tracey, as Farrell checked his phone.

'Some anonymous tip-off has come in about Thomas.'

Farrell glanced at Tracey, sensing everything slipping away from them. 'What sort of tip-off?' said Tracey, keeping her eyes focused on Robertson.

'I'm trying to find out. I'm being kept out of the loop and I don't know why. A team has been sent to his house now. Have you heard from him today?'

'I spoke to him earlier,' said Farrell.

'Did you?'

'Just wanted to update him on the drug case.'

Robertson nodded, then said, 'What the fuck?'

Farrell looked around to see Thomas walking up the stairs, a guest pass around his neck. 'I thought my ears were burning,' he said.

'You're early,' said Farrell.

'Yes, well, I got Rebecca to pick up Noah. Can we talk?'

Farrell looked at Robertson, who said, 'I'll leave you to it. Good to see you, Thomas.'

'Come on,' said Farrell, guiding him to an interview room.

'Can you come as well, Tracey?' asked Thomas.

'Sure,' said Tracey, as if nothing was the matter.

The second they stepped through the door, Thomas dropped a plastic package on the desk. 'Is this why you were so eager to talk to me on the phone earlier?' he said.

'What is that?' said Farrell.

'This is what was left at my house. I found it not long after we spoke to one another.' Thomas opened the bag to reveal six tightly wrapped bundles of fifty-pound notes. 'Sixty thousand pounds,' he said.

Chapter Forty-Nine

It was one of those picture-perfect Weston days Louise remembered from her childhood. Her memory was distorted that way because her parents only used to take her and Paul to the seaside town when the weather was like this: the clear blue sky an indication that the day was going to be full of brilliant June sunshine.

After Amira's testimony had run until after lunch on Thursday, the judge had taken the decision to adjourn for the weekend. Amira had left the witness box, shaken and furious at the approach the defence team had taken. Both Meades and Knight had shrugged off her concerns, but Louise had sensed some indecision in them, as if they hadn't been expecting the switch of tactics.

It was now 6 a.m. on Saturday, and Louise hadn't yet had a chance to buy the day's newspapers, but the court reporting was already out online and the defence's counter-accusation against Amira and Louise was now public.

Louise was sitting in the garden of the house she shared with her parents and Emily, drinking a cup of builder's tea and eating dry toast. She was alone, save for the manic energy of Molly who was using the rare opportunity of being alone with Louise to bring her different toys as a means to encourage her to play.

The rest of Thursday and Friday had been spent scouring the CCTV images from the museum in an attempt to find the person responsible, and attending meetings with top brass and members of the local council as they decided whether or not to proceed with the weekend's air show.

It had been a tough decision, but it was only ever going to go one way. There was too much effort involved to cancel the event, and even with the incident at the museum, the consensus was they couldn't be seen to be giving into threats of terrorism.

By yesterday evening, confirmation had come in that the device used in the museum had been of a similar type to that used at the school. All available resources were being utilised to find Walton-Renwick, but after the rashness of him showing his identification at the youth hostel, he'd gone back to being elusive.

Thirty minutes later, Louise was in the centre of Weston organising the teams of uniformed officers from both headquarters and numerous local stations, who would be searching as much of the town centre as they could for signs of IEDs before the crowds descended. The main focus was on the beach lawns behind the promenade, and the beach itself including the Tropicana building, where events would take place later.

For now, all they could do was make sure nothing had been placed in advance. Once the area was as secure as it could be, they could turn their attention to containing the thousands who would descend on Weston that day.

Louise had the help of the specialist search teams who began organising everything. Sniffer dogs had been brought in, and two helicopters were sweeping the area and would remain a constant presence over the weekend.

It wasn't long before the crowds started rolling in. The air show brought tourists from all over the country, and with the promise of good weather for the weekend many had arrived early in the week. People were already out making the most of the sunshine.

The beaches were busy, the outdoor cafés and bars doing a roaring trade as anticipation built.

Despite the obvious police presence, and the explosion at the museum, everyone seemed oblivious to the potential threat. Louise had never ceased to be amazed at the extent to which certain parts of the population could put their own enjoyment ahead of other concerns, but now it was as if everyone was oblivious. Families walked hand in hand along the promenade, groups of teenagers played cricket on the sand, and younger adults gathered in the beer gardens on the front drinking as if it was early evening, and not just before lunch.

Louise made her way to the beach next to the old aquarium, which was now a restaurant, where the first event was due to be held. She was on constant alert, looking out not only for Walton-Renwick but for signs of anything suspicious. The metal pylons beneath the old aquarium had been checked and uniformed police were positioned there. Bag searches were being conducted as people entered the beach, and Louise was sure everything had been covered, but still it was a difficult hour watching the event.

It was hard not to expect an explosion to ring out at any second, and Louise felt every muscle in her body tense as a car backfired while she was crossing the road. It was going to be a long weekend, and the first airplane had yet to take to the sky.

That happened forty minutes later, and one by one a number of vintage aircraft passed over the seafront. As the first plane flew overhead, its engine a low growl, it became apparent that the air show was the perfect distraction. As she looked around, nearly every face was turned upwards – the police and emergency services included – creating a number of opportunities to plant a device.

Once the first plane disappeared towards Brean, Louise radioed through to the team leaders to explain, giving the instructions that all police officers should maintain their eyes away from the sky at all times.

As the fifth plane of the day – the T67 Firefly – took to the skies, Louise received a call from one of the team leaders on the north side of the seafront. 'Sorry to bother you, ma'am, thought you'd want to know. We appear to have a potential jumper on top of the Weston College building on Knightstone Road. Looks to be a single white male. Early twenties. Currently sitting down on the cusp of the roof, feet dangling over the edge. Emergency teams have been dispatched.'

Louise let out a sigh, her head falling to her shoulder. It was probably nothing, while being a distraction she could do without. 'Eyes down,' she said to a pair of uniformed officers as she made her way back down the promenade, dodging groups of tourists blocking her path, staring wide-eyed into the sky as if UFOs were circling above them.

An ambulance and fire engine turned on to the seafront and made slow progress as Louise walked past the Grand Pier, which was lined with eagle-eyed tourists watching the air show. The Firefly plane made another lap of the area while she rounded the corner into Knightstone Road. Despite her earlier warnings, Louise couldn't help but look up at the plane. She wondered again if that was how it would happen. Everyone distracted by the planes, and the offender dropping the device and setting it off before anyone had a chance to react.

A team was already set up by the time she reached the college. Once more she looked up, this time to the sight of a man sitting on the ledge of the building that was ten storeys high. A former colleague of Louise's, Inspector Baker, was currently organising everyone. He didn't hide his surprise at seeing her. 'Louise. I thought you would be busy with the air show,' he said.

Baker was relatively new to the Weston team. When he'd joined, they had clashed over his approach to policing in the town. His remit had been to rid Weston of some of its more anti-social problems, and he'd gone about it with an evangelical zeal that at times had hindered her investigations. The clash was forgotten now, but she still had the sense that Baker saw himself as being above her somehow. 'You know how it is, Dan, thought I could do with a break. Do we have a name for him yet?'

Baker scowled as if disappointed by her comment. 'We have someone on the way to the roof now,' he said, handing her a pair of binoculars.

Louise took the binoculars and held them to the roof, blinking as she accidentally caught the glare of the sun. Adjusting, she alighted on the figure, and played with the zoom until she could make out the man's face. 'Dan, you may want to hold back on sending anyone up there,' she said, handing the binoculars back as she accessed a photo on her phone.

'Why?' said Baker.

Louise showed him the photo. 'I think our jumper is Martyn Walton-Renwick.'

Chapter Fifty

The evacuation started immediately as extra police were called in to do a sweep of the building. It was no easy task with over ten floors and numerous offices and classrooms.

Louise called Robertson after notifying Adam King who was on standby in the area.

'You sure it's him?' said Robertson.

'Same face as the passport photo. We are trying to get a phone to him now so I can talk to him.'

'What the hell is he playing at?' said Robertson, to himself. 'I'm on my way.'

Another plane flew by as Louise lifted her binoculars once more to Walton-Renwick. His face was unreadable as he stared blankly into the distance.

Thankfully, it was a Saturday, and the building only had a skeleton staff working, with a few students using the library and IT facilities. But what if Walton-Renwick's plan had been to draw everyone here so he could set off an explosion? With so many people in the surrounding area and still in the building, the damage could be catastrophic.

For the first time, she saw a hint of emotion in his face, as he turned to look behind him with a panicked expression.

'Martyn? Is it Martyn?' came the voice of one of the team on Louise's radio.

'Go away, or I will jump now,' said Walton-Renwick.

'I can help you, Martyn.'

'Now,' screamed Walton-Renwick, getting to his feet as everyone below held their breath.

'OK, Martyn, OK,' said the voice. Louise pictured the officer backing away as he added, 'I'm just going to leave this here for you. There is a pre-installed number. You can call me at any time.'

Walton-Renwick disappeared from Louise's sightline for a second. On the radio, she heard him speak as he presumably picked up the phone. 'Blackwell,' he said.

Seconds later he returned to the edge of the roof, the thinning crowd gasping once more as he took a seat, the phone in his hand.

Louise asked Baker for the number.

'Do you think this is wise?' he said.

'Do you have any better ideas? He asked to speak to me. He's sitting on the edge of the building, and he's more than likely responsible for a number of recent explosions in the area. This is connected to me, you know that. He's Max Walton's son, for Christ's sake.' Louise was surprised to find herself shaking with rage. 'I killed his father, Dan,' she said, through gritted teeth. 'You want to tell him no?'

Baker shot her a reluctant look before giving her the number. She didn't waste any time, connecting her phone to her earpiece so she could continue watching Walton-Renwick through the binoculars.

Walton-Renwick stared at the phone in his hand as if confused by its being there. 'Yes,' he said, answering.

Listening in on the radio, and hearing his demand to speak to her, Louise had thought he'd sounded in control and sure of himself, but her opinion changed the second he answered. He sounded distant and confused, and her first thought was that he was on something. 'Martyn, this is DI Louise Blackwell. You can call me Louise.'

'Louise,' said Walton-Renwick, slowly, as if testing the name.

'Martyn, I'm here to help you. We're really worried about you. Would it be possible to step away from the edge of the building?'

Louise saw Walton-Renwick smile as another plane flew by, the illusion created by the binoculars making it appear as if the man could reach out and touch the plane. 'I like it up here,' he said. 'Where have all the planes come from?'

Walton-Renwick's slurred speech and slow responses were enough to convince her that he had taken some sort of drug. He was gazing into the sky and didn't appear to know what was going on. In one way that could be a positive if it meant he would be too incapacitated to take any further action, but if he'd already set up an IED in the college then all it could take was the running down of a timer or a call from another mobile phone to set it off, and considering he was sitting at the top of a lethal drop, it appeared he didn't care too much at this point about his own life. 'It's the air show this weekend, Martyn, remember? Why don't you come down now?'

'You killed my dad,' said Walton-Renwick, still staring out at the procession of three Spitfire planes.

Goosebumps prickled Louise's skin at the comment. 'We can talk about that, Martyn.'

'What is there to talk about. You killed him. I thought I hated you for that,' he added, his words drifting away from him.

'Martyn, please come down. I can help you, I promise.'

'I wanted to be like him, you know. But I'm not,' he said, getting to his feet.

'Martyn,' said Louise, more urgent now as Robertson arrived and stood next to Baker, his eyes drawn to the wobbling figure on the top of the building.

'I'm not like any of them,' said Walton-Renwick, stepping off the roof and falling, in what looked like slow motion, to the ground.

Chapter Fifty-One

The majority of the bystanders had already left the scene before Martyn took his walk over the edge, but those still behind the police cordon stared in disbelief, having witnessed something that would stay with them forever. Even Louise was momentarily stunned, the phone she'd been speaking to Walton-Renwick on by her side as she lowered the binoculars.

It would have only been a couple of seconds, but it felt like she'd been standing there for an age next to Robertson and Baker, who were equally as shocked, before she clicked into action, running towards the area where Walton-Renwick had landed.

She didn't hold out any hope, and one glance at the impossible angle of the fallen body was enough to tell her that Walton-Renwick was no longer with them. She stopped in her tracks, calling the line that would need to be kept until the SOCOs arrived. While it was clear Walton-Renwick had taken his own life, he'd been intoxicated at the time and she couldn't rule out the possibility that he had somehow been coerced. She was reminded of one of her earlier cases in Weston when she had investigated a suicide cult where young women had been induced to take their own lives. This felt different, but she wasn't going to take any chances, especially considering Walton-Renwick's final words: *I'm not like any of them.*

'*Them?*' she said to Robertson, as a pair of uniformed officers secured the area surrounding Walton-Renwick's broken body.

'I heard it. Maybe he meant Karl Insgrove?' said Robertson.

'I think that is a given, but he said *them*, not *him*. There must be someone else.'

'He could be referencing his father? As in, he's not the same as Insgrove and his dad. *Them?*'

Louise shook her head. 'No, I don't think this is over. We need to go through every inch of that building,' she said, thinking that an explosion could go off at any second, like at the museum.

Them. Was it possible Walton-Renwick had been working with Insgrove from the beginning? He'd told her that he'd come to realise he wasn't like his father, but what had he set in process before taking his life? 'I need to see Joanne Harrison,' said Louise, thinking the headteacher would be the only one to know if Insgrove had contact with Walton-Renwick.

Robertson didn't argue, and Louise was heading back to her parked car when she caught sight of one of the bystanders watching from the sidelines. 'Justin Walton,' said Louise, under her breath.

Walton-Renwick's cousin must have noticed he'd been spotted, for as Robertson turned to look, he began backing away. 'Stop that man,' shouted Louise to the officer guarding the tape as she began moving towards Justin, who'd started running up Lower Church Road.

The uniformed officer gave chase. Louise took Wadham Street hoping to cut Walton off at Grove Park. Part of working in the same town for so long was knowing where all the previous crimes had been committed. Although she'd only been in Weston for a few years, she carried a catalogue of crimes in her head. She could enter nearly any street in the town and know what had previously happened there. Grove Park was no exception. Her arm began to itch as she recalled the man who'd been attacked in the park by the same person who'd given her the scar; the same person she'd chased to the top of the park only to have them disappear into the shadows.

Justin Walton wasn't going to be as lucky. His head was turned, searching for the uniformed officer who'd been chasing him, and he didn't see Louise coming. He'd only reached the bandstand when Louise caught up with him. As another Spitfire passed by low ahead, distracting Walton further, she didn't waste any time, launching herself at the man.

Walton was winded by the attack, but Louise wasn't taking any chances. As the uniformed officer caught up, Louise turned Walton on to his side. She cuffed him and read him his rights before asking, 'Now Justin, would you like to tell me what the hell is going on?'

Chapter Fifty-Two

They should have been in Weston helping Louise and the others with the bomb threat, but instead they were camped outside Oblong Distribution's headquarters in Bristol going through last-minute preparations. Farrell could see everyone was on edge and he was doing his best to manage the situation.

After Thomas had come into the station and dumped the £60k on the desk, Farrell had been forced to get Robertson involved. Telling the DCI what had been happening over the last few days had been one of the hardest things he'd ever done, and it had been compounded by having Tracey in the office with him.

'I would have expected better from both of you,' Robertson had said, the disappointment in the low rumble of his Glaswegian accent a hundred times worse than any bollocking he could have given them. As it was, he'd let them continue, but now it was an official case. Eddie Perkins was on the Ghost Squad's watch list and DS Kent Mooney from the team was with them as they carried out last-minute checks on Thomas's wire.

'You ready?' said Farrell.

'Are you?' said Thomas. They couldn't have asked for a better person to be going in for them. They'd explained the surveillance on Perkins and Sinclair that had led them to Thomas's old boss,

Wheatley. Thomas was still angry about it but didn't appear to be taking it personally.

'Remember, you can stop it at any time and we'll be there in seconds,' said Tracey, brushing down Thomas's collar as if she was sending him off to an interview.

Thomas frowned and walked towards the business centre. 'I feel like shit,' said Tracey, as he walked away.

'You hear this?' said Thomas, testing the one-way wire, the decision not to let Thomas have an earpiece a safety precaution.

'It's not great, but what else could we have done? We had no way of knowing Thomas would get this involved,' said Farrell.

'Louise doesn't even know.'

'She has enough to deal with at the moment.'

'That's hardly the point, Greg, is it. They're obviously going through some sort of difficulty and here we are using Thomas as bait.'

Farrell rubbed his forehead. She was right. He'd got carried away with the operation and was now risking his friendship with Thomas, and his professional relationship with Louise, and by the looks of it, with Tracey as well.

'Oh, hi Tom,' came a female voice, caught on the small transmitter under Thomas's collar.

'Hi Jane. Is he in?'

'Umm, I'll check.'

'No need,' said Thomas. A few beats passed as he must have made his way to Wheatley's office.

'Tom, good to see you. What brings you here on a Saturday?'

'Cut the shit, Trent.'

'Jane, could you get security in here,' said Wheatley.

'Do that and I go straight to the police.'

'The police, Tom? I think maybe you should be looking for your job back, don't you?'

'Balls on this guy,' said Tracey.

'If anyone comes in here, I'm going to the police about the £60k you left for me at my house.'

There was a pause. Farrell would have loved to see Wheatley's reaction. 'I don't know what the hell you're talking about.'

'I have security cameras at my house, you dipshit,' said Thomas.

This time, Farrell could picture the scene as Wheatley began to panic. 'Not to worry, Jane. Look, I don't know what to say. I felt bad the way things had been left with us and wanted to give you a little something.'

'Oh, fuck off, Trent. Stop wasting my time. Why did you do it? Is there some sort of evidence on the money? Something linking me to more drugs. Who put you up to it?'

'I don't—'

'Stop,' said Thomas. 'The police are after me. They know about the money. Now, you need to tell me who is trying to set me up and why.'

'No one is trying to set you up. They wanted to buy your silence. Eliminate you so you couldn't cause any trouble. I'm sorry, Tom, I'm over my head here.'

'Why did you hire me when all this shit was going on?'

'That's the thing, I didn't know anything about it. A few of the team have been using our vans to deliver stuff and they pissed off the wrong guys.'

'Why did they come after me?' said Thomas.

'I don't know. I think it's to do with your old colleague.'

The line went silent, and Farrell grew concerned that Thomas was going to go for Wheatley. 'Louise?' he said, eventually.

'I know you're seeing her, I'm sorry. They gave me the money, told me to drop it at your place. They threatened my family, Tom. I had to do it.'

'Who?'

'I can't give you any names.'

'You tell me, let me deal with it my way, or you tell the police.'

'There's two of them I know. Sinclair and this other guy, don't know his name.'

'Anyone else? If I find out any different then it won't end well for you.'

'Jesus. One of your lot,' said Wheatley, the pleading voice changing to something much sterner.

'Who?' said Thomas.

'Perkins, OK? Eddie fucking Perkins.'

Farrell let out a breath. 'Everyone, go,' he said, over the radio.

Chapter Fifty-Three

Justin Walton made an elaborate show of catching his breath. Louise watched him dispassionately as he coughed and spluttered his way to speaking. After all that, his first word was 'What?'

Louise hoisted the man to his feet, using the cuffs on his wrists as leverage. Walton groaned at the manoeuvre, coughing again as he bent over. She waited until he'd composed himself and had stood back up straight. One look at his eyes, and she could tell he was still on something. His pupils had contracted so much they were like tiny dots on his eyeballs. 'What have you taken, Justin?'

'What haven't I taken?' said Walton, giggling to himself.

It felt pointless trying to reason with the man in this state, but back at the college a team of officers were risking their lives clearing the building when any second a bomb could rip through the structure. 'I saw you at the scene. Your cousin was there. Did you see him, Justin? Did you see him jump?'

'I saw him,' said Walton, suddenly straight-faced as if he'd been shocked sober.

'Were you here with him?' asked Louise, wondering what the hell had happened to the surveillance on Max Walton's nephew.

'No.'

'You just happened to be walking by?'

'No, but . . .'

'What, Justin? Why were you there?'

'I was trying to stop him, OK?'

'You knew he wanted to kill himself?'

'He called me last night. He was out of it. I didn't understand what he was talking about. Said something about not being like them.'

'Who was he talking about?'

'How the hell would I know. Listen, I don't even know the lad. We were friends on Facebook before he turned up here. I said I'd meet up with him when he came to the UK and gave him my phone number. I knew him when he was a kid, but I don't know why he called me last night beyond him being my cousin.'

Louise didn't think it was an act. She didn't believe Justin had the mental dexterity to pull off such a story, and definitely not when he was in his current state. 'Why are you here then?'

'I was supposed to meet him, wasn't I. In the park. Said we'd go for a few drinks. I get here and notice all the commotion and walk over to see him dangling over the edge of the college.'

'And you stayed for the show?'

Walton stepped back as if she'd insulted him. 'He was my cousin. There wasn't much I could do, but the least I could do was be there for him. I prayed he wouldn't jump.'

He sounded so sincere that Louise felt sorry for him. 'I need to take you in for questioning, Justin, but you could really help me by answering some of them right now.'

'Can I sit down? I feel sick.'

Louise nodded at her colleague to help Walton to the ground. He sat there for a few seconds, his head between his legs. 'Who was Martyn working with?' she said, as he looked back up at her.

Walton shrugged his shoulders, his movement curtailed by his cuffs. 'I told you before, I don't know nothing about any of this.'

'People have died, Justin. And I am worried more could die as a result of what Martyn has done. I know he wasn't working alone.'

'I told you, I don't know. What about that caretaker guy? He offed himself as well. Maybe it was him.'

Nothing beyond the vague link of Karl Insgrove being in the Falklands with Max Walton linked him to Walton's son. That they had now both killed themselves suggested a link beyond that, but the answer felt further away than ever.

As Justin Walton was driven back to Portishead, Louise returned to the scene where Martyn Walton-Renwick's body lay at its impossible angle. Janice Sutton and the SOCOs were managing the scene. Louise asked Janice to inform her if any suicide note was found, before heading back to headquarters.

Above her planes still flew overhead, and the tourists roamed the lawns and streets of Weston, oblivious to what had just happened. It would be easy to lose focus with Walton-Renwick out of the picture, but as Louise messaged the team leaders to update them, she reminded them to be as vigilant as ever. She reiterated Walton-Renwick's use of the word *them*, reminding everyone that the risk was far from over.

◆ ◆ ◆

The full greeting party was waiting for her back in Portishead. DCI Robertson had driven ahead and was sitting with Assistant Chief Constable Brightman and the two officers from CTU.

Louise stood up straight as she walked into the office. She was drained and had been lacking in energy recently, but wasn't about to let it show.

'The positives are, we are one day down and, so far, no further explosions,' said Brightman, as Louise took a seat.

301

'And one less potential suspect,' said Robertson, so straight-faced that it was hard for his fellow officers to tell if he was commenting on Walton-Renwick's death with gallows humour or not.

The ACC paused, as if letting that information settle, before continuing. 'You exchanged words with Justin Walton when you arrested him?' he asked Louise.

Louise relayed the conversation she'd had with Max Walton's nephew. 'He claims he was meeting Martyn for a drink. He seemed quite shell-shocked, but he had definitely taken something.'

DI Faulkner smiled and Louise felt her stomach turn. 'Walton-Renwick's last words were "I'm not like any of them"?' he said.

'That seems to be the consensus,' said Louise, wondering at her negative reaction to Faulkner's smile.

'And we think *them* relates to . . . ?' asked the ACC.

'That's what we need to ascertain. Possibly Karl Insgrove. But *them* obviously suggests more than one person,' said Louise.

'Max Walton?' said Faulkner. 'His dad.'

Louise stopped short of sarcastically thanking Faulkner for clarifying the relationship between Max Walton and his son. 'Could be. Could be he meant his cousin, Justin Walton. Or someone else.'

Louise peeled away from the meeting and made herself some white tea in the canteen. She needed to compose herself before speaking to Justin Walton again, had to work out a strategy to gain his trust and information. Three people were dead due to recent events, and every time she heard the sound of a phone ringing, she expected to be informed about another explosion.

'Everything OK?' said Robertson, making her jump.

'Jesus, Iain, don't sneak up on me.'

Robertson's lips parted into something resembling a smile. 'You want me to sit in on this interview with Walton?'

'You think I'm not up to the job?' said Louise, regretting her words instantly.

Robertson didn't even react. 'Could be good to have someone to fall back on. To ask the questions that might piss him off.'

Louise nodded. 'Sorry, you're right, that would be good.'

'What the hell is that you're drinking?' asked Robertson, glancing at her cup.

'White tea?'

Robertson's forehead broke out in lines. 'Fucking white tea?' he said, under his breath. 'Don't let the others know you're drinking that shite or they'll put you away,' he added, wincing as he drank the lukewarm coffee that had been out for hours.

◆ ◆ ◆

Justin Walton failed to make eye contact as Louise entered the interview room with Robertson. He was sitting scrunched up in his chair, as if trying to hide behind his body. As Louise started the interview, introducing those present including the duty solicitor appointed to him, Justin Walton looked up at her. The contracted look of his pupils had faded and it was clear he was coming down from whatever drugs he'd taken.

The red light of the camera caught Louise's peripheral vision as she began questioning Martyn Walton-Renwick's cousin. 'When was the last time you saw Martyn?' she asked.

'Haven't seen him since we were children. I told you that. I only knew him from Facebook.'

'How old were you when you last saw him?'

'I must have been thirteen or something. He was a few years younger than me. There was some sort of family get-together. Over in . . .' Justin's voice petered out, as if he'd lost track of his thoughts.

'Over where?' said Louise, trying to imagine what such a dysfunctional family get-together would look like.

'The farm,' said Justin, glancing at his solicitor as if pleading for forgiveness.

Louise kept her eyes straight ahead as the farmyard smells of excrement and decay seemed to drift through the air while she recalled that night she'd been at the farm with Finch.

'You're talking about Max Walton's farm?' said Robertson.

Justin nodded. He could have offered a dig at Louise at that point, could have reminded her how she'd shot his unarmed uncle, but either through fear or consideration he didn't make a comment.

'You've been in contact with him since, via social media?' said Louise.

'Not really. I'd see the odd post about his life in South Africa on Facebook, but that's it.'

'But you knew he was coming back?' said Robertson.

'I already told you this,' said Justin, finding his voice out of nowhere.

Robertson furrowed his brow. 'You taking that tone with me, son? With all the trouble you're in?' he said, as Justin shrank back into his chair.

'You know about what's been happening in Weston,' said Louise. 'The explosion and fire.'

'You question me after every incident, so of course I do.'

'Why do you think Martyn would have been involved in that?'

'You'll have to ask him, won't you?'

'Let me remind you, Mr Walton, three people are dead, one of whom was murdered, and you are currently our number one living suspect,' said Robertson.

'What?' said Justin, the sound coming out as a high-pitched squeal, as it dawned on him how much trouble he was in.

'You're the only link we have,' said Louise. 'In fact, it all started with you, didn't it?'

'What do you mean?' said Justin, looking pleadingly at the duty solicitor who appeared shell-shocked by developments.

'Nearly two weeks ago, I find out you're planning a civil case against me on behalf of the Walton family. Not long after, we're receiving bomb threats demanding I leave my position as detective inspector.'

'Going to be difficult to explain that one away,' said Robertson. 'Especially with your little cousin dead.'

'Fuck off,' said Justin, before adding: 'Sorry, sorry. Listen, I admit the court case idea may have come from Martyn. He sent me all the details about how to proceed before he arrived. I didn't really know what I was doing.'

'He emailed you?'

'Facebook Messenger.'

Louise looked at Robertson.

'Anyway, there is no case anymore. I dropped it.'

'Why did you drop it?' said Louise.

'It was bringing me too much trouble. The solicitors were hassling me about cash, and Martyn wasn't answering his calls.'

'Why didn't you tell us this before?'

'I don't know. I wasn't doing anything wrong. You did shoot my uncle you know,' said Justin, squirming as the words left his mouth.

'You agreed to meet Martyn today?' said Robertson.

'Yes.'

'When was that agreed?' asked Louise.

'He called me last night. Out of the blue, said he was in the area and wanted to meet for a drink.'

'Where did you agree to meet?'

'On the seafront to watch the planes, that sort of thing.'

'Was that before or after you planted the next device?' said Louise.

'Oh, come on.'

'He wasn't working alone, Justin, was he?'

'Well, he wasn't working with me. I told you, after the solicitor stuff he didn't answer any messages until last night. That caretaker, he's the one. He was at that school. They were working together by the sounds of it.'

'But why?' asked Louise.

'I don't know. It wasn't anything to do with me.'

Louise rubbed her eyes. 'You want some time alone with your solicitor, Justin?'

Justin frowned. 'No, why?'

'Come on, you must know how this looks? You've set all this in motion, Justin. It's obvious. You launch a civil case against me, then try to get me to resign. Somehow you get Karl Insgrove involved. I imagine you were selling Insgrove drugs and he owed you a favour perhaps? You hear Martyn is coming over, so you enlist his help?'

'What? I don't understand. Why would I do this? Why would I hurt those people? I'm not like them.'

Louise stood up straight as Justin lowered his face. 'Who aren't you like, Justin?'

'Whoever has done all this. Martyn, and that caretaker bloke.'

'I don't think that was what you meant, son, was it?' said Robertson.

Justin raised his head. His eyes were blood red, pricked with tears. 'I'm not like Uncle Max, that was what I meant.'

'You said *them*,' said Louise.

'You think Max was the only one? He was fucking depraved, man, they all were.'

'What are you trying to tell us, Justin. Are there members of your family who were involved with Max Walton and his killings?'

'Family? Probably, I don't know. You know the shit he was into. It wasn't just the killings. They were into some horrible stuff. I've tried to blank it out as best I could, but I saw some of the stuff that went on at that farm. I'm not like that,' said Justin, breaking down.

'I think it would be a good time to end it there,' said Justin's solicitor.

Justin had been right about Max Walton's crimes not being limited to the numerous murders he'd been held accountable for. Tens of people had disappeared over the years within a short radius of the Walton farm, and one of Louise's enduring regrets over Walton's untimely death was the fact that they had never been able to fully question him over the missing persons cases. Rumours had persisted over the years about strange practices at the farm. The place had been derelict for a long time before Walton's death, and although bodies had subsequently been found on the Walton farm the investigation into Max Walton's crimes had suffered from a lack of people being willing to speak against him. Louise had long suspected that Walton hadn't worked alone, but after his death she had never been allowed to progress further on any investigation into him.

'Did Max do something to you?' asked Louise, ignoring the solicitor.

Justin shook his head as tears streamed from his eyes. 'No,' he said, as if trying to convince himself.

'Who else was involved?' said Louise, softening her tone, understanding now what might have led the young man to the life he lived.

'I don't know,' said Justin, breaking down to such an extent that his solicitor finally insisted that the interview come to a halt.

Chapter Fifty-Four

Louise returned to the incident room, convinced she still had unfinished business with Justin Walton. They had been on the brink of a revelation, and if it hadn't been for his duty solicitor finally finding her voice, Justin would have cracked.

'Good job, Louise,' said Brightman, just on the right side of patronising.

'Not good enough. He knows more than he's letting on.'

'Let me speak to his solicitor,' said the assistant chief, standing.

'There were other suspects during your investigation into Max Walton?' asked DCI Hartson, speaking directly to Louise for the first time that evening.

'Walton was always our prime suspect but there had been reports of other things going on in that family for years. Social have files on them inches thick. Reports of abuse a mile long, but nothing had ever stuck beyond a couple of distant cousins being put away in the eighties for their part in a paedophile ring.'

'But did you ever get a feeling that Max Walton was working with someone else? Maybe his wife was involved?'

At the time, they had incontrovertible evidence that Max Walton was responsible for the murders of three people. All teenagers who had been travelling through the area. Their bodies had been found with DNA matching that taken from Max Walton during his previous arrest. All their energies had been focused on Walton, and a potential accomplice had been low down on the list of concerns. 'The mother wasn't involved, at least not directly. She knew what Walton was like, we got that much from the interviews. Tried to leave on a number of occasions after Martyn was born, but Walton kept dragging her back. It was only when he was forced to go on the run that she managed to escape him for good.'

'And, after his death?' said Faulkner.

Louise glanced at Robertson. She understood the question. There had been an inquiry, then an ongoing investigation after she'd shot Walton. More bodies had been found at the Walton farm, deaths attributed to Walton, but as far as she was aware no accomplice had ever been uncovered. 'I'm afraid I wasn't allowed access to any subsequent investigation into Max Walton, as I'm sure you're aware,' she said to the two CTU detectives.

'So who was?' said Hartson.

The woman wasn't that ignorant, thought Louise as she tried to control her temper.

'The disgraced former DCI, Timothy Finch,' said Robertson. 'And we'll be getting shit-all out of him any time soon.'

'I could speak to him if it would help?' said Faulkner, his smile on overload.

'No, son, that's not going to happen during his trial. If he does have anything to share then it will come at a price that's too high.'

The ACC returned. 'Justin Walton is with Medical. They have recommended we leave it until the morning until speaking to him again.'

'You're kidding me,' said Louise.

'It's frustrating, but that's the way it is. I suggest we all get some rest and come back here at first light,' said the ACC, leaving before there was any time for objections.

Louise waited until the two CTU officers had left before speaking to Robertson. 'I'll have another crack at Karl Insgrove's support group in the morning, as well as Mrs Harrison. I'll need to speak to Justin first thing though, Iain,' she added, leaving no doubt what she expected of him.

'I'll sort it. Now get out of here,' said Robertson.

She was in the car park when her phone began ringing. 'Shit,' she said, looking down at the name *Glyn Rhinehart*, the journalist from *The Times*. She was about to answer when someone called her name.

'Hey, what are you doing here?' she said, turning to see Thomas leaving his car.

'You going to get that?' said Thomas with a smile, pointing to her ringing phone.

Louise glanced at the phone. 'No, that can wait. Fancy a drink?'

They drove to a late-night bar off Park Street in Bristol. Louise felt nervous and tired as Thomas ordered them both soft drinks. It was like a first date all over again, and Thomas couldn't hide his concern. 'Nice and public,' he said, half smiling. 'Is that in case I throw a wobbly?'

One of the things she'd always liked about him was the knack he had for defusing a situation with ease. 'I don't think I've ever seen you throw a wobbly.'

'It's not a pleasant sight, believe me.'

Louise chuckled. 'I've been a bit distracted of late.'

Thomas shrugged. 'That's understandable. You've had so much on, and I imagine you were warned to steer clear of me?'

'Well, not completely.'

Thomas scratched behind his ear, something Louise had learned he did when nervous. 'Was it my suggestion that we get the kids together?' he asked, turning his attention to the label on his bottle.

'It took me by surprise, but it shouldn't have. Did you notice?'

'Sometimes you are mysterious, DI Blackwell, sometimes you're an open book.'

'Sorry, I shouldn't have reacted that way. In truth it's something we should have done before.'

'You don't need to apologise. I can rush into things sometimes.'

'And I can be a bit too hesitant. So, what were you doing at the station?'

Thomas told her about what he'd been up to over the last few days. At first, she thought he was joking about the undercover sting, but it soon dawned on her that he was telling the truth. 'How was I not made aware of this?'

'In your defence, you've been rather preoccupied.'

'In my defence?'

Thomas laughed. 'Just go easy on Tracey and Greg. I asked them not to get you involved.'

Louise pretended to pout. 'Fine,' she said. 'Let's get back. Luckily for those two it's a bit late in the evening for a reprimand.'

'You going to stay at mine?'

Louise smiled. 'Sounds like a plan.'

Chapter Fifty-Five

Louise woke alone, taking a few seconds to acclimatise herself to her surroundings. Light peeked through the curtains of Thomas's bedroom. Suddenly panicked, Louise reached for her phone, relieved to see it was only 6.30 a.m. At that precise moment, there was nothing she wanted to do more than roll over and go back to sleep, but she forced herself up and, pulling on a spare dressing gown from behind the bedroom door, made her way downstairs where Thomas was making breakfast.

'Thought you'd need to get out and about early,' he said, as the beeper went off on the coffee machine.

Louise smiled and wondered at her stupidity at taking so long to talk to Thomas about her concerns. It felt so right being here that she couldn't believe she'd come so close to destroying it. Not that she wasn't pissed off with Tracey and Farrell, who'd both left grovelling messages on her phone that she'd yet to reply to.

'Do you mind if I have a tea?' she said, as Thomas went to pour her a coffee.

'My God, how long has it been since I last saw you?'

'I'm going through a phase, what can I say.'

'You still eat eggs though?'

'It hasn't been that long, Tom,' said Louise, taking the plate from him. She tried not to rush the food, wanted to spend as much time as possible with Thomas, but despite the early hour she was already itching to get back to work. If she could get through today, the last day of the air festival, then maybe it would all come to an end. If there was someone else other than Insgrove and Martyn Walton-Renwick involved, then today would be the most likely day for them to attack again.

'Where are you going first?' said Thomas, as Louise washed down her eggs and toast with the tea.

'I'll see if I can speak to Emily's headmistress before heading into the office. I'll update her on recent developments and see if that jogs her memory.'

'I wish there was something I could do. I'm supposed to be going to the air show with Noah later, but I'm not sure I want to risk it.'

'Try and keep him home, Tom. I'm telling my parents the same.'

Louise skipped upstairs and showered, pleased that she still had a change of clothes at Thomas's house. Kissing him goodbye, she marvelled at how quickly things had changed back to normal; how much time she'd wasted dithering and worrying, when she should have realised how happy she was.

◆ ◆ ◆

She arrived at Joanne Harrison's house just as the headteacher was leaving, the sound of dogs barking drifting towards her from inside. Mrs Harrison was dressed in a flowery summer dress that made her look a good ten years younger than she was. 'Glorious day,' she said, as Louise approached.

'I am sorry to bother you on a Sunday morning, Mrs Harrison, but I would be grateful if you could spare me a few minutes.'

'I'll be late for church.'

'Please, five minutes.' Louise wasted no time in telling Mrs Harrison what had happened in the last couple of days, the head-teacher squirming as she told her about Martyn Walton-Renwick's suicide from the college building.

'When will this tragedy end, Detective?' she asked.

'I wish I knew.'

'I'm afraid I don't quite understand, though, what has this to do with me?'

Louise tried to explain Martyn Walton-Renwick's dying words. 'We think Martyn was working with at least one other person, probably two. With what happened at the school . . .' said Louise, noticing the way Mrs Harrison cringed at the words. 'I know you don't want to hear it but everything still points to Karl Insgrove being involved. If we can find out who else he was working with, we could stop any further incidents. And with both Karl and Martyn taking their own lives . . . I do think it's possible they were under duress somehow. We could help clear Karl's name, or at least explain why he did what he did.'

'That sounds wonderful,' said Mrs Harrison, walking towards her car, 'but what has that to do with me?'

'I need you to think, Mrs Harrison. I need to know who Karl could have been that close with. Who could perhaps have had such a negative influence on him.'

'I've helped you all I can. It was that bloody war that changed Karl. That's your negative influence. It changed me as well. I wasted a lifetime waiting for something to happen that was never going to happen. Waiting for the real Karl to come back, when he'd all but died that day the ship was blown up. Now, if you'll excuse me.'

Louise watched the woman drive away. She knew the church she went to but was in two minds whether to follow. There seemed so little to be gained but Holy Trinity was the same place where Karl Insgrove had attended his war veterans group, so there was a chance she would be able to speak to Bryce Milner and others from the group before she had to return to headquarters.

The roads were already packed with tourists and locals making their way to the centre. The uniformed teams would be out in force on the seafront and lawns, and would be making random stop checks like they did yesterday. Martyn Walton-Renwick's death had been tragic and avoidable, but if they could get away with another day of relatively minor trauma then Louise would gladly take it. She'd never been a superstitious person, or the type of cop who worked on hunches, but she couldn't deny the hollow feeling in the pit of her stomach that suggested so much worse was to come.

She parked up opposite the church and watched as Mrs Harrison joined the others congregating outside the building. Emily's school was non-denominational and wasn't affiliated to any church, but did have close links to Holy Trinity and had held a Christmas carol concert there last year. Even so, Louise was surprised by the number of parents she recognised mingling outside the building, including Graham Pritchard who was wearing the same suit from the other day. There was a sense of community in the way everyone was mixing that was absent from the mornings in the playground, and Louise felt as if she had somehow been excluded from this group.

As the churchgoers began filtering inside, she looked over at the church hall where she'd met Bryce Milner earlier in the week. A caretaker was opening the building but there was no sign of Milner, or any of the others from Karl Insgrove's counselling group.

Robertson called as she was deciding whether or not to head into the church, and informed her that Justin Walton had been cleared for interview. Still she lingered, as if what was happening behind the stone walls of the church held the answers she was looking for.

'You coming?' said Robertson, on the phone, jarring her into the present.

'I'll be there in thirty,' said Louise, tearing her gaze away from the pretty courtyard and setting off for Portishead.

◆ ◆ ◆

Tracey and Greg both greeted her as she entered the CID. 'Oh, I remember you too,' she said, looking from one to the other in mock surprise. 'What have you been up to aside from harassing Thomas and keeping secrets from me?'

The pair looked comically sheepish, making it hard for Louise to keep a straight face. 'We thought you had enough on your hands without getting you involved?' said Tracey, wide-eyed as Farrell failed to meet Louise's gaze.

Louise let them suffer for a few seconds. 'It all worked out for the best, I guess. And you're both here now. Could be lots to do. Come on,' she said, leading them to the incident room where she briefed the full office. 'We're not going to spend the day waiting for something to happen. I want us out there speaking to everyone we can,' she told the team, giving Tracey and Farrell the specific duties of rounding up the members of Karl Insgrove's counselling group as well as Justin Walton's social cohort.

'Bagsy the old men,' said Tracey, after the meeting had been dispersed and it was just the three of them.

'There is a joke in there somewhere,' said Farrell.

'If there is, I'd advise you not to use it,' said Tracey. 'You want us to wait until you've spoken to Justin Walton again?'

'No, that's OK,' said Louise. 'I'm sure Robbo wants to sit in anyway. Get going, I'll let you both know as soon as I have some news for you.'

Robertson appeared from his office as Tracey and Farrell headed for the lifts. He nodded towards the interview room. 'They're ready for us,' he said. 'Doc says we need to go easy on him,' he added.

'We have to go easy on hangovers now?'

'Exactly. That solicitor won't say boo to a ghost so we should be OK,' said Robertson, opening the interview room door for her.

Justin Walton looked less downtrodden than the day before, but was still hunched in on himself. His eyes appeared more alert as they looked briefly up at Louise before returning to stare at something invisible on the ground.

'Good morning, Justin, I hope you're feeling more with us today,' said Louise, starting the interview and introducing those present, before adding, 'I hope you've also had some more time to think.'

Justin shrugged, and Louise felt a tightness in her spine. 'You know we've been receiving threats all week. I say *we*, but those threats have been centred directly on me. Someone wants me out of a job, or at least they're using that as an excuse to commit some terrible crimes. I think Karl Insgrove and Martyn had a part to play in this, but I don't think you did. Do you understand me, Justin?'

Justin lifted his head and looked at her. 'Why do you want to speak to me then?'

'Because I think you know who else is responsible. Who it is that's behind all this.'

'I don't,' said Justin, shaking his head.

Louise felt as if she was back at the beginning, and feared she would be forced to endure the same never-ending conversation with Justin Walton for an eternity. Perhaps she was in some sort of purgatory where she was being punished for killing Max Walton, but then what god would punish her for doing that? 'Do you know what I thought at first? At first, I wondered if somehow Max Walton had come back from the grave. Ridiculous, hey? But that's the sort of sway people like him can have on you. Seeing them dead isn't enough. They continue to haunt you forever. You ever feel like that, Justin?'

Justin placed his right hand under his chin. Louise couldn't tell if he was listening or not but continued unabated. 'You began to tell me last night about what happened over at Max Walton's farm,' said Louise.

Justin took in a deep breath, his hands moving over his face.

'I know this is a hell of a lot to face up to now, and if we could do it any other way then I would, but people have died, Justin. Karl Insgrove, Martyn . . . Hana Sanchez, an innocent mother of two. And can you imagine if we hadn't got to the museum in time? There were so many families in there, and the things they'd put in that bomb,' said Louise, shaking her head. 'I know you wouldn't want anything to happen to these innocent people, but if you don't help us now, I fear something like this might happen again today.'

'Can't you stop this?' said Justin, moving his hands away from his face to plead to his solicitor, his cheeks damp and red.

'This is a very forceful line of questioning, DI Blackwell,' said the duty solicitor.

Louise had purposely kept her voice low and even. 'No one is being forceful here. I just want what is best for everyone, Justin,' she said.

'But I don't know anything,' said Justin.

'I know this is so hard for you, but try to think back if you can. You told me you used to go to the Walton farm when you were younger.'

The heat in Justin's face dissipated in a flash, and Louise thought he might be sick. 'You told me Max Walton was there, but who else can you remember? Was there anyone else, maybe someone who was close to Max?'

Justin started mumbling, his lips twitching as he began swaying on the chair.

Louise looked at Robertson, who nodded. 'I am so sorry, Justin. You have my word: I will protect you and put away whoever was responsible. Just tell me his name.'

'I don't know his name,' said Justin, his mouth trembling as if he was having a seizure.

'Can you remember anything about him, anything about the way he looked, or spoke?'

Justin stopped moving. 'He had an accent. I remember that. I didn't know what it was at the time, but now I guess it was Welsh.'

Louise took a sharp intake of breath. Taking out her phone, she searched for an image as her mind started making connections. 'Is it this man?' she said, showing Justin an image of Bryce Milner from the eighties.

Justin took one look at the photo, and promptly turned to his solicitor and vomited over her.

Chapter Fifty-Six

Robertson grabbed a set of keys for a patrol car, and within minutes they were hurtling through the village towards the M5. 'You've met this Milner character before,' he said, as Louise posted images of Milner to all the team in Weston.

'Just the once. CTU cleared him,' said Louise, hating the defensiveness in her voice. 'He set up the war vets group Karl Insgrove attended. Bit aloof but came across as being helpful.'

The siren screamed as Robertson joined the motorway, Louise receiving notification that cars had been sent to Milner's house in Ashcombe. 'No record?'

'None. Counter Terrorism noted some misdemeanours during his time in the army, but nothing suggesting any involvement with Max Walton.'

'And his name never came up during your investigation into Walton?'

'Jesus, what is this, Iain? Of course it didn't.'

'Sorry,' said Robertson, his eyes focused on the traffic giving way for him.

'Milner's in his seventies now. He would have needed help if he is responsible.'

'Looks like he got that with Insgrove and Walton-Renwick.'

'Let's hope it was just them.'

They'd reached the junction to Weston when notification came in that Milner wasn't at his house. Robertson agreed that they had enough justification to warrant entry into the property, and Louise gave the orders.

'Get everyone available onto the seafront. If he's got something planned for today then he might go and watch his handiwork.'

'Let's go to the church first, where they have their meetings,' said Louise.

'You were there this morning?'

'Yes. I didn't see him, but he could have been there. They had some sort of afternoon fete planned, to watch the planes. Could be he's made his way there.' She called Adam King as Robertson sped through the back streets.

'I'll head towards the church as well,' said King. 'In case that's his target.'

Robertson turned off the siren when they were a few streets away, not wanting to announce their arrival. The same crowd from the morning were now gathered in the courtyard where tables and stalls had been erected, with food and games for the children. Louise briefly wondered why Emily and her family hadn't been invited to the gathering, as she received glances from a number of parents from Emily's class.

'Louise, how are you?' said Graham, his face soon losing its smile as Louise dismissed his greeting with, 'Have you seen Mrs Harrison?'

'I think she's in the church hall,' said Graham, crestfallen as he looked from Louise to Robertson.

Louise felt momentarily dizzy as she walked across the courtyard. The temperature must have been in the high twenties, and she hadn't had anything to eat or drink since breakfast that morning with Thomas. The cool interior of the church hall was a welcome respite, and Louise caught sight of Joanne Harrison in conversation with the vicar. 'Mrs Harrison, could I speak to you?' she said, interrupting their conversation.

Louise waited until the vicar had moved away before introducing Robertson. 'We're looking for Bryce Milner. It is important that we speak to him immediately.'

'Bryce? Why?'

'Was he at the church service this morning?'

'No, I haven't seen him all day.'

'Does he usually attend these events?'

'I would have expected to see him, yes, but his health is not great at the moment. That's why I'm not that surprised he isn't here. Anyway, what is this about?'

Robertson cursed, a number of heads turning in his direction. 'Can you think where he can be, Mrs Harrison? I can't stress how important it is we see him,' he said.

'You've tried his home?'

'Yes,' said Robertson, his patience clearly at breaking point.

Mrs Harrison shrugged. 'Oh,' she said, inspiration striking. 'You could try his allotment. I know he loves spending time there.'

'His allotment?'

'Yes, on Bath Street. You could probably walk it.'

◆ ◆ ◆

Robertson called for backup as they ran towards the allotments. The heat was oppressive, Louise's throat dry as she made the short journey through the back streets. The smell of cut grass hung in the air as they headed towards the gate. A battered wooden sign displayed a map of the small allotments. It was clear it hadn't been updated in ages, and none of the names were visible.

The first plane of the day had taken to the air in the distance behind them as Louise and Robertson edged along the dried mud pathway, Louise alert to the tiniest of movements while insects buzzed around her hair. She was desperate for a drink now, her eyesight blurred by the sunshine as she tripped over a loose stone.

'You OK?' said Robertson.

Louise nodded, glancing towards movement at the foot of the hill. She couldn't quite make out the person moving behind the overgrown vines blocking the entrance. They crept down the hill, Robertson grabbing the rusted gate and creaking it open as Louise stepped through.

Bryce Milner was digging next to a patch of vegetables fifty yards from where they stood. He was bent over, his foot resting on the long-handled shovel in his hand as Louise took a step nearer, Robertson following close behind.

Milner pushed himself up straight with a groan, dropping the shovel as he turned and limped his way towards the small wooden shed at the other end of the allotment, seemingly unaware of their presence.

'Mr Milner, DI Blackwell and DCI Robertson,' shouted Louise.

The allotment was surrounded by fencing along its perimeter. Although it was less than two metres tall, she doubted Milner would be able to escape over it. He stopped walking and turned slowly towards them, smiling. 'DI Blackwell, how nice to see you. Do come in,' he said, gesturing with his hand for them to follow him to the shed.

'I'd like you to stop where you are, Mr Milner,' said Louise, as Milner stepped towards the entrance.

'Just getting some water,' said Milner, without looking around.

'Shit,' said Louise, in unison with Robertson as they both began running to the shed, only to stop five metres from the door as Milner turned.

'It really is lovely to see you again, Louise,' said Milner, the shotgun he held in his hands shaking as if being moved by the breeze. 'Who told you about me? Was it Max's son?'

'You were working with Martyn?' asked Louise.

Milner laughed, the shotgun swaying precariously in his hands. 'What, you want a confession before I kill you?'

Chapter Fifty-Seven

'Louise,' said Robertson, gently, as he moved towards her.

The last few moments had passed in a blur. Robertson attacking Milner with the shovel, only for Milner to respond by producing the thick metal wire and pressing it to Robertson's throat. It was a wonder her colleague was still alive, and Louise thought how easy it would be to pull the trigger now, to put an end to all the misery caused by Milner.

'You've broken it,' screamed Milner in breathless agony, his injured arm twisted behind him in the cuffs.

'Louise?' said Robertson, again.

Louise shook her head, the gun still pointed at Milner's head. 'Your confession,' she said.

Milner was prone on the ground, his face contorted. 'I done the lot,' he said, his laugh once more turning into a cough.

'You were responsible for the explosions?' said Robertson.

'One way or another. Yes, I used Karl and Martyn. They both had their demons which I could exploit to my own ends.'

'Why?' said Louise.

'Is that important?'

'You asked me to give up my job. Is this all because of that? Because of what happened to Max Walton?'

It was as if the comment had flipped a switch, going by Milner's face, the smiley facade disappearing as Louise again saw the hard ruthless interior she'd only glimpsed the last time they'd talked. 'You ruined what we had together.'

'You committed crimes with Max Walton?' asked Louise.

Milner shook his head, returning to the present. 'You really think this is about you?' He spat on the ground again. 'I could have snuffed you out at any time I wanted. You, and that stupid fucker on trial now as well. You're nothing to me. You understand that? Nothing. I used you as a distraction. I was planning something big and I needed their help.'

'Karl and Martyn's help?'

'I couldn't do it myself. Karl was easy enough. He owed me, and he was carrying a lot of grudges around with him. Against authority, you understand. That said, he was a fucking junkie and would do anything for some skag.'

'And Martyn? If you liked Max so much, then why would you involve his son?'

'Look at me. Can you imagine me carrying explosives around, sneaking into buildings and planting them? Maybe twenty years ago. I've been in contact with that lad for a few years. He was always confused. Didn't know if he wanted to follow in his father's footsteps or not. It wasn't difficult to get him over here. I told him Finch was on trial, and that we could do something about you. Stupid little shit really thought we could get rid of you without causing any casualties. His heart was never in it, really, but he did what was asked of him.'

'But why?' said Louise, as Milner started coughing again.

'Why? Fucking *why*? Because no one knows me, that's why. All they know is Max, and those boys and girls he killed. Jesus, you don't even know the half of it. What we got up to . . . Hell,' said Milner, shaking his head as if lost in memory.

'You're doing this for notoriety?' said Louise, unable to hide the disbelief in her words, as her finger worked its way to the trigger.

'I guess you can say that. I missed it though as well. You know, being with Max. The things we did. I'm not a young man anymore, but I can still enjoy things. You understand? That reminds me, what time is it?' said Milner, lifting his head from the ground.

'Two fifteen p.m.,' said Robertson.

'Forty-five minutes and this will be over.'

Louise's arms began to tremble. 'What have you done, Milner?'

'You'll see.'

It was enough for Robertson. He moved towards Milner and grabbed his injured arm. 'What have you done?' he said, spittle falling from his mouth as he spoke through gritted teeth, his voice hoarse from the metal wire that had left a mark around his neck.

Milner was doing his best to laugh, but the pain was evident on his face. He mumbled something inaudible as he struggled on the ground.

'We don't have time for this,' said Louise.

Robertson nodded towards the gun, a silent instruction for Louise to lower the weapon, but she ignored him. She thought about everything that had happened. Not just the two suicides, and the murder of Hana Sanchez, but all the countless deaths that could have occurred and could still occur. She took another step towards Milner, the gun now inches from his face.

'Louise,' said Robertson, the words all but lost as Louise fixated on Milner.

'You came to my niece's school,' she said, in her mind's eye picturing her finger pulling the trigger.

'You don't want this, Louise,' said Robertson.

Louise kept her focus on Milner, who appeared bemused rather than scared at the gun. It wasn't only the damage he'd caused in the last couple of weeks. The man was a one-time accomplice of Max

Walton, and had all but admitted to a string of atrocities going back years. He deserved to die, but Louise wasn't going to let him take her down with him. 'Pull him up,' she said.

Robertson lifted the man, pressing his fingers into Milner's wound. 'Tell us,' he said.

Milner's body jumped, and floundered, as if he'd been struck with electricity. Robertson kept the pressure on for a few more seconds, Louise checking for the sight of backup, knowing that if anyone witnessed what was happening, they would both lose their jobs.

'Where is the bomb?' said Louise, the gun still pointed at Milner, Robertson's fingers still on the wound. For a second, Louise wondered if Milner was going to remain silent. The gun felt heavier than before and she had to use all her strength to keep it in place without her arms shaking. 'Last chance,' she said.

Milner closed his eyes. 'OK, OK,' he said breathlessly.

'Where?' screamed Louise, pushing the gun into Milner's forehead. Like Max Walton had been, Milner was unarmed, but she needed to know where the bomb was located.

Milner twisted his neck so he could display his soulless grin. 'The pier,' he mouthed. 'Take me there and I'll show you exactly where we planted it.'

◆ ◆ ◆

A paramedic insisted on joining them as they drove to the Grand Pier. Robertson sat in the back with Milner, who was smiling as the paramedic tended to the wound. Louise drove, giving orders over the radio that the pier be evacuated.

They pulled up at the entrance to the Grand Pier ten minutes later. Inspector Baker was already at the scene, and had begun cordoning off the area and organising the evacuation. It was no easy feat. The pier could hold thousands, and on a day like this it was likely to be at capacity. The main risk was causing a panic which could lead to further injuries. As Louise left the car, she saw parents urging their children down the walkway, the elderly and disabled being assisted by her colleagues, while some people clung to the sides of the pier, their attention focused on the aircraft still circling the skies.

'Has King arrived yet?' asked Louise, managing to control her mounting panic.

'They were here before us. They're searching for the device now but we need to get everyone clear. There must be two thousand still inside,' said Baker, as the sound of fire alarms rang out in the air.

Robertson pulled Milner from the back of the car. 'What time is it due to detonate?' said Louise, under her breath.

'Where's your gun now?' said Milner.

Robertson pulled hard on the cuffs, and Milner gasped in pain. 'What time?'

'I told you, three p.m. Thank you for bringing me to watch. I hadn't planned to come, but I'm glad you changed my mind.'

There was no point trying to understand him. All that mattered now was that they find the bomb and neutralise it. 'Where is it, Milner?' said Louise.

Milner continued smiling, gazing up at the planes as if he hadn't seen the sky in years. Louise had never felt so restless. Robertson gripped the cuffs again, but there was no way they were going to get an answer from Milner with everyone watching.

'I'll take him up,' said Louise, as Milner continued his non-committal sky-gazing.

'No way,' said Baker. 'I'm not risking any more injuries, and you can't take a prisoner in custody into such an environment.'

Louise glanced to Robertson, who looked more dishevelled than she'd ever seen him, his hair matted against his scalp as sweat poured down his forehead. His hand went to the mark still visible on his neck. 'He's helping us with our inquires, aren't you Milner?' he said, nodding to Louise.

◆ ◆ ◆

It was the strangest journey along the pier Louise had ever made. Although they hurried, Milner almost floating in the air as she and Robertson jogged either side of him, she had a few moments to remember all the times she'd made this journey before. Recent visits with work aside, they were mainly pleasant memories. She recalled the times she'd visited as a child, and the breathless anticipation as she and Paul had gazed through the cracks in the wooden boards at the sand, or occasionally the water, as they hurried their parents along. The pier had seemed so long back then, the promises of the noise and excitement, the games and prizes, always just out of reach. She tried to ignore the panicked look of the citizens moving in the opposite direction, their terror heightened by the sight of the crazed prisoner being dragged along towards the fire alarms.

'What the hell are you doing here?' said King, as they arrived in the main building on the pier.

The interior of the pier was chaotic. The fire alarms were doing battle with the sounds of the arcade and fruit machines, and the anxious chatter of the hundreds being marshalled out of the building by the uniformed officers.

Both King and Mitch Norton were wearing their full gear, Arnie ready for action.

'This man knows where the device is but isn't speaking,' said Louise.

King pulled off his helmet and stared at Milner. 'You're ex-forces,' he said to Milner, a statement rather than a question.

Milner nodded. 'Welsh Guards,' he said, his head held aloft.

'Lance Corporal King. What the hell are you playing at?'

Louise was amazed to see a look that resembled shame form on Milner's face. After what he'd done, and was willing to do, all in the name of notoriety, it seemed ludicrous that an accusation from a serving member of the army could affect the man in any way, but Milner looked more than uncomfortable.

'You know what you're doing. To detonate that many devices in such a controlled manner. That takes some doing, even with help. But you need to stop now. I don't know exactly what you went through, but this is no answer. Innocent people are going to get hurt. You don't want that,' said King.

Louise could tell Robertson wanted to shake a response out of Milner, and she was inching that way herself, but they had to wait. Milner was staring at King, open-mouthed, the voices in his head all but visible. Louise glanced around. Uniformed officers were searching as best they could but there were so many places where a bomb could have been placed undetected. There were two main floors to the building, and a number of sections such as the ghost train and fun house that were out of sight. The problem was intensified by all the belongings people had left behind in their panic to leave the place.

'We used to come here. Me and Max,' said Milner.

Louise lowered her eyes. The thought of Max Walton being let loose in this building turned her stomach. She tried to think where would be the likeliest place for Milner to have put the device, but the thought of the ticking minutes was a distraction. She closed her eyes and thought back to Justin's testimony, shivering as she recalled what he'd described at Walton's farm when he'd been a child.

'Upstairs. There's one of those soft-play areas, right?' said Louise.

'There's a café there,' said Robertson. 'Is that where you used to go, you sick fuck?' he added, tugging at Milner's cuffs.

'Get out of here,' said King, moving with Norton as they guided the bomb disposal robot upstairs to the soft-play area on the top floor.

Louise and Robertson began helping with the evacuation, Louise calling off the search for the device and freeing up the other officers. People were running down the walkway now; Louise pleased to see the numbers were thinning.

'Look at them go,' said Milner, as they made their own way down the pier. 'I hope they make it in time.'

Robertson pushed him forwards. Louise had half a mind to take Milner back to the main building and to leave him there. As it was, she was trying to access King's and Norton's body cams on her phone when a thunderous sound roared out above them, causing the structure of the pier to shake.

Blue, white and red smoke filtered through the air as the Red Arrows passed overhead, the sound ringing in Louise's ears.

'We've located it,' said King. 'Sending Arnie in.'

They reached the foot of the pier, Robertson instructing one of the team to take Milner away as Louise loaded the robot's camera on to her mobile phone. 'What sort of monster would do that?' said Louise. Arnie moved towards the stanchion at the rear of the soft-play area, its caterpillar tracks not missing a beat across the soft material. If they had never located Milner then the place would have been full of children. And by the looks of it, the set-up was similar to that of the museum. The device was wedged out of sight and must have been placed there earlier in the week, possibly by Martyn Walton-Renwick.

King and Norton wasted no time, the robot sending a blast to neutralise the device as the Red Arrows made another deafening pass by above them.

Chapter Fifty-Eight

'Some pretty good timing,' said Thomas, showing Louise the article in the morning newspaper.

'All part of my master plan,' said Louise, taking a sip of tea before scanning Tania Elliot's hastily put together article about yesterday's events. Thomas was right, it couldn't have come at a better time. Despite everything that had gone down between them, Tania was now painting her as some sort of hero for her part in stopping the explosion on the pier, and even went so far as to say that her actions would hold her in good stead when Louise was on the witness stand later today. 'Say what you want about her, but she's not scared about switching sides,' she added, closing the paper before reading Tania's second article where she ripped into Tim Finch.

'Nervous about today?'

'Not really. All I can do is tell the truth. It's all I could ever do.'

Thomas cleared the table and put the dishes away. She'd gone home for a couple of hours last night to see Emily and her parents, but had spent the night here with Thomas. She still didn't understand why she'd tried so hard to create distance between them, but there had been nowhere else she'd wanted to be last night, and no one else she wanted to drive her to the courthouse today. It felt good admitting that, even if it was only to herself.

A crowd was waiting at the courthouse. This time the press were mainly shouting questions about the evacuation of the pier, while inside, Louise's team gathered to support her. Robertson, Tracey, Farrell and Simon Coulson greeted her like they hadn't seen her in ages. It could have made things daunting, but she took strength from their being there, and even more so from the sight of Amira Hood. 'I guess I'll just try and do what you did,' said Louise.

Amira hugged her silently, and together they walked into the courthouse.

It went better than she could have ever imagined. There were some awkward moments when the prosecution barrister, Amanda Knight, had her recounting the night of Finch's arrest, but what she had told Thomas had been correct. All she had to do was tell the truth. There had been no ulterior motives, no sense of revenge. Yes, she had long wanted to see Finch get his comeuppance for the terrible wrongs he'd committed on so many people, but there had been no master plan that night, no elaborate entrapment. Amira had gone to see Finch and things had got out of hand. When Louise had arrived, it had been clear that he'd planned to kill her and if he'd had his way would have killed Louise too.

It felt so good saying it out loud, even better when she caught Finch looking over at her. She sensed the defeat in Finch's barrister the second he started questioning her. Boothroyd accused her of setting the whole thing up, for waging a war on Finch for the perceived injustice of her being moved to Weston, but stopped short of mentioning Max Walton's death at the farm on the outskirts of

Bridgwater. By the time he'd finished, it was clear that any potential character assassination Finch's team had planned must have been shelved.

'That must have been a calculated decision,' said Antony Meades, afterwards. The jury were always told to ignore news stories about the case, but it wouldn't have escaped their attention that Louise had only yesterday arrested one of Max Walton's accomplices; someone who was suspected of running a long-term paedophile ring with Walton.

'You think they would have mentioned Max Walton's death if it hadn't been for yesterday?' asked Louise.

'We expected it, but I don't think this has gone the way they were hoping. Amira was fantastic last week, and you . . . Well, with you I think we've got him.'

Epilogue

Louise sat with Amira in the courthouse café, as Thomas went to get them drinks. 'This bit never gets any easier, does it?' she said.

The jury in the Finch case had been let out an hour ago. It was still relatively early as there were multiple charges they would have to discuss, but every minute that went past ratcheted up the tension. It was always the way when waiting for a jury. However cast-iron you thought your case was, there was always a nagging feeling that the jury would see things differently.

'I don't miss it, that's for sure,' said Amira. 'I'll be glad when this is all over, and I can forget the name Tim Finch for good.'

Finch was so close to becoming just another bad memory that Louise could taste it. After Thomas's undercover work, Eddie Perkins, the last of Finch's corrupt former colleagues, had been arrested for his work on the drug operation at Thornbury and beyond. It was as if the old order was in its death throes. Now all they needed was a guilty verdict for Finch.

Louise caught Amira's eye, and seeing the doubt there she still wondered if either of them would ever be able to escape Finch's shadow. For Amira, it would be that night at Finch's house that would be hard to shake; the memories of being trapped there, believing any second Finch would take her life, would haunt Amira for a long time to come. For Louise, she doubted she would ever forget that night at the Walton farm. Over the last few days, she'd learned even more about the depravity of Max Walton, yet nothing he'd done made her feel any better about his death. Finch had coerced her into that action, and she would never forgive him for that. If they'd kept Walton alive that night, then so much future tragedy could have been stopped. They would have found out earlier about Bryce Milner and would never have had to face the events of the last two weeks.

Milner had admitted under interview that he had masterminded the bombings in Weston. As he'd told her and Robertson at the allotments, he'd used Karl Insgrove and Martyn Walton-Renwick to do his dirty work. They now had records of correspondence between him and Walton-Renwick going back years, where Milner had subtly laid the foundation for Walton-Renwick's revenge. Milner had ruined that boy's life as much as he had ruined Justin's, creating the idea that Louise should pay for what she'd done to Walton-Renwick's father, when all he'd ever wanted was to use the boy for his dubious ends.

With Insgrove, he'd deployed a different type of mental pressure. He'd manipulated Insgrove's experience from his time in the navy, and his old dependency on drugs, to tragic effect.

The wonder of it all was the years of preparation since Max Walton had died, and in all this time Bryce Milner had been hankering for something even he found difficult to define. He still claimed he wanted to be known, in the same way Max Walton was known, but Louise wondered if it was something else. They had started talking to his old colleagues, and like Insgrove, Milner had seen some gruesome things during his years in the service. In the Gulf War, he'd been present for an explosion at an oil refinery that had killed dozens of people. The psychologists would no doubt be discussing that with Milner in due course, and it would probably be used in mitigation. But whether it had started there or not felt irrelevant at that moment. He was behind bars, and would stay like that, one way or another, for the rest of his life.

'We've been called,' said Thomas, placing his hand on Louise's shoulder and bringing her back to the present.

This was the hardest part of all. Louise grabbed Amira's hand and together they walked into the court. Louise tried to contain the adrenaline as Finch was shown to his position, but it hit her in waves. All she could do was consider what would happen if he was found innocent, and her legs almost buckled as everyone rose for the judge.

Amira's hand was sweaty in hers as the clerk stood and addressed the jury, going through Finch's charges one by one. Relief surged through Louise, Amira gripping her hand tightly, as the guilty charges kept coming through.

'And to the charge of the attempted murder of Amira Hood?'

The churlish part of her wondered if the lead juror was an amateur dramatist, such was the length of the pause before she gave her verdict. She even made a point of glancing at Finch before speaking, sending shock waves of worry through Louise that the jury were going to find in his favour.

'Guilty,' said the woman, after an eternity.

The sound of the celebration from the gallery took Louise back to the pier, and the noise of the Red Arrows flying above her. She stood up too fast, and had to sit back down, the world spinning out of focus for a second until Thomas was leading her out and giving her some water outside.

'Sorry, the moment must have got to me,' she said, drinking the water as the heat on her skin dissipated.

'How about that time off now?' said Thomas, eyes full of concern.

'I think this time you may have a point. But first, I need to get back in there and see Amira and everyone else.'

◆ ◆ ◆

Finch didn't want to give them the satisfaction, but he couldn't help it. They'd shoved him off the van and he'd landed squarely on his bad leg, which crumpled on impact.

'You pissed or something, Finch?' said the guard, an unpleasant piece of work called Rutland who'd been harassing him ever since he'd been bundled into the van in the middle of the night.

The journey to the Cat A prison had been a never-ending litany of abuse and threats. Finch understood it was a way of conditioning him for what he was about to face, and it didn't really bother him. He already knew that Eddie Perkins had fucked up and had been arrested along with members of Terry Clemons' team, but Rutland had taken some delight in reminding him. 'No one on the outside for you now, Finch. Those days are over. No one on the inside for you either,' he'd added, informing him that Clemons would also be on the move to an undisclosed Cat A prison and was blaming Finch for the trouble.

Finch pushed himself from the ground, the walking stick he'd been allowed at the courthouse now denied him. The cloudy darkness seemed to envelop the imposing prison building as Rutland and his colleague shoved him towards the gated doors where he was processed, before he was led to a second, damp room that was colder than outside where he was made to take off his clothes.

The indignities of the strip search were always the hardest thing for him to endure. The incarceration he could handle – that was simply a state of mind – but being made to bend over for these bastards was difficult to stomach.

'Don't be shy now, Finch,' said Rutland, as he was told to squat. 'We can't be too careful.'

Perkins and Clemons hadn't been the only victims of late. His one-time jailer Derek Wilson had lost his job after revelations about how he had facilitated Eddie Perkins and Clemons working together, and now he was facing criminal charges. That had been no accident. And neither had transferring Finch this far away from Bristol. Rutland had made it clear that none of the staff here were corruptible, that Finch would be receiving no help from any of the guards, and that his former roles made no difference to how he would be treated.

That last part, at least, was a lie. Ex-coppers were treated with equal disdain by convicts and screws alike. Finch was prepared for that. Accepted that it would take time to assert his dominance in whatever wing they put him in. The threat of violence wasn't something that fazed him. He would take the inevitable beating he was due, would wait until his past became an irrelevance, and would start building again. However sure of himself Rutland might be, the real truth was that Finch did have support both inside and out. Eddie Perkins and Derek Wilson weren't the only people he had dirt on. That list felt pretty endless.

'None of that easy Cat B shit for you now, Finch,' said Rutland, once he'd got changed into his new prison clothes. 'There won't be an easy way for you to do time here, but there will be a hard way for you to do it, and an even harder way. You understand me?'

Finch didn't grant the guard the satisfaction of an answer as he was led to the cells where the prisoners were waiting to greet him. He kept his head up as he was led past the gesticulating inhabitants, and allowed the whistles and jeers, the obscene insults and threats, to wash over him. He'd spent a good decade all but running the whole of Avon and Somerset. These thick bastards were nothing in comparison.

'Your new home for the next fifteen to twenty years,' said Rutland, opening the cell door to a cramped room. 'Breakfast in twenty minutes, sweetheart,' he added, locking the door behind him.

At least he was alone, though the bunk bed was an ominous warning. Finch sat on the lower bunk, trying to ignore the smell from the toilet bowl that would be less than a few feet from him at all times. Try as he might, his mind turned to the reason he was here and the oversight that had allowed her to thrive.

So overjoyed had she been by his guilty verdict, Blackwell had all but fainted and had been carried out of the courthouse by that non-entity Thomas Ireland. Finch's failings where she was concerned had taught him that he could never be too ruthless. He'd thought her broken and beaten after that night at the Walton farm, but she'd kept coming back.

He wouldn't make that mistake again, he told himself, as the bell rang and his door was unlocked; the thought lost as soon as it had arrived as three inmates let themselves in through the open door.

'A little welcome present, DCI Finch,' one of the men said, striking Finch to the ground before he had a chance to respond.

It wasn't quite the Majorca holiday Thomas had planned, but it felt right walking along the main beach in Weston after all that had happened. Louise was hand in hand with Thomas, as Emily and Noah did their best to follow the wild movements of Molly as she chased the sheets of sand blowing along the shore. There was no sense of hesitancy as they walked beneath the Grand Pier, the place now fully opened after the previous scare.

The town moved on as it always did, and it was heartening to see so many people out in the July sunshine. Close to the promenade, a group of children were being led on a donkey ride, as further along a group of teenagers started a game of beach football. As they emerged on the other side of the pier, Molly a blur of action as she seemingly chased every grain of sand at once, Thomas grabbed Louise's hand tighter.

It was the first time Emily and Noah had met and Louise was surprised by how easily they played together, Molly acting as a shared focus.

Although the children were oblivious, they were out celebrating Finch's sentence. Louise had insisted on waiting until she'd heard the sentence before agreeing to some time off. Life had definitely felt easier with Finch on remand, but knowing he would be behind bars for a minimum of fifteen years changed everything for her. It felt like her career had been given back to her, and her parents aside, she couldn't think of anyone else she wanted to share that feeling with.

'Shall we grab a coffee before heading back?' said Thomas.

'Maybe a hot chocolate,' said Louise.

'Oh yeah, I forgot about your new phobia. Remember, I've worked with you before. God knows how you'll cope without your daily hits of caffeine.'

Louise let go of his hand, and double-checked the children were out of earshot. 'Actually, I did a bit of research into that,' she said.

'Don't tell me, going without caffeine is good for you. Well, you can count me out on that. Coffee is one pleasure I can't go without.'

'No, you fool,' said Louise, laughing as he pretended to be wounded by her comment. 'I was looking into why I'd gone off coffee.'

'Oh.'

'Yes, oh. It seems that can often be a side effect of being pregnant. Something about the smell of coffee beans. You don't need to know the details.'

Thomas's lips parted slightly as he let the words settle. 'Are you saying . . .'

Louise nodded. 'How does that make you feel?' she said, studying Thomas as closely as she would any suspect in an interview.

'How does it make me feel? Are you serious?' said Thomas, pulling her close.

Behind him, Louise watched Emily and Noah catching up with Molly. Holding Thomas tight, smiling as the dog jumped up at the two delighted children, she said, 'I guess you feel the same way I do, then.'

ACKNOWLEDGEMENTS

Huge thanks to everyone who has contributed in some way to *The Pier*.

The wonderful team at Thomas & Mercer: my amazing editor, Leodora Darlington, for her help in shaping this book, Sadie Mayne for the perfect copy-edits, Gemma Wain for her detailed proofreading, Tom Sanderson for his beautiful covers, Nicole Wagner for all her behind-the-scenes assistance, and Bekah Graham and all the marketing team for helping the books reach as wide an audience as possible.

My wonderful development editor, Russel McLean, who always pushes the book to the best level it can be.

To Graham Bartlett, for his peerless police procedural advice, and Simon Andrews for his bomb disposal expertise (any mistakes in the novel are mine only).

To Alison, Freya and Hamish for being my inspiration.

And, as always, many thanks to the lovely people of Weston-super-Mare for putting up with me writing scary stories about their beautiful town.

ABOUT THE AUTHOR

Photo © 2019 Lisa Visser

Following his law degree, where he developed an interest in criminal law, Matt Brolly completed his Masters in Creative Writing at Glasgow University. He is the bestselling author of the DCI Lambert crime novels, *Dead Eyed*, *Dead Lucky*, *Dead Embers*, *Dead Time* and *Dead Water* and the Lynch and Rose thriller *The Controller*. In addition, he is the author of the acclaimed near-future crime novel *Zero*. The first novel in the Detective Louise Blackwell crime series, *The Crossing*, was published in 2020. Matt also writes children's books as M. J. Brolly. His first children's book was *The Sleeping Bug*. Matt lives in London with his wife and their two children. You can find out more about him at www.mattbrolly.com or by following him on Twitter: @MattBrollyUK.